VENGEANCE OR DEATH

VENGEANCE OR DEATH

TEAM SAVAGE™ BOOK THREE

MICHAEL TODD

MICHAEL ANDERLE

VENGEANCE OR DEATH TEAM

Thanks to our Beta Readers
Kelly O'Donnell and John Ashmore

Thanks to our JIT Readers
Peter Manis
Dorothy Lloyd
Jeff Eaton
Diane L. Smith
Micky Cocker
Dave Hicks
Paul Westman

Editor
The Skyhunter Editing Team

DEDICATION

*To Family, Friends and
Those Who Love
to Read.
May We All Enjoy Grace
to Live the Life We Are
Called.*

CHAPTER ONE

He disliked having to make house calls. Humans had invested considerable time, effort, and money into creating enough technology in the world to ensure that face to face interactions were only necessary when the people involved wanted them to be. Despite this, however, there were still those who demanded they be a part of their everyday life.

Mason Banks had never enjoyed being around other people. He was one of those people who liked the term introvert. In simple terms, he felt uncomfortable around others. They were hard to read and tended to be unpredictable monsters who could become deeply involved in one's life without one having much say in the matter. It had been a problem in the past—one that had resulted in an ex-wife. They had parted amicably as both had been of the same mind at around the same time, and Mason hadn't found it in him to attempt to date again.

Which meant social interactions were limited to those his work as a lawyer demanded—which in his case, unfortunately, was a significant number. He was a good lawyer, but people didn't merely take his word on it. They didn't even take his firm's word on it. No, they wanted to meet face to face to discuss their matters in person. These meetings were sometimes at his office and sometimes at theirs. He had a special place in his heart for those who wanted to discuss it over a meal they were willing to pay for. Unlike most of the other partners at his firm, he hadn't come from money, and when it came to food, like beer, free was best.

This home call was the kind he really hated. It made him drive all the shit-fucking way out to the middle of nowhere and forced him into places where phone reception was spotty. In this day and age, you'd think they'd have that shit fixed by now. But no.

Banks scowled at his phone and the pathetic two bars displayed on it. That would change soon if his experience with prison visits was anything to go by.

That said, this particular place of incarceration looked more like a resort than most prisons did. Golf courses, tennis courts, indoor pools, and even access to the beach all masqueraded as punishment. Being in prison when you were rich really wasn't a fair deal, he thought. He knew that even a place like this would be hell for someone who came from the kind of money his client had, but it was still a whole lot better than where criminals usually went.

Hell, a lot of people paid to stay in places worse than this.

Banks shook his head and strode over to a guard. The man was tall, overweight, and lacked any visible deterrent other than a radio at his hip.

"Reason for visit?" the man asked, pushed himself up

from his seat, and paused the movie playing on his phone.

"I'm here to visit my client," he replied with a small, businesslike smile. Just because he didn't like being there didn't mean he couldn't be professional. That was what people hired their lawyers to be, right? Professional?

"Name of your client?" the guard asked while he quickly filled out a form on the computer.

"Evan Carlson." He placed the man's file on the counter, and the guard eyed it like it was a snake.

"That won't be necessary. I'll only need to see your ID, and if you could sign your name, I'll issue you a visitor's badge," the man said with a chuckle and printed out the form for Banks to sign with somewhat surprising efficiency.

If only visiting every other prison in the world were this easy, Banks thought as he signed where indicated and pinned the badge on his lapel.

Well, most of the prisons in the world wouldn't be as empty, that was for sure, he mused. There weren't that many criminals with the kind of bank balance required for up-market incarceration. He shrugged, made his way into the facility, and followed the yellow line through the halls as indicated at the entrance. The facility appeared to be almost fully automated. Most of the doors only required him to press his badge to the keypad on the side. There were a large number of cameras, though, so they had that going for them.

Banks stepped into the visitor's center. Even this room was pleasant and calm. Tables and chairs were provided, and a couple of guards sat in the corner of the room, obviously stationed there for the purpose of watching the interactions to make sure nothing that wasn't allowed was passed to the prisoners. They looked more engaged with what sounded like the newest Candy Crush game than they were on their task, however. Would they ever stop making those games?

Not so long as they made money, he assumed.

He sat, retrieved his files, and laid them out on one of the tables. Again, having it all on some kind of digital storage device would be easier, but the clients liked to see the files in person. The paperwork made them feel safe and comfortable like it was more real to them or something. He could understand that, he supposed—a certain fear of change and a mistrust of the digital age they'd actually been in for decades by now, which meant he needed to lug paper around everywhere he went.

Banks leaned back in his seat and smiled at the symmetrical organization of the papers in front of him. Maybe it wasn't all bad. There wasn't the same feeling of symmetry when you simply placed things on the surface and tried to keep everything neat and organized in a pile. It was also a way to keep his mind occupied while he waited for his client.

The door at the other end of the room buzzed and, a little irritated, he looked up from the table where he still applied minute corrections to the organization of his paperwork. He reminded himself that his client—the actual reason for his visit—had arrived. His need for perfection now set aside, he leaned back in his seat, straightened his coat, and looked at the man who approached.

There was something about these people that said they

came from money, he acknowledged as Carlson limped over to him. Banks had heard about what happened and how he had been shot on the plane he'd planned to abscond on shortly before his arrest. The fact that they had allowed him to have full reconstructive surgery on his knee as well as a cane was astounding—full mahogany too, from the look of it, with an ivory grip. He couldn't help a soft shake of his head. It certainly paid to be rich in these parts.

It was somewhat hypocritical of him to think that, he supposed. He made upper-six figures in base salary before the addition of performance incentives and bonuses. This year alone, he had already put seven figures away with much more to come.

Still, an air of old money hung around Carlson. Even in prison, his hair looked like it had been styled by New York pros and boasted the salt and pepper look people called distinguished. His shoulders filled the eyesore orange jumpsuit prisoners wore regardless of where they were imprisoned. He looked like he could be a model for the damn garment. Even walking with that limp, he carried himself with the kind of grace people like Banks only saw in movies.

The prisoner took a second to situate himself on his chair and scowled and groaned as he settled into place. His knee was still stiff and unable to bend if the way he sat was any indication. Banks tried hard to feel bad for him, but he'd also seen why Carlson had been targeted like that.

Still, he was professional enough to not let his personal feelings interfere with his business and simply smiled and proffered his hand to shake Carlson's.

"Mr. Carlson, my name is Mason Banks, Esq," he said to complete the formalities. "I've been assigned your case by the firm that has represented you, Statten-Whitney, on the request of a mutual client of ours."

The man nodded. There were less than pleasant implications involved in providing details of who the client was. Considering that these conversations were all recorded, there was no point in taking any chances. He already knew who the unnamed client was anyway.

"Of course," Carlson said with a small quirk of the lips and shook his head. "Are there any updates on my case?"

"Well, the FBI is still processing your testimony since it was considerable," Banks said and ran his finger over the redacted files he had been given by the FBI. "I know it's not my place to ask, but how does someone in your position get that deep into organized crime?"

"It's not the crime itself," Carlson explained with a soft chuckle. "A person in my particular situation tends to have trouble with the law—mostly the IRS—so it's usually a good idea to have something like a get out of jail free card, just in case. I make a few connections, launder a little money, and keep the receipt in case I ever need to give it to someone who will reduce any sentencing that might appear in my future."

Banks nodded. "That sounds like a good plan. How has it worked out for you so far?"

The prisoner shrugged and offered a noncommittal grunt. "They put me in here to work on improving my handicap while they process the testimonies I've fed them. It's rather like witness protection in style, you know what I'm saying?"

He nodded because he did, in fact, know what he was talking about. The FBI was notorious for treating cooperating witnesses like VIPs. In this instance especially, considering the names given up in his testimony, they had thought it would be better to keep him in custody for the duration of their investigation. Of course, in this case, it could be years. There had been something in the files that said his previous attorneys had been the ones to suggest putting him in this facility. There hadn't been any mention of why, but that was one of the reasons for this meeting. Carlson was afraid of someone—or something. Banks could only assume it had something to do with the bullet that had resulted in a seemingly endless series of surgeries on his shattered knee.

There was no point in guessing, though. From what he'd seen of the videos and the transcripts of his testimonies, the man struck him as the kind of person who liked the sound of his own voice.

"Well, I assume I can speak freely," Banks stated when both the guards moved a little farther away from them and the cameras in the room suddenly went dead. "Here's the short version of it, Mr. Carlson. Our mutual client is annoyed by how long it's taking for you to get out into the world and do the good work, as it were. Their words, not mine. Your minions in Pegasus have tried to put up a fight but they've failed miserably, to the point where the client is losing too much investment with too little gain."

Carlson ground his teeth. The lawyer had also assumed the man was the type who would dislike being given orders like this, but he knew he was in no position to be pissy about it. Promises had been made by the man to people whom you didn't want to disappoint. And he had disappointed them. Banks knew that even though he didn't know many of the details involved. He was merely the messenger.

"I won't leave here until certain matters outside have been dealt with," the ex-CEO said and looked visibly tense under his baggy jumpsuit.

"If you're referring to the criminal enterprises you might have angered with your testimony, you have nothing to fear," he responded with a small and hopefully reassuring smile.

"What, do you think I care about what a couple of small-time Italian mobsters can do to me?" The man leaned forward and whispered despite knowing they weren't being listened to by anyone who mattered. "Please. I have more resources at my disposal than the whole of the Cosa Nostra."

"Then color me curious," Banks said and shifted in the uncomfortable seat. "What makes someone with your kind of resources hide in federal custody?"

Carlson didn't like that question. He had worded it in a precise fashion to rub him the wrong way, and he could see his words had exactly that effect as the prisoner settled back in his seat and adjusted his jumpsuit the same way he would have adjusted a sport coat.

"I assume you're aware of the actions perpetrated by Colonel James Anderson and Dr. Courtney Monroe, the duo that currently runs Pegasus in my absence?" he asked, his voice still low.

"Of course," the lawyer replied and allowed a warm and hopefully professional expression to light up his face.

"They are the reason why your exit from this facility is being facilitated."

"What you don't know, I suppose, is that they have worked with a pit bull," the man continued. "Well, not an actual pit bull, but an enforcer—muscle they brought in to make sure their takeover was successful."

"We knew they had muscle, but are you saying it's the work of only one man?" He'd seen the kind of damage that had been wreaked on their investment, but he always assumed that it had been the work of a highly-trained team.

"Well, I assume he has a team, but I only met the one man," Carlson confirmed with a scowl. "The motherfucker put a bullet in my knee and walked away, leaving me to eat the charges as some kind of lesson, I think."

"Oh, right, I remember that." Banks scanned the file until he found the section that covered the incident. There had been a couple of questions raised over it. "How did that happen again?"

"He shot me," he explained with exaggerated patience but looked and sounded exasperated. "What the fuck else do you need to know?"

"Nothing that's not already in the file," the lawyer said quietly with a hasty glance at the guards who still made no effort to listen in. "I merely need to understand what happened from your perspective so I can spin it for your hearing for a more accessible kind of confinement."

He nodded and winced as he shifted in his seat. "So, what can you do to help me with that?"

"To help you eliminate Anderson and Monroe?" Banks asked and narrowed his eyes.

"Eventually, sure, but to get to them, you need to get to their muscle first," the former CEO replied and rolled his eyes as if this much at least was obvious. "The man called himself Savage when we talked. Before…you know." He pointed at his knee.

"Right." The lawyer read quickly to see if there was any mention of this Savage character in any of the testimonies that had been submitted. He wasn't surprised to find there wasn't. The prisoner seemed genuinely terrified of this man, and he wasn't the kind of man to scare easily.

He wasn't the kind to get casually kneecapped like that either, Banks thought and rubbed his eyes as his mind worked the possibilities.

"Okay, Savage…that sounds like a fake name," he said decisively.

"It probably is," Carlson agreed. "But he was American and definitely had experience in the intimidation business. From the look of him and the way he operated, he might even have a military background. That should be enough for you to start with, right?"

"Do you have any pictures of him?" At this point, even grasping at vague straws might provide somewhere to start with his search. "Or maybe remember what he looks like?"

"If there were pictures, they were scrubbed," the man said and shook his head. "He has support staff, that much is obvious, but there has to be some kind of image of him out there. He…had green eyes, although I guess he could have worn color-changing contacts, I suppose. Other than that, he had brown hair—a very average-looking Caucasian male. Not too bulky and not too tall. Nothing really stood out about him, now that I think about it."

Banks made notes of what little description the client provided. It wasn't much, but he had been known to find people with less. He was a tenacious bastard, something taught to him in his early days as an attorney. If this enforcer had been in the military, those bastards tended to keep the records on their operatives very dutifully. If the man was one of Anderson and Monroe's associates and had been seen with them, there would be pictures to work with somewhere. If he could find those, it would be a start.

He had been told to meet with Carlson and make sure he was ready to work with them again, and it seemed like eliminating this Savage was the way to do it. The lawyer had to resist the urge to roll his eyes as he gathered his paperwork again.

"I need you to dig deeper," the prisoner said and obviously sensed that his time was almost up. "Find the man, find his weaknesses, and use them to take him out of the picture. With him still around, you'll never get to Anderson or Monroe. He's too good a buffer."

Banks nodded, finished packing up, and pushed himself from his seat. He extended his hand for Carlson to shake as the guards moved closer again and the cameras came back to life.

"I'll see what I can do," he said with a small but non-committal smile. "I'll let you know."

Plans already churned in his mind. He didn't wait for Carlson to push his lame ass up from his seat before he headed to the doors that buzzed to let him out.

First, find the muscle, then find the muscle's weaknesses. Use those weaknesses against the muscle somehow.

It wasn't anything he hadn't done before.

CHAPTER TWO

It hadn't been an easy recovery. They never were, but there was something about this one that made him feel…devastated.

He had taken a considerable beating. Even he wouldn't deny that. But he had taken beatings in the past, some of which had been worse than this. Savage could remember a couple of times when he had walked away with gunshot wounds, treated them himself, and been back in action after only a few days of recovery. He had been young then, of course. His body had felt like a machine that would keep on going forever.

And he felt the effects of that now. The punch to his kidney had seemed to be the worst of it, and after he'd reached the hospital, there had been problems with internal bleeding he hadn't detected at first. It had required surgery, which left him laid up for a little longer than he would have liked. The damage had been extensive.

"You should see the other guy," had been something he found himself saying more and more after a couple of visits. He wasn't wrong to say it, of course. It had been a tough fight for them both and he had certainly come away the winner. He'd needed to play dirty to achieve his victory, though. Then again, any fight against the monster of a human he'd paired off against was ridiculously tilted toward the man's favor. He certainly didn't feel bad for pounding him where every man wanted to be treated nicely and then gouging his eyes out. It had been a matter of survival at that point, and the person who walked away from the bout was the one who survived.

He walked away. The other man didn't.

Well…he'd been carried away, pure and simple. He'd had difficulty moving after the adrenaline in his system had worn off and he'd winced and groaned while Terry had helped him to get to the hospital. It had culminated in a hefty dose of painkillers and him eventually put under as the MRI showed bleeding in his kidney as a result of the punch. There were other injuries in there too, which were treated at the same time.

Savage didn't like that there was a part of him that seemed to not want to recover. It was taking too long, and he alternated between trying too hard and not trying enough. The doctors told him the momentary bouts of depression could have been a result of the medication he was on, but their lack of certainty was telling. Or it felt telling, anyway.

It was a good day when, three and a half weeks later, he was given the all clear by the doctors. Thankfully, the bills could be transferred to Pegasus for Anderson and Monroe to deal with. As Jeremiah Savage, he hadn't thought to look into the variety of insurances he would need to have in order to be a functioning human being in the United States. Health insurance was one of them.

Back to the real world. The thought brought a scowl as he packed his personal effects. Terry had the presence of mind to make sure he didn't have anything incriminating on him when he was delivered to the hospital. Anderson had advised them over the phone as they drove into the place and gave them a story that wouldn't involve any cops in their business. It had worked, although the doctors had still needed to fill out paperwork that meant his condition would be delivered to the police should it become relevant to any open cases.

Savage doubted that would happen. Terry had managed to take care of the bodies before the police arrived to investigate the gunfire. It wasn't like it had happened in a populated neighborhood, and the few who were in the area probably wanted to get clear of it themselves before the cops showed up.

Things had been tied up in a neat little bow. Alvarez had taken care of Stafford, and that meant all the money that had originally gone into the attempt to kill Anderson had gone into the Mexican's bank account.

Terry and Sam had both come in to visit him a couple of times to make sure his recovery was progressing as it should. Anderson did too, and while it seemed that Monroe's business in the Zoo kept her occupied, the former colonel told him that the woman had sent her best regards and both of them told him to focus on recovery above all else. His money would still come in while he was in bed.

He had put on a brave face for all of them. His doubts

about his own body's ability to recover from the beating it had taken were put aside and hidden until he could actually do something about it. Compartmentalization. That was key.

Savage would have declined the use of a wheelchair to get him to the lobby, preferring to get there on his own two feet instead. The orderlies were insistent, though, and he had to allow himself to be wheeled to the elevator. A couple of papers were waiting for him at the lobby, mostly to make sure Pegasus would cover his medical bills. Paperwork was something a man with his particular history wouldn't be used to.

When he reached the lobby, a familiar face waited for him. Not one of the faces he had expected, of course. He had always assumed that the former colonel had better things to do than to make sure his employee was recovering well, but there he was—Anderson, the tall, lean, dark-haired man with well-disguised burn scars around his neck and hands. He wore jeans, boots, a flannel shirt, and a leather jacket, but he looked uncomfortable in those for some reason. He seemed like the kind of man who would be uncomfortable in anything that wasn't a uniform of some kind. Even a suit and tie would probably feel better.

"Savage," Anderson said with a smirk, pushed up from his seat, and put the magazine he had been reading to pass the time aside. He approached quickly to shake his hand. "I love the wheels."

"Anderson." The operative chuckled and shook the man's hand firmly. "Yeah…they basically made me do it. I can walk fine, but I guess they want to make me feel like an invalid for as long as possible. What the hell are you doing here, you crazy bastard? Don't you have a home life to get back to? A kid and wife who need your attention more than me?"

"I'll be honest with you, I needed a break from the home life," he admitted and looked a little guilty. "And you're the only one I've actually opened up to about that, so you're the only one I can be honest with about it."

"Damn," Savage grumbled as they made their way to where the paperwork waited for him. "Does that mean we're friends now? Because I don't think I can handle the pressure."

"I'm afraid so." The former colonel chuckled and left him to sign his name on all the documents. He finished with it less than a minute later, and both men moved toward the sliding exit doors.

"So what have you been up to while I've been laid up?" he asked as Anderson brought them to a halt at the front where a car was brought around for them. "Fending off more attacks from Carlson's minions? Have you put Sam and Terry through their paces?"

"In order, no, and yes," Anderson said and gestured to a gleaming, polished Mustang GT that stopped at the entrance. Both men took a moment to appreciate it and Savage pushed himself gratefully from the wheelchair. "I don't know why or how, but it seems like Carlson's people have laid low after Stafford's death. Which…okay, I assume you had something to do with?"

Both men stepped into the car and the ex-colonel looked like he was enjoying himself a little too much—to the point where his companion wondered if he needed to give the two a room.

"Do you really want an answer to that?" he asked and leaned into the leather passenger seat with a soft sigh that was both a little relaxation and a little pain. His body was still sore, but he didn't allow that to limit his appreciation for how comfortable the seat was. "Oh, by the way, our friend Alvarez says hi."

"Who now?" Anderson asked and started the car with a satisfying roar.

"Remember? The guy in the bar?" he asked and fiddled with the controls on his seat until the other man glared at him. "The Mexican Sam and I were sent to recover some of our stolen merch from."

"Oh…right. The man who got me into the VIP section of a club for the first time," Anderson said with a chuckle and eased the car slowly out of the parking lot.

"That…that's sad, dude," Savage replied and gave Anderson a comforting pat on the shoulder. "I assume a big part of what you want me to do is provide you and Monroe with all the plausible deniability the police know and love, so I'll leave out the part where Sam and I tore through this guy's complex like he owed us money." He grinned cheerfully as they pulled out onto the road. "Which, you know, he did."

"Well, keep assuming that," Anderson replied and fed the beast they were riding a little more gas as they headed deeper into the city of Philadelphia. It was mid-afternoon, meaning the peak of the rush hour was still a few hours away, but the streets were far from empty, They wouldn't be able to enjoy the full power of the car but then again, they didn't need to. It was enough to simply revel in the ride. Savage didn't know what Anderson was doing with such a family-unfriendly car, but he had no intention to complain.

There weren't that many pleasures in the world equal to that of riding around in a muscle car. It was in the middle of autumn, meaning it wasn't convertible weather, but it was still a nice drive all the way to the apartment the operative had called home during those times when he wasn't called to travel all around the country for work.

They pulled into the underground parking lot of his building in almost complete silence. It hadn't been uncomfortable, even though Savage knew they needed to have a talk about what he would do next now that he was out of the hospital.

"So, these paces you've put Sam and Terry through," Savage said as they stopped in one of the empty parking places. "They wouldn't have anything to do with keeping your family safe, would they?"

Anderson shrugged his shoulders. "Sam and Ivy have really bonded. Ivy hasn't had many female friends since we've recently moved out here. Terry and Damon really get along too, so I assumed it was what they wanted to do. Besides, having them take care of the family gave me more time to work with Anja and find out what Carlson's people are up to."

"And what did you find?" he asked as they moved to the elevator of the building.

"More than I expected although less than I hoped," the other man admitted. "Like I said, they've gone to ground more and more over the past few weeks. There have still been a couple of incidents of lab materials going missing, smaller stuff like that. Anja had worked on containing them as much as she could from her end of things, but there has been some need for fieldwork."

"You weren't able to take care of that?" Savage asked when the elevator arrived and they stepped inside. He punched the button for the seventh floor.

"Well, no," Anderson grumbled and shook his head. "Courtney had a couple of choice words to share about me heading out into the field on my own."

"And you took that from her?" He raised an eyebrow in genuine surprise.

"Yep." The man shrugged and seemed to completely lack shame on that particular issue, and Savage nodded.

"She is a terrifying woman," he said with a firm nod.

"Right. Anyway," the ex-colonel said when the elevator came to a halt and they stepped out into the hallway leading to the apartment. "I sent Terry and Sam in to deal with what they could. Anja says they have all the right training, but they're not as easy to work with as you are. I think she missed you, although she didn't say it outright."

"That's fair." He chuckled, retrieved his keys, and opened the door. "She's not the kind of person to share her feelings much anyway, so you have to read into what she says."

His companion nodded as they entered. It wasn't an overly expensive apartment—nothing like a penthouse, of course—but even one like this in the center of Philly wasn't cheap. It wasn't all that small either, with a kitchen that connected via a bar to the living room. In addition to a guest bathroom, the single bedroom had an en suite bathroom of its own.

Savage looked at Anderson, who had narrowed his eyes

as he inspected the room. He wasn't sure what the man was looking for. He always made sure the place was clean before he left and didn't keep much in the way of fresh food that would go bad after a long time away. He made sure to eat healthy, of course, but he always purchased only what he needed when he needed it, given his unpredictable schedule. Aside from the necessary appliances in the kitchen, the apartment was purely utilitarian, and the only visible furnishings were a couple of couches surrounding a widescreen TV.

It was still clean although it had collected a little dust. Savage opened the curtains and turned to see Anderson still making a careful scrutiny of the space.

"You really don't like decorations, do you?" the man said abruptly as if he'd suddenly realized what it was he found strange. The operative looked around and nodded. There weren't any paintings on the walls, no plants, fake or otherwise, and nothing to indicate that an actual human lived here. It looked like a picture straight out of a real estate magazine, an empty canvas meant to elicit the artistic nature inside every bored housewife who saw it.

"I never saw the point," he said with a chuckle. He sauntered over to the fridge in the kitchen, pulled out two long-necks, untwisted the caps, and handed one of them to his companion. "I won't spend what little time I have off staring at paintings or taking care of plants."

"Fair enough." Anderson accepted the beer with a smile. "You can't deny this place needs a woman's touch, though. Something…hell, a tea cozy or a bowl of potpourri. Anything. And are you sure you should drink with the medication you're supposed to be on?"

He shrugged with every intention not to answer. After a moment, he dropped onto the couch and indicated for the other man to do the same. "If they didn't want me to drink, they should have told me."

"And if they had told you?" the former colonel asked.

"Then I didn't listen, same difference." He grinned, clinked his bottle to Anderson's, and took a long swig from it. "Think about it. With the life I live, dying of liver failure or something like that is probably preferable to getting shot or having my skull bashed in anyway."

"Well…that's depressing," Anderson replied with a shake of his head. "You really need a better outlook on life, you know. And like I said, get a woman's touch around here."

"I don't generally bring the women I meet back here," he replied matter of factly.

"Well, that's obvious enough," The former colonel chuckled. "If Jessica Coleman could see this place, she would go full in on the nesting instinct."

"Why would she ever come here to see it?" he asked and cringed inwardly when he realized a little too much bitterness had entered his voice as he spoke, which in turn made the other man study him closely before he responded.

"Ah…well, she's back in Philly, actually. I assumed you knew." Savage shook his head to indicate that he didn't, in fact, know. "Yeah, Courtney called her in to give her and the board an overview of the labs she's been overseeing. She was the one who alerted Anja to some of the robberies and attempted robberies, so she does need to update them all and make sure none of them see what's happening as any sign of weakness. There was something to do with stock shares and the fact they're selling the shares that belonged to Carlson in a little while, so they don't want any price drops. Something like that."

He would be the first to admit he didn't know much about stocks and shares or anything, but it did make sense. News of robberies at newly established labs had the potential to send the stock prices down.

"She'll give her presentation tomorrow," Anderson continued when he noted the operative's sudden interest in the conversation. "It'll be at the Pegasus building. As a security consultant whom we have on retainer, I'm sure nobody would be surprised to see you in attendance."

"I can basically guarantee Dr. Coleman will be surprised to see me there," he responded with a grim chuckle and took another sip of his drink. "She didn't even let me know she was back in town," he grumbled and sipped his beer as if to punctuate his thoughts. "But you know what? This has all been about learning and growing through experiences and shit. I bet meeting her is probably the best thing to do, right?"

"It makes sense to me," the other man said and kept his voice soft. "So will you be there tomorrow?"

Savage nodded. "Yeah, I think I will. But I think that's enough emotional talk. My DVR is filled to busting with games I missed while I was in recovery. Let's do that and not talk."

"It sounds good to me." Anderson chuckled as Savage turned his TV on, selected one of the first games he had missed, and leaned back in his seat.

CHAPTER THREE

Mistakes were made, Savage realized as he settled into his seat in the conference room where the presentation would be given.

First of all, he felt like a fish out of water. The other men and women in the room looked like they belonged in an environment like this. Three-hundred-dollar haircuts were somehow the cheapest parts of their attire but still managed to be understated at the same time. They looked serious and talked in hushed whispers about what might as well be quantum physics for all he really knew about it.

He wore a suit with no tie and felt as uncomfortable in it as Anderson had been in casual clothes. Admittedly, the coat he wore was a good cover for the pistol snuggled into his side. It was good to be armed again. There was a certain reassurance to it, he realized. The people around him seemed as comfortable in their expensive clothes and with their overpriced watches as he did merely having that oddly-shaped pistol tucked into the underarm holster hidden beneath his jacket.

That was the difference between him and them, he realized and leaned back in his seat, a little more at ease now that he'd thought things through. The feeling almost immediately disappeared when he looked up to see who walked over to the head of the conference table.

She hadn't changed much, but there was still a hint of a jolt in his chest when he saw her there. Her hair was different, he realized and decided that platinum blonde suited her. It gave her an edge, a rigidity that lent her confidence. She wore a pantsuit instead of a lab coat, and the glasses looked new too.

Jessica had changed, Savage amended and focused his gaze on the table. He suddenly didn't feel quite as confident as he had a couple of seconds before. She looked around the table and touched her glasses the way she had when they had talked before. It was a trick, she told him, which gave her a moment to think and to look around at everyone she was addressing before she actually spoke.

Her gaze settled on him and she paused for a half-second. She looked momentarily startled and her right eye twitched before she adjusted her glasses again quickly. Her finger pushed them onto the bridge of her nose as she turned and looked around at the rest of the assembled group, who had apparently missed her little pause.

"Ladies and gentlemen, thank you for taking the time to be with us here today," Coleman said. Her voice carried well, and she didn't sound at all fazed by her audience.

"Here with us?" one of the board members asked, a hint of hostility in her voice. Savage made a note to look into her later. Carlson still had many loyalists on the board, and while they were content to keep their heads low and follow the status quo, he didn't doubt that they would surge forward at the first chance they had. People like this could sense weakness the way sharks could smell blood in the water.

"Yes, here with us," a voice said from the screen behind Coleman which displayed Monroe, speaking from the Zoo. She looked tired and a little bruised besides and wore glasses and a lab coat as she listened in on the meeting. "I'll be here to oversee proceedings, but Dr. Coleman will run the meeting. You can treat her words as if they came from my own mouth."

"Thank you, Dr. Monroe," Coleman said, and her lips quirked up as she turned back to the others. "Shall we begin?"

A handful of assistants and aides entered the room and passed the meeting's agenda around to each participant. Savage took a moment to peruse the details. There wasn't much said on the paper he was given. He doubted that much of the conversation would be about him anyway, despite his assumed status as a security consultant. Protecting wasn't really in his job description these days unless you counted the best protection as a good offense.

In which case, he was a fantastic protector.

The meeting proceeded and from what he could understand, she went through the paces of delivering the status of each of the labs. Part of this was to make sure each of the board members knew that despite the attempts at sabotage and robbery, they were still on track to resume work on the projects they had been given. He noted that most of the projects affected by robbery or attempted robbery were those dealing with the government contracts sent to them by the Pentagon and delivered almost directly from the Zoo. There would undoubtedly be a fair amount of contention about it, but he'd learned to trust his gut.

And right now, his gut told him that anyone who tried to interfere with Zoo projects did so on Carlson's orders.

Educated guesses were still guesses, right?

Savage sucked in a deep breath as Coleman finished her presentation and immediately opened the floor to questions. There weren't that many, he realized and wasn't sure whether to be surprised or not. They might be in charge of the running of the company, but that didn't mean they knew what they were doing. What they were good at was delegating all the actual work to competent individuals like Coleman and himself and reaping the rewards.

They didn't have much to say. After a couple of questions, mostly involving the cost of her proposals—which were almost entirely covered by Courtney as she had the data on that—the board members all began to leave. He'd been engrossed in his own thoughts and didn't realize the meeting was over until he saw them all stand.

He had no intention to be caught in there alone with Coleman because he wasn't good at dealing with old flames. One of the reasons he had elected to take on a couple of extra tours in some of the most dangerous places in the world was so he wouldn't have to deal with his ex-wife and the complications that had separated the two of them. It wasn't something he was proud of, but he wouldn't try to hide that truth about himself either.

His attempted retreat didn't work, though. She saw him try to slip out without talking to her, and she stepped between him and the door with a smile. Her quick thinking had him caught and she knew it. He tried to force a smile, but it came off poorly and he gave up the attempt after a couple of seconds.

"Hey there, Jer," Coleman said and cocked her head to the side as she watched him look around hastily as if to find another way to escape.

"Hello, Jessica," Savage said finally and resigned himself to his fate. He would have an uncomfortable conversation one way or the other, it seemed. "Your hair looks great."

"Thanks. It's nice to see you again too," she said and squeezed his shoulder lightly.

"I honestly hoped you wouldn't see me," he replied with an awkward chuckle. "I'm not great at this kind of conversation."

"Well, that's obvious enough," she replied with an understanding smirk. "Although in the future, if you find yourself in a situation where you would rather not be seen, I would suggest you try to avoid sticking out like a sore thumb. You could not have been more out of place in the meeting."

"I don't disagree." He had actually begun to wonder what it was he had hoped to accomplish by attending, and with no answers forthcoming, he shook his head.

"I think we need to talk, Jer," she said with another firm squeeze to his shoulder. "I'm not too happy with how we left things, and I want to set that right."

His jaw tensed instinctively, even without him thinking about what that might mean. He had practiced this conversation a hundred times in his head, and he had always alternated between cold and hot burns. In one scenario, he'd always be cold and collected and cut her off with his calm yet icy retorts. In the other, he'd be hot under the collar with a few curses tossed in for good measure and play to her guilt for having left him behind when a better offer showed up. Neither was particularly classy, but he'd never been classy, to begin with.

The lack of class was a moot point, however, since neither seemed to fit in this situation. She did seem genuinely regretful over what had happened and how, and the look on her face pleaded for a chance to explain. These effectively swept aside the need to vent at her and release the emotions he'd successfully repressed over the past few months. In all honesty, he wasn't actually angry at her. He understood why she'd made the choice, and he wasn't about to criticize her for putting her career in front of her love life. It wasn't like they had even been in a long-term relationship.

He sighed and nodded. "Yeah, I think we need to talk too."

She noted his hesitation but didn't appear to want to press him for an explanation. She smiled and ran her fingers down his arm before she let her hand drop to her side. "What do you say—should we have dinner tonight? It'll give us time to talk over a nice meal and in a location that can provide enough booze if the night demands it. And I'll pay for myself, obviously. It's not like it's a date or anything."

"That sounds fair. Should I pick you up?"

"I think it's better if we meet there," Coleman said as they made their way toward the elevator. "Do you know the Marmont? On Market Street?"

Savage nodded. "Around eight? That should give us time to talk and drink if that's the case."

"It's…not a date," she replied with a grin as the elevator arrived. She stepped inside and narrowed her eyes when he hesitated. "Are you going down?"

"Yeah, but I think I'll take the stairs." He gestured vaguely at the stairwell door. "It's not that I don't enjoy palpable tension, but…I think the walk will do me good. I've been in a hospital bed for the past three weeks or so and I could use the exercise."

"Suit yourself," she replied, chuckled, and pressed the button for the lobby. The doors closed to hide her from view. He nodded and remained where he was for a few long seconds before he stared his reflection in the elevator doors in the eye.

"Yeah," he grunted and headed over to the stairs he remembered all too clearly from his first visit to this building. "That went about as well as you could have expected, dumbass."

He sighed, shook his head, and began a slow descent. It wasn't the worst decision he'd ever made. He could feel his muscles begin to loosen and limber up after the first two floors. It seemed he really did need exercise and he decided he might actually visit the gym before going out to dinner. If nothing else, he could work up an appetite so he wouldn't dread the meal quite so much.

Banks hated being in Washington—the capital city, not the state. He actually liked the state. It provided a variety of open spaces to go fishing, where he could spend long hours in silence while he waited to catch something he could cook with his own two hands. There was a cause and effect aesthetic to the idea which he found appealing.

The city, on the other hand, was something else entirely. It was populated with the people he held responsible for why he disliked humans and any interaction with them. And they seemed worse around there too. There was something about this city that made everyone a little greedier, a little meaner, and a little less understanding. If he didn't know any better, he would have said each one of these bastards hated other people as much as he did, and this was their punishment for the rest of their race.

If that was the plan, well…it was one hell of a plan, he had to admit.

He looked up from where he arranged his folders on the coffee table in front of him when Congressman Alfred Jenkins stepped out of his office. The man laughed with a couple of aides and other members of Congress as he sent them off with messages to be distributed to their various colleagues and subordinates. There were a couple of bills they needed to pass before they could retire for the Thanksgiving weekend—or fail, possibly. Banks wasn't sure which and honestly didn't care.

He wasn't there to talk politics. Jenkins was a long-time member of the House Armed Services Committee, the kind of person who would oversee the financial spending in the Pentagon and the perfect person for him to meet. He had studied Jenkins for some time to determine what kind of price the man would demand when someone asked what Banks had to ask.

It hadn't taken very long for him to decide the price was too high and he would go a different route. His choice wasn't based on any dislike for the concept of bribery per se. It was a necessary, if skeevy, element of how governments were run. But time was of the essence, and they didn't have enough of it to cater to the demands of a sly and greedy politician.

"Congressman Jenkins," he said and offered his hand, which the congressman took almost automatically. "I'm Mason Banks, Esq, and I've come at the request of a client of mine—friends of yours, I understand. Pegasus Incorporated?"

"Pegasus, of course!" Jenkins exclaimed with a laugh. "I always have time for my friends at Pegasus. I'll catch up with you guys later." The other aides nodded and made their way out as the congressman invited his visitor into his office.

"Well, the appropriations committee is due to meet in a week, and I think you folks will be quite happy with the contracts that will come your way," he said with a chuckle.

"I'll be honest with you, Congressman," Banks said and closing the door. "I don't actually represent Pegasus itself. There is enough time to run through the various problems that come with this, but I'm sure they will be irrelevant by the time I've finished saying what I've come here to say."

The man tilted his head and opened his mouth as he reached for his phone, probably to call security. The lawyer calmly withdrew a file from his briefcase—which he'd stored above all the others so it could be easily accessible—and placed it on the desk. Jenkins examined it intently and narrowed his eyes when Banks drew one of the pictures out and slid it on top of the folder. The image was of the congressman himself, very clearly drunk and stepping out of a building downtown with a woman who was equally as clearly not his wife—and semi-nude, as well.

"Before you launch the inevitable questions of how I obtained these and your denial that it's you, I'll point out that it wouldn't take much to convince a jury to believe that young woman there is underage." He retrieved a couple more of the pictures. "Do I have your attention, congressman?"

Jenkins looked like something dark had passed over his grave and leaned forward. He frowned as he touched the edges of the pictures as if to make sure they were real.

"What do you want?" he asked finally.

"I need you to find someone," Banks replied and pulled another picture out of his briefcase. With a slow, deliberate movement, he placed it on the desk and turned it so Jenkins could see it. The headshot was obviously blown up and what he assumed was the selfie it started out as had been cut from the finished image. It presented the face of a man in his...well, he had to assume it was his thirties, although it could have as easily been late twenties or early forties. He had brown hair and green eyes and was of average height and build—nothing overly dramatic about him. Banks felt he could come across the man on the street and not recognize him.

He still didn't know how his client's resources had found the original picture considering the weak description Carlson had provided him with. Then again, he no longer underestimated what his client could do.

"And who am I looking at?" Jenkins asked quietly.

"I don't know. That's what I'm asking you." He smiled to hopefully soften the blow. "Now, these pictures of you wetting your dick are the stick, as it were. There is a carrot to this whole thing too. You're running a reelection campaign that could be severely damaged by the evidence in front of you. Well, except this one, I suppose." He pointed out the picture of Savage. "The kind of campaign that could use a generous amount of anonymous donations as well as endorsements by my client."

"And who might your client be?" the congressman asked.

"The person who has your balls in a vice," Banks said, repacked his briefcase, and turned to the door again. "Carrot and stick, Congressman. I know you'll make the right choice. When you do, you can find my comm line on the back of those pictures."

Jenkins wasn't even remotely brave. He was accustomed to being in charge, but when he lost his power, he wasn't the type to bend.

"Aren't you going to take the pictures?" he asked as his visitor reached the door.

"Those are printouts, Congressman." The lawyer turned to face him again. "We have the original images stored online. You should keep those, though, to remind you who has your balls in a vice."

He gulped and Banks smiled, stepped out, and closed the door again. He had no doubt that he would hear from Jenkins again.

CHAPTER FOUR

Savage had to admit he wasn't sure how to do this. He hadn't been on a date in a long time, which made the fact that he wasn't going on a date rather fortunate. Still, the fact remained that he didn't know what he was supposed to do in terms of dress code.

He shook his head, irritated by himself and the situation. While he hadn't been alone since Coleman had been gone, there had never been any dating involved. His love life had mostly been drunken encounters that had culminated in quick one-night stands in hotel rooms or the women's homes, which had enabled him to leave hastily the next morning. As it turned out, being dark and mysterious overcame his usually unobtrusive appearance. He didn't fully understand the apparent allure but he had no desire to argue with it.

Finally, prompted in part by his mental wandering, he came up with the idea to dress casually. It wasn't like he looked good in a suit and tie anyway. Not anymore. There was a time way back when proms were still something he actually cared about and he looked rather snappy in a tux. Very James Bond-like, according to his mother.

Those times had passed, and he felt too uncomfortable in a suit and tie. That discomfort would simply not happen tonight. Savage also felt there was no uniform attire he would feel comfortable in and therefore look good in. Even though he hadn't felt awkward in the ceremonial uniform from his time in the military forces, he doubted that he would be seen anywhere near that particular uniform any time soon. It was the inevitable result of the fact that he was dead to everyone who had ever seen him in one.

It wasn't a particularly inspiring mindset to be in when he had to head out to have a meal with his ex, but Savage was good at compartmentalization. He could put this mindset aside for the moment. It worried him more that he didn't even know what he would face with Coleman. As he stared at himself in the mirror, he acknowledged a trace of ice in his veins—much like he usually felt when he knew he was going into combat.

He had no idea why he would feel like that given that this was simply a social meeting. The overflow wasn't good compartmentalization either. It was essentially drawing on something entirely separate to manage an unrelated issue.

It wasn't healthy. He knew it but wasn't sure what to do about it.

Savage dragged himself reluctantly out of his apartment and headed down to his car. He didn't like that he had time to think about this. It would be obvious to anyone who ever met him that he'd had a workout and cleaned himself up for this. He didn't like the subtle implications it carried.

A part of him was relieved that he'd dressed casually. Jeans, boots, and a button-up shirt were definitely preferable to a suit. As a last-minute decision, he'd shrugged into a leather jacket Sam had given him as a joke—but which he actually really liked—to complete the outfit with a little something extra. He reached his car all too quickly and paused to look at it with a small smile. His car. It was a pleasant affirmation of how far he had come, even if it wasn't remotely impressive—certainly, nothing like Anderson's Mustang.

It was a hybrid. He didn't care for them but the mileage was decent, which meant fewer trips to the gas station. It was simply a tool to get him from point A to point B. If he ever got his hands on something he could really treat well, that was when things would change.

He stepped inside and reversed out of the garage and into the street. The rush hour was still noticeable but it had died down enough in the inner city to allow him to reach the restaurant Coleman had selected for them without unnecessary delays.

It was a good call as restaurants went, he decided. The bar at the very front attracted considerable attention. Three or four bartenders were there at all times, while the restaurant was in the back. He could see she was already at the bar, halfway through the gin and tonic she'd ordered while she waited.

Savage cleared his throat and took a quick look at himself in some of the nearby reflective surfaces before he pushed inside and tried once again to anticipate what she would say when he reached her.

He should have been able to guess.

"Hey." She smiled and took a quick sip from her drink. "Do you want to move to the table?"

"Hold your horses there, Coleman," he said with a chuckle and slid hastily onto the seat a couple of the nearby single men were eyeing. Depending on how patient they were and how the night went, they might actually have their chance later on, he mused.

"Don't you want to get to the meal?" she asked and regarded him curiously. "I hear the Steak au Poivre here is really good."

"And I look forward to finding out what the fuck that is," he said with a nod. "But if this meal will go the way I think it will, we should probably avail ourselves of as much alcohol as we can get our hands on."

Coleman chuckled and nodded agreement as he waved one of the bartenders over. "Double of bourbon, neat, please."

"You got it," the man replied briskly and delivered the drink in a few seconds. Savage paid for it and settled into his seat before he made the double into a single in one sip. It wasn't something he usually did, but the night wasn't a usual one, was it?

She appeared to feel the same and drained her gin and tonic and requested another one in quick succession.

"For the meal," she said with a smile.

He shrugged. "I'm not judging." He really wasn't. The only reason why he hadn't lubricated as quickly himself was because he was on an empty stomach. If there was anything thing worse than talking to your ex about your relationship, it was talking to your ex about your relationship while completely hammered.

They moved to their reserved table by unspoken mutual agreement. The restaurant definitely wasn't the kind of place he usually went to, but that wasn't the highest of bars to clear. He was the kind of person who could cook for himself, and when he wanted something different, he would get a burger or a steak at a sports bar and that would be that.

From the menu that listed first course, second course, dessert, and wine, he could tell this was a classier establishment than he was used to. Well, it wasn't like he couldn't afford it anymore. With the stipend Monroe and Anderson paid to retain his services for when they needed him to apply a little pressure to the opposition, he could afford to eat there once or twice a month.

Both chose the ceviche for a starter, something Coleman had ordered and he simply went along with her choice. She made a show of studying the wine menu and ordered a dry Riesling.

Savage knew it was some kind of white wine, but he didn't want to appear as though he relied on her for his order.

"I'll…have a beer," he said with a firm nod and handed the first-course menu back to the waiter.

The tall, lean man smiled politely in response. "And what kind of beer does the gentleman prefer?"

"Whatever you have on tap," he insisted and pushed the drinks menu into the man's hand.

"We have a variety of beers on tap here, sir," the waiter replied. Savage couldn't be sure in the dim lighting, but he would have bet the kid was toying with him. Coleman obviously thought the same thing because she stepped in to rescue him.

"Something to go with the ceviche," she said and with a firm nudge, insisted the server take the menu. "An IPA, for instance."

"An IPA it is." The waiter's smile clearly indicated that he liked her more than Savage and he retreated quickly to relay their order.

"So," Coleman said once they were alone.

"So," he replied. "What the hell is a ceviche?"

She laughed and shook her head. "It's basically fish that has been cured in citric—lime, in this case—liberally spiced and served with a couple of dips like mango and avocado. Something appetizing and light to start the meal off."

"Couldn't we have gone to a sushi joint for raw fish?" he asked as their drinks arrived. He did have to admit, the aggressively hoppy taste of the beer she had ordered for him—the IPA?—was a good way to get his appetite going.

"It's not raw, it's cured." She laughed, sipped her wine, and made a pleased face. He wondered for a moment if he should have gone for the wine too. "Besides, this is only a starter. We came here for the steak, right?"

"Right, the steak au pwah?" Savage asked with a grin.

"Poivre," Coleman corrected. "It's French, so about two-thirds of the letters in the writing will be silent for some reason."

"Well, color me impressed." Savage looked around a little awkwardly. He'd noticed she'd had more or less the same idea as he had and arrived in what looked like a casual outfit. She still looked stunning in a summer dress, and it did remind him of their mission together in the hotel. "I'm...not really used to restaurants like these if it wasn't obvious already."

"I only know about it because of my parents, to be honest," she said with a dismissive shrug. "They liked to put on a show of how classy they were and made sure I knew everything about it too when they entertained guests in their home."

"That sounds...boring," he observed but further comment paused when their waiter approached with the food they'd ordered. He wasn't sure what he expected, but he held what resembled an overturned bowl of slices of cured fish tangled in citric sauce. Small, decorative dots of yellow and green represented the dip she had mentioned.

"Bon Appetit," the waiter said and beat a hasty retreat.

"So..." Savage said and raised an eyebrow.

"It's better than it looks." Coleman laughed and used her fork to toy with the fish a little and mix it with the sauces. "Give it a try. This is a classy establishment, so they won't judge you if you leave most of the food on your plate. We're here for the steak, remember?"

After a moment, he nodded and followed her example to mix the food with his fork a few times before he tried a small mouthful. It smelled like lime and he grimaced when he first tasted it. The flesh was a little slimy, but it also tasted like lime plus a host of other herbs and spices, which made it light and refreshing if you could get past the fact that you were eating semi-raw fish.

At that point, he could look past a lot of shit. He hadn't eaten much all day.

His plate was empty in less than five minutes. Coleman wasn't halfway finished with her course and she grinned at him while he cleaned his plate with some of the bread supplied in a basket.

"What?"

"Well, here I was thinking you might have something against the ceviche," she replied and her grin widened. "I'm glad you enjoyed it, though."

"Enjoy might be too strong a word." Savage waited until his mouth wasn't full anymore before he spoke and dabbed his mouth clean lightly. "It wasn't terrible, though, and I've certainly had worse. I had a couple of runs in a certain South American jungle where we ran out of food supplies."

"This won't be one of those 'slimy yet satisfying' stories, is it?" Coleman asked.

He had intended to tell her about how they'd raided a couple of termite mounds and roasted the insects over a hastily built fire for food. Considering the company they were in, however, it might not be the right kind of story to tell. "I...yes, I suppose it was. Although termites end up more crunchy than slimy—which is a word I would apply to this ceviche stuff."

"Fair enough." The waiter returned and they placed their order. Once again, they concurred on their meals and both chose the Steak au Poivre she had raved about. He also went with her red wine suggestion for them both, which saved them from having to deal with the conde-scending waiter.

Savage took a single bite of the steak and closed his eyes. "Well hot fucking damn, that's a good fucking steak. And I don't care if it isn't the right kind of language for this place. When you make a steak this good, you have to expect some red-blooded folks to curse their way to a compliment."

Coleman couldn't help a laugh, but she didn't respond as she chose to focus her attention on consuming the medium-rare piece of meat. The peppercorns formed a tasty crust that complemented the flavor as well as the thick, creamy, cognac-y sauce paired with bacon-wrapped asparagus. This time, she finished before he did, which indicated that they were both equally famished. The second course finished, they allowed themselves a little time to enjoy the wine.

"I need to come here more often," he said with a chuckle and shook his head as if to almost make it a joke. "So, what have you been up to?"

"Smooth segue there, Jer." She grinned at him, tilted her head, and took a sip of her wine. "Well, Monroe has run me ragged. When she realized I was one of the few researchers she could trust, she jumped me from one lab opening to the next. Basically, I had to identify fires started by our good friend Carlson and put them out. I heard he's gone to jail, but that doesn't seem to have done much to cool the fervor of the dumbasses who take his money."

Savage shrugged. "It might seem odd to say this, but for some reason, these folks are loyal to the man. For the life of me, I don't understand why."

She looked thoughtful as she cleaned her plate with some bread. "You don't get as high as he did without acquiring a couple of loyal followers, I suppose. Things have quieted over the past few weeks, which is why I was able to come here and report instead of being flown to another lab that needs my help. I assume what you and Anderson have done is working."

"We…might have made a couple of statements," he said with a nod. "We stole back stolen material, caught a few rats trying to steal stuff, and sicced a couple of Mexican hit squads on some loyalist board members."

Coleman grinned. "Am I supposed to know about any of this?"

"Probably not, but it's not like you'd be able to prove any of it anyway." He smirked. "Besides, if you tried to do anything about it, Anderson would send me your way."

There was a hint of an awkward silence between them and he regretted what he'd said almost immediately.

"I'm sorry," he said finally while the plates were cleared. "It's not really something to make light of."

"It's okay," she replied. "It's just…for a second there, I almost forgot what you do for a living. Hell, what we do for a living. God, my life is so much more interesting than I'd like these days."

"You don't mean that," Savage challenged with a grin before he finished his red wine. His phone rang in the silence that followed, and he reached into his pocket to press the button that would send the call to voicemail.

"Well, the jury is still out on that." She chortled although her expression remained partly serious. "But that's the official story I'm sticking with anyway."

He smirked and immediately thought of a comeback but lost it when his phone buzzed again. Irritated, he pressed the voicemail button again and tried to return his attention to Coleman. His phone buzzed once but only once to tell him a text message had arrived.

"Do you need to get that?" she asked.

"Give me a second to see what it is," he replied and scowled. "It might be Anderson to say he's fallen and can't get up."

He pulled the phone out. The number on both the missed calls was blocked. So was the one behind the text message, but the origin quickly became clear when he read the message.

Answer your fucking phone – Control

"Who is Control?" Coleman asked when he showed her the message.

"Oh, it's Anja," Savage replied, pushed out of his seat, and placed his napkin on the table. "It's…an inside joke we came up with. She felt left out after we started to build a team, so we made it up to make her feel better. I'll explain the full story later, but I think I need to take this."

"Of course," she said. "I'll order us dessert."

"I'd appreciate it." The device vibrated again and he grimaced. "Get me something with chocolate, okay?"

"Will do." She smirked as the waiter came over with the dessert menus, and he hurried to the exit while the phone continued to ring.

CHAPTER FIVE

He moved outside the bar, away from the road, and finally chose an alley behind the restaurant as a quiet and secluded location appropriate for taking a call from Anja.

When he answered the damn thing and put it to his ear, he could already hear the Russian hacker. She sounded angry and cussed at him for a few seconds in Russian before she reverted to English.

"Goddamnit, Savage. Don't you answer your fucking phone anymore?" she asked but didn't slow enough for him to slip an answer past her barrage of assumedly foul language. "What, are you in the middle of something? I think you can take a couple of minutes out of your busy schedule of picking up skanky drunk chicks to answer your damn phone."

Savage nodded. "I was…with company."

"Are you on a date right now?" Anja asked.

"I…no," Savage said. It wasn't a lie, not really. He and Coleman had both agreed that it wasn't a date.

"You do know I can look you up based on the GPS signal on your phone and simply look into the security cameras, right?" she asked and revealed the reason why he really regretted having lied. If he'd simply said he was at a bar hooking up with someone, she probably wouldn't have gone further than to berate him a little more. That much, at least, was evident by the fact that she hadn't tried to find a camera view of him already.

"Aw, is that Dr. Coleman? Jessica?" she asked and confirmed that she'd already accessed the camera feeds. "I really liked her. What happened between you two kids anyway?"

"That's none of your business," he retorted and paced the alley in irritation. "And before you threaten me with hours wasted on digging through my personal life, might I ask if there was a point to you calling me repeatedly?"

"Oh, right," the hacker said with a chuckle like she had almost forgotten the matter in light of more intriguing possibilities. "I have sleeper programs in place all over the databases in the US government. The purpose is to make sure they don't access certain files and break out certain documents I would rather they keep secret. I would explain, but there's no time for that. The down and dirty of it is that your personal file in the Pentagon has been raided."

"I have a personal file in the Pentagon?" Savage frowned as he considered that. He'd thought his tracks had been covered more efficiently.

"Well, Jeremiah Savage doesn't have much in the way of anything like files anywhere," she said. "You're welcome for that, by the way, and thanks for taking such good care of your online profiles. It's surprisingly easy to keep you off the books. Anyway, Savage is a ghost. Jeremiah Johnson, on the other hand, has a number of files in place—as the Pentagon usually does since they like to keep thorough tabs on the killers they've spent millions and millions of dollars training and developing."

"Okay," he said. "Were you able to stop it?"

"I can't stop anything," Anja grumbled. "Any action on my part would raise all kinds of red flags that would have the government databases swept for the bugs I've put in all over the place. In addition, it still wouldn't stop someone from accessing the files after the sweeps have been done. No, I couldn't fucking stop them, Jer."

"There's no need to get snippy. What kind of damage are we talking about? I'm supposed to be dead, right? Everyone thinks I'm dead. That was the whole point of faking my death."

"Well, I did a little back-tracking on that, actually, and found a few problems." She tapped her keyboard and rocked on the office chair that squeaked loudly enough for him to hear. He wasn't sure if he missed or dreaded the sound these days. "Right, they didn't come looking for your files—not directly, anyway. They ran a database-wide search based on a photo. I can't tell, but it looks like a selfie with you in the background that I must have missed. I really hate the information age sometimes. Selfie cameras have a far higher res than when I was growing up."

"Isn't your expertise based on the information age, though?" Savage asked.

"I said sometimes," Anja corrected herself. She sounded annoyed and frustrated, and it had been a while since he had heard her like that. "Anyway, I was able to take a peek at what they were looking for—which turns out to be basic shit about your past. They seemed to know what they were looking for, too, and selected your service record, the people you served with, where you served, the people who trained you and who you trained with, your family, place of birth… Essentially anything they could get their hands on, I suppose. It sounds like someone is working Sun Tzu's method of knowing their enemy."

For a second, he couldn't hear anything she said. A ringing sound filled his ears, and he wondered briefly if it was the tinnitus he had previously been treated for. He dropped to his haunches in the middle of the alley when the reaction in his ears was joined by the suddenly erratic beating of his heart in his chest. He had a hard time breathing, and he couldn't tell if this was a heart attack or not. The doctor had said it was one of the very rare side effects of the medication he was on. Considering that he had all but ignored their suggestion to avoid alcohol while on his painkillers, he might have increased the risk of something really bad happening.

Savage extended his free hand in front of his eyes. In the dim streetlight seeping into the alleyway, he could see it trembling. This was a new feeling and perversely, it brought a small, distant smile. He'd faced fear before and always had the faith that his training and his abilities, as well as the help of his support, would be there to give him a chance at survival. Fear wasn't necessarily a bad thing since it did have the side effect of pumping his body full of adrenaline, which made him faster, sharper, and better overall at what he did.

But this wasn't fear. This was something he had always been told to avoid since it was what would get him and anyone who depended on him killed.

This was panic. Pure, unadulterated, body-freezing panic. There wasn't anything to train you in what to do when your family was suddenly in the crosshairs of killers the likes of which seemed to gather around Carlson and his goons.

"Jer? Savage, are you still there?" Anja said, her tone concerned, but he needed a moment to collect himself before he spoke again. He dragged in a deep breath and went through the effective mental techniques he'd committed to memory and which usually calmed him when he was too worked up. While he'd never quite had this situation in mind, he assumed they would have a positive effect.

After what seemed an eternity, his heart still pounded in his chest like a runaway rabbit but the shaking had ceased and he could hear again.

"Yeah, I'm still here," Savage said and winced when he heard his voice was cracked and soft. "That part about my family—did they get all the details on them?"

"From what I can see, yes. They got everything," she replied. "I can't find anything specific, though. I was locked out of the 'names' sections of the files. Why do you ask?"

"Because it sounds like someone is coming after me," he said and cleared his throat roughly to bring his voice to his normal pitch. "And given the history of the people we're up against, I think they'll try to use my family and the people I care about against me."

A long and very tense silence ensued and he could tell

she thought about asking him who it was he thought might be in danger from the information that was now out in the open. He wouldn't talk about it if she asked because he wasn't ready for it. His entire world seemed to have been upended and he hung onto sanity by the barest of threads. Quite simply, he didn't know what he would do if he was pressed. It could be anything from rampaging through the restaurant or stealing the nearest car and driving all the way to Seattle. He needed a moment to collect his wits and gather himself physically. The priority was to pull himself together—for the sake of his family if not his own.

"What will you do, Savage?" Anja asked suddenly, her tone worried.

"I can't simply charge off," he said, more to himself than to her. "I need to know what I'm doing and take a moment to think and plan before I act. This is not the time to act impulsively."

"That sounds about right, yes," she affirmed.

"Can you track down where the leak came from?" Savage asked once he'd managed to slot his brain back into the cold, compartmentalized place he took so much pride in. "A name or a location—something for me to start unraveling this thread."

"I'm working on it," she said. "I'll call you back when I know more."

"Thanks, Anja, you're the best." His voice was satisfyingly steady and he pressed the end call button. First things first, he decided. Coleman was still in the restaurant, ordering dessert he didn't have an appetite for anymore. He wasn't sure how he would break the news to her.

Honestly, he didn't even know if he would.

His numb fingers fumbled to shove his phone back in his pocket but he finally succeeded on the third try and made his way into the restaurant again. He ignored the noise and the other patrons as he walked over to where she was still seated.

"Jer, there you are. I couldn't decide on the chocolate lava cake or the mousse, so I ordered both and thought we could share and see which one was better," she said and turned to face him. She quickly realized that sharing a dessert was the last thing on his mind when she saw his face. "Hey…is everything okay?"

Savage opened his mouth and actually considered simply telling her the truth. *My ex-wife, her new fiancé, and my kid have had their connection to me revealed to the kinds of people who actually attack families to get at the people they want out of the way.*

He shut his mouth again and stood silently behind his chair.

"What happened, Savage?" Coleman asked and pushed up from her seat. "What did Anja want?"

"Something's come up," he said softly and gripped the back of his chair firmly enough that the whites of his knuckles were visible. "I…can't say what it is exactly, but the fact remains that I need to leave right away to take care of it. I know we didn't get around to talking about what we scheduled this dinner for, so I'll have to rain check you on that one. And I won't be able to take you up on that dessert either."

She nodded and touched his shoulder gently. "I understand, Jer, and that's fine. I think we both know I can wolf down anything made of chocolate in no time flat."

He smirked, which was all the mirth he really had time for as he located his wallet in his pocket and withdrew the necessary bills to cover his half of the check, a generous tip included.

"Let me know if you need my help," Coleman said, her voice laced with real concern. "Believe it or not, my time working for Monroe has brought me a fair number of contacts in all kinds of walks of life."

Savage nodded. "Thanks, I might actually take you up on that."

"Be safe, Jer," she whispered and he turned to make his way outside. He knew he wouldn't really enlist her help or be safe, so there was no real point in pretending otherwise. His was a very dangerous line of work, and if he had to do what needed to be done to keep his family safe, he had to put himself in harm's way.

Being safe wasn't really an option.

He stepped into his car and stared at the steering wheel for a second before he yelled as loudly and as hard as he could into it. His vocal protest continued until his lungs were empty and he leaned his head into the horn, gently enough that it didn't sound off. He needed the release, even if only for a few seconds, before he could regain his focus, start the car, and head home to pack.

CHAPTER SIX

Banks looked out over the city of New York as the sunlight faded from the sky and the nightlights flickered to life and repainted the tapestry before him. He wasn't one of those men who took the job of partner in the firm only for the perks it brought. The corner office in the high rise, the assistants at his beck and call, the right to pick and choose which clients he wanted to represent, and the obscene amount of money.

Well…he certainly hadn't taken the job for those, but they had factored into his decision.

The position had, of course, come with strings attached. He had earned every advantage of it, but his lack of traditional connections had, for years, meant others were undeservingly promoted thanks to relationships cultivated by years and years of family friends and connections. He had seen others rise in the ranks while he remained on the menial end of the task pool and was forced to watch others fuck up what he knew that he could easily accomplish.

When the offer had come with the connections to push

him to the highest levels of his profession, the strings attached were clear. Certain favors would be owed to people who wanted those favors granted by someone in the positions he wanted to attain. Despite this, he hadn't thought twice about taking the opportunity. It hadn't been easy since then, but not once had he ever regretted making the decision that had led him to the seat he now occupied.

The view, the help, and the pay were merely cherries on the cake. All he really wanted was excellence and recognition for his efforts.

Banks drew a deep breath. An examination of Carlson's paperwork had revealed a wide variety of problems he would have to present to his client before too long. He doubted it was anything they didn't already know, but that was what he was there for. To assist them to see whether or not Carlson was still with the program and then, possibly, to start the process needed to move him back into a place where he could benefit their plans better.

The videophone rang and he turned his chair to look at the desk. It was the congressman, obviously, and the man was already a little late with the call. It wasn't like they were on a timetable or anything, but it was of the utmost importance to keep the man on his toes. Having someone in his particular capacity under their heel was something the client felt was important. Therefore, Banks thought it was important.

"Mr. Banks, nice to see you again," the man said, his words as fake as his smile. "How's life in the Big Apple?"

"I can't complain," he said and did a decent job of masking his contempt. "I have a great view of the sun setting over the city, which reminds me that you're taking your time in getting me the information. Have you made any progress on that?"

"Actually, yes. I was able to get my hands on the file of one of the special forces members who matched the facial recognition on your Savage character," Jenkins said, and Banks watched as a selection of files appeared in his inbox. "Here's the thing, though. He's been listed as killed in action for months now."

The lawyer didn't respond initially. He wasn't sure how the government treated their retired special forces members, but he did have a feeling that Savage—or Sergeant Jeremiah Johnson, as was on his file—would be one of those who hadn't actually died. It was a hunch and thus not guaranteed to help, but it was very obviously the same man as the one in the picture provided to him by his client's contacts. He didn't trust the US government to tell the truth, the whole truth and nothing but the truth, so help them God. He did trust his client's contacts to provide him with good information, though.

It would require thorough validation, of course, but he wouldn't be at all surprised it if turned out that Johnson was alive and well.

"Thank you, Congressman. You have been most helpful," Banks said and returned to his call.

"We're even now, right?" the man asked and leaned forward, the small hopeful smile on his lips no longer fake. "You will destroy the…uh, embarrassing pictures of me minding my own business?"

"Is that what you call it?" he mocked with a chuckle.

"Please," his caller pleaded.

"To answer your question, no, we are not even, not by

the proverbial long shot, Congressman." He smiled again and actually meant it this time. "But it is good to know you're on board with the program, and I think this is the start of a very long, very profitable relationship for both of us. Tomorrow, I think you'll find a handful of small-time celebrities will endorse your re-election campaign, as well as a sudden influx of anonymous donations to that same campaign."

Jenkins narrowed his eyes and blinked a few times as if he didn't know what he should do. The lawyer could understand. The rumor was that the congressman had difficulty with his campaign as another younger and more vital candidate had presented herself. It really was a fairly common occurrence, or so it appeared.

"You can thank me later after you verify that everything I told you is the truth," he said. He tilted his head in what he knew was a superior and even arrogant challenge and merely waited for him to hang up. Jenkins didn't appear to get the message, though, so he sighed and resisted a cutting comment. "You have a nice evening, Congressman. We'll be in touch."

The idiot still didn't hang up, so Banks obliged and cut the communication. He could understand the man's trepidation over the whole situation. Understandably, he'd want to try to keep himself off the hook for prostitution charges with the possibility of statutory rape thrown in as well. All these would culminate in the end of his marriage and political career.

While a part of him wanted to feel bad for the man, he simply couldn't manage to actually manifest the emotion.

He disliked politicians in general, and Jenkins was one of the worst as far as he was concerned.

Savage—or Johnson, rather—had been a busy bee during his time in the special forces. He'd been all around the world based on the contents of his file. It fit with much of what they had described of his actions. The man was a professional fixer with substantial experience under his belt, which made actually getting to him a difficult prospect.

There was something in there that might be a passport, though. Savage had left the service early and indications were that the reason had something to do with a wife and a kid. A divorce was mentioned too, and the soldier had thrown himself deeply into his work again. It wasn't unheard of, naturally. Men who wanted to avoid problems at home often did so by signing up for a couple more tours, so that wasn't entirely unusual.

An ex-wife wouldn't draw much of an emotional response, but a daughter? This little treasure of information was all he really needed. Banks lifted his phone from where it was still connected to his computer and dialed his client to confirm that he had a green light to get the ball rolling on what he had learned.

Savage finally reached his apartment after what felt like an interminable trip, but the comforting simplicity of it wasn't enough to calm him. He went to the fridge for a beer and reconciled himself to the knowledge that he would work through the night. Sleep definitely wouldn't be an option, so he might as well get something done that didn't involve tossing and turning in his bed until the sun finally rose.

Fuck that. Fuck all of it. He would track the sons of bitches and turn the best defense into a good offense, as it were.

It wasn't his family's fault. They hadn't been a part of his life for years, and someone now targeted them for something he had done? It wasn't a fair or honorable way to go about things. Then again, they wouldn't have a fair playing field either with him in the mix.

Why did he even try to rationalize their behavior? They had set their sights on his family and he intended to kill the sons of bitches and about three or four generations of their family in response. While that might seem a little hypocritical and counter-productive, his instinct was to go on a rampage at this point. No one would be spared.

He dropped to his knees beside his bed to retrieve a locked suitcase he'd stored under it. It wasn't necessarily the right thing to keep a small arsenal for himself when Anderson and Monroe provided enough weapons for his work, but the need was instinctual. Always being prepared for a rainy day something hard-wired into him.

The stash contained his pistol—the one they'd given him and he had simply refused to return. He'd managed to acquire a couple more strips of the needles it fired, so he had more than enough ammo to tear through the equivalent of most military installations. In addition, he had the shotgun, of course. The remainder was comprised of a small rifle he probably wouldn't use, a knife, another pistol in case of emergencies, and a couple of the 1911s, still with their suppressors attached.

Savage used almost an hour to clean the weapons. The ritual of it was rather soothing, he had to admit, and it put him in the mindset he needed to be in. The calm, collected killer who wouldn't be ruffled by anything, even the knowledge that his family was on the line.

His hands still shook a little as he placed the weapons into the duffel bag along with the fake IDs, credit cards, and cash that wasn't fake. The silence was deafening as he slipped out into the living room of his apartment. He drew the pistol from the underarm holster and checked it one last time while he ran his gaze along the comforting lines and grooves in the weapon.

When his phone buzzed, he answered quickly and didn't bother to check the caller ID in case it was Anja. Anderson was the one who greeted him, however.

"Hey, Savage," the former colonel said and sounded like he had been woken from a deep sleep. "Anja called me to let me know what's happening."

"Yeah." His tone was almost a growl and he scowled at his weapon. "I think I'll have to take time off work. I know I just got off medical leave, but I think I'm about to have something of a family emergency I need to deal with urgently."

"Yeah, like I said, Anja filled me in," Anderson responded, and he sounded concerned. "What will you do, Savage?"

"I'll take care of it," he said and deliberately kept his tone even and also tried not to let anything slip. Giving

Anderson and Monroe some plausible deniability was still essential, even when he wasn't on the clock.

"I understand that," the man replied softly. "You do what you have to do, okay? And let me know if you need any help. Anything you need, it's yours."

"Thanks." His voice, cold and distant, almost startled him. "I think I might take you up on that."

"Stay alive, you hear me?" the ex-colonel ordered. At least he'd kept his expectations a little more realistic than Coleman's. "We still need you here."

"Will do, boss. I'll call you." Savage ended the connection and made another cursory inspection of the weapon in his hands before he slid it into his holster and pulled his leather jacket over it and made his way to the door. He was careful to lock and secure everything before leaving too. The chances were high that he wouldn't be back for a while.

He shouldered the duffel bag full of shit to kill people with and made his way to the elevator, but he didn't go to the garage of the building. He went to the lobby instead and nodded peremptorily at the guard who was too interested in what was showing on his TV to really pay attention to anything happening around him. Anja had told him what the poor man earned. He wouldn't pay much attention to his job either if he was paid so little.

There were certain things he needed to do and didn't want them tied to his Savage name. He liked it and had already begun to build a life around it, which meant he wouldn't waste it on this. Of course, he would if he had to, but that wasn't plan A by any means. This clarity was what he needed, yes—to think straight and make the smart decisions that would keep him and everyone else alive. The alternative of charging in half-cocked against people who were better armed, better prepared and, more importantly, working with cooler heads was not an option.

He fully intended to survive this shit and make it out the other end with the blood of those responsible on his hands.

Which was why he had purchased a car. Not his hybrid, of course. That was in his Savage name. The one he'd managed to acquire had papers under one of the names on an ID he had stored in his duffel bag. It had been purchased in cash, second-hand from someone who had wanted to unload a perfectly functional car because it was simply a little outdated. Old enough, in fact, that it lacked any of the standard tracking and GPS devices other cars had and that could have activated by someone with a computer and Anja's level of skill.

It meant he had to walk a couple of blocks to reach the parking complex where he'd put it, but the activity helped him cool off further. He let the relative peace seep into his inner tension while he wandered through the streets that were almost abandoned by now. The quiet was no surprise, really. It was almost midnight, after all, and it was still a work week, although it would be cut short by Thanksgiving for some if not all.

He showed his fake ID to the guard, who nodded and allowed him through before he turned back to his TV. Savage wondered what was on that had so many people interested, but he thought it was better not to ask. He was quite content to let them watch if it meant he would be ignored.

The steel-gray Subaru was parked in a corner where it wouldn't easily be noticed but which also afforded a hasty exit if needed. Like the hybrid, it was merely a tool to get him from point A to point B and was still common enough on the country roads that it wouldn't turn any heads. He made sure there were no witnesses and he flipped his bag quickly into the trunk and slipped into the driver's seat. Before he started the engine, though, he removed an earbud from his pocket, pressed the button on the end to activate it, and eased it gingerly into his ear.

"Good evening, Jer." The familiar voice with a Russian accent was comforting by now.

"Evening, Anja," Savage replied, started the car, and eased out of the parking space into the lane that would take him out of the garage. "How is this evening treating you?"

"It's actually almost morning here," Anja replied. "And small talk? Really?"

"Well, I thought I would give it a try," he said. "I've needed to simply talk. To let my lips move without really giving much thought to what I actually say is like a white noise machine I create myself. It doesn't work as well without someone to bounce it off, though, or you come off as that crazy person who talks to himself."

"Are you doing it right now?"

"A little, yeah, and it is working." He reached the crossbar and waited impatiently for the guard to open it.

"Do you want to know what I found out?" she asked as he pulled out of the building.

"Lay it on me," he said and deliberately focused on the road and on controlling his breathing.

"Well, I'm still working on digging for actual details of whoever leaked your information, but I do have some news if you're already on the move. And I can see you are. Anyway, you can head to the I-95 because I can see the leak came directly from the Pentagon, so it has to be someone who's physically in Washington. I have a couple of names I'm tracking down, but they're all merely aides and assistants, so I have nothing solid yet. I'll let you know."

"Thanks, Anja." Savage circled and redirected the vehicle based on the signs which told him how to access the I-95 heading south. "I really appreciate what you're doing for me."

"You don't need to thank me, Jer," she said and he could hear the smile in her voice. "I like to think we're friends, and when it comes to family, there's nothing I won't do to help you. So…from what I can see, we're in for another fun road trip, eh, Jer?"

"It sounds like it," he replied and managed a small smirk. He gripped the steering wheel tighter and felt the old leather groan under the strain. "Do you mind if I get real for a second here, Anja? This isn't white noise talking."

"This is a safe space, so talk away."

"The thing is," he began, then paused for a moment before he spoke slowly and deliberately since he had practiced this speech in his mind. It was a way he had been taught to calm himself by rationalizing the emotions rushing through his head. "The thing is, I've taken this whole job—and most of my life, if I'm honest about it, which includes even personal relationships, I guess—at a half-assed setting. I've put too much effort into something that wouldn't net me much more than a little money.

Getting some assholes votes back home has never been much of a priority for me. The only time I actually gave a crap was when my brothers and sisters in uniform counted on me, and…"

Anja had seen his file by now, he assumed. She would have known what happened the last time his brothers and sisters in uniform had trusted him to get them in and out of a dangerous mission alive. He squeezed the wheel again and allowed his body to relax after a few seconds.

"To find out some pencil pusher in Washington has put my whole family in danger and in the crosshairs of people who won't hesitate to use them to get to me—and all for something that has everything to do with me and nothing to do with them…" He paused again and found it hard to stay focused on the road as he accessed the traffic on the highway. "It's like a giant hand from heaven came down to earth and turned an invisible knob inside me to push me from half-assed to quadruple-assed."

"Wow," Anja said and chuckled. "That's like eight times the ass. And you'll simply leave that invisible knob comment hanging out in the open like that?"

"You know it." He grunted derisively and leaned back in his seat as the car settled into the speed limit and he put it into cruise control. "Let me know when you have someone for me to punch until my fists bleed."

"Will do, Jer," she replied. "You know I have your back in this, right?"

Savage nodded. "Yep, I know. And I know you have my front too since that's where all the fun stuff usually happens."

"Is that where you had your kidney punched out of you?" the Russian asked, and he laughed aloud.

"Touché." He grinned. "Also, it's a low blow. You know that punch landed me in the hospital for three weeks, right?"

"Well, maybe avoid giving him your back, then." She sounded more cheerful than usual, and he wondered if she did it for his benefit in an attempt to raise his spirits. If so, he could appreciate that.

"You can bet on it," he said softly and watched the odometer as the miles were slowly eaten up by the old yet still very efficient vehicle.

CHAPTER SEVEN

He hadn't liked it much the first time around and Banks wasn't at all happy to be back. Visiting prisons was never a pleasant experience, no matter how light the security was. The fact that Carlson still refused to be released into open custody—which would allow Banks to meet with him at a house arranged by the FBI—was something that annoyed him immensely.

It annoyed the client too, Banks thought, but for different reasons. Carlson used prison to hide from this Savage character, and despite the news that they were working on eliminating him, the ex-CEO had insisted that his lawyer bring him the evidence of what he claimed. He'd stated unequivocally that he wouldn't leave the prison until he did. Every time someone arrived to transfer him, he claimed he had more information to share and wouldn't do so if he was removed from the prison.

Annoying rich prick. Banks couldn't help the thought as he slammed the door to his car and marched over to the guard who already waited for him. He'd called ahead as he wanted to do this as quickly as possible. In addition, he'd notified the FBI handlers to inform them their prize pony would leave the prison in short order and be moved somewhere more civilized.

He stepped into the prison and went through all the same motions he had on his previous visit. For some reason, he felt more on edge than he had then as they stepped through the doors. This was the first time he'd done something like this for his client. He knew, of course, that this kind of thing wasn't unusual and assumed he would be called upon to do it eventually. While he had prepared for this eventuality, he was still nervous. To initiate an attack on someone as directly and as violently as he now did against Savage was new. It was exciting too. Like a chess game for keeps.

When he entered the room with the tables and chairs, he noted the cameras were already off and the security guards huddled on the other side of the room. There was only one topic to be discussed in this conversation, and nobody wanted it to be heard.

Banks didn't have time to organize all his paperwork on the table before the prisoner was led into the room. The manacles around his wrists and ankles were removed quickly. The man limped to the table and still used that ridiculously expensive ivory and mahogany cane he had seen him with before. Carlson looked wired and anxious as well, which bit into the calm and aloof air he usually wore to set everyone around him on edge. The lawyer assumed the man hadn't felt like this in a long time, and he still couldn't find it in his heart to feel bad for him. He was the one who had forced him to make the trip all the way out there, driving to Pennsylvania from New York and then having to drive all the fucking way back.

Let him feel bad.

"So…Banks, right?" the man asked as he lowered himself into his seat slowly and thoughtfully. He very noticeably spared his bad knee any weight as he settled in.

"Mason Banks, yes," he responded with a small, annoyed quirk of the lips. It wasn't quite a smile or a scowl but a chilling mixture of both. He continued to set his papers out.

"You said you had my Savage situation handled," Carlson said and leaned forward with a frown, obviously unused to having anyone give their paperwork more attention than him. "I look forward to seeing what you have to show me."

"You won't take any calls, Mr. Carlson," Banks replied and still made no effort to look at the man. "You won't accept electronic messages, and you won't help me help you get out of this place."

"As I've told the FBI, the people who have targeted me —Savage included—have significant resources." He slapped his open palm on the metal table between them. "I don't pretend to understand how any of it works, but if you want me to survive my time in here and my time out there, you need to assure me that you have my situation under control."

Banks sighed. He'd completed his meticulous arrangement of documents but still wasn't comfortable enough to look the other man in the eye. "I have to ask something here. I can handle the likes of Savage, as you call him. He's a tough cookie, make no mistake, but he's not invincible and certainly not immortal. More importantly, he has weaknesses that can be exploited. But what makes you think Anderson and Monroe won't simply find someone else to do their dirty work for them?"

"Well, I'm sure they will find someone else." Carlson shrugged as if he found the question irrelevant. "You have to understand, Banks. I've been around military people my whole life. I've dealt with military defense contracts since before I entered the world of business. I know these people. They're all tough fuckers, reliable, and can get the job done. I actually have nothing against them. But once or twice in a generation, you have someone with exactly the right mixture of will and remorselessness that makes them the perfect killers. It might be something genetic, I don't know. But they become the best killers of their time. Of course, they're not always celebrated as such."

Banks had to resist the urge to roll his eyes while the prisoner went through what had to be a rehearsed speech. He rationalized why he would rather play golf with his older friends instead of taking his place in the world again and making a difference. The lawyer liked this side of the man even less than the other arrogant asshole persona. Let him be afraid in private all he wanted as long as he had the balls to keep himself in the game.

This Savage seemed to have really knocked the fight out of him.

"So please tell me you actually have the means to get Savage out of the way and for me to get my ass out of this fucking place," Carlson finished belligerently. He leaned back and watched his attorney closely.

"We were able to locate some evidence of him," he said.

He drew the picture of Savage out, placed it in front of the man, and watched his reaction closely.

It wasn't quite what he had expected. The ex-CEO avoided touching the picture, a look of anger and disgust in his eyes, and the way that his nostrils flared indicated clearly that he still wasn't over being shot in the knee.

"That's him." His voice was a little hoarse.

"You're right, if it's any consolation," Banks continued. "He does appear to have some help in keeping his record—legal and online—clean as a whistle, so it took a fair amount of digging before the client found a picture our friend's friend missed. Using that, we were able to obtain his file in the Pentagon. This is it."

Carlson was more willing to touch that than the picture and rapidly read the various details of Savage—or Johnson's—life during his time in the military. He looked a little more relaxed as he did so. The lawyer wondered if this was merely a result of now knowing what he faced and not having to deal with the unknown of it. It could also be that he had started to feel better, knowing what had beaten him and feeling more at peace with that.

He didn't know much about the man's psyche, so he wasn't sure which was more likely. It could even have been a combination of both.

"Well, that was some interesting reading." The prisoner smirked and placed the file on the table. He watched Banks return it studiously to its place in his little organized pile. "Knowing that Savage, or Johnson, is an actual human being is something of a relief, but I still don't know how we can eliminate him. You told me the situation was handled. This is progress, not handled."

"You didn't read the full file," Banks said and opened it to the section he had in mind. "He has a family—an ex-wife and a kid his pension was sent to after his alleged death. I assume it means he still cares about them and thus, they can be used as leverage to bring him into a position for our maximum opportunity."

Banks' confidence dropped suddenly when Carlson's face paled dramatically and his usually confident demeanor completely vanished. He seemed to recoil with each word.

"Are you fucking crazy?" the prisoner demanded and shoved his chair back a little farther.

"I don't understand your response. You're talking to me like this, but I know you've done this kind of thing in the past—used your enemies' loved ones as leverage—and not too long ago, either."

"Yes, and do you know what happened to me the last time I tried it?" Carlson asked and somehow managed to speak through clenched teeth. "I was shot in the knee and ended up arrested for fraud and a shithouse full of other charges. Savage entered my plane and he told me very clearly that my decision to target Anderson's family made it personal. Then, he shot me in the knee and left me to be arrested. And that was what he did when I attacked someone else's family and he wanted to teach me a lesson. What kind of shit show do you think we'll be in for when he finds out we have targeted his? I'm warning you, don't do this. Find another way."

The lawyer shook his head with a soft sigh. "The client has grown impatient with your wishy-washy attitude regarding her investment. Remember, she's the one who keeps you nice and comfortable in a prison that has the kind of amenities most resorts lack. She can take it away too. It's something you might want to keep in mind."

"I don't think you've heard me," the other man said and narrowed his eyes as Banks began to collect his papers. "What I'm saying is that I've met our client. I've also met Savage, or Johnson, or whatever we call him now. I'll take my chances with the client. Did you not hear me when I told you what kind of bastard he is?"

"I tried to ignore you, honestly," Banks said. "If you want to go against the client, believe me, it will be your funeral. For my part, I'll continue to work to move your ass out of here, although whether it will be for you to continue your work or for the client to kill you with her own two hands remains to be seen."

He placed the last of the documents in his briefcase and wondered why he had wasted so much time to set them up. It was a little ritual of his that helped to establish himself as a pro to the people he met with but honestly, he didn't think the man was worth the trouble. He certainly wasn't worth the trouble he'd been put through to save the bastard, but he was paid to do it for someone who had a bigger vision. He was merely a puppet, and she pulled the strings.

When he reached his car, he muttered a few exasperated curses and tossed his briefcase into the back seat while his mind tried to decide what he would do. Despite the fact that the ex-CEO was a spineless freak, Banks still knew the man had a point. The plan to eliminate someone like Johnson meant they only had one opportunity to succeed. To give him the chance to retaliate would put him in a similar situation as the other man had found himself in. Banks really didn't want to have his knees capped.

And again, Carlson was right when he assumed Johnson had gone easy on him because it had been someone else's family. His actions had been a lesson, not a rampage. It wasn't rocket science to correctly assume the retribution would be considerably more intense the more personal it became.

But it wasn't like he intended to try to kill the family either. They merely did this to draw the operative out into the open, not to plan an assassination. The plan was simply to hold them, keep them alive, and threaten their lives until Daddy came in to rescue them and walked directly into a killing zone that gave them all the advantages. Banks wasn't sure what would happen to the family afterward, of course. The client wasn't the kind to leave witnesses alive. Which meant…yeah, they would probably die anyway.

Savage had to know that—or Johnson, rather. Dammit, it would be hard to switch them around. The name Savage was already well and truly stuck in his head.

He debated the topic with himself in the car all the way back to New York. Sometimes, he actually talked to himself on the highway when the car assumed the responsibility of driving. It wasn't an easy debate. Having Savage earmark him for vengeance wasn't something he wanted for himself, but there would be enough time to deal with that once—if—he actually found himself in that situation. The client would want him to be creative and precise about this.

When he reached his office, he told his assistant to make sure to clear his schedule for the rest of the day, settled at his desk, and pulled the phone up to open a comm line.

"Banks, how was your visit to Carlson's prison?" The woman's voice was chillingly familiar, hardly surprising since it had been a part of his life for the past six years or so.

"Well, he didn't like the plan to involve Savage's family," he replied and scowled because there was no face to face contact with the woman on the other side of the comm link. "He said he won't leave the prison until we've dealt with Savage. I think he was really broken."

"Well, I have my doubts about him being our man anymore anyway," she replied. The distinctive sound of screaming echoed in the background. He couldn't tell if it was fun or pain that caused the screams, and he had no desire to ask. "But we'll cross that bridge when we get to it. It would be much easier to kill a free man than an FBI prisoner. That doesn't alter the fact that we need to eliminate Savage. Get it done, Banks."

With that peremptory command, the line cut out. He shook his head. Unlike Carlson, he hadn't met Savage, but he had met the client. It wasn't part of his agenda to risk pissing her off. With that in mind, he started dialing another number rather hastily.

CHAPTER EIGHT

It wasn't the longest drive Savage had ever made. There were upsides to having a car that lacked most of the modern conveniences, especially for someone in his particular profession and involved in what he intended to do. A car no one could track would enable him to slide through the country off the radar while he traveled with a small arsenal in his trunk. If he stuck to the speed limit, he would avoid the attention of the local cops—and, he suspected, they didn't like to pull a car like his over anyway.

But there were downsides as well, he realized. While the cruise control maintained the correct speed and some motion sensors prevented him from tailgating someone a little too closely, the electronics were considered ancient by current standards. There were no auto-driving features, which meant he needed to keep his hand on the wheel at all times, and no auto braking features either. The radio he used was an old FM/AM radio with a screen but no access to the newer bands that shared TV programs.

All this made for a very, very long three-hour drive

from Philly to Washington. Anja wasn't around for most of it. The adrenaline from the rest of the night had begun to fade, and he struggled to keep his eyes open as the hours wound up from midnight.

By the time he could see the lights of the city brighten the evening sky ahead, he decided it was time to call it a night. Anja clearly didn't have anything for him yet or she would have contacted him to warn him to stay loose and ready. While that irked him, he also acknowledged that he would need to sleep at some point. A couple of motels were advertised around the entrance into the city, and he decided against using any of them.

There was no GPS in his car but there was one in his phone, so he found a safe place to pull off and quickly called the nearest three star-hotel that accepted cash and didn't ask any questions. He was directed to an establishment barely inside the city that was exactly what he needed. Cash for the night and a little money discretely added on top of that persuaded the late-night clerk to write him in as a returning customer by the name of John Doe.

He didn't exactly have money to burn, but it was better to have a somewhat respectable place to spend the night instead of having to check the bedroom for insects. Worse was the strong possibility that he would come away from the night's sleep with an aching back because the bed itself had seen better days. He'd experienced too many of those to even consider the prospect.

Despite his weariness and the hour, he still needed help getting to sleep. The problem with someone as smart as him was that his mind wasn't something he could simply turn off. Inevitably, he'd be stuck in a situation where he would replay the same worst-case scenarios over and over in his head, try to find some way to change them that would make everything better, and fail most of the time.

Thankfully, there was a solution to that particular problem, Savage found as he paced the room at about four in the morning. A small fridge in the corner of his room provided his medication of choice in convenient tiny bottle form. He started with only a nightcap, and as the pain in his side and shoulder worsened, he kept going until he dropped onto the bed, still vaguely conscious but not for long.

What dreams he might have had erased themselves rapidly from his head as he slipped in a semi-drunken stupor. The hours passed until he was dragged into consciousness when something buzzed in his ear. He slapped at the side of his face in an effort to shoo the bug away and waved his hand to make sure the tent door was still intact.

When his hands found nothing but cotton sheets, his eyes opened. He wasn't in the middle of a jungle, nor was he sleeping in a tight and uncomfortably cramped recon tent. His gaze focused to confirm that he was actually in a hotel bed—albeit laying across it, which explained why his right leg hung over one of the sides.

He grimaced and rubbed his eyes. His mouth tasted like shit, and his head pounded in protest when he pulled himself into a sitting position on the edge of the bed. He yawned, shook his head, and immediately regretted it. Clearly, he wasn't ready for that shit yet.

"Good morning, Savage," Anja said softly. "I'm sorry for

buzzing in your ear, but I tried to call you like a regular person and you weren't up yet."

Savage nodded even though he knew she couldn't see him. He didn't much care anyway. It was unlikely he would be able to force any reliable words out of his mouth with the way it tasted.

"Well, you had a long night, I guess, so I actually wondered if I should let you sleep," the hacker said apologetically. "Which I did by not waking you every time I had an update. But some are more important than others, and this is definitely a top of the list important one."

He found a tiny bottle of complimentary mouthwash in the bathroom and gargled quickly. She suddenly fell silent and remained so for the full minute he needed to complete the process and spit it out.

"If you could refrain from doing that to me…forever," she grumbled, "I'd really appreciate it. I don't like having to listen to your nasty ass making whatever nasty-ass sounds you choose to. I do have some sensibilities and as of right now, I feel the need to hurl."

Savage sucked in a deep breath and tried not to lose his temper. She had to know he was a little hung over, and he suspected this was some kind of revenge or payment she exacted from him for her letting him sleep in. If that was the case, he was more than thankful for the rest he'd been allowed and decided to let the other ride. A hasty glance at his watch told him it was already a quarter past one in the afternoon. It had been a late night and a fairly traumatic one, and he had definitely needed the rest.

"Do you know I had to listen to you snoring all morning?" Anja asked and sounded like she tried to push his buttons. "I had to simply listen in and hear you go on like a damn chainsaw. I didn't have to listen to it all morning, of course, since I can turn your feed on and off as I choose, but I still like to stay in contact with the people I'm handling from afar. So, yes, that pissed me off."

"Was there a point to all this?" he asked and now regretted not having brought the painkillers the doctor had prescribed for him at the hospital. Too late, he now remembered they were in the cabinet in the bathroom at his apartment.

"Oh, right, did I forget to mention something?" The hacker chuckled ironically. "Damn, now what was it? Ah, now I remember. I found the source for the leak. Jer, remember how that's what we're here for?"

"I remember," Savage muttered acidly. There weren't any painkillers in the cabinet above the sink. He'd hoped for an aspirin or maybe a acetaminophen but it seemed he would have to deal with a pounding headache for most of the day. Or until he could get to the nearest drugstore, which immediately became a priority.

"Check your phone. I emailed you all the info on the man we're looking at as the source of the leak." She waited patiently while he limped over to where he'd left his phone on the nightstand the night before. The battery was still good, although he would probably have to charge it in the car.

Sure enough, a message waited in his inbox. Anja's chair squeaked irritatingly as he opened the file she had sent.

"Congressman Alfred Jenkins?" he asked and dropped

on the bed again. He suppressed a groan and held his head to reduce the pain the movement had triggered.

"Yep," she replied. "A twenty-year veteran of the House and member of a handful of Committees, including the House Intelligence Committee as well as the House Armed Services Committee."

"Which explains how he accessed my file, I assume. The dumbasses in those committees are given all kinds of leeway in the intelligence and military communities. People seem to think that because they have a say in how those branches are run, they actually care about the people who are caught in the middle of what they do."

"Right." The Russian slid past that comment as she sent him another two files. "There isn't much to say about the people who did the dirty work for him, although I'm not sure why he didn't simply go through the regular channels to access the paperwork himself. He didn't have to go through all the channels he used."

"Elected officials always look for ways to cover their asses," Savage explained absently. He leaned against the headboard and read the files, even though the process made his eyes hurt. "If he hasn't gone through the regular channels, it means he's tried to cover up what he's done so it can't be traced back to him if something bad comes out of it. Which in turn means he's anticipating something bad will come out of it. The bottom line is that he knows what he's done can have negative blowback."

"And the fact that he's had a difficult reelection campaign against a popular up-and-comer might have something to do with it too," Anja pointed out with a chuckle. "I've run checks on the campaign to see if there are any trails in there for us to follow."

"You have good instincts, but I doubt there will be anything there for you to find." He rubbed some feeling back into his eyes before he turned his attention to the files again. "It's ridiculously easy to bribe elected officials through anonymous donations to their campaigns. While it might be a little more difficult for the politicians in question to use the money for anything other than their campaign, if that's all the guy wants the money for, it's not really an issue."

"It sounds like an issue to me," she protested. "It's more a matter of principle, although the fact that they don't have anything to track properly does sound like it could be a problem."

"Don't I know it." Savage chuckled and shook his head, then immediately winced. "But that's a problem for another day. The real issue is if we can't find a way to find the actual people who want the information on me, we'll have to extract it from the man himself. And, for what it's worth, I won't be nice about it, either."

"Wait, wait. Hold up," Anja said and laughed nervously. "Are you really talking about putting the screws to an elected official? Of the United States?"

"The guy put my family in danger," Savage reminded her, amazed at how he could say that without a tremble in his voice at all. Even his hands held the phone firmly and lacked any of the tremors that had plagued them the night before. "He's lucky that all I'll do here is pay him a visit in search of information."

"That's fair." Her voice sounded soft and tentative.

"We've never actually talked about your family before. I think you mentioned having one at some point, but you never volunteered any information beyond that."

"For someone in the kind of position I find myself in, you have to understand that much of the information about my personal life will be shared on a need to know basis." He dropped his phone beside him, his mind already working on what needed to happen. First, he would need to do recon and actual surveillance on the man himself. Second, he'd have to familiarize himself with his security. An infiltration was a complicated situation, especially if you did it in a populated area where any random grandmother who couldn't sleep could see him climb over a fence and call the cops. That, simply put, was all it would take to guarantee failure. There was no way to plan for something like that. It was a variable, something beyond his control.

He needed to find a way to limit the variables, though. His objective was to find a way to reach the man without being detected. Considering the number of people and cameras that surrounded elected officials these days, it definitely wouldn't be easy.

"You do know I can simply look into the records myself and find out, right?" Anja asked to break the silence. "I don't even need to go through the government files. I already know your real name, so all I have to do is run a couple of nation-wide searches. Nothing's hidden in the world anymore. You know that better than most."

"I know," Savage said and stared blankly at the ceiling above him. "But there is a chance that this has nothing to do with them. A chance that this is only about me and might pose no danger to them whatsoever. After everything I've put them through, they deserve the chance to remain uninvolved in my life. So I'm asking you as a friend—please leave them out of this for as long as possible."

It was important to have a small amount of hope. There was a chance that this had nothing to do with either of them and he wouldn't destroy that by being overly paranoid. The regular amount of paranoia would do right now.

"Damn it, not as a friend." She groaned and must have leaned back because her seat squeaked in protest. He could almost hear her roll her eyes. "Okay, fine, but if I do this as a friend, you can expect that I'll take it out on you later."

"As long as I'm the only one you take it out on." Savage chuckled. He knew someone who was as privacy-conscious as she was wouldn't mind letting him keep his for as long as was necessary, but that didn't mean she would be nice to him about it. He could take her punishment.

"Okay, can I assume you've started to work on a plan for how to reach this elected official of ours?" she asked. "I'm already digging into the plans of where he's living, as well as the various security he has, but considering the location I see here, you might actually have to head out there to eyeball the place in person. Do you think you can do that, wasted as you are?"

"I'm hungover," he protested and pushed himself slowly from his prone position on the bed. "Wasted is what I was last night. So yes, I think I can do it, as long as I have coffee and aspirin in me."

"Well, isn't that nice," she replied. "I'll text you the address. Let me know when you get there."

CHAPTER NINE

Savage hated the suburbs. Too many rich, entitled people lived there, all safe and smug in their socially acceptable homes. He'd only had to deal with the likes of it a couple of times, and even then, only for a few months at a time. Dealing with homeowner's associations had been something of a nightmare. It was amazing how so little power could still go to people's heads, and he'd narrowly avoided fights with the assholes who virtually measured the grass for any tiny infraction they could find as an excuse to assert themselves.

But if there was anything he could give to these people, it was that they were vigilant about the security of their homes. This was something he couldn't fault them for, even if it was inconvenient for him at the moment. He arrived in his car and drove around the neighborhood a couple of times to familiarize himself with the area. Even this early in the afternoon, there were still people out and about in the neighborhood—the kind of people who would definitely notice if an old Subaru parked outside their homes for extended periods of time.

He wasn't someone who usually aroused suspicions in these kinds of communities as he didn't really need to take pictures of the target location. Still, there was no point in taking an unnecessary risk. One call to the cops and he was done for. A search would reveal the weapons—for which he did not have a permit—and he would find himself in prison faster than he could snap his fingers.

"Okay," Savage said softly as he completed his third circuit. He still hadn't identified a suitable place where he could stop without being called on it. "I think we need to change tactics. I won't be able to stop for any actual surveillance of the house without someone calling the cops on me. I need a place where I can park without arousing suspicions. Even simply driving around here has already generated a little interest. My third drive-through probably didn't help, so I definitely can't risk another."

"Give me a second," Anja replied and sounded like she was already working on that problem. She was good at that —anticipating the kinds of issues he would face and already working on a solution before he even asked. It made her much quicker with her response times when it turned out that he did ask for her help. "I pick up three different houses that have calls in for assistance—two plumbing issues and one with the satellite dish. Do you think you could pass yourself off as a plumber?"

"That won't work." He grunted and turned the car. While he had no intention to make another sweep, he couldn't simply park anywhere. "These people all know the plumbers and technicians they've worked with for years.

They'll always expect a familiar face to first introduce a new guy. Besides, that would include getting a paneled van and disguises, which I really don't feel comfortable with considering the timetable we're on. We need to find another way."

"Damn," she muttered. "Who knew that casing a house in the suburbs would be more difficult than breaking into Fort Knox?"

"Well, that's not really true," he corrected her as he steered his Subaru into the parking lot of a nearby supermarket. "Breaking into Fort Knox is virtually impossible, but it doesn't have many variables. Breaking into a house around here is difficult because it has too many variables."

"So, what do you suggest?" she asked.

"Uh…" Savage paused. He needed a moment to think. Bringing the art of spycraft into the sleepy world of suburbia was something he never thought he would do, and it was surprisingly challenging. He would have appreciated it under any other circumstances, but in this case, where time was something of an issue, he wished it was a situation where he could simply charge in without too much thought involved.

"Okay, I have an idea," he said finally. "Can you look into houses in the area that have been for sale for an extended period of time? In the area of the congressman's house, obviously, and been on the market for more than six months."

"Okay." After a few seconds, his phone buzzed in his pocket. She had sent him four addresses. "Those are the ones closest to the house in question. Will you tell me why

I'm looking for the objects of sadness for divorced couples?"

"Well, houses that have been vacant for more than six months still need maintenance. This is usually covered by the insurance of the real estate companies, which are rarely as expensive as those the people living in these houses can afford," he explained, drove the car out of the parking lot, and headed to the first and closest address, which had been vacant for eight months. "You'd be surprised what you learn when you look through homeowner's association manuals in search of loopholes."

"I have a standing order for everyone around me that if they ever find me reading through a homeowner's association manual, they are to find the largest gun within a five-mile radius and shoot me with it," she replied. "I'm extending that standing order to you too."

"That sounds about right." Savage pulled into the driveway and looked around the area for a few minutes before he decided that the nearby adjacent wall was where he would find the key lockbox. "Although I'll settle for the nearest knife or blunt object. Those manuals are boring pieces of literature." He found it where he thought he would, hidden from view but near enough to the door to make it accessible. It required a key of its own to open, of course, but it was fragile enough that he was able to force it open with the butt of his pistol. After a few attempts, he finally managed to pry the key free.

"But you've apparently learned a lot from them." Anja chuckled as he stepped into the abandoned house. "Like knowing how to magically locate keys to empty houses."

"That is actually a trick I learned from my ex-wife," he

said. "I was in a college dorm she didn't like and she was still living with her parents. She worked as a real estate agent and knew the agents always left the keys somewhere near the house in case they needed to show without having time to head back to the office to get the keys. Of course, in her case, she and I only did it—"

"I don't need a play-by-play," she protested. "I think I have the gist."

"What you have is a dirty mind." He laughed and circled to the part of the house that gave him a view of the congressman's home. "So did she."

"Ew. I don't need to think about that. You need to stop it. Also, let me know when you have a good view of the place."

"I have a good view of the place," Savage said immediately as he drew a small scope from his pocket and peered intently through it. "Congressmen don't have the protection of the secret service when they're not on government property, but I see a fair level of security hanging around his house—one van and two armed guards. It would seem the man thinks someone's gunning for him."

"You would be right about that," the hacker replied. "I'm looking through the congressman's finances, and I see considerable spending on security. He upgraded the alarm system across the whole building—which wasn't cheap given that the place was built about a hundred years ago. And then he brought a security company in to have people physically guard the house. And the real kicker? All the payments were made about three hours after I detected the leak of your file."

"That recipe does not spell an innocent man, I'll tell you

that," he grumbled and continued his scrutiny. "With that confirmed, the security team on his house will complicate matters. Are they only there for the time he's away? Do they take any time off?"

"Nope. I've accessed the company's records, and it appears they have three teams working a twenty-four-hour shift on the place."

"Shit." He shook his head in irritation. "Simply charging in there won't work. And I had really hoped I could charge into something. All this thinking is exhausting."

"Still hungover, huh?"

"Yep. Any attempt to storm the place will mean we— and by we, I mean I—will get to meet literally every cop in the city. We need to play this smart."

"Do you have any ideas?" Anja asked.

"Yeah, I have a couple." He lowered the scope and fiddled with the dials. "There are too many variables involved in getting into the house, but there is a way to circumvent the whole security system."

"And how is that?" Anja asked.

"The security system," Savage replied with a chuckle. "Ironic, I know, but hear me out. The team out there is acknowledged and known by the people of this delightfully regulated slice of heaven. That actually seems like the best way in."

"Do you think you can pull it off?" She sounded dubious.

"No, but I think you can help me with it," he said with a grin. "It actually reminds me of the first time we worked together."

"I'll work on it." She sounded less than excited. "You

might want to consider not drinking yourself into a stuporous coma the night before your first day on the job. And get a damn aspirin. You can't show up hungover either."

"I'll keep that in mind." He locked the door of the house behind him, headed to the car, and started it. She had a point, but he doubted he would need to drink anyway. He had taken some solid steps in the direction of reaching the people responsible for putting his family in danger. He wouldn't be surprised if he slept like a baby tonight.

After a couple of aspirins, he reminded himself. Anja was right. The state he was in would probably continue until tomorrow if he didn't do something about it.

***

He had made a habit of staying late at the office. It wasn't something he particularly enjoyed, but it wasn't like he had much going on at home to get back to. The apartment he called his own was rented and furnished by the firm until he found better accommodation. Given that it was a penthouse overlooking Central Park, he doubted he would find anywhere as good.

Well, he could, but Banks had never put too much importance on a big house. It would be empty most of the time anyway.

Maybe he could find a way to get involved in the nearby bars and work himself into the local scene. The only drinking he did was social anyway. He might as well get good at it on his own time. But it would be a while before he was on his own time these days. Very little time was his own since he became a partner, and that was the way he liked it.

His phone rang and he realized that the sun had set and there weren't any lights on in his office. He turned the desk light on and lifted the phone to his ear rather than connect it to his computer this time. It honestly wasn't worth the effort, not after the day he'd had. Involvement in the dirty business of kidnapping for money wasn't what he was accustomed to. He was anxious to the point where he considered breaking open the bottle of Blue Label that had been gifted to him when he'd been promoted.

"How has your day been, Banks?" The smooth, dulcet tones were almost a trademark of the woman to whom he owed most of his successes.

"I've worked to make sure that our Savage problem is taken care of," he said and leaned back in his seat. The ergonomically padded leather supported his weight easily and comfortably. "I've contacted one of the communities that were suggested to me by your contacts and opened the account for payment for the kidnapping of the child and her mother. I wasn't sure what you wanted me to do with the fiancé, so I left that up to the discretion of the professionals who were available."

"The fiancé probably won't matter to Savage, so that was a good call," she replied. "We need the leverage in this situation. Having a hold over him is the point of all this, so I suggest they stay alive. They're no good to us dead."

"I've made it abundantly clear in the contract that any harm done to either of the targets will be returned in kind to the guilty parties," he said and kept his voice firm. "I can assure you, the professionals involved will deliver their targets on time and without any undue fuss."

"I knew I could trust you Banks." She chuckled. "You've fulfilled your role rather well, considering the position you're in. I've begun to wonder what you could do for me when in a more advantageous role."

"I'm glad you approve, ma'am," Banks said and tried not to preen too much from the compliments. "I would like to ask, what do you have in mind for Carlson? Once Savage is dealt with, do you think he'll be the right person for the job he had before?"

She sighed. "I doubt it. Savage broke him in ways I actually envy. But we need to be delicate with Carlson. He's smart and he's been in the game long enough to know that he needs insurance to ensure that people don't try to mess with him. Rather like the game he's playing with the FBI."

"Is there anything you want me to do in the meantime, ma'am?" he asked and surveyed the files and folders laid neatly out on his desk with a critical eye.

"Keep working his case and update me on his interaction with the FBI," she said. "When the time comes to deal with Carlson, one way or another, I'll let you know. Keep up the good work, Banks."

The line went dead, but he held the phone to his ear for a few more seconds. The woman was still rather terrifying, even over the phone and even when she was pleased with his work. He wasn't sure he liked working for someone who intimidated him so completely. Unfortunately, he also knew he was in too deep and he would have to continue to play this ridiculous little game of hers to completion, one way or the other.

Coming to terms with one's fate was a liberating process, but he needed something to calm his nerves. He had turned to smoking back in law school—nicotine, not marijuana—but he'd shaken that habit a long time ago. It had left a hole in his life he'd ignored until this moment. He stood, retrieved the bottle with silver and blue markings forged into the glass itself, and walked to the wet bar neatly and unobtrusively set up in his office.

Crystal glasses had come with the office too, and he dropped a couple of ice cubes in one before he poured the dark amber liquid over them until it was well above the four-finger mark. As meticulous as ever, he replaced the cap on the bottle and only then took a long sip. Damned if it wasn't worth the elevated price tag. That was some smooth whiskey.

"You're doing this for your career," Banks told his reflection in the nearby mirror. "You wouldn't have made it this far without taking risks. This is merely paying your dues, and it's fucking worth it."

He took another slow sip of the whiskey and scowled to see the two gulps had emptied the glass. Without hesitation, he poured another drink, a little more generously this time. He knew that if he reminded himself constantly of how he would benefit, he would actually start to believe that it truly was worth it.

CHAPTER TEN

As security gigs went, things could have been much worse. Leaving the military had landed Jordan Fraser in hot water. He'd had some good times in uniform but when he returned to the States with that much experience under his belt, most of the people who had interviewed him stamped the "overqualified" mark on each of his applications. In this economy, people didn't want to pay more for qualified personnel. They wanted to hire someone who was underqualified, train him or her up to the level where they were useful, and still pay them the same amount throughout.

Landing a job with a security company had been something of a godsend. His wife wanted to send their kids to a private school, and with the kind of cash Tower Security paid him by the hour, he could now afford any school Tammy wanted. He didn't even need to read the brochures and could leave all the work of scouting and selection to her. Considering that she would be the one to drive their two little ones to and from the place, he knew she would choose someplace nearby.

In the meantime, he could spend most of his time with like-minded individuals since Tower mostly hired men and women recently out of the military and in need of work. His wife knew he needed to bring the bucks in and would complain less. It would also leave her with more time to use his credit card, but she was working now too, so much of the money she spent was hers anyway.

She was a stand-up gal, Tammy.

He spent most of his days in a van with one of the men he'd toured Afghanistan with. The company had nothing resembling the kind of authority they'd had while in the Corps, so it wasn't a bad way to pass the time. Their food and drink were a part of the budget, and all they had to do was check all the security features of the house every three hours or so, fewer when the congressman was at home.

It was honest work, and they had fun while conducting it. It wasn't even too difficult to access the house's unblocked Wi-Fi so they weren't restricted only to the sites Tower thought weren't timewasters.

A man could get used to this kind of work, he mused as he chewed some of the pizza left over from their lunch.

And it was almost time to go home too. They had given most of the Thanksgiving weekend off for the team members who had been around for longer than six months, which meant they would use the time to let the desk-jockeys have fun training the new guys. Jordan had made plans to take Tammy and the kids to a Redskins game on Sunday.

All in all, it sounded like the kind of week he didn't mind having from time to time.

It was his turn to be up front, and he had the entertainment system tuned to a sci-fi show Tammy wanted him to catch up on so they could watch it together. He was two seasons in and damned if it wasn't intriguing. It wasn't like her to suggest anything with this much full-frontal female nudity, but the solid script and good acting were enough to allow her to look past it and now, they had something to watch together. Not with the kids around, of course. They were addicted to their Disney shows anyway.

He looked up from the screen when the commercials came on. The replacement car pulled up behind them, and he grinned at the perfect timing.

The man in the driver's seat was easily recognizable, of course. Buck Castle, a former Navy man who was heavy around the waist, and his baldness was halfway through treatment with the new Zoo shit that made everything better. Jordan had heard it had the kinds of benefits men and women had only dreamed about before, but it was still too far out of his pay bracket for him to acquire any. Give it a couple of years, though, at the current rate in which he rose through the ranks, and he might try it too.

The man he didn't recognize looked new and he had the ex-military look about him. He wasn't young but was only recently out of the uniform. He still had the look of someone who waited for a superior officer to show up before he snapped a salute. That would fade, along with the crisp black and white lines on his new Tower uniform. He even wore the cap and a hint of brown hair, still not having outgrown the regulation cut, peeked out. At a cursory glance, he filled the uniform well but he still looked lean and not overly tall.

"How's the shift going, Jordan?" Castle asked at the window while the new man came around the other side and slid into the shotgun seat. "Meet Elliot Hardison, new recruit."

"No kidding." Jordan chuckled, turned, and shook the man's hand. He looked firmly into his timid green eyes. "Nice to meet you, Hardison. Jordan Fraser. Where did you come out of?"

The newcomer chuckled nervously. "That obvious, huh?"

"You look like you're waiting for a superior officer to come along before snapping a salute, son." Castle laughed. Jordan was about to scowl at having the joke stolen before he could voice it, but he remembered that the older man had cracked the same joke when he had trained him. He couldn't blame the man when he'd been about to steal what was originally his line.

"Just out of the 75th Ranger Regiment. I did a couple of tours in the 'stan," Hardison said and looked a little more confident.

"Damn, you guys must have lowered the hiring standards in the office to allow dogfaces like this in," Jordan chuckled, and the new man smirked. Military jokes were one of the ways to let the newbies feel welcome in their new place of business. "I spent some time in Afghanistan as well, so maybe you can keep up with a Marine after all."

"We'll see about that," Hardison said readily but he still didn't seem comfortable enough to joke around with people who had been there far longer than he had. They would get that out of him, Jordan thought. Eventually.

"Is there anything to report?" Castle asked as Jordan stepped out of the driver's seat and his partner, Gordon, slid out from the back.

"We had word back on the suspicious vehicle called in yesterday," Jordan replied. He stretched and groaned gently after having spent the last three hours in the seat. "It turns out it was only one of the realtors running an inspection on one of the empty lots down the street so nothing to worry about. Other than that, it was simply another slow day at the office."

"Fantastic." Castle chuckled, patted him on the back, and handed him the keys to the other vehicle. "Slow days are the best for training rookies. I'll see you tomorrow, Jordan."

"Have a good one, Castle," he responded briskly and jogged to the car that Gordon had already boarded. He couldn't help but smirk when the new kid jumped out of the van and set off toward the nearby supermarket. Castle had made him do the walk for coffee on their few times in the field together, and he wouldn't even let the kid use the van. He might have some steel in him yet.

He pulled the car out of park and turned back to the Tower offices, where they would print out a report of nothing to report, punch out, and head home. Another good day, he decided, in which all was right with the world.

Sometimes, Jenkins absolutely hated the holidays.

He couldn't complain about the time off from his day job that could be spent either with his family or getting ahead on his campaign dues, but the fact remained that it was a whole week of the year during which no one on Capitol Hill wanted to work. The inevitable result was that they needed to complete two weeks' worth of work in one week.

There were people who took advantage of that, of course, and slipped subtle edits into bills that would reach the floor. One had to keep one's eye on the other congressmen and women since none of them would think twice about using the increased workload to slide something past everyone's notice. Not only did they have to work twice as much, but they had to be extra careful about what the people on the other side tried to pull out of their hats. All this while trying to pull a few tricks of their own, of course.

Unfortunately, he didn't have time for tricks. Garcia was running him ragged in the reelection campaign, which meant he had his hands full trying to deal with his job and keep his job, all while needing to conduct favors for his new overlords. Banks had made it clear in no uncertain terms that, while they would help him keep his seat, they were still the ones in the driver's seat of this relationship.

He'd told Carol he would be home later than usual. He'd left a voicemail and sent flowers to mollify her since they had planned a family dinner during which they would discuss their Thanksgiving plans. She hadn't liked that. Usually, she responded to his voicemails in kind, but she'd answered with a text and simply said she would take Jason out to eat since he wouldn't be there for it.

It had stung a little, but the thought of being able to have a brandy and a cigar in his office after a rushed meal of whatever they had in the freezer eased the instinctive resentment. He could afford to celebrate a little. Even with all the work and the stress from work, there was good news to come out of this. Thanks to all the work put into improving his image and the various celebrities who now endorsed his campaign, things looked better and better for him in the polls. The younger ages were the only demographics he'd had trouble with, and with the help of his new friends, they began to show support in the polls. He had even trended on Twitter.

Jenkins waited for the driver appointed to him by the Tower Security company—which also provided most of his other security—to open the door to his car to let him out. It had been a long time since he'd had a driver of his own. He definitely appreciated how convenient it was and he could afford it, but his campaign manager in Wisconsin had told him that to be seen with a driver would hurt his image.

That fear was gone now, thank God.

He glanced at the paneled van that had been parked outside his house for the past few days. It had the Tower logo on the side to indicate to all the assholes in the homeowner's association that they could shove whatever stick they had up their collective asses deeper in. He had simply upgraded his security and they couldn't fuss about that. There didn't appear to be anyone in the van at present, but that probably meant they were securing the property and checking all the security systems to make sure nothing was tampered with.

The driver appeared to feel the same way, as the man didn't look overly concerned. His training, of course, reminded him to keep his hand on the weapon tucked under his arm at all times, and his sunglasses-covered eyes scanned the windows while he stuck close to Jenkins.

"Do you mind if I do a quick sweep of the house, Congressman?" the man—whose name had escaped Jenkins already—asked as they stepped inside. The house was unlit. It was unusual, but Caroline had a habit of turning all the lights off when she left the house and was angry with him. She thought it would make him feel lonelier in an empty house and encourage him to apologize to her faster.

The woman had a degree in psychology and damned if she didn't know her stuff. He would make sure to buy her something extra special for Thanksgiving.

"Can I at least go the kitchen for a beer?" he asked and heard the frustration in his tone. The man nodded and removed his sunglasses.

"I'll mostly check the third and fourth floors," he clarified and locked the door behind them before he started a quick sweep of the ground floor.

The congressman turned the light on in the kitchen. It could be a real pain, sometimes, to have this much security, but a shot in the back would hurt more. If it even hurt at all. It would all depend on precisely where that shot was delivered. Still, having to wait around in the kitchen while he sipped a beer and wondered what he would have for dinner was better than dealing with the medical bills that came with getting shot.

At least he assumed so. He'd never actually been shot before.

He retrieved one of the dark ales he'd picked up on his trip to Belgium and popped the cap. It wasn't even a twist-off. They were so classy about beer there. He wondered if he could open a brewery once he was finished with politics. It couldn't be long now anyway. He was owed a lot for the efforts he'd put into the different groups that had sponsored his various election campaigns, and he would collect once he was no longer a public servant. They would pay him through a handful of speeches held at corporate events, merely to keep things above board. Once he had the capital from that, he could look into what investments he could make that would keep them thriving through his retirement. Opening a Belgium-styled brewery seemed like one of the ways he could do that. Or maybe it would be better to invest in an existing brewery and have them produce the same brews.

Jenkins froze when he heard a thud from his den. He put the beer down, his fingers suddenly shaking, and he listened intently into the ominous silence.

The next noise wasn't the same, but it did sound like a struggle was in progress. A soft, growled cry of pain. A clatter as a weapon was knocked out of someone's hands. The distinct sound of a fist hitting flesh and a hard thud, followed by what sounded like a body crumpling.

"Shit," he gasped. He had a gun. Any self-respecting elected official would have found some way to protect himself should the worst happen, but it was in his desk. In his den.

There was a gun in the car. He'd seen the man—what the fuck was his name again?—put a weapon in the glove compartment in case of emergency and pointedly let Jenkins see him do it. There was a phone there too. He could call the police and drive away.

Panic almost overwhelmed him as he scrambled toward the door. While he'd played lacrosse in college, those days were long behind him and too many dinners at Michelin-starred restaurants had put a little too much padding around his middle. He still had the muscle and muscle memory, but it took him a couple of steps to build up to his full speed.

A surging sensation of hope as he reached the entrance hallway and had the door in sight was snuffed out of existence when a hand grabbed him by the collar of his American-made suit and dragged him off his feet. He landed with enough of an impact that the breath was knocked out of him. Even in the dim light from the kitchen mingled with the fading light from the sun setting outside, he could see the elongated weapon in the shadowy figure's hands as he aimed it at his head.

The congressman closed his eyes and raised his hands in front of his face in a futile attempt to keep the man from firing. He held his breath but the sound of a bullet sent to end his life didn't come. It was replaced with the man's boot pounding into his ribcage. The kick wasn't hard enough to break anything but was more than enough to double him over. His attacker grasped him by the collar again and hauled him over the smooth oak surface Carol had allowed him to choose for the floors.

It wasn't a long way to his den, and the man tossed him inside like he weighed less than a body pillow. A couple of lights were on and as he pulled himself up from a painful and ungainly sprawl, he caught sight of his driver, battered and bleeding and unmoving on the floor. He was clearly unconscious, perhaps dead. Jenkins hadn't heard a gunshot, but there were other ways to kill a man.

Guns were a good choice, though, he was suddenly reminded when he felt the barrel of one press into the back of his neck.

"Take a seat, Congressman."

Jenkins would have preferred some emotional inflection to the intruder's voice. The almost inhuman calm considering what the man was doing there felt wrong. With little choice in the matter, he pushed himself slowly to his hands and knees and crawled to his comfortable chair beside the unlit fireplace. When he turned, he expected to see a masked man but instead, he was faced with features he was actually familiar with. Not that he'd ever met the man, of course, but he had spent the past few days worrying about a picture of him so it was all but imprinted on his brain. Now, the man in the image was there in the flesh in a Tower uniform and stared at him with implacable coldness.

He gulped as he settled into his seat and looked into the eyes of Jeremiah Savage—or Jeremiah Johnson, as had been revealed by the file he'd found on the man.

The weapon in his hand resembled something out a sci-fi novel, and the congressman was almost tempted to test the man based on the vague and extremely stupid notion that it simply couldn't be real. The fact remained, however, from what he'd read in the file he'd found, that the intruder could probably simply beat him to death with his fists and not even break a sweat, so there was no point. The gun was most likely as deadly as the rest of him.

"We need to talk." Savage dropped onto a nearby chair and straddled it so he had the back pressed up against his chest and used this to prop his gun hand up and aimed at his captive's knee.

"Do you know who I am?" Jenkins blurted without thinking. "Do you really think you can get away with killing a sitting member of the United States' House of Representatives?"

"You put my family in the crosshairs of barbarians who wouldn't think twice about using them as leverage to get to me," the man stated calmly, and not a single hint of emotion crossed his face. "You have a family, Congressman, one you appear to love a great deal. What exactly would you do to keep them safe?"

That was a good point, he thought and gulped again as he gripped the arms of his chair to stop his hands from shaking. His gaze flickered to his desk in the other corner of the room when he thought about the gun he had in the top drawer. He doubted he would be able to reach it without a little guile, but if he could convince Savage to let him go there…

His captor's gaze drifted to the desk and he smiled when he divined what Jenkins thought about. He reached back and drew a pistol from where it had been tucked into his pants—a Smith and Wesson M&P45, American-made.

The congressman blinked and jerked his hand to push some of his thinning black hair out of his face as he looked down the barrel of his own gun.

"There has to be some kind of curse for a man to be shot by his own gun," Savage said thoughtfully but with a mocking edge to his tone. "Maybe you'll be shamed in the next life for it. I don't know. Or maybe knowing that, if I can shoot you in the temple at precisely the right angle, I can simply put the gun in your hands and the cops will think that it was a suicide."

A hint of a smile played on his lips and made a chill run down Jenkins' spine.

"Then again, if I shoot you in the knees and gut a couple of times, I won't be able to get that story past the cops, but it will be far more satisfying for me," Savage continued and gestured with the weapon. "But this doesn't need to happen to you, Jenkins. I can let you out of here scot-free. All you need to do is tell me who's behind the leak of my file. Who wants to know about me?"

He was no hero and honestly wasn't even marginally brave. He was smart, and he had the kind of face people liked to trust, but when a gun was aimed at him, every good intention went the way the wind blew. And right now, it blew Savage's way.

"Banks," he hissed through clenched teeth. "His name is Mason Banks. He's a lawyer. When he first called me, he said he worked for Pegasus, but he lied about that. The messages I sent to him were addressed to a firm in New York called Statten-Whitney so I looked him up. He was recently made a partner in that firm. I got the feeling that he didn't do this for them, though. There was a mention of a client, but I'm not sure if he meant a client of the firm or a private one. They had some information on me that... well, they made me an offer I couldn't refuse."

Savage scowled at him and his expression suggested he didn't quite believe what he'd heard. He tilted his head as if listening.

"Control, can you confirm any of this?" he asked. Jenkins narrowed his eyes but quickly realized he was talking to someone who wasn't in the room. They were probably in a van outside somewhere or over a comm link. "Yes, I'm talking to you. Can you confirm any of this?"

He glanced around and wondered if he was expected to do anything at this point. He hadn't lied, and if the man's sources were anything resembling good, he would be able to confirm that.

And then what? The chilling question needed to be answered.

His captor turned his attention to the present and stood to fix him with a hard look. "Well, it appears you can tell the truth after all, at least about names. I'll leave you intact for the moment. If I have to return for you—either if you're lying, or if you tell anyone about this little conversation—the only clue you'll have is your brains plastered on whatever you happen to be looking at in that moment. Look in my eyes and tell me that I'm lying."

Jenkins did look into his eyes. There was absolutely no emotion in them. He didn't doubt that the man could reach him again. He was unquestionably a professional and excelled at what he did. Besides, it wasn't like Jenkins could invest in much more security before eyebrows were raised.

"Please," he said and jerked up from his seat as Savage

started to make his way to the door. "Leave my family out of this. Don't hurt them…and they don't have to know."

Savage sneered in response. "Don't make the mistake of thinking I'd hold a man's mistakes against his family. I'm not like you and your ilk."

And with that, he was gone and the front door opened and closed a few seconds later.

The congressman remained motionless for a few minutes until his knees were able to support his weight again.

"That motherfucker," he said, annoyed that his hands were still shaking. "He took my fucking gun."

CHAPTER ELEVEN

Savage stepped out of the house, closed the door carefully behind him, and jogged to the van. He'd drugged the coffee he'd bought for the man who'd come to train him on his first day. No doubt the people at Tower would figure out what happened eventually. Either Jenkins would fill them in on the details, or they would get the story from the trainer—Castle, that was his name—and they would know their system had been hacked and their clients compromised.

He knew corporate America well enough to know they would do everything they could to make sure the story didn't become common knowledge. Jenkins also seemed like the kind of man who wouldn't spread the news that he'd been forced to give up sensitive information, especially on someone who had blackmail material on him.

While he couldn't afford to make any assumptions, an educated guess could be made that suggested he might have a couple of days at the most before Banks knew he had been identified.

With that said, he also knew the lawyer couldn't be his priority at this point. The man could be dealt with in due course. Now that he knew who he was after, he needed to make sure the people who needed protecting were out of harm's way.

"Hey, Anja," Savage said as he slid into his car, which he'd left parked in the supermarket parking lot. He removed the uniform a piece at a time.

"Mission accomplished, right?" she asked.

"More or less." He started the car and pulled onto the road. "I mean, yes, but I have another mission on my shoulders now. Can you put me through to Anderson on this connection? It must be a secure line. I need to be on the move right now and I can't be pulled over for talking on my phone while driving."

"A little bit bossy today, aren't we?" Anja asked. He knew she tried to push his buttons to lighten his mood, but he really didn't have time for it. She was one of the people who would try to help him when she thought he needed help, whether he agreed with her or not.

He actually felt better now than he had when this whole thing started. It helped to know who he was dealing with. Well, he had a name and knew the hacker would turn it into all kinds of knowledge they did and didn't need. While she worked on that, and while he could probably have Sam and Terry run point on an operation against Banks, he knew his priority right now needed to be helping his family and keeping them safe.

"Hey, Savage?" Anderson spoke through his earpiece. "Anja said it was important and that you found whoever accessed your files?"

"She wasn't lying," Savage replied and eased onto the highway. "We had a chat with the congressman responsible for the leak, and he spilled the beans on who was behind it. Apparently, he was blackmailed into sharing the information by some lawyer called Mason Banks. Anja can fill you in on the details."

"Mason Banks?" Anderson asked. "Am I supposed to know who that is?"

He shrugged. "I don't. But Anja said she is working on uncovering what she could on the man. Well, not in so many words, but the fact that she hasn't actively joined this conversation tells me that's what she's doing. Anyway, that's not what I wanted to talk to you about. I…have a favor I need to ask of you. And possibly Monroe too."

"Name it," the former colonel said immediately.

"You don't know what it is that I intend to ask," he pointed out.

"You were there for me when I needed your help to save my family, Savage," the man grumbled and obviously didn't like that he had to spell it out explicitly. "What the hell kind of man would I be if I didn't help you do the same thing for yours?"

"Well, maybe you'll be the man who can talk Monroe and maybe even the board into giving me access to one of those corporate planes we used to travel all around the country?" Savage asked. He grasped the wheel tighter as his heart rate quickened again.

There was a slight pause on Anderson's side of the line. "You need a private jet?"

"I need to fly to Seattle," Savage explained. "I can't let my family know I'm alive, but I need to make sure they're okay. I wouldn't be able to focus on anything else until I know they're safe, and what better way to do that than in person, right?"

Another pause dragged on a little longer than the last. "I don't understand why you can't fly commercial. First class, of course."

"My comfort isn't the problem," he retorted. "I'm headed there with a small arsenal—the kind the TSA doesn't appreciate being brought on their planes anymore. I'd like to keep it instead of wasting time to rearm myself once I'm there."

"I understand. I'd approve it myself, but I'll need to run it past Courtney first. She'll be able to make sure it's all cleared with the bureaucrats around here. I'll call you when it's done."

"I appreciate it, Anderson."

"You know it," the former colonel replied and hung up.

Savage continued in a tense silence until the sound of Anja's voice broke through the tedium.

"I've sent what I could find on the surface about Banks to Anderson for intel," she said and sounded a little more subdued than before. "I have bugs running traces and digging deeper, so we'll know more about him soon."

"Thanks, Anja," he rumbled and kept his eyes focused on the road.

"I've known you a little while now, Savage," she said haltingly and didn't seem too confident about what she was about to say or ask. "I'd like to think I know you better than most people. Hell, I know most people better than most other people know them."

"I don't doubt it." He chuckled.

"Anyway," she continued, "you seem like the kind of guy who would have charged off to attack Banks personally, made sure you reached him first, and taken him by surprise. I'm not a specialist in any of this, but it seems to me that would be the best move. Banks is in New York, about three or four hour's drive away. Why are you heading to Seattle?"

He didn't want to answer that and knew he wasn't thinking clearly right now. But he had meat in the game, to speak metaphorically, which meant every decision he made would probably be biased one way or another, and that was a recipe for disaster.

"I know I should probably eliminate Banks first," he said, his voice soft, and despite his best efforts, he couldn't keep the emotion from it. "I should force him to stay away from my family and kill him if I have to—be the savage Anderson and Monroe hired me to be. Hell, you'll probably find Carlson's behind this, and that'll finally give me the excuse I need to confront the bastard and finish him off once and for all."

"But you're going to Seattle," she pointed out.

"Yeah… Well, Sam and Terry can handle Banks," Savage snapped and shook his head to quell the rising irritation. "The man's a lawyer. They can take an afternoon break from babysitting Anderson's family and deal with him. It'll give the colonel an excuse to hang out with his family."

"While you hang out with yours?"

Savage sighed. "Yeah. Well, I can't actually hang out with them, obviously, but… I need to make sure they're okay. I just…need to know. Is that too much to ask?"

"No, it's not," she said softly. "Sam and Terry can start

tracking Banks. They're close to Anderson's family, so it might be a trial to tear them away from their current charges, but I think I can manage it. Or maybe Anderson will have to. You go to your family, kick the ass of any poor bastard who crosses their paths and tries to bring them harm, and celebrate by taking them out for pizza."

"They can't know I'm still alive, though," he reminded her belligerently. "But aside from that, I really like your plan."

"Why the hell not?"

"The US government wanted me to be dead to the world for a reason," he explained. "And they won't take it easy on the people who act against their interests. I won't put them in that kind of danger either."

"Wow, you're really intent on being a martyr about all this, aren't you?" the hacker muttered. He didn't answer and simply drove in silence until she patched Anderson in on the other line.

"Hey, Savage," the colonel said. "I talked to Courtney, and she approved the plane for you. I'll text you the details. She also extended her best wishes with the situation and said she would join the hunt for Banks herself but she's too tied up in the Zoo to be able to make an appearance. She has approved sending Sam and Terry in too."

"I appreciate it, Anderson," he said again. "Will you spend time with your family?"

"Yeah, I guess so," the man confirmed. "The sacrifices a man has to make, right?"

Savage couldn't resist a smirk. He knew his boss didn't mean it and that he loved his family, despite the real conversations the two had shared during their road trip almost a month before.

"You be safe, Anderson," he said.

"Break a leg, Savage," Anderson replied. "Hell, treat yourself. Break two. Not yours, of course."

"Of course." He chuckled and the line went dead.

It had been a long night thus far. He wasn't sure how long he had been at it, but he knew it would be longer. He still waited for confirmation that the contract he had put out for the kidnapping had gone through.

Thankfully, none of it required him to actually talk. He merely waited for an email to confirm it through the various third-party agencies that had sent the money through to advise him of a green light. It was fortunate since Banks was about two-thirds of the way through the bottle of whiskey and he didn't think he would be able to say anything without slurring. He needed something like this. Hell, if the bottle was finished in less than an hour, he thought he would climb into his car and find a nearby bar.

No. Not his car. A cab. He was nothing if not responsible.

The thought teased a smug smile as he poured more into his glass. The ice had run out a couple of hours before. It merely slowed him down at this point anyway. He'd taken to adding coke from the bar to the drink too and paced himself through the bottle. That had helped. The smoothness of the liquor effectively masked how hard it would hit him fifteen minutes later, so it was better to dilute it a little.

The annoying buzzing sounded again. Banks looked around and narrowed his eyes as he scanned the room for the source of it. It took him longer than he would have liked, which left him wondering if he should take a break from the drink and maybe start on preparations for the hangover he knew was coming. What could he prepare when it came to hangovers, though? He'd heard something about adding coconut water ice cubes in his drink instead of regular ice cubes, but it was a little late for that. Maybe he should take some painkillers once he was done drinking. Oh, right, hydrate. Lots of hydration.

Buzzing? Oh, right. His phone. Fucking phone. Who called him at this hour of the night anyway? he checked his watch and scowled at it. This hour of the night was nine in the evening, apparently.

"Fuck, I'm getting old," he grumbled and shuffled to his desk where his phone had almost vibrated itself over the edge. He managed to connect it to his computer after he tried and failed a few times to press the accept call button. That accomplished, he cleared his throat, straightened his shirt and tie again, and let the call come up on the screen.

The face that greeted him wasn't one Banks had thought he would see for a while. He'd assumed the client would handle the congressman from this point forward. The information he had used to leverage the man into cooperating had been provided by her, and the proverbial carrot had been provided by the same source.

"Congressman Jenkins," Banks said and worked hard to keep the slur from his voice as he leaned back in his seat.

"How nice to hear from you again, but if you're calling me in thanks for securing your re-election campaign, I'm afraid you have the wrong number."

"I'm not calling to…thank anyone." Jenkins scowled. From the look of the half-empty glass of brandy in his hand and the well below half-empty bottle in the immediate background, he had to think the man was almost as drunk as he was. The annoyed, anxious tension in his caller's body language told him the drinking wasn't in any kind of celebration, however.

"If you have any kind of complaint or legal information you need help with, I'd suggest calling the firm during business hours," he advised him coldly. He'd suddenly lost interest in the conversation although he'd heard about this sort of thing happening, of course. They'd threatened to reveal his philandering, and if the man had trouble with keeping it a secret, he would turn to his blackmailers as the only ones he could actually talk to about his situation. "They'll be able to assign you someone who can help with your…particular case."

"What?" the congressman asked and shook his head in apparent bewilderment. "What are you talking about?"

"What are you talking about?" Banks retorted.

"Savage was here."

Savage? Oh…Savage. Right. His heat rate ticked a little faster, and he leaned forward. "Savage was there?"

"Yes," Jenkins confirmed resentfully. "The man broke through my security and put a gun to my head. He said that by uncovering his file, I had put his family in danger. I don't know what the fuck he was talking about."

"I do," Banks blurted without thinking.

"What?" the man asked sharply.

"Nothing." He shook his head. "What did you tell him?"

"Everything," the congressman snapped. "What, do you think that because you have some pictures of me I'll cover for you when I have a gun to my head?"

The lawyer nodded. That was a good point.

"It's not like I know that much anyway," Jenkins continued. "Only your name and the name of your firm, but he had some support on the line who didn't think it was much of a problem. If I were a betting man—and if you have actually targeted his family—I'd definitely put money on him coming for you with a slow, painful death in mind."

Banks nodded. He didn't actually agree with anything the man said, however. His mind was already on what he could do to cover his tracks to keep himself out of Savage's crosshairs. He realized he should have seen this coming, but not in his worst nightmares did he think the cat would be out of the bag this quickly. The reality was that he'd believed they would have handled Savage before he ever had to worry about him.

"Well, I'll assume your silence is you considering how fragile your mortality is," the man said finally, his tone resentful. "Just so you know, this is me done. Warning you is my debt repaid in full. You all need to leave me alone now."

"Yes, that sounds fair," he replied but still paid little attention to what he said. "We'll be in touch. You have a fantastic Thanksgiving, Congressman."

Jenkins tried to say something before the lawyer closed the connection, but he was too slow. Or maybe he wasn't, but Banks didn't really give a shit. The man had sold him out—a gun to his head notwithstanding—and he now had bigger problems to deal with than making sure the client knew the congressman's debt was squared away.

"Shit," he mumbled and thumped his fist on the arm of his chair. "Well, this fucking complicates matters."

CHAPTER TWELVE

The plane jostled hard enough to jerk Savage awake. He shook his head to clear it, looked around, and wiped a touch of drool from his lips. While he had said that having the comforts of traveling first class wasn't important, he had to admit it did factor in. He'd slept in all kinds of places, some of which weren't necessarily where people usually slept. When you had spent most of the day lugging about fifty pounds of equipment and weapons up and over dunes, you would be surprised by where you could manage to fall asleep. After a while, you simply adjusted to it. Your body adapted quickly to the kinds of stress it was put through and by now, he'd reached a point where he was able to basically sleep on demand. Most of the time, anyway, unless his brain had engaged high gear and wouldn't decelerate.

That said, the comfortable plush seats in the private jet were a definite improvement to being strapped into a cramped seat in a Goliath aircraft. Dinner had been served immediately after takeoff, and the stewardess had directed him to the bar should he need anything else and told him to let her know if there was anything he needed from her. That was essentially all he remembered of the overnight flight—or seven-hour flight, anyway, he noted when he checked his watch.

When the lingering traces of sleep slowly faded, he registered that the fasten seatbelt sign was already on. The jolt he had felt was most likely from the plane starting its descent.

Another thing you learned from spending days, weeks, and sometimes up to months out in dangerous territories in the world was to be a light sleeper. It hadn't paid off in this case, though, he acknowledged wryly. He groaned, rolled his shoulders, and took a second to stretch before he strapped himself into the seat and adjusted it into the upright position.

The stewardess entered the passenger area and paused before she turned back the way she had come. He assumed she had intended to alert him that they were starting their descent. His mind began to turn and he leaned back into his seat and stared through the window while the plane thrust through the low cloud.

It really did pay to be rich these days, Savage thought with a small smirk. Or have rich friends, anyway. He had heard the story of how Monroe and Anderson had become tangled in this mess only once and he honestly didn't remember much of it. All he needed to know was that they were in the Zoo together and decided they needed to change Pegasus from the inside to make it an organization or company that wasn't the epitome of evil in the world, or something like that. Things had merely spiraled from that point forward.

He didn't even want to think about what kind of shit the pair of them and their friends in the Zoo would have been in had he not been brought on. Considering that Anderson's home had been attacked with his wife and kid inside, there were some things even a man like him didn't want to have to consider.

The thought was immediately pushed aside, and he focused on his current situation rather than the nightmare that hovered below the surface of his calm. He gripped the arms of his seat as they touched down. As soon as he was cleared to do so, he disembarked and breathed in the icy evening air before he shouldered his duffle bag. The stewardess told him she hoped he enjoyed his flight. He'd left her a generous tip—generous by his standards, anyway. He wasn't sure how much millionaires tipped after they had a pleasant cross-country flight.

Either way, it was the best he could do at this point. He moved away from the plane and realized when he looked around that he had lost a couple of hours on the trip to Seattle. It had been late before the plane had been prepped for the trip, and yet according to his clock, only three and a half hours had passed, more or less. The airport they had landed at was a private strip outside the city of Seattle and he wondered if he would have to call a taxi or an Uber or something. Then he saw the Audi parked out near where the plane taxied into a hangar.

Signed rental papers had been left on top of it, with a message from Anderson that he should deliver the car to the company when he was finished with it and keep his refueling receipts.

The man had apparently missed the fact that he'd rented an electric car. Savage snatched the keys up from where they had been placed on the roof. The details of the vehicle were included with the rental papers and confirmed that the car was delivered with a full battery. On the top of the vehicle, solar panels were fitted to keep recharging it throughout the day, but a small gas-powered engine was stored in the back, just in case. It was designed to be a fully electric car.

It wasn't his favorite kind of car, but he wouldn't turn his nose up at one that was better than the two he still technically owned. They were both in fake names, of course, which was the next best thing to a rental for anonymity. He heaved the duffel bag into the trunk and slid into the driver's seat. When he reached the exit of the small airport, the GPS activated and directed him into the city, although there weren't any actual destinations marked on the map.

"Oh, dang, are you already on the ground?" Anja said and yawned for a few long seconds after she'd asked the question.

"Evening, Anja," Savage said and resisted the urge to join her in the yawn. It was more difficult than he thought it should be.

"Evening, Jer." She yawned again.

"Did I wake you?" he asked and turned the car onto a long, winding street that descended from the elevated location the airport was on. The silence of the electric motor was a little unnerving, but he simply needed to get used to it. He gave himself fifteen minutes to adjust to the new lack of noise.

"I needed sleep, and since everyone is either out of reach or resting themselves, I thought it was as good a time as any." The hacker chuckled. "I managed about five hours, which is more than I get most nights. I'll find coffee in a while too."

"Well, I had about five and a half hours, so there." He chuckled. "I win."

"Yeah, Jer one, Control five hundred," Anja replied with a trace of a sting in her voice. "It's good to see you starting to cut into my lead there. I thought I was playing on my own for a while."

"Aw, don't feel bad." He smirked and guided the car onto a more-heavily populated road. It looked like the city of Seattle had begun to come alive with the morning rush hour. He knew the city well enough that he didn't need the GPS to order him around. It had been a while—a few years —but you didn't forget a city like this one.

"How long has it been since you left?" Anja asked and appeared to read where his mind was at in the silence.

"About a year and a half." Savage shook his head. He remembered having to be recalled to this city. It wasn't a pleasant memory. Off time was supposed to be spent with your loved ones, or lacking that, getting yourself wasted in preparation for resuming your tour. He had been pulled back to Seattle almost against his will.

"I grew up around here, but both of my folks are gone," he said and decided that she was ready to hear the truth about what he was doing there. "We weren't really close with the rest of my extended family. I think I have a couple of uncles and aunts living somewhere in Texas, but I never really knew them, never really cared to, and the feeling was mutual. By the time I was sixteen, it was only me and Jules. We'd been together since our sophomore year in high school.

"We married a couple of years later when she got pregnant but we separated after Abby was born. Things were… complicated. She was anti-military and had been supportive of my time with the Army despite that, but with a kid, she became a little more insistent, to the point where I decided against my second tour and came back home instead. I found a job and felt a little resentful about it too, I guess."

She didn't say anything. He didn't know if she was actually listening or if she had turned his connection off until he was done sharing, but the floodgates had opened. She'd asked to know about it before and he now obliged. It was up to her whether she wanted to know or not.

"Anyway, things got tense, and she told me if I wanted to go, I should go." Savage pressed forward and pretended he was merely talking to himself to make the whole process easier. "And I did. I picked up another tour and was out of the country again less than a month later. When I went home for some time off, I asked if she wanted a divorce, and she said no. I think she wanted to maintain the marriage at least until Abby turned eighteen. When I got back again a year later, though, she called and said she'd changed her mind and she did actually want a divorce."

"Shit," Anja interjected, which confirmed that he wasn't merely talking to himself. The conversation helped to distract him from rising irritation when traffic slowed to a crawl through a construction zone.

"Yeah, she met a lawyer, actually," Savage continued. "Andy…something. I forget his last name now. Anyway, they started dating, he proposed, and she accepted. She was still technically married to me, so they needed me back there to sign papers before they could get the marriage plans underway."

He fell silent as the memories surfaced, still a little raw around the edges. Rather than dwell on it, he focused his attention to stare at the cars ahead which moved as best they could in the usual stop and go pattern that defined heavy traffic. He removed his hands from the wheel and turned on the auto-drive features that had been developed for traffic jams exactly like this one. It would keep him moving steadily along the road until he needed to take control of the car again once they could increase speed.

"I wanted to hate him so much when I heard about it," he said softly into the silence. "I needed him to be an asshole—a rebound who Jules would realize wasn't right for her so she'd come back to me. But he's awesome, and that's the truth. He's a great lawyer and has his own practice and everything. He's successful, treats Jules like a queen, and Abby adores him. The man was a fucking boy scout. He did the triathlon in college and he still runs a marathon every year."

"How do you know all this?" Anja asked. She sounded curious but also a little hesitant as if she didn't want to push.

"What, do you think I'll let a man live in the same house as my baby girl without making sure I know every dirty little detail of his life?" Savage asked with a scowl and thumped an open palm on the steering wheel. "My first CO was out and in the FBI at the time, and he agreed to run a couple of background checks on the man when I asked."

"Did he find anything?"

"He was busted for possession a couple of times in college."

"Why do you sound so disappointed about that?"

"It was pot possession," he grumbled in response. "Nothing serious or life-threatening that might rear its head later on and be a problem they need my help with. I think I would have preferred it if he was merely some boring-ass choirboy. But no. Not only is he perfect Mr. Lawyer, but he also has a trace of bad boy—a hint of a dark side, enough to make him exciting."

"So, while we head in there to deal with the threat against your family, will we save his life too?" the hacker asked.

"Only if it's on the way," he replied. "If I have to choose between saving Jules and Abigail and saving Andy, I'll leave him behind without a second thought or a hint of regret."

"That sounds fair," she agreed. "So as of right now, we'll work to keep Jules and Abigail safe, yes?"

"I have a feeling you already knew who we were coming here for." He glanced into the rearview mirror at the seemingly endless stream of cars. "That you might have looked into my personal life anyway despite knowing I wanted to keep my family's privacy intact."

"It's adorable that you think there's any privacy in this world of ours." Anja cackled and almost sounded like a

Bond villain. "But I like to let people think that basically, everything about them isn't readily available online these days. It makes them feel a little more comfortable around me."

"Right." He knew he should have felt annoyed—or even insulted—that she hadn't respected his wishes, but he should have known that telling her not to look into something was like telling a kid not to touch the giant chocolate egg on the counter and then leaving kid and egg alone for a couple of hours. While he could hope she would have stopped herself from accessing the information, he really shouldn't have expected it.

"Anyway," Savage said when he decided to simply move past it. "We're—and by we, I mean me, of course—here to make sure Jules and Abby are safe and sound. I don't really care what happens to Andy. He can die or get kidnapped for all I care."

"You don't really feel that way, do you?" the hacker prompted.

He smirked when his mind went back to the last time he'd had a conversation like this—in the steak place, sitting across from Coleman. Her words at the time sprung to his mind at this point too.

"Well, the jury's still out on that," he murmured under his breath, knowing she could still hear him. "But that's the official story and I'll stick with it."

"Okay, big guy." Her voice held an edge of amusement. "How do you want to do this? I have the street address where the ex and the kid are living with the lawyer. I have the addresses where the ex works, where the lawyer works, and the school where the kid is."

"Is it a school day?" he asked.

"Yeah, Thanksgiving is tomorrow, so all the schools are still open. I can look into Abby's schedule right now if you'd like."

"I don't think that's necessary—" he started to say, but he could already hear her clattering away on her keyboard.

"It looks like she has classes all morning," Anja said. "But she's been given a pass from classes later—she's earned it due to good grades—and will be at soccer practice all afternoon."

"Okay." He rolled his neck to ease the tension creeping in. He didn't know how he would take this. If having a discussion with Coleman had been difficult, he wasn't sure what to expect from himself in this situation. While there were feelings involved when it came to Coleman, this was his baby girl. The apple of his eye. The single person in the world who would turn him from mildly violent to over-the-top genocidal.

"I should probably do a couple of sweeps during the morning," Savage said as a plan came together in his head. "I can check the house and make sure there's nothing there for me to deal with. Look up Jules' workplace and maybe even Andy's practice too. With that done, I can circle back to Abby's school and make sure she's okay. And once I've established that everyone's alive and well, I can mount a defense for them over the next few days while we decide how to deal with Banks and make him leave them alone. If he's actually targeted them, of course."

"It's nice to hear you all unreasonably optimistic about how well today will go." The Russian chuckled. "But that sounds like a plan, Daddy-O. I'll patch your day into your car's GPS with all the addresses."

"Daddy-O?" He narrowed his eyes and wished she could see his disapproving expression. "You've never said that before in your life, have you?"

"Nope," she confessed cheerfully. "What do you think? Does it suit me?"

"Nope. In fact, I'm of the opinion that the never-er you say it, the better."

"Duly noted," Anja replied, and he could have sworn she grinned while she said it.

CHAPTER THIRTEEN

He'd spent most of the day out and about and reacclimated himself to the city of Seattle after his time away, and it was enough to settle him and restore his sense of familiarity. The adjustment gave Savage the confidence that he was capable of taking on the task he was there to accomplish. Anja might as well have been a superhero based on her abilities behind a keyboard, and as long as he was able to fulfill the physical demands of the mission, he would be able to resolve the whole situation if he was called upon to do so.

A trace of hope remained alive in his mind that there was nothing to worry about. At times, he almost convinced himself Banks had accessed his file only to know what he was up against at Carlson's behest. The hope that the ex-CEO had learned the very pointed lesson he'd been taught when they met face to face in the plane remained obstinately alive. After all, he'd left a bullet in the man's knee to ensure he would not forget it.

On the whole, though, common sense retained

supremacy and he didn't feel overly hopeful. Carlson did seem like the kind of man who thought the rules that governed the actions of the rest of the world didn't apply to him. He would try again and even believe he could be smart enough to get away with it too.

He hated that kind of person. In his less calm and rational moments, he wondered if he should have simply put a bullet through Carlson's neck and another in his head, just to be sure, and left the FBI out of it. Frontier justice had a strong appeal.

But Monroe and Anderson had insisted, and Anja listened to them more than she listened to him. That had left him with only a warning shot and the cops. Now, the bastard had targeted his family too—his instincts told him he could be sure of this. He had already made up his mind that he wouldn't let them call the shots on the field if his inner certainty proved correct.

He drove past Andy's practice first. Andrew Devers, Esq, was the name on the plaque outside the office. The car Anja had identified as his was parked outside in one of the reserved parking spots, and after about fifteen minutes, the man appeared and talked to one of the receptionists who had stepped out with him.

His gaze focused and intent, he studied him carefully, looking for any indication of stress or nervousness. He appeared to be his usual confident self, and there was no sign of surveillance or any indication that things weren't exactly as they should be. Satisfied, Savage drove to where Jules worked. She wasn't in the real estate business anymore. It had merely been a job to pay for her college education.

Now that she had her business degree, she had been hired to help organize the finances of a marketing company. It was small but seemed to make significant waves in the industry by the looks of it. According to Anja, they could anticipate a very profitable year, which could result in a couple of buy-outs next year. He didn't know much about how all that played out, but she seemed to know what she was talking about.

Things were going well for his ex-wife, and that was good enough for him. Unfortunately, her offices were on the fifth floor of a building with solid security, so he wasn't able to manage a visual. After Anja ran a couple of checks to make sure nothing hinky was happening around the building, he headed off.

He took a long lunch at a nearby shopping mall's food court to get himself a burger while the hacker updated him. Terry and Sam had already relocated to New York, where they had eyes on a certain Mason Banks. Anja had run facial recognition software and found cameras around Jenkins' office that placed the lawyer there a day or so before the leak happened. So far, everything confirmed the story the congressman had sold him.

Which was a relief. Savage doubted that reaching Jenkins a second time would be as easy as the first. You couldn't necessarily trust a man who talked with a gun to his head, so it was good to know that so far, the story he'd been given stood up under scrutiny. His teammates ran surveillance on the lawyer for the moment and Anja kept track of his online activity, which had registered the files arriving in his work email.

It seemed as though he hadn't even anticipated that

anyone would come looking for answers. There were hints that he'd passed the data on to third parties, but thus far, the Russian had a little difficulty in tracking the possible contacts.

All in all, it had been a productive day of stalking for the crew. Anderson had stayed home from work with his family to keep an eye on them with Terry and Sam away on their mission. Monroe was still out in the Zoo and appeared happy to delegate the day-to-day running of Pegasus and the challenge to whip it into shape to Anderson and Coleman.

Savage was Anderson's delegate. He was very clear on that, and the operative saw no reason to complain.

After lunch, he had made his way to the school where Abby was supposed to have soccer practice. It was a good school—a private school, the kind a lawyer could afford these days.

"Interesting," Anja said as he pulled up at the gated entrance. "The security is essentially as good as you can find out here without being military grade."

"Many rich or even simply well-off people send their darling heirs here to be educated," he pointed out and displayed a police badge to get through the security checkpoint. The guard manning the gate ran a quick check with the Seattle PD to confirm that they did, in fact, have a Detective Brian Jackson working in their department. Thanks to Anja's intervention, the department was able to vouch for him and he was waved through quickly.

"How would they get security like this, though?" she wondered aloud as he guided his Audi to the parking lot in view of the soccer fields. He could already see a team outside, starting practice.

"Well, these parents probably don't mind paying a little extra so the school can afford enough security that Mommy and Daddy don't have to worry about their kids. It must be a relief to them while they're off doing whatever it is they do to earn the money to pay for it in the first place." His tone sounded more than a little snarky but he ignored his slight resentment, donned a pair of sunglasses, and ruffled his hair a little. He didn't think Abby would recognize him, mostly because she wouldn't look for her dead father at soccer practice, but there was no point in taking chances. If she saw him—even if he managed to get away before she could actually confirm it—she would probably tell Jules about it. That would open all kinds of worm cans he wanted to leave unopened.

"So, what are we looking at here?" Anja asked and drew him away from that unpleasant thought.

"Middle school league soccer." He moved in close enough to see the activity on the field. "It's merely the first step in athleticism where various middle schools are probably already scouting talent that can be turned over to the high schools and then college. You'll find the school system in the US is actually something of an assembly line for all kinds of sports, from baseball, basketball, hockey, football, Olympic sports and, in more recent years, even soccer. That last one is thanks to Beckham showing up and making the sport somewhat popular in this country."

Savage located his gum in his pocket and popped a strip into his mouth as he watched the practice with little enthusiasm. He wasn't keen on the sport itself, but thanks to

Abby's interest, he'd acquainted himself with the rules and the more famous characters of the sport. He hadn't managed to keep up with her for long, but the lessons seemed to stick. From what he remembered, he could deduce that the kids on the team—which was co-ed, probably due to the low interest in the sport—played what looked like a game. Half wore red vests and the other half wore blue. They all raced around with the ball, except for two who were dressed in individual uniforms with longer sleeves and gloves. The goalkeepers, if he remembered correctly.

There was no mistaking Abby, though. She wore one of the blue vests and was the only kid on the field with bright red hair. As always, it was long—the way Jules insisted on despite his protests—and held in a ponytail. Of course, he hadn't been Jeremiah Savage in those days and had the time to complain about a little girl's hair length.

And damned if she wasn't good at the game too, he thought with a small smile. She streaked across the side of the field and handled the ball deftly until she reached the chalk marking of the big area in front of the goal. Still in motion, she cut one of the kids away from the ball, and as the goalkeeper rushed out to try to take it from her, she darted back and chipped it over the taller, burlier opponent's head to nestle it in the back of the net. The other kids cheered as she celebrated what was apparently a very nice goal.

"Now there's a part of you that I'm not used to seeing," Anja said with a chuckle.

He looked around hastily and wondered how she could

see him but also realized there was a silly grin plastered across his face that he couldn't seem to remove.

"Like I said," she responded and seemed amused at his effort to see how she had a visual on him, "these people are ridiculously paranoid about their security, ironically enough. Most of the school is covered by cameras."

Savage nodded. "Do you think you can take a look around to make sure there's nothing to indicate that someone of Carlson's ilk is stalking the grounds?"

"Like I said, I have eyes all around the damn school, Jer," she retorted briskly. "I already have a couple of searches running and I'll let you know if I find anything. You know, for a place with this much digital security, you'd think that they'd want to keep it off the grid. But no, simply plug into the Wi-Fi, and voilà, I have access to all the damn security cameras. Someone needs to rethink this place."

"After we're gone," he quipped and drew back a couple of steps into a small grove of trees when the soccer coach blew a whistle, which brought both teams to a halt. They didn't look like they were finished with the game, so maybe it was halftime. He didn't know and couldn't tell, at this point.

He kept his eye on Abby as she rushed over to the water fountain, shouldered and elbowed her way past some of the other kids to get there first, and gulped the icy water like it owed her money. She walked away and wiped her mouth with the back of her arm.

Savage narrowed his eyes as the goalie she had scored against marched over to her. The kid had about ten pounds and a few inches on her, although Savage couldn't tell if it was a boy or a girl. They were all kids, none of them older than ten, and this one had long, wavy hair.

"It's nice that you can play like that with your feet, Devers," the kid said and sounded distinctly masculine despite the distance of about thirty yards the operative maintained between them. "I guess you have something to rely on since your brains and hands don't work right."

Savage narrowed his eyes. Devers? Since when did fiancés get to add their name to the kids of their spouses?

"Shove off, Walo," Abby retorted and attempted to circle him, but he moved faster, grabbed her by the shoulders, and shoved her hard onto the ground.

Something clicked in Savage and he started to take a step forward, spurred on by the sudden need to feed the boy a few of his own teeth. He stepped out from under the trees and started to make his way over to where some of the kids began to gather to watch the show.

Abby pushed herself up, her face red.

"What's the matter, Devers?" Her tormentor laughed. "Are you going to cry? Do you need Coach to get your daddy for you again?"

Abby wiped her forearm across her cheek again and brushed the dirt off her freckled cheeks. "No, Walo. My dad—my real dad—always told me I should never start a fight, but I should make sure I end one."

Walo looked a little confused for a second as she advanced on him, her clenched fists at her sides. Her father had been in enough fights to know what was coming, even when it was little kids who did it.

She ducked under a heavy haymaker from her adversary and pounded her fist into his gut. When he doubled over, she took a step back and stamped her cleated foot on his instep. He gasped and tried to back away but doubled over as he was, she had time to step in and punch him firmly in the jaw, which tumbled him effectively into an awkward heap. The kids around them cheered and jeered as she stepped closer. Savage began to wonder if he would have to keep her from killing the kid.

"Savage, remember what you said?" Anja reminded him. "You know, about not letting your kid see you?"

In that moment, he simply didn't care. He couldn't stand around while his baby was involved in a fight.

But Abby didn't continue her attack. She looked at Walo, who still struggled to regain his breath as he rolled and groaned dramatically.

"You shouldn't have said anything about my father, Walo," she said, closer now because he had moved from his previous position. "You should be glad he wasn't here to hear you. He'd make sure you didn't talk for a month."

Well, maybe not a month, Savage thought and backed slowly toward the trees again. He hadn't thought clearly at all. Hell, he'd been about to charge in there and drag her away from a bully she apparently had dealt with for a while. Understandably, his first instinct was to be there with her and for her, but there were serious implications to his precipitous response. It wasn't the wisest move to reveal to a ten-year-old kid that her assumedly dead father was alive and well and had appeared from nowhere to rescue her from a fight. That would take more time and therapy to heal than the altercation would.

He couldn't help a smirk, though, as he watched the teams run onto the field. They looked like they were having fun. All except Walo, of course, who still hadn't found his feet. He wiped dirt from his knees and scowled when Abby seemed to forget all about him and rushed away to start the game again. The players switched sides and formed up. Everyone seemed to have forgotten about the boy until the coach noticed he had a goalie missing as the game started again. He turned to see the kid still on the ground outside the chalk lines of the field and jogged over to see what had happened.

Walo shook his head. For whatever reason, he refused to snitch on Abby, but the coach appeared to know they had some kind of feud as he turned to look where she waited for the ball to be passed to her.

Savage jogged over to him as he put the whistle to his lips. He dragged him around to face him and conveniently pulled the taller, more corpulent man between him and where Abby stood.

"Hey," he said with a grin.

"What the f…fudge do you think you're doing here, pal?" the coach snapped and took a step forward. He didn't bother to give the man the satisfaction of taking a step back like he was intimidated.

"I know what you're about to do, but I think you should give the kid a break, don't you?" he said with his most charming smile.

"You know…what…who the f— Who are you?" he demanded and looked and sounded flustered as Walo rushed past them and jogged to where his goal stood open. The players continued with the game.

"Oh, did I forget to say?" Savage asked and chuckled. "That's my bad." He pulled his fake badge from inside his coat pocket and flipped it open for the coach to see the bronze shield as well as the nametag that showed him to be a member of the local police force. "Detective Jackson. I'm actually here to see Abigail Devers' father. I don't suppose you'd know when he's coming to pick her up, would you?"

The sight of the badge apparently calmed the coach down a little, although he took it to inspect it more closely. It was all for show, of course, as he doubted the man knew what to look for to identify a fake badge. It was an excellent fake anyway, so would have passed more stringent scrutiny. After a moment, he handed the badge back.

"Oh… Right. The practice goes on for another half hour," he said with a firm nod and looked around instinctively for a higher authority. "If you like, you can wait inside the school building until he comes. I can tell him you're looking for him, Detective…"

"Jackson," Savage said with a smile and patted the larger man on the shoulder. "Brian Jackson. You do that. I'll be waiting inside…where, exactly?"

"There's a visitor's room," the coach said. "Ask the people at reception and they'll show you where."

"I appreciate it, Coach," he said, patted the man's shoulder once more for good measure, and turned to head quickly to the building before any of the players noticed his presence.

CHAPTER FOURTEEN

The two young women at reception seemed uncertain how to react when he flashed his badge. After a little gentle prodding from Savage, they were able to direct him toward a small room, isolated from the rest of the building by one-way glass, with a few tables, chairs, and a handful of vending machines. It actually looked like a teachers' break room, but it seemed classes were over for the rest of the day, and as such, it was empty for the moment. He settled himself in his seat, made sure to look busy on his phone, and even enlisted Anja's help to hold some official-sounding conversations.

After about a half-hour of waiting, movement from outside the room caught his attention. The coach guided Abby to one of the couches outside in the lobby. He couldn't tell what was said, but he could guess from the way she had her chin jutted out like she dared the man to do something. It was what she always did when she knew she had done something wrong but wasn't ready to admit it—a habit she had acquired from her mother, along with her freckles and fiery red hair.

A few minutes later, a blue Mercedes SUV pulled up outside and a face that had Savage already on edge stepped out. Andy looked like he'd come directly from work, although he couldn't tell if that was how he dressed for business or if the suit and tie were merely his general look. The coach was outside to greet him. Devers looked angry at first and then confused as he looked inside. He had obviously been told there was a member of the police force waiting who had asked to talk to him.

A couple more words were exchanged that he couldn't make out, but they looked like they had something to do with why this detective had come to his daughter's school instead of to his place of business.

Stepdaughter, he reminded him mentally as he adjusted his clothes, and without thinking, brushed his hair quickly into place from when he'd ruffled it before. He needed to look good in front of the ex's new man. It was simply something he needed to do.

Andy followed the coach inside and told Abby to sit when she stood as he needed to do something really quickly before they could leave. It looked like there might be some bribery involved—probably ice-cream—that kept her in her seat as he followed the coach into the waiting room where the operative was still seated.

Savage still had his sunglasses on as the two men entered and closed the door behind them.

"Mr. Devers, this is Detective…what was it again?" the coach asked.

"Brian Jackson," Savage said and painted on his most

charming smile as he removed his sunglasses and offered Andy his hand to shake. The lawyer's face paled immediately and his eyes widened when he realized who he was about to shake hands with.

The coach noted the sudden shift in his face, but his expression clearly indicated that the tall, thick-set man had no desire to be caught in the middle of anything complicated. This was between the cop and the parent, and he didn't want anything to do with it.

"Mr. Devers, I'm sorry I had to reach you through your daughter's school, but after I share what I came here to say, I'm sure you'll understand," Savage said quickly and tightened his grip on Andy's hand to convey a subtle warning. "Do you mind if we take a minute to talk? Alone?"

The last word was directed indirectly at the coach to encourage him to leave the room. He looked around a little helplessly. "I'll make sure Abby has some water. She played her heart out in practice today."

"Of course," the lawyer said. He still looked more than a little stunned as the other man made his way out to check on the child who waited outside.

"Please, take a seat," Savage insisted and pointed toward the chair opposite the one he had claimed for himself. His choice would allow him to keep an eye on his daughter.

Andy looked like he was in the process of working through shock, but he recovered quickly enough that he already had questions lined up when Savage took his seat across from him.

"H…how?" Devers asked and leaned forward in his seat. "How…the fuck are you here? You're supposed to be dead. As a doornail. As in I went to your fucking funeral."

"Reports of my death were greatly exaggerated," he responded with a polite smile and offered his fake badge to Andy, who took it numbly and shook his head like he couldn't believe what he was looking at.

"Don't worry," Anja said into his earpiece. "I've made sure none of the microphones or the cameras in the room are working."

He nodded his thanks subtly while the other man continued to shake his head.

"What…what are you doing here? Are you here for Abby? Is this some kind of threat? Do you want to be with your daughter again?" He rambled a little as if the filter between his head and his mouth had suddenly gone missing. Openly anxious, he ran his fingers through his thick black hair.

"Don't worry, Andy," Savage said and tried to keep his voice as calm as possible. "I'm not here to stage any kind of…to take my family back. Abby doesn't know I'm here. She can't know I'm here."

"I…don't understand." The man blinked slowly and looked like he still tried to decide whether his visitor was a ghost or not. "You're supposed to be in a military graveyard in Maryland. I went to your funeral."

"That's really not important right now, Andy."

"What the hell are you doing here?" the lawyer asked quickly, then paused when he remembered he'd been assured this wasn't an attempt to reclaim his family. "I mean…how can you keep your death a secret? Jules still cares for you, obviously, and hell—Abby spent three or four months after your funeral saying you faked your death. How fucking ironic is that?"

"They can't know I'm still around," he insisted, but the other man shook his head sharply.

"Who gets to decide that?" Andy snapped. "You? They were hurting for months after news of your death reached them. I remember that because I was here to make sure they both stayed in one piece."

"The US government decided that." He deliberately made his voice hard. "The biggest killer of them all decided it needed me to retire and faked my death to cover their asses. The last thing I want to do is hurt Jules and Abby by getting you all in their crosshairs, do you understand?"

"Wait, aren't you putting me in danger by talking to me like this?" the lawyer asked.

"Don't take this the wrong way, but are you really surprised that I don't really give a shit about what happens to you?" Savage demanded, spurred on by a hint of annoyance. It was a lie, but it seemed plausible enough that he didn't question it.

The man paused, nodded, and shrugged. "Fair enough. So…why are you talking to me?"

"Because I need help." He leaned forward and propped his elbows on the table between them. "I can't go into too many details about it, but the long and the short of it is that I've done covert work since my death, working undercover to eliminate some really shady motherfuckers. As it turns out, those shady motherfuckers realized who I am, put the pieces of my life before death together, and found out I have a family that might be used as leverage against me."

Andy narrowed his eyes, and Savage lowered his head.

"I know," he said and raised his hands. "I know, this is all my fault. This is my business, and I have no right to endanger you three because of my actions, but the fact of the matter is that it happened. They are in danger because of me, and I'll do everything I can to keep them safe, but…" He paused and closed his eyes, hating the fact that he was about to say this. "I need your help to make it right."

His companion nodded cautiously. He appeared to understand what had been said, and despite everything, he appeared to believe him too. Savage really needed to give the man credit for taking it all in stride as easily as he was. He didn't know what he would have done when faced with the specter of his fiancé's dead ex who showed up and told him they were in danger because of him.

No…not fiancé anymore, he realized when he saw the wedding ring on the man's finger. It still had a faint gleam, which told him it was relatively new to his finger.

"Uh…hey, congratulations," he said softly and indicated the ring.

"Oh, thanks." Andy was momentarily distracted and ran his fingers over the ring. "We were engaged anyway, and it had been a while. We decided to go for it and elope. Just us, my parents, her parents, and Abby. She was the maid of honor and the ringbearer. I…have pictures, if you want."

"I'm good, thanks," Savage said, maybe too quickly.

"That's fair." Andy chuckled. "Look… I don't like this, Jerry. I don't like you faking your death and then showing up less than a year later to say my family is in danger. But I can move past it. All I want is for them to be safe here. We're building a life. I don't want anything to come between Abby and everything she wants to accomplish, do you understand that?"

He nodded and ground his teeth at the man's apparent

insistence on describing them as his family. Of course, he wasn't wrong to use it. They were his family, and if what he'd seen of the man's finances was any indication, he had put more than enough time, effort, and money to earn the right to say it. But it still ground on his nerves.

"She's really good," he said finally and glanced quickly to where Abby still waited for them—no, for Andy, rather. "I managed to watch some of her practice today."

Andy couldn't help a small smile, a gesture that burned Savage to his very core. He wished he could hate the man, but there was genuine sentiment in his smile. It seemed to say that he knew Savage loved Abby too and would do anything to keep her safe.

"What can I do?" the lawyer asked and pulled his companion's attention back to the present.

He drew a deep breath and forced the distractions aside. "I'm still assessing the threat at the moment. I have a team focused on the people responsible, but since they're on the other side of the country at the moment, I decided to look in on you guys myself. Just...take Abby home. Make sure Jules makes it home safe too. Keep an eye on them. Be paranoid about security—a little more paranoid than usual. I might call you from a blocked number, so greet me as a friend or a family member Jules won't want to be involved with. You know the type. Stay alert and I'll be in touch."

Andy nodded, sucked in a deep breath, and finally smiled. "I think I can do that. Good luck, Jerry."

He offered his hand across the table to Savage, who took it and shook it firmly.

"You too, Andy," he replied.

CHAPTER FIFTEEN

"Well," Anja grunted. "That couldn't have been easy."

Savage didn't respond, but she was right. It was, in fact, hellish to watch the man leave the room, walk out there to hug Abby, and chivvy her toward the car while she talked excitedly every step of the way. He assumed she was asking him about the delay in heading home. Andy would have said that it was nothing and come up with some bullshit excuse grownups usually used before he told her he would make up for the delay with ice cream to make her feel better.

She jumped up and down the way she did when she was excited and left tracks across the marble floors inside the school. They exited and continued to Andy's SUV. Savage assumed she was talking about how practice had gone as she gestured animatedly and imitated her moves with her feet. Judging by the motions, she probably told him about her goal, and Andy offered her the appropriate excited response to what she had told him. The story was cut off when she disappeared into the vehicle. The lawyer cast one last furtive look at the school before he slipped into the driver's seat, turned the vehicle, and headed toward the exit.

"Did you get what you needed, Detective?" a voice asked from the entrance of the room, and Savage was brought back to the here and the now. The coach appeared to want him out of the building as quickly as possible. He assumed there was probably some stigma involved in having police on the premises that made them not want to have him linger for any longer than necessary. It was perfectly understandable.

"Yes, I have all I need," he said with a smile, replaced his badge in his pocket, and smiled before he left the room. His gaze followed the SUV until it reached the gate and turned out onto the street. He narrowed his eyes when a paneled van immediately eased out of the parking lot of a nearby building—one that didn't have any definitive logo—and moved quickly in the same direction as Andy had. He jogged to his car and the inner voice prompted him to follow the vehicle.

"Is everything okay, Jer?" Anja asked as he started his car and pulled it out of the parking lot as quickly as he could without drawing undue attention.

"I don't want to talk about it," Savage uttered coldly and gripped the steering wheel tightly to quell his irritation when the guard took what felt like his sweet time to raise the barrier and allow him through.

"Well, if you don't want to talk about your feelings, would you maybe care to discuss why you're trying to get out of that school like you owe it money?" she pressed.

"I thought I saw a van follow them as they left," he

explained and gritted his teeth as he pressed the accelerator. If there was one thing to be said about electric cars, it would be that there was virtually no lag between pressing the "gas" pedal and the actual acceleration. The tires screeched as he pulled clear of the school and out onto the road. He turned in the direction Andy and Abby had gone and strained to catch sight of the two cars as he pushed the vehicle down the road, well above the speed limit. The street was fairly empty at this time of the day and he soon found his quarry, but both vehicles were a long way away.

"Can you run a plate check on that van?" he asked when his brain clicked into gear.

"I'm already on it," she assured him and he accelerated even more to literally hurtle down the road at high speed. He kept his gaze glued to his targets but they pulled off of the side street they were on and onto a street that had more traffic, now going in the opposite direction. Both cars rushed past him before he swung after them, but by the time he was on the right street, they were already too far ahead.

"The van comes up as a rental, currently assigned to a shell corporation based on a shell corporation, and so on and so forth," the hacker informed him. "I'll keep digging, but I doubt I'll be able to find anything substantial."

"Well, I know where Andy's going," he said, increased his speed a little more, and wove gently through the slowly intensifying traffic. "I'll keep going and if they have any trouble on the road, I'll be able to catch up."

Savage continued his somewhat reckless pace and played the dangerous game of weaving through the traffic and staying under or at the speed limit to avoid drawing the attention of the local police. The fake badge he had flashed to the people in the school was good enough to pass a quick visual inspection, but the badges these days had RFID chips in them to make sure nobody did what he tried to do. He would be caught the moment he tried to flash it, and the fact that he had weapons and ammo, cash, and more fake IDs would land him in all kinds of trouble.

He also had the feeling that the Pentagon's tolerance for their supposedly dead operatives showing up in police stations looking like they planned an invasion of Canada wasn't very high. Still, he assumed it would be marginally lower than their tolerance for supposedly dead operatives letting their friends and family know they were actually alive.

Either way, he didn't want to test the goodwill of the people who ran the kind of operations that could never be fully disclosed before the ruling bodies of elected representatives. There was no telling what they would try to do in that case. Either they would merely leave him alone to live his life—meaning they didn't see the point in spending more time and effort to kill someone who was already dead—or they would decide that the risks of someone like him possessing the secrets he did and trying to share them for a quick payoff in the form of a book or a movie were too great. Worse, the decisions were made arbitrarily and usually on the spot. He honestly didn't want to risk it either way.

"Okay," the hacker said and intruded on his less than pleasant wonderings. "I've patched into the security systems of the houses around...the one we'll cover. Andy and Abby haven't made it home, and I'm still running a search around the area to make sure they're not being followed."

"They've gone to get ice cream," Savage explained. "Abby's favorite is a place off East Pine Street. There are dozens of cameras there, so you should be able to locate them."

"I should?" Anja queried. "Aren't you going there?"

"I'd like to, of course, but I should probably set up somewhere near their house. I need someplace where I have a good view of the place without attracting any attention." He turned off the highway into the suburban neighborhood where Andy and Jules had created their life together.

"I have to hunt for more abandoned houses, don't I?" she demanded, and he could almost hear her shaking her head. "Okay, I have eyes on the Devers SUV pulling up at the ice cream shop. Andy and Abby have stepped out. There's no sign of the van, though. I'll keep an eye out while I find you a home to hole up in."

"You're the best, Anja." He chuckled.

"Flattery won't get you anywhere with me, Jerry," she mumbled. "But you really shouldn't stop trying."

"Don't call me that," he protested gruffly, but she simply cackled in response. She'd found a button to press and he had a feeling she would make use of it often.

Savage wasn't about to let Anja forget how good she was at her job considering that she made a habit of reminding him on a daily basis as well. Not only by saying it but rather with regular displays, to the point where he was almost a little numbed to how awesome and terrifying her power was. He was only happy that she used her powers for good—or for his good, anyway. There had to be more than a few people out there who thought she was a force for evil.

"I've found you a place," The hacker fed the address to his onboard computer and displayed a couple of pictures on the screen. He held off on checking on them until he reached a red light, then he studied them quickly. "There are no alarm systems in place," she continued. "It's been on the market for a couple of months now. Nobody has scheduled to look at it this close to the holiday weekend, which means you'll probably have the place to yourself."

"Probably?" he asked and turned into the street in question.

"I'm literally on the other side of the planet, Jerry," she snapped in response. "That house doesn't have any cameras on it, so I can't tell if there are any squatters or if someone has decided to do an impromptu viewing. You'll have to work that out using your own two eyes."

"Okay," he said, calmly and coolly. "And I know that you're serious right now, but I have to ask you to stop calling me Jerry."

"You let Andy call you Jerry," she pointed out. "And here I was thinking you and I were a lot closer than you are with him."

"It's what Jules used to call me." Savage scowled and turned cautiously into the target driveway. "He calls me that because she does, I assume, and while I'm not in the mood to correct him, I am in the mood to correct you."

"Ugh, fine, fair enough," Anja grumbled. "How will you get into that place?"

He didn't answer and instead, stepped out of the car,

drew his jacket closer, and removed his duffel bag from the trunk. He handled it gently and placed it beside the front door. Once he'd picked the lockbox that hung neatly from the doorknob, he retrieved a knife from his bag and used it to force the box open and pry the key free. It all took only a few seconds before he opened the front door and entered, taking the ruined lockbox with him.

"You'll need to teach me that trick." The hacker chuckled, and he couldn't resist a small smirk as he paused inside the house to close the door behind him. It was a two-story home and appeared to have been recently renovated and cleaned. Most of the furniture was still present. The real estate company probably anticipated a quick deal, considering that it looked like they either planned to sell or rent with the furniture included. Or they could have simply taken pictures to post on their site. This was a prime real estate location, he thought as he familiarized himself with the layout. It was close enough to the city to make it a comfortable drive while still outside the city limits with good schools nearby. Many younger well-to-do families with either old money or newly acquired wealth would fight each other for a place like this.

"How long did you say this place has been on the market?" Savage asked. He found an accessible corner for the duffel bag, removed the rifle, and began to assemble it.

"A couple of months, why?"

"It should have the bodies of young couples piled around it in the battle to acquire it." He finished with the rifle and checked the sight. "Did someone die here or something? Is that why it hasn't sold?"

"How the hell am I supposed to know?" she asked. "All I

know is that it's empty and it's on the market. Do you really want me to scan all the police reports on this location? Because I can do that."

"I assume you have better things to do," he responded and took a few moments to peer through the scope before he stretched and eased his back. "I was simply curious, is all."

"Are you looking to buy property, Jer?" the hacker asked.

"I'm looking to invest some of the money I've been paid for this job," he replied. "That and some of the money the Pentagon gave me for dying. Real estate felt like the safest bet. I'm simply planning for my retirement."

"Do you actually think you'll retire?"

"You always plan for success in this job. Okay, so where am I at? Where can I position myself to look over the house?"

"The west side. There should be a window on the second floor that gives you a clear view," Anja replied but sounded a little distracted. "You don't seem like the kind of man to drop everything and find a sunny place to spend your twilight years, is all."

Savage climbed the stairs slowly and familiarized himself with his surroundings as he moved to the bedroom on the west side. Sure enough, a window looked directly down onto the Devers' house.

"A man like me probably won't have twilight years," he said idly and drew a chair closer to the window. "Most of my time will be spent on the run or staying one step ahead of the bullet that has my name on it. But you do have to plan for survival. Maybe I end up injured and unable to live this life anymore. It's always a good thing to have something to fall back on. If anything happens to me, it'll all be locked into a blind trust that will go to Abby when she turns eighteen. That way, it can be something for her to fall back on."

"Planning for the future, Jer," she said, and her voice sounded almost wistful. "I think I like it."

"I'm glad you do." He focused his attention on the target location. Even if the Devers didn't notice a man with a scope watching them from across the street and over the hedges that separated the properties, someone else might be able to see him instead and call the cops. He didn't actually know if anyone around there would look out their windows long enough to see him, but what the fuck else was there to do out in the suburbs?

He looked around, drew the blinds down over the window to prevent anyone from seeing him, and retrieved a small pair of binoculars to train them over the driveway. His work had necessitated many long waits before, and he settled comfortably into his seat with his eye to the scope, prepared for the tedium that lay ahead.

Ice cream took about a half hour and the SUV turned into the driveway soon after. Abby looked like she'd smeared much of the chocolate on her jersey, and he could imagine Andy promising they would clean it quickly before her mother saw it and flipped out. The lawyer obviously still had the warning in his head and a hint of paranoia showed when he looked around. There wasn't a trace of trained instinct in the man, but then again, that was the reason why Jules had chosen him—or so she had told Savage during one of their many, many shouting matches.

She arrived in a Mazda about an hour later, and Andy and Abby came out to greet her. They pulled her into the house quickly and all the lights came on inside. It appeared that Andy's version of keeping them all indoors and safe was to cook a meal for them. There were also preparations for the next day's meal too, Savage noted, but for now, it looked like Andy prepared a family stir-fry—and he seemed damn good at it too. He used a real wok and chopped ingredients with the skill of…well, maybe not a professional chef, but certainly someone who had paid attention in adult cooking classes.

"So, let me get this straight," Anja said into the earpiece after she'd left him alone to continue his surveillance. "This man is a lawyer—and a top graduate from law school, no less—has his own practice, is rich enough to buy his own house in a prime location outside the city, and he can cook like a pro? That must hurt to watch, eh?"

He didn't respond. The silence might actually have been preferable. When it was quiet, it was easy to let his mind wander and time would pass without him paying attention to the details that weren't important to the case.

"I know you've accomplished some shit in your life, Jer," she continued like she didn't mind that he hadn't participated. "I've looked into your file. I know you told me not to, but sue me, I'm a curious person who lives and breathes information—ones and zeroes. So yeah, I've seen your file. You've done stuff that would drop jaws for the right and wrong reasons all around the world, and yet, watching your ex shack up with a man who has everything figured out with his life, is settled, and even cooks for her… You have to be a little jealous, don't you?"

Savage knew she was only ribbing him and attempted to distract him and maybe to get a rise out of him. But it didn't change the fact that she was absolutely right.

"I don't disagree," he said finally, his voice low and not only because he tried to keep a low profile.

"You know, it's not as much fun to tease you if you don't fight back, Jer," she grumped.

"Yep, I know." His response was automatic but distant, superimposed on an unspoken warning that resonated within him. Something wasn't right. He could feel it climb his spine and raise the hairs on the back of his neck.

"You know I don't mean any of it, right?" the hacker asked. "This lawyer might have it all figured out, but when it comes down to the facts, he still needs you to help keep him and his family safe."

"Safe from a threat I brought on them, remember? Look, I…I know you're only kidding and poking fun at me to keep me light. But staying quiet is a good way to let me focus on the job and also to pretend it's any other job—something impersonal and normal."

"Right." She sounded a little put out. "Sorry. I'll shut up."

"Well, I didn't say that." The words seemed to speak themselves without any need for him to pay attention to what he said. Something was definitely wrong. It hovered barely out of reach on the edge of his mind, waiting for him to discern it.

"You don't want me to shut up?" she asked suspiciously. "Did I seriously hear you say that?"

"Oh yeah, I totally agree." What was wrong? What was off? He wracked his brain… Lights. The second-floor lights had been on fifteen minutes before but they were off now, and the whole family was still downstairs in the kitchen.

"Jer, you're not making any sense. Do you have a gun to your head?"

"Shit, they're in the house already," Savage whisper-yelled and dropped the rifle when the rest of the lights in the house went out.

"Ah, so you weren't even paying attention to me," the hacker said.

"Don't feel bad," He yanked the blinds up and opened the window. "You make a fantastic white noise machine."

"Asshole." He vaguely registered the lilt of amusement in her tone, his attention already focused on the ground. The house was newer and lacked any arching ceilings and high rises, which meant it wasn't much farther than ten feet from the window where he stood. He'd made longer drops than that—usually in some kind of power armor, of course, but the concept remained the same. Without hesitation, he heaved himself onto the windowsill and after a few quick breaths, pushed himself clear.

Just like riding a bike. He dropped quickly and landed with loose knees and his feet pointed down, continued smoothly into a roll over his shoulders, and found his feet easily. He'd felt an uncomfortable jolt when he hit the ground, but he shrugged it off. He had left all his weapons in the house except for the pistol under his arm. Thankfully, he still had a ski mask he'd shoved into his jacket pocket, one he had acquired for exactly this kind of situation. He was rather thankful he hadn't left it in the duffel bag as he'd originally intended to do.

Savage yanked it on quickly using only one hand as the

other drew his weapon from its holster. The mask covered most of his face except his eyes and hugged his skin closely enough that it wouldn't impede his vision.

"Are you all right?" Anja asked. "You're making that weird noise you make when you're limping."

"It's called breathing, Anja," he snapped and shoved unceremoniously through the hedges. His mind scanned rapidly through the various problems he faced at the moment. If they were there to kidnap, they wouldn't risk dragging the family out the back. It worked well enough as an entry point, but when you had to move a family out, there was the possibility that the neighbors would see you and either call the cops or try to intervene themselves. This was America, after all. People had guns and ached for the excuse to be a hero with them.

No, they had another escape plan. They would choose a way out they could use quickly and without too much inconvenience. Out the front door was what usually worked, he thought as he sneaked through the garden between him and the Devers' house. It still carried the possibility of police involvement, but it would give them time to get away without too much trouble. They would be able to switch vehicles once they were far enough away.

"The van," he muttered. "The paneled van. Did you find anything on the plates yet?"

"No, nothing yet, why. Do you see it?"

"Nope." He shook his head and jogged clear of the neighbor's house to emerge on the road. As he scrutinized the streets in the fading light of the setting sun, a pair of headlights flashed on and tires squealed as a larger than usual vehicle hurtled across the asphalt faster than it should have. "Well, I stand corrected."

"Do you or do you not see the fucking van?" Anja hissed.

"I don't know if it's the same van, but it's a van and it's headed directly for me." Savage held his weapon ready and narrowed his eyes. It was a little difficult to actually judge the distance considering that his eyes were slightly blinded by the headlights, but he didn't need to be accurate.

Spray and pray, he thought calmly. He held the weapon with both hands, squared his hips, and narrowed his eyes to squint through the lights as he pulled the trigger. The soft whoosh of the unique needles the weapon fired, sent off with the help of the electromagnets, brought a sense of calm. The weapon responded with only a hint of a kick as he pulled the trigger over and over again. It was supposed to be accurate at up to…two hundred feet? Three hundred? He wasn't sure, but again, accuracy wasn't exactly his intention right now.

After about the tenth or perhaps the twelfth time he pulled the trigger, the van jerked and turned. The tires screeched once again, the sound shrill in the quiet, as the driver lost control and crashed into a mailbox three houses down.

"Savage?" Anja asked. "Are you still there?"

"Yeah." He checked the weapon hastily to make sure he hadn't burned anything out by firing so many times and so quickly. "I made sure our kidnappers don't have an escape vehicle."

The sun slid below the horizon and the streetlights

came on around him almost immediately. He moved hastily into the shadows cast by the hedges.

"Well, that's good news, right?" she asked.

He nodded and kept his voice low. "Yep, but now comes the difficult part."

CHAPTER SIXTEEN

"The difficult part?" The hacker sounded confused.

Savage couldn't risk saying any more. The people in the house would be waiting for their van to pull up outside before they brought the hostages out to keep the time they were exposed and when people could see them at an absolute minimum. He assumed, of course, that these were professionals brought in for a large amount of money. That was the hope, anyway. Professionals would keep their fingers clear of their triggers when things went wrong. The large payday meant they would think twice about simply cutting their losses and killing the victims in order to escape.

He had to hope that—no, he needed to. Otherwise, he would have to charge the house and risk losing people he wasn't willing to lose.

This was the moment when he had to stay calm, he reminded himself. He had to remain focused on what he was doing there and to do that, he needed to stay calm. It was not the moment to do anything stupid. He sucked in a deep breath and closed his eyes. Sweat trickled down his spine and from his grip on the weapon. He dragged in more deep breaths as he fought the same panic he remembered from when the news about his family first came to him. His heart hammered in his chest and his ears rang. The impending panic attack threatened to usurp the control of the situation and leave him helpless. He needed to stay in control.

"Come on, Savage," he whispered roughly and managed to hold the urge to barrel into the house at bay. "Stay focused. This is exactly like any other job. Remember that time in Bogota? It's exactly like that. No, it's better than that. Easier than that too. Keep your mind on the prize— no, bad idea. Keep your eyes on the target. That is what's important. Kill these motherfuckers. Kill them all, and everyone else walks away alive. Stay on target."

Anja didn't comment on the fact that he was talking to himself, and for that, he was grateful. He knew he barely held on by a thread. There was no telling if her customary teasing and ribbing would have the unforeseen effect of sending him into a spiral that would end up with too many people dead. Maybe him and probably Andy too, now that he thought about it. He knew what he was capable of, and he didn't want to push himself to that edge.

What was amazing was that Anja didn't want to push him to that edge either.

"Where the fuck is the van?" a voice demanded from inside, very clearly and without an American accent.

"That asshole is late. I told you we should have used—" The second comment was immediately cut off by what might have been a snort of derision.

"Your friend? Right. Like he's fucking Mr. Dependable."

He couldn't place an exact location in the house, and they all had different accents. One sounded vaguely European, and another had a tell-tale Afrikaans twang. The west coast of the US was enough of a melting pot that people tended to lose their accents there over time, which gave them the kind of accents anyone could mark down as American but nothing more specific. The fact that these men still had theirs was an indicator that they were new to the scene.

See? Keep thinking like that and you won't have to think about how one of these motherfuckers has a weapon pressed against your daughter's head.

"Get out there and see what the problem is," the first man shouted, the apparent leader of the group.

"Which one of us?" the third asked.

"We're on the fucking job. That means no fucking names, dumbass," the leader pointed out. "You! The one I'm pointing my fucking gun at, that's who. Get outside and see what's holding the fucking van up."

Savage had to thank his lucky stars that they didn't use any comms. Of course, the sheer number of Wi-Fi spots in an area like this would make it impossible to hold a line with anything that wasn't military grade.

He tightened his grip on his pistol and withdrew deeper into the shadows. It wasn't difficult to find enough places to obscure him. The driveway would usually be awash with lights from the kitchen and he could make out dedicated lighting from the garage to light the driveway when needed. But with all the lights cut, there were more than enough darkened corners to hide in and he was able to remain low and away from the door when one of the men stepped outside.

Shadows worked both ways, though. Only basic shapes were visible as the operative remained as still as he could manage. He barely even dared to breathe while he watched the man step out into the subdued lighting from the street-lamps, the glow insufficient to highlight any details. The kidnapper wore a ski mask too, with black clothes and combat boots, judging by the heavy footfalls as he crossed the driveway. He carried a pistol in his hands, and the silhouette outlined the elongated barrel that signified a suppressor. The make and model were, of course, hidden in the darkness.

While he searched the street from halfway down the driveway, Savage remained in place, tense and focused. He sucked in a slow, noiseless breath and remained utterly motionless.

The man looked around but didn't move far enough along the driveway to see what had happened to the van. If he did, Savage would have to kill him and hope he could do it quietly enough that he wouldn't draw more of the attackers out of the house.

There was no need, fortunately. The man cursed softly and returned inside.

"It's not there," the scout declared unhappily. The operative used the cover of the shadows to move cautiously closer to the door.

"We can't stay here," the second voice said. "We should simply kill them and get out of here. Cut our losses."

"No one will touch them," the leader commanded harshly. "None of you idiots will hurt a hair on their heads.

You read the contract. If any of them is hurt, none of us get paid and there will be serious pain for anyone involved. They want these…people alive and unharmed. Let's get them out of here. Maybe we'll take the family car to the drop off point instead."

Savage sucked in a deep breath as a surge of hope entered his body. He pressed himself tighter against the hedge to his back. Someone was being smart—get moving, stay out of sight, and use the family car.

He could hear the sound of movement from inside, soft cries from Abby, and a curse from Jules.

"Next time you touch her, I'll kill you myself," he heard her familiar voice say.

"Do what they say, Jules, please," Andy pleaded. "Nothing will happen to us, I promise."

The man clearly had his thinking cap on. He knew Savage was around and probably realized that he was the reason why things hadn't gone smoothly or according to plan.

Dammit. He still wanted to hate the bastard but, as always, the emotion was lost in the fact that he actually liked him on some level.

"Keep moving," the leader snapped. "You, dad-guy. I want the keys to the SUV outside."

The jangling indicated that the keys changed hands. The door opened and Abby was the first one out, shoved through although she kept her balance smoothly. She tried to run but was quickly caught by the man who emerged first.

Jules came out next, a firm hand on her shoulder as a second attacker moved through behind her. Andy was the last one with another man directly behind him and a pistol pressed into his back.

Savage had an odd moment of clarity. He could step in and raise the alarm. Or he could save the family, pull his mask off, and let them see who he was. He could win his family back, exactly like in the movies

The moment passed as quickly as it had come. He didn't like that it had even occurred to him. Doing anything like that would simply put his family in a different kind of danger, and that was the line he would never cross.

He was still a monster but not the kind who would give his own daughter trauma that would last a lifetime.

The group moved past him and he acted smoothly to snake his hand out and yank the hand that held the weapon away from Andy. His first instinct was to aim it at one of the other attackers and make the man pull the trigger, but in this kind of darkness, there was no telling who would be caught if he missed.

Instead, he pressed the barrel of his pistol to the man's head and the kidnapper's weapon fired harmlessly into the ground with the tell-tale cough and snap of a suppressed weapon. He still couldn't tell what make it was.

It really didn't matter now, he decided and pulled the trigger. He both felt and heard the whoosh of the needle as it exited the barrel. A splatter of blood soaked through his mask as he hauled the man aside and shoved Andy out of the way when the other two men turned to see what was happening. He raised his weapon and a sudden calm infused his body. The man who held Abby was the first to die. Savage brought the pistol to bear and pulled the trigger twice. The comfortable non-kick of the weapon tapped his hand. His target stumbled and his weapon fell from already lifeless fingers before the body toppled in slow motion.

The third man, clearly the brains of the operation, saw what was happening and immediately avoided the first shot in his direction. He tried to circle Jules and use her as a meat shield and ducked his head continuously to create a difficult target in these conditions. The operative lowered his expectations as well as his aim.

The kidnapper screamed as a pair of needles drilled through his knee. He lost his balance and landed with a thud. His hand flailed at his pistol which spun from his grip and skidded away across the driveway.

Savage wanted to say something badass at this point. Jules grabbed Abby and dragged her to where Andy was still on the ground.

You wanted to hurt my daughter, you son of a bitch? If you want to go for the pup, you'd better make sure the hound is put down first. Asshole.

Yeah. Something like that.

But he couldn't. The fact that he wore a mask was the only reason why he hadn't been made as a dead man. No words were allowed, only actions.

The man began to crawl to where his gun lay. Savage raised his weapon again and punched two needles casually through his forearm, then one through his hand. He uttered another piercing scream, barely human anymore. Blood splattered across the driveway. Jules would have covered Abby's eyes and maybe her ears too.

It was best to bring an end to this. Still, he couldn't resist delivering a round into the man's other knee before he finally put him out his misery and killed him with a double tap to the head. The kidnapper sagged and lay still.

He'd needed this, he realized. There was nothing quite like being able to blow off steam at the expense of people who really, really deserved it.

In the silence that followed, he took a moment to collect himself. He dragged in a deep breath and checked the strip of needles he still had available. There were more than enough, exactly as he'd suspected.

His gaze drifted to the family he had saved and possibly traumatized and studied the three of them. Abby was all right. Her mother had covered her eyes and ears as Savage had suspected. Jules looked okay as well. Her bright red hair was a mess, though, and a few tears were visible, reflected in the streetlight. She tried to be brave, but she was as terrified as Abby was.

Andy looked rather terrified too. He knew the thoughts that ran through the mind of the masked man in front of him, the desire to pull the mask off and show his family that he was still alive. The lawyer's expression stiffened as if he could envision the scene—differences set aside, a passionate kiss, and a happy ending with the little girl reunited with her real daddy again. Savage could see it in his eyes. Andy was afraid for his family but he was also afraid of losing them.

He didn't need to worry about it. The man had always been a better father and husband to them, anyway.

"Is everyone all right?" he asked as he scanned each one again but directed the question to Andy. He managed to mask his voice in a low, rough cadence.

The lawyer nodded and drew his family into a warm embrace. He nodded again, this time in thanks.

"Call the cops," the operative rasped. The crashed van outside would bring the police there anyway, but if they registered a call of their own, it would reinforce that they had nothing to hide from all this. "Get the girl inside. She doesn't need to see what happened out here."

Andy caught and held his gaze for a moment and the two men shared a silent agreement before he and Jules pulled Abby into the house again. He looked back one last time to where their rescuer waited in the driveway.

"Thanks," he whispered. Savage couldn't do anything other than nod. He needed to get out of there. People had begun to stir, wondering what the commotion was about, and they would call the police if the Devers didn't. He needed to get clear. There was no reason for him to get involved with the police.

When he crossed the street, he noticed the van was gone. He had no idea who had been in it, but apparently, he hadn't killed at least one of the members of the kidnapping team and they'd managed to get away. Or maybe there were more than one. Anja would have to help him track the motherfuckers down. Maybe he could handle them with a little more dedication without having to worry about police or trauma to what was once his family.

Savage snuck through the houses across the street again and avoided the lights that clicked on all around him to slip through the hedge. He moved hastily and earned himself a few scratches from the shrubbery, but he didn't have time to waste. His heart thudded but he reached the abandoned house without incident. His refuge was the only one that didn't have people talking about calling the police.

He slipped inside, rushed to the room where he'd watched the Devers' house for most of the afternoon, and packed his weapons. His movements were quick but precise. The adrenaline pumped through his veins and did an excellent job to make him faster and sharper than usual but lacked the jittery edge that would have caused mistakes on his part. He went through the motions almost on autopilot as he collected his things and made sure there was nothing left behind that would provide a clue to his presence in the room.

A few minutes later, he eased out the front door and closed it behind him, then locked it quickly. The ruined lockbox still lay inside the house as there was still someone who needed to make a living from selling this place. He did feel a little guilty about having to break into the house but made sure he left the key where it could be easily found.

Not for the first time that day, he thanked his lucky stars that Anderson had rented an electric car for him. He pulled quietly out of the driveway and accelerated away, careful to keep to the speed limit and not arouse any attention, and yanked the mask up and off his face hastily as he went. Very few things in the world were quite as suspicious as a man driving away from a crime scene at high speed while still wearing a mask and gloves. He couldn't forget the damned gloves.

Anja had a habit of knowing when to keep quiet and knowing when he was in danger and needed to stay focused. She also seemed to know when he was out of said danger.

"I have a question, Savage," she asked when he finally left the suburban area and joined the more heavily trafficked roads. The wail of sirens—what sounded like dozens of them—approached rapidly.

"Fire away, Control," Savage said and eased his gloves off while he kept the car moving.

"Well, I know we've played the gang violence excuse to cover for you upping the number of people killed by firearms within the borders of the United States," she stated. "But the men you killed were professionals and are probably known to the cops who will go there to bag and tag the bodies as we speak. You also killed them in an upscale residential neighborhood on the doorstep of a kindly lawyer and his lovely wife and adopted daughter. Considering all that and also that the cops will find needles instead of bullets in the bodies, how do you think they will manage to write this shit off as random gang violence?"

He had actually wondered the same thing but there had been no time to clean up. There had been even less time to guide the investigation away from him and Pegasus. The needles shattered on impact so they wouldn't be identified completely, but they were trademarked by Pegasus. If anyone happened to know a thing or two about weapons development, they might be able to put two and two together.

Luckily, if it ever came to that, Pegasus had notified numerous officials across the country about missing company material in their development labs. Monroe, Anderson, and now Coleman too could simply blame it on stolen company property and even demand that the needles in question be returned to them under some kind of legal claim to stolen property once they were no longer relevant to the investigation. He wasn't sure about the actual details, but he felt fairly certain Monroe would figure it out.

But it didn't matter right now. What did matter was that he would leave the area as quickly and as subtly as he could, which meant his number one priority at this point was not to get caught.

"I don't know," Savage said because he doubted even Anderson, with all his contacts, could float the gang violence vote this time. He checked his rearview mirror to confirm that the flashing lights indicative of the police arriving in force definitely headed in the opposite direction. "I'm sure they'll find a way."

CHAPTER SEVENTEEN

There was too much to easily process what had happened that evening. It had still been reasonably early when Anja had shared the news that there was no sign of the police even trying to come after him, and no indication that they might have tried to track an electric Audi that had driven away from the scene of the crime. There had been a couple of videos caught of it, mostly on the nearby security systems, but she was quick to scrub the evidence. The houses in the neighborhood might have fitted some of the best security on the market, but when it came down to it, she had hacked government security systems since her early teenage years. Access to the nanny-cam level systems these homes ran was something she could do in her sleep.

That wasn't simply an assumption on his part. Those were Anja's own words as she gave him a play by play update on what she was working on while he headed back into the city and away from most of the sirens that still screamed loudly enough to be heard a good distance away.

From what he caught on the radio, there was a fair amount of news coverage of the incident as well.

"We have live reports coming in from just outside the city of Seattle," declared a young, attractive woman who had recently bleached her hair blonde. "These shocking reports are from the charming suburb of King County, where the inhabitants of a quiet neighborhood of family homes have been exposed to shocking images of violence."

The image cut to shaky cam footage of the police surrounding the Devers' driveway with tape as curious onlookers gathered. The three bodies were covered in tarps and footage included them being examined by paramedics.

"From the firsthand witness accounts of the neighbors, the shooting occurred sometime between 6:45 and 7 in the evening, just as the sun was setting," the reporter continued as the cameras focused on her once again. "Three gunmen invaded the home of Andrew Devers while he and his wife and daughter were preparing dinner and attempted to kidnap them, according to police reports."

"Stepdaughter," Savage corrected with a gentle shake of his head.

"Other reports suggest that a van that crashed into the mailbox of a neighboring home might have been involved. As the family was dragged out into the driveway, another group of gunmen, whose numbers are still unknown, assassinated all three with a weapon the investigating officers still haven't been able to identify."

The image cut to a tall, well-built man in a police uniform with only a hint of male pattern baldness in his greying hair. "We have our detectives looking into the details of what might have happened, but initial reports point toward the rising surge of gang violence spreading into the city."

"Called it." He grinned and Anja cackled into her comms. He supposed joking about the death of three men by his own hand probably wasn't in good form despite the fact that they had aimed to harm Jules, Abby, and Andy. But when someone had been involved in the life as long as he had and faced death as often as he did, they needed ways to see the humor in it, even if the dark variety was all they could find.

The camera returned to the attractive reporter. "The officers in charge of the investigation have taken the Devers family into custody for their own protection, as well as to provide more detailed statements on their attackers and the mysterious group that saved them from being kidnapped. As yet, there is still no indication as to whether Andrew Devers was involved in any criminal organization that might have made him a target for such an attack."

"Is that the story they're running with?" Savage asked and scowled. "Seriously, you could not find a more vanilla guy. I'm absolutely certain he comes to a full stop at every stop sign."

"That is what you're supposed to do, right?"

"Yeah, but nobody actually does it. Cops tend to turn a blind eye unless it's done blatantly and puts lives at risk or something like that."

"Well, they have to do something to keep the ratings up," the hacker commented. "The truth is very rarely as dramatic as we'd like it to be, and sometimes, they need to come up with some random and crazy prediction based on the facts available to persuade people to tune in next week."

"Honestly, you should know by now that the truth is often a lot crazier than people give it credit for." His chuckle was dark. "Seriously. You're a Russian hacker living, from what I can tell, a hop and a skip away from an alien-spawned jungle that's out to kill everything even remotely human that enters it. For myself, I'm a former black-ops operative who has had his death faked by the government. But when you tell the American people any of that, they're quick to write you off as a crackpot conspiracy theorist living in the mountains while wearing a wide assortment of aluminum foil hats."

"Isn't it tin foil hats?" Anja asked seriously.

"Hats of many assorted foil types," he grumbled. "Either way, these people ignore the real stories as being too crazy and out there, and when they're presented with the truth of the matter, they scoff and write you off as crazy. That is some bullshit right there."

Anja chuckled. "Well, you clearly have feelings on the matter."

"You are Goddamn right."

He pulled into a nearby hotel she had identified as the kind he should stay in. By that she meant it had enough vacancies to allow him to get a room of his choice while it was full enough to make sure he didn't draw too much attention. It was also the kind that was upscale enough to have decent enough service while it lacked the kind of security that would be dangerous for him. Most importantly, it was amenable to cash bribes to ensure they didn't need to put a name into the registry.

But considering that Savage traveled under another fake ID anyway, that part wasn't so important to him on this trip. He warned the bellboys away from his weapon-filled duffle bag for long enough to check into a quaint little room on the fifth floor.

"Okay," the hacker said when he was in the elevator. "I'll put my contacts through the griller to find out where this contract on your family is and see if I can't have it reversed somehow."

"That sounds like a plan," he said, stepped out, and strode toward the room he'd been assigned.

"What will you do?"

"Well, at the last place I confined myself to my room, but tonight, I think I need a little liquid therapy, so I'll visit the bar I saw in the lobby." He pressed the keycard to the room's lock and entered. It wasn't anything to write home about, but the queen-sized bed and the notification of free Wi-Fi above the TV were all he really needed. He tossed his duffel bag onto the bed and turned toward the door.

"I might need your help as the night wears on, so I'll ask that you don't get too drunk," Anja said quietly.

"I didn't intend to anyway." He chuckled. "I only need a little something to take the edge off. It's been a long day."

"Oh, and keep your earpiece in," Anja said. "If I have to call and text you on your damn cellphone again, I'll make sure the Internet is flooded with porn with your face and name attached."

"Understood." He didn't believe she would, although he had a sinking feeling she could very easily deliver on the threat. Either way, it wasn't really worth the risk. If she wanted to listen to him getting mildly sloshed, that was on her.

They'd told him that involvement with a professional team like this would be hard work but the pay was good, and he would be able to retire in a couple of years with more than enough money to pay off the loans he'd taken against the house. More than a few of his army buddies had recommended he enter the freelance business, even if it was part-time. He didn't have a family to maintain, and he needed the money. It had been relatively easy to decide he might as well get into the business that, so far, had been populated mostly by criminals who couldn't do the job right.

A team of trained and experienced members would wipe the floor with the competition, make a lot of money, and pull away before things went bad.

But things had gone bad—very bad, and in the most spectacular way.

Charles Tells—once known as Charlie but since nicknamed Chucky due to the scars left on his face after a landmine had gone off a little too close to him—wasn't the kind of man to scare easily. He'd been through tough spots before, including ops that had gone sideways and had shifted from a clear objective to a get out and survive kind of deal. All in all, he'd been through all kinds of hell.

But this was supposed to be the easy part. The promise was that he would cash in on all the training the government had given him while they forgot to deliver the kind of money he was owed for his particular skills.

There weren't many people in this business. Fewer still who had the skills they did.

Of course, most of their team was now gone and had burned themselves on the job. Reports already started to show up on the news about three bodies and a crashed van nearby. They didn't appear to have any pictures of the van itself or the plates, but that would only delay the police for a limited period. When rich people like those living in that neighborhood were involved, the police had ways to make sure that virtually anything that was missing could be found.

But none of that really mattered anymore. They were finished. It had been a six-man team and they were down to two. Braken had been driving and had been shot two or three times by the man they had barely seen in time. The stranger was dressed in black, wore a mask, and carried a gun.

Chucky had been seated in the passenger seat. Grant was in the back, waiting to help them get the family inside. It had been a solid plan but someone had fucked them over. The man had waited for them, already in place to protect the family.

The merc grimaced. He had been hit in the shoulder too, although he couldn't find any bullets in his wound. In fact, he wondered if his wound wasn't actually caused by some of the broken glass. There was a lot of it inside the van, especially after it had crashed into that damn mailbox. Braken was killed on impact and he'd managed to get himself together, drag the man out of the way so he could take the driver's seat, and get them the hell out of there. Grant, their man in the back, had walked away with a bump on the head and maybe a concussion, and he was the lucky one. Chucky had gotten them out of there, ditched the van at the drop-off spot, and driven away in the new one to take them the hell out of Dodge.

Only then had they had the time to check the news and their wounds. Chucky still couldn't find any bullets in his shoulder, and while he'd initially assumed it was glass, when they tried to haul Bracken's dead body out of the van, they didn't find any slugs in him either. He had heard about weapons currently under development that didn't leave much in the way of shrapnel or bullets behind, but those rumors had been around for decades, probably since the Kennedy assassination.

"What the fuck happened in there?" Grant asked while he pressed ice to the side of his head. "I thought we were in clean. Who was there to protect them?"

"That's what we need to find out." He probed his shoulder gently. Every time he moved, he could feel something dig in deeper and bite, much like a splinter that had gone way, way deeper than they tended to go.

"How?" his companion asked.

"The contract was posted online." He scowled as he thought things through. He remembered seeing Alfonso run through the details that had been sent to them. "If there were other teams looking into it who declined because they knew something we didn't, I'd want the information out there, and so would all the other teams who work jobs like this. It's a common and professional courtesy issue. No one wants to work for someone who doesn't post the full operational details and uses that to underpay in the contracts."

Grant shook his head. "What happened?"

"Someone was covering the family," Chucky said and stated the obvious. "Someone good enough and well equipped enough to knock us out of the running, and from the news, kill Alfonso, Eddie, and Murdock. The family's safe in police custody, but I think we can put money on this person still covering them, so another attempt is pointless now. We need to make sure no one else tries the contract without knowing what they're walking into. It'll be a charnel house otherwise."

"Professional courtesy?"

"I'd want to know if I was walking into a trap." He logged into the online auction site that doubled as their host site on which to find clients in need of their services. It was partly because he wanted to make sure their fellow illegal operatives didn't come within a mile of this contract. But he also wanted to screw the contract initiator who had gotten his friends killed.

And maybe, just maybe, he could find out who the asshole was who actually did the killing.

***

"How sloshed are you?" Anja asked.

"I only had two drinks," Savage protested cheerfully, thankful that he was alone in the elevator. "You of all people should know I have a higher tolerance than that."

"You weren't drinking on an empty stomach, were you?"

"Please, Anja, it's like you don't know me at all." He grinned. "The hotel has a kitchen too. I had dinner before I went to the bar. Weren't you keeping an eye on me?"

"I ran an Internet-wide search on any sites that might have issued the contract on your family," she explained sharply. "I also kept an eye on the developing police case to make sure they haven't realized that you're involved in any way, all while also making sure your family is safe from attack. All things considered, I'm running two or three other operations at the same time. I don't have time to keep an eye on you every second of every day. That, plus the fact that the cameras in the bar and restaurant area are down for repairs and you paid your tab in cash, so I couldn't be sure what it was that you bought."

"Huh." He grunted to conceal his laughter. "So, you're telling me you tried to keep an eye on me, and when you couldn't, you decided to do all that other stuff?"

"Shut up," the hacker retorted. "Stop talking to me while you're out in the open like that. People might be listening from their rooms and think you're crazy."

"We wouldn't want the truth about me to be out there, now would we?" He grinned but she was right. He kept his voice low when commenting as he headed into his room and locked the door behind him. "Now that it's only you and me, is there anything you can update me on?"

"Do you really expect to be able to get anywhere near anything you would be able to shoot, stab, or punch?" she asked.

"I'm a nasty kicker too, don't forget about that." He drew his pistol from the holster, removed a towel from the duffel bag and laid it out on the bed, then placed his weapons onto it one by one. "I simply thought that you have an innate need to talk while you work, being your own white noise machine like I am, and I wouldn't mind having my mind eased by knowing what everyone else is up to."

"Ugh, fine." She sighed and the soft squeak from her side of the comm line told him she was rocking in her office chair again. "Well, the cops have your family in custody. They're taking statements, but it doesn't look like they've tried anything along the lines of tying the investigation to whatever ties Andy might or might not have to the mob. Despite the captain's statement on the news, no one seriously thinks there are any actual gangs involved. I assume that's mostly because they've identified the three men you killed through fingerprinting and have them listed as ex-military from Bosnia, South Africa, and Italy."

"Mercenaries." It made sense given the nature of the contract.

"Yep. More importantly, mercenaries whose DNA and fingerprints have been found at a variety of crime scenes across the country, which means they have done considerable work in the US for about five years."

"Professionals," Savage concluded and began to take his weapons apart.

"Stop summarizing my updates in one word," she snapped. "You wanted me to be white noise so I'm being white noise. Do you want me to stop?"

"Nope, by all means, keep talking." He inspected the pistol and cleaned it carefully. There wasn't much residue left behind when the needles moved magnetically through the barrel, but this routine was what he'd learned way back when he was taught how to use weapons. There was a sense of ritual to it, he supposed, and found the idea calming.

"Well, I'm facilitating the process of getting your family into protective custody," Anja said. "Moving it to the top of the pile, as it were. They should have it finalized before the night is over, although they might have to spend the night in the police station to be safe."

"In the police station is better than dead," Savage said cheerfully. He hadn't drunk that much. His steak and fries with a side of salad—none of which had been half bad but not fantastic either—were accompanied by a beer. He'd followed with a double of scotch as a digestif. That was the right word for it, wasn't it? As a result, he was slightly buzzed, not enough to leave him impaired in any way but he definitely felt more relaxed. He would have growled and rolled his eyes excessively at her antics otherwise.

"Agreed," the hacker continued. "But there's only so much I can do on that front from here, so I've looked around and…"

She paused and he frowned as he focused on the odd sound that came next and wondered what it was. It sounded like a chuckle but not quite like anything he'd heard from her before.

"What is that?" he asked as he completed his inspection of his revolver and fed the needle strip in. "Are you laughing?"

"Oh yes." She chortled, a more recognizable sound.

"What are you laughing at?"

"Would you believe me if I said that it was need to

know?" she asked. "You tried that shit with me, remember?"

"No, I wouldn't," he replied and turned his attention to the shotgun. The routine to clean and oil it was soothing. "And you do remember how well that worked for me, right?"

"Well, let's be honest." The hacker paused, still chuckling uncontrollably. "You don't have anything like my skills at uncovering people's dirty secrets."

"Get to the fucking point," he commanded and this time, he did roll his eyes.

"Ugh, fine." She groaned. "You're no fun today, you know that? Give me a few minutes and check your phone. I'm finishing this up. You'll love it."

Savage simply nodded. He knew she couldn't see him but didn't really feel too charitable toward her at the moment. For a minute or so, he continued to work on the shotgun, then switched to the rifle before his phone buzzed. He leaned over, picked it up gently, and peered at what Anja had texted to him.

"What am I looking at here?" Savage asked when the link directed him to an online auction house.

"You'll find the capture contract on your family if you put in Andy's home address in the search bar," she explained. He did so, his expression one of distaste.

"Nobody buys anything on this site that doesn't have a picture on it, especially when they have a price that high," she explained when his search brought up a piece of art that had no image and only the street address named. Mixed into the description, which was longer than it needed to be for that purpose, were the words **Capture**

Alive. It was an interesting system and difficult to penetrate unless you knew what you were looking for.

"Under the description, you can see people asking about the delivery system which is code for the payments and details on the job mercs would be interested in," she continued. "Look at the bottom—last comment, added less than an hour ago."

"Huh." He snorted. "Worried about delivery system. Who is running point on security? And there's already an answer, but not from the person who posted the contract."

"That would be me." She sounded like she was grinning.

"I'm glad to see you're being professional about it, Pain-DianaJones." He chuckled. "And this link you posted…"

"It's a storage site that holds the resumes of most of the pros in the country," Anja clarified. "Basically, it's a way for people in the business of hiring professional criminals to be able to do so across the country with a marginal degree of certainty and verification."

"And this is…a page for The Savage." He scanned the variety of operations assigned to his name. "Houston, LA… yeah, I remember those. Rio, Lisboa…uh, I sort of remember those. I don't think I was ever in Seoul, though. Or Bangkok. Or…most of these countries, actually."

"In fairness, I managed to make up half the jobs in there based on ones you were actually involved in, either before or after your time in the government. But I felt I had to pad the numbers. I found old pictures of you and altered them slightly to help me with the verifications. It took considerable work, but I think I got the point across. A significant number of people have already checked the details about you and that made sure the whole contract turned radioactive overnight. No one will come forward to fulfill it, and that gives us time to deal with Banks the right way."

"How sure are you that this will work?" Savage asked. "There have to be some people who can verify whether or not I was on certain jobs. Especially the people who actually did them."

"Well, it's a risk, I'll admit, but I made sure none of the jobs I chose were claimed by anybody else," she pointed out. "I've planned for something like this for a while, so I had a list ready. But worst case, it's enough of a bluff to give us time to handle Banks and nullify the contract anyway."

He nodded, his weapons maintenance now complete.

"Look, we're staying in town for the night anyway," she assured him. "I'll make sure they're safe come the morning, and if our cover is still solid, I'll let Anderson know you're ready to head back to New York to confront Banks. I have a feeling you want to exchange a few words with him."

"Words, yes," he agreed, packed his weapons away, and pushed the duffel bag under his bed before he stretched out comfortably. "I'd like to exchange bullets with the man too."

"I'm sure we can arrange that." She laughed and he couldn't help a small smile of his own as his eyes drifted closed.

CHAPTER EIGHTEEN

Savage scowled at the phone. He didn't want to make this call. It was a part of the life he had put away in the closet, and over this past week, he'd been forced to bring it out and display it like dirty laundry. It wasn't a good look on him. He liked having the mystique of someone who had no earthly attachments. It made people think he was somehow invulnerable, which in turn made it difficult for them to read him. Even the likes of Anderson and Monroe seemed to hold him in a little awe. Anja was the only one to whom his secrets weren't secret, and he'd made peace with himself over her particular kind of irreverence.

Despite his reluctance, he knew it was something he had to do. He dialed the number into his phone and held it gently to his ear. They were supposed to leave the police station at any moment now, so they would have their personal effects. Anja had made sure there would be a police detail on their house and with them at all times for another couple of weeks at least. It would be a little inconvenient for them, but it was better than being temporarily relocated, and certainly better than staying at the police station until they found the man or men who had survived to drive the van away.

The line took a few seconds to connect as Anja patched him through a couple of secure channels, but eventually, it rang on the other end.

"The phone is on the move, so he might be driving," she said. "If he puts it on speaker, you'll know to hang up."

"How am I supposed to tell if it's on speaker?" he asked.

"I'll know if you don't and I'll kill the connection." The phone continued to ring.

"Hello?" Andy finally answered. Savage wasn't sure what he could say to make sure the line wasn't being shared with anyone else, but the fact that it remained open for another few seconds said that Anja hadn't killed the connection yet. "Hello?"

"Do you know who this is?" Savage asked and masked his voice in case anyone else might overhear.

"Yes," the man said and a slight change in his voice indicated recognition.

"Am I on speakerphone?"

"No," Anja grumbled and sounded impatient.

"No, you're only talking to me, don't worry," Andy said. "We're in the car at the moment. It's nice to hear from you again Steve. It's been a while."

He tried to remember if they had agreed on a name or any codes, but by the sounds of it, he was on the line with Andy and Abby and Jules were close by, probably in a car with him.

"Is everyone all right?" he asked.

"Yeah, it's been a tough night, but we're leaving the

police station now." The man managed to keep his voice upbeat. "They're driving us home in the back of a police car, something that's been on Abby's bucket list forever—right, sweetie?"

Savage nearly cracked when he heard Abby cheer in the background. So much of him wanted to at least hear her voice again. He didn't even need to talk. If he could simply listen to a recording of her reading the phone book, he was sure he would find it fascinating.

He cleared his throat quickly.

"Is everything all right with you?" Andy continued. "How's Sally?"

Savage had no idea who Sally was, but he assumed her addition to the conversation was for the benefit of the other people listening in. He could roll with that.

"Sally is…great, dude." He shook his head and focused on the reason for the call. "Anyway, we've cornered the people responsible for what happened, and we've isolated the attackers. While you should probably stick with your police protectors, you should be clear to go. If all goes well, by the time the police pull the protection detail off you guys, the whole situation will be resolved, one way or another."

"What do you mean by that?" he asked. "And how did you know…about that?"

Clearly, the lawyer was no professional in this and had almost let slip what they were actually talking about. He realized he would need to cut the conversation short.

"You'll receive a text message a few minutes after I hang up. There will be a phone number on it. If you see anything odd or anyone following you, or even if you feel particularly paranoid and need to be reassured, call that number. Let it ring three times and hang up. I'll call you back as quickly as I can, you got it?"

"Yeah, I'll let you know about that softball game," Andy replied. "Look, we're pulling up at my place. I'll give you a call about it later, all right?"

"Yeah, stay safe," Savage replied. "Oh, and I already gave you the whole hurt them and I'll kill you speech, but I want to make sure it's still fresh in your mind, you hear?"

"I'll let them know you said hi." The man chuckled. Savage nodded and hung up, then stared at his phone for a few long seconds. He wouldn't let them know he said hi. Well, not him-him. He'd simply say that Steve, their family friend, said hi, which would sustain the narrative they tried to sell but didn't help how he felt.

"How're you feeling?" Anja asked after he had stared at the phone for a little longer than he would have cared to admit. "Oh, wait, let me guess. You don't want to talk about it?"

"You're getting good at this." Savage set his phone on the nightstand and lay on the bed. "If you couldn't make your money with computers, I would suggest being a fortune-teller."

"I know you don't mean that, so I'll let it slide," she replied with a hint of warning in her tone. "But don't try me, bitch."

He couldn't help a small smirk as he stared up at the ceiling. No, he really didn't mean to get snippy with Anja. Despite everything, she was the closest friend he had after his death, and he didn't know what he would do without her, both on and off the job. It was annoying that she was halfway across the world at this point since he would have liked to buy her a beer at some point.

Although her being distant was probably for the best. He knew himself well enough to know he would say or do something stupid before too long that would simply make everything so much worse. Maybe it was better that their friendship remained long-distance.

"It's been a while since anyone's called me a bitch," he said softly and folded his arms behind his head.

"Well, you earned it, buddy. I'm only trying to keep it real. You can push everyone around you away all you want, but we're stuck together. Mostly because I'll still be working for Monroe and with you and Anderson anyway, so we might as well stay cordial with each other."

"Agreed." He pushed up quickly. "So, before we start braiding each other's hair and talking about boys, what say you we go over what the plan is to eliminate this Banks character once and for all?"

"Well, Sam and Terry are running point on that operation, and they're taking their sweet time reporting in this morning," she advised him. "Considering that it's already midday in New York, they're very late in getting back to me about Banks' movements yesterday. So, either they're in trouble and need bailing out, or—"

"Or they're so wrapped up in bickering that it must have slipped their minds." He knelt beside the bed to pull his weapons out and began to prepare for his trip back. He still had time before his checkout, of course. That would be at midday for him, three hours away. Still, there was no point in lollygagging around there when the work in this part of the country was resolved, for the most part. He packed his few belongings, tucked the pistol into his underarm holster, and stowed everything else safely in the duffel. After one final survey of the room, he snatched his jacket off the chair and headed to the door.

"Aren't you supposed to do something like wipe your fingerprints from the room before you leave or something?" Anja asked as he pulled the door shut and locked it behind him.

"That would be necessary if someone was specifically tracking and targeting me," Savage explained as he strolled to the elevator. He was leaving so didn't really give a shit if any of the other hotel patrons heard him talking to himself. They would probably do what normal, sane people did and assume he was talking into a Bluetooth headset or something. "The whole point would be to cover up the fact that I was in there in the first place. But considering that most hotel rooms aren't cleaned very well between guests, there will be at least a hundred or so different fingerprint partials in there, overlapping each other and obfuscating any evidence of me having been there. If I ran a wipe of the room to clean my fingerprints, I would also clear the hundred or so others there too. That would be a more obvious indicator of my presence than if I had simply left everything as it was."

"Huh. You learn something new every day."

He nodded and made the sound effect of a rainbow coming across a TV screen as he entered the elevator.

"What the hell was that sound?" the hacker asked.

"It's the The More You Know rainbow," he explained. "Didn't you see the PSAs while you were growing up?"

"I grew up in St. Petersburg, remember?" she reminded

him. "I...well, there's probably some kind of joke about how the PSA's saw us, but I didn't grow up in Soviet Russia. Things were tough but not really that different for regular folk like my parents while I was growing up than it would have been for the people in most of Eastern Europe."

"Fair enough. And that's an opportunity for another The More You Know rainbow right there."

"I know about that. I didn't know what the hell that sound was. I've only ever seen the visuals."

"Oh, right." The elevator opened to let him out at the lobby, and he made his way to the front desk to check himself out.

It had been a long night—not the first one he'd spent in the office this week, and he doubted it would be the last. Having to keep track of what was happening in Seattle had been stressful enough and realizing there were fires that needed to be put out on that front had been annoying. The entire debacle had left him to make calls and try to obtain action reports from people who weren't exactly careful in their note-taking, another added stress he could do without. A combination of pills and coffee were the only things keeping Banks awake at this point, and as he watched the situation devolve on the news and online, he knew he needed to cut his losses.

He didn't really need to worry about the fact that it appeared some members of the team had survived. That was what he had thought at first. Everything had been done away from his location by a third party, courtesy of the client, which allowed him to keep his hands clean and clear of the whole process. For all anyone who could run online tracking knew, his IP was simply one that had viewed the details of the contract which had been cleverly disguised as an antique nobody would think to actually buy.

The problems started a couple of hours after the mission had effectively failed. It had been all over the local news, but the story seemed to be focused on the involvement of gang ties, something that had been on the rise in the country over the past few months. The failure was annoying, of course, but the fact that nothing about it led back to him wasn't a bad thing. They could simply find another team that could get it done and perhaps add a little extra cash to gain access to those that didn't mind going through a couple of levels of police to reach the targets. The whole situation could be solved relatively easily.

His complacency faltered when one of the surviving team members had added a comment to ask about the security surrounding the family. It was well-masked enough to make sure anyone who wasn't directly involved in the operation wouldn't know what was discussed. On its own, it was a minor detail. But less than five minutes later, someone with the screen name of PainDianaJones entered the conversation and asked outright why the first attempt failed so spectacularly. They also gave anyone who had questions about the kind of security assigned to the family knowledge about someone called The Savage.

Banks immediately followed up on the link. He couldn't verify the man's resume, but he remembered some of the jobs listed as being in the file the congressman had sent, which meant that at least some of the kills and operations were true. He had no idea if all were, but at this point, it didn't really matter. No comments followed the link, but the lack of responses during the night—even though he upped the price on the contract three times to the tune of seven figures—clearly indicated that nothing was happening. He could always bring a foreign team in, a group of real pros. There were special forces belonging to some despot in central America or another that could be flown in, but it would take them too long to get there.

The contract obviously would no longer get any nibbles. That harsh truth effectively meant his plan to use the family to draw the operative into a trap was dead in the water. That plus the fact that the man now knew his name and probably everything else about him was a worrying thought. In fact, it had caused a handful of panic attacks as the night wore on and turned into morning, and all Banks could really think about doing was telling the client he'd failed in his task.

He was starting to realize what Carlson had meant when he said he was more afraid of Savage than he was of the client. At the time, he had thought the man foolish but that hasty judgment had definitely been amended.

There really was no other option, he realized. He picked his phone up, punched in a number he had found during one of his panic attacks during the night, and closed his eyes and rubbed some sensation back into them as the line started ringing.

"Hello?" The voice wasn't one he was familiar with, even though he knew the name of the man behind it.

"James Anderson?" Banks asked.

"Speaking," the man replied.

"This is Mason Banks," he said. A slightly uncomfortable pause ensued, although the sound of breathing on the other end told him the line was still open. "I take it you know who I am."

"The name does ring a couple of bells, yeah," Anderson said, a hint of tension in his voice.

"I'd like to open discussions," the lawyer said. "A parley, if you will. I'm working at the behest of someone who has targeted you and Dr. Monroe and I can tell you everything you need to know about them. In exchange for this information, I want an assurance that Savage will not act on any plans he might have to seek revenge against me."

An odd sound was the only response. It took him a couple of seconds to realize it was Anderson laughing—an angry, disbelieving kind of laugh that did little to build confidence.

"You've gone and fucked yourself," the man said once he was capable of speech again. "Do you think you can go after someone like Savage and try to talk your way out of it? Like some kind of witness protection deal?"

"It worked for Carlson," Banks said and immediately regretted it.

"We know where Carlson is," the former colonel retorted. "Savage gave him a warning, and so far, there's been no real evidence to suggest he's ignored it. Until now, of course."

He nodded and took some comfort in knowing that if he went down, he would take the ex-CEO with him.

"Do you want my suggestion?" Anderson asked, and

Banks nodded, although he gave no verbal indication. "I would suggest a nightcap of .45s to the head. Now you know what it will take for you to avoid having Savage come over and ruin every facet of your life before he kills you. You were dead the moment you targeted his family."

The line went dead, but he kept the device pressed to his ear for a few more seconds before he placed it carefully on his desk with shaking hands.

"Well, fuck," he muttered as he ran his hand over the stubble that had started to grow on his cheek. What the hell could he do now?

CHAPTER NINETEEN

He was awake this time when the plane started its descent but kept his eyes closed as he felt himself return from the temporary haven the flight had provided. Savage brought himself slowly back to the topic of what he was there to do. It was pleasant to take the plane across the country. The seats were comfortable, entertainment was available in the form of conversation with Anja—with whom he still had a connection thanks to the woman's genius—as well as a couple of films, series, and Internet access. It was an enjoyable little isolated paradise up in the clouds, and now he had to come back to earth. He needed to return to the mindset of the man who would kick ass and chew bubblegum while forgetting to bring bubblegum.

Compartmentalization. He had to put everything else behind him. He needed to be…well, to use the character Anja had more or less pulled out her ass, The Savage.

He actually rather liked that. There was a reason why he had chosen it as a last name to begin with and having it as a moniker wasn't a terrible thing. There were worse nicknames to be saddled with. He remembered one man on a team he'd been on called Chucky thanks to his face being scarred from an encounter with a landmine. Imagine being lucky enough to walk away from a landmine exploding, only to be nicknamed for a killer doll thanks to the scars the encounter had left?

The landing was a little rougher than he was used to and he gripped the arms of his seat as they touched down. The pressure against his seatbelt left him uncomfortable. He didn't like that. It felt like he was going soft. Memories surfaced of the massive carriers used to ferry troops from one place to another, the kind that felt like earthquakes when they touched down. The pilots would always laugh and mock the newcomers who had the gall to complain about the roughness involved.

Savage shook his head, unbuckled, and stood up from his seat. He collected his bag on his way out. The stewardess hoped he had a great flight, and he nodded with a small smile because he didn't want to have to make small talk. He wasn't in the best of moods thanks to the odd sense of nostalgia that persisted. There was a reason for it, of course. Having been around his family would inevitably have consequences, even under the best of circumstances. He simply didn't have the kind of mental power to keep it from affecting him. While that irked him as much as the emotions, he reminded himself he was only human, after all.

When he disembarked, a car was already waiting for him. It was a BMW, one of the newer M models with a powerful engine and powered by gas, unlike the Audi he had left to be delivered to the rental agency.

Sam sat on the hood and looked like she enjoyed a little sun out in the open a few miles away from the city of New York, which he could see in the distance. Terry stood outside the driver's seat as if to claim the driving rights for himself and make sure his British counterpart wouldn't try to steal his thunder.

"Hey, it's the boss man," Sam called when she saw him. She tilted her sunglasses down a little when she saw him move down the stairs toward her and grinned at him. "Coming off a private plane, no less. What do I have to do to get that kind of cheese coming my way?"

"Have your family put in danger," he retorted but he chuckled when she jogged over to him and wrapped him in a hug.

"Hell, my family live in the darker, meaner parts of London, so I expect they're in some kind of life-threatening danger at least once a week," she replied with a grin, released him, and brushed her hand over his jacket. "Now can I use the private jet?"

"Would you use it to head over to help get them out of the life-threatening danger?" he asked as they strode to the car.

"Probably," she replied. "You know, eventually. First, I need a vacation somewhere sunny with numerous beaches and where the gents are all shirtless, sweaty, and in possession of abs I can wash clothes on."

"You'd need to talk to Anderson about that," Savage said. "Although I can assure you he'll respond with a very emphatic no."

"What kind of boss man are you anyway?" she protested as he reached Terry and shook the man's hand.

"The kind whose paychecks still need Anderson's signature," he replied with a cheeky smirk.

"Holy shit, she's sassy, right?" Anja said into his earpiece. "I like her."

He didn't bother to give her a response.

"It's good to see you again, Savage," Terry said. "We heard about what's happening to your family, and we're here to help, whatever you need. Within reason, of course."

"Don't worry, I won't ask you to do anything more demanding than risk your life, Terry," he replied with a small smile, and the sniper nodded.

"I think I can live with that." A rare smile touched his lips as he indicated for Savage to take his place in the back seat of the monster of a car they had gotten their hands on.

"This is a nice car," he said and ran his hands over the leather seat as his teammates joined him in the vehicle. Terry started the vehicle and headed toward the entrance of the airfield. "How did you two get your hands on it again?"

"Anderson essentially gave us a blank check on everything we needed to keep tabs on Banks," the other man replied. "Sam here said the area where we would track the man would be thick with cars like these, which I suppose she was right about."

"The idea was to be able to blend in," Sam explained and glanced at Savage in the back seat as they approached the bridge that would lead them to the heart of Manhattan. "We wouldn't be able to do that in a Prius or anything like that. Besides, the BMW has a sturdier engine than most of the cars they have around there these days. The German make will ensure that it will be able to endure almost anything in case of a chase."

He nodded. Anderson had shelled out to get him a good car in Seattle, so he doubted the man would make any noise about the rental the two had selected for themselves. Monroe might have something to say about it, of course. Anderson was leading with his heart a little on this one, but Monroe would be the one who actually had to sign off on all the expenditures.

She wouldn't be too harsh about it, though, he thought. She seemed like the kind of person who realized that, while this was very personal for Savage, it was also a part of the overall reason why they were there in the first place —to clean out the rot in Pegasus caused by Carlson and his ilk. It had been problematic so far but not impossible. They were taking all the right steps and definitely moved in the right direction.

Savage let his gaze soak in the view of New York that drew ever closer to him as they crossed the bridge. It was a fantastic city, one he hadn't actually had the opportunity to spend any time in until now. One hell of a time to visit the place, but it was bound to happen eventually, right? He'd been all over the rest of the world, why not end up here?

His gaze flickered to two cars that pulled in behind them. Every city had its own individual kind of traffic and flows were unique to the various cities. Sometimes, even cities had different patterns between one section and another.

Either way, the fact remained that two cars of the same make and model—dark-blue sedans—now drove behind them.

"Hey, Control, do you have a visual on us right now?" he asked, his eyes narrowed.

Anja took a few moments to answer. "Oh, Control. That's me. What's up, Savage?"

"I asked if you have a visual on us," he repeated. Terry and Sam looked at him and followed his gaze to the two cars that maintained a steady pace. "Maybe camera access?"

"Give me a sec." She returned after a few seconds. "Okay, what am I looking for here?"

"There are a couple of sedans following us," he said. "Or…I think they're following us. I feel like I'm in something of a paranoid state of mind. Two cars behind, same make and model, and keeping the same kind of distance. Do you think you can run the plates?"

"I'm already working on it," she grumbled. "Yeah, they're both rentals from the same agency and rented by the same people. That's not uncommon, though. It's a corporate rental, so it could basically be any corporation that has sent people into the city."

Savage nodded, still unable to shake the feeling in the back of his mind. Maybe he was a little too paranoid in this case, but he'd learned to listen to this instinct. In the past, it had meant the difference between death and survival.

"Could they be following us?" he asked.

"I'll keep an eye on them," Anja said.

He nodded. It was all he could really expect from her at this point, but he reached surreptitiously over to the duffle bag on the seat beside him, unzipped it, and checked that the weapons inside were loaded and ready. He made sure they were easy to retrieve from the bag in an emergency. The shotgun, rifle, and pistol were ready for action, and he pulled the knife clear, slipped it into his right pocket, and checked to ensure that the clasp that kept his pistol in place was loosened too.

"Do you really think we're being followed, boss?" Terry asked. He held Savage's gaze through the rearview mirror.

"I'm in a paranoid mood at the moment, so let's leave it at that," he responded loudly enough for the two of them to hear. He had learned to trust his instincts, but the fact remained that he hadn't exactly been at the top of his game lately. His recovery had been slow, and he was barely out of the hospital, not to mention a little rattled over the recent events. He hated feeling like this. His job had always required him to be absolutely certain on his calls and to be able to act on them at a moment's notice without any hesitation.

And, dammit, he now felt hesitation.

They left the bridge and proceeded into the city where the afternoon traffic wasn't quite as heavy as it would be come rush hour. The two sedans still followed them, which didn't help his feeling of suspicion. He faced his two teammates in the front of the car.

"There's no harm in coming up with a game plan in case we are ambushed, right?" he asked, and neither of them voiced any complaints. "No offense, Terry, but Sam is the specialist behind the wheel and we'll need you to cover any potential long-distance problems we might have to face. If something happens and we're forced into a stop, you two change places. What do you guys have in terms of weapons?"

"Pistols," Sam said. "Both of us. We left most of our hardware back at the base."

"Shit. It's a good thing I brought enough to share. Terry, I have a small hunting rifle here. Can you make it work?"

The man shrugged to indicate that if they were in a situation where someone took shots at them from a distance, there wouldn't be much of a choice, now would there?

"Okay." Savage looked around as they started to weave through the maze that was Manhattan. He didn't know the layout of the city so he wouldn't know a route to their base of operations that would avoid choke points where ambushes were more likely to happen.

Choke points…like the one they'd just driven into, he realized when he saw two SUVs blocking the other end of the narrow street they were on. Terry pulled the Beemer to a halt but it was too late. Both sedans drew in behind them to block the exit.

"Shit," he muttered. Sam and Terry were already moving to unbuckle their seatbelts and scramble quickly across the narrow space between the seats. They had switched places in seconds, and Savage was ready with the rifle.

"Where did you get this?" the sniper asked as he checked the weapon and its scope hastily. "Your hunting trips from your teenage years?"

"It…was an impulse buy," he replied and shook his head. That wasn't important. Terry made a few hurried adjustments to make it somewhat useable before he flicked the safety off. His first order of business would be to make sure they didn't have anyone shooting at them from above, which meant it was down to his teammates to cover them in the meantime.

The men disembarked from their cars, eight from the SUVs in front of them and six from the sedans behind. Savage removed the shotgun from the bag and handed it to Sam, who took it with a small, manic grin as the men unloaded assault rifles from their vehicles. They appeared to be in the mood to take their time and make sure they did this right. They looked like professionals and a formidable challenge.

He drew the pistol from his holster and the Glock from his bag before he twisted to look behind them. The trunk would have to give him enough cover from the lead that would rip through the car at any second.

Terry fired, aiming up at a nearby building, and everyone seemed to take that as a signal that they were ready for a fight. Savage left the Glock on the seat beside him and aimed the needle gun at the men near the sedans. He pulled the trigger to punch small but visible holes through the Beemer's back window. Sam did the same, although she fired from the side window. Savage assumed it was because she didn't want to damage the windshield too much in case an escape was still an option. They couldn't move until Terry had made sure they weren't at risk from above.

Savage could see flaws in his plan as he initiated a series of volleys as rapidly as his cutting-edge weapon could fire. It was effective enough, but it had taken the men coming from the sedans a few seconds to realize they were under fire. The problem came when one of their team dropped as the needles drilled easily through the body armor he wore and eliminated him in seconds.

The others opened fire from the rear, and he ducked

quickly behind the back seat and covered his head as bullets erupted all around them. The idea had been, of course, to force the men attacking them to take cover in order to buy them some time. So much for that, he thought, picked the Glock up again, and pulled himself up to start shooting. His ears rang as the firefight continued with a vengeance. Sam had dropped into the driver's seat to reload but the windshield started to show a variety of holes that forced her to slide down into the relative cover of the massive engine in front of them.

"We're clear on top," Terry shouted, spun, and opened fire at the men in ahead. His accuracy was on point, as always, and the head of one of the men popped like a melon. Sam, still under the cover of the engine, thrust hard on the accelerator and the vehicle lurched forward. If they had been covered from the top, all it would have taken was a shot to the engine with a high-powered rifle to disable it and leave them stranded. Of course, there would also have been the issue that they could pick the driver off whenever they decided to.

Now that they were clear and knowing there was no way to win the battle outright since they were in a bad position, outmanned, and outgunned, their only option was to get the hell out of there. Savage shifted to aim his weapons out the front. A couple of rounds impacted the trunk and he wondered when one of their attackers would manage to hit the tank.

"Anja, we need a way out of here as soon as you can," he shouted. The concentrated firepower from the three was focused on the men in front of the SUVs and forced them to take cover, which brought a measure of relief to the defenders.

"Tell her I'll need some help with the car too," Sam shouted.

"Heard you both, working on both," the Russian replied crisply.

Sam raised the shotgun as they came in close to the SUVs but still pushed the Beemer as fast as it would go. They closed on the larger vehicles and she guided the smaller car to the back of the one on the left, powered hard into it, and spun it into a skid to move it far enough to allow them to escape.

There was a downside to this plan, Savage realized when all the airbags deployed at the same time and cut the engine immediately. He helped to clear the airbags in the front as she levered herself up to lean through the open window and fired the shotgun at the men who now gathered around to try to pick them off while they weren't moving.

Cars like this—and most modern cars, really—were designed to cut all power to the engine as soon as an impact occurred, thanks to a fuel pump shut-off switch to avoid the nastiness that came with spilled fuel after the collision. While necessary for most accidents, it could be rather annoying in the event of an escape attempt.

Anja worked quickly and well and started the car almost immediately. Sam dropped into her seat and immediately careened through their newly opened exit line.

She cackled and patted the dashboard of the Beemer. "Hah! What did I tell you? German engineering is the fucking best."

"I've set the GPS for an escape route and a location to stash the car," the hacker said. "I'm keeping track of the police band too. There are notifications of shots fired in your area. The cops should be there in less than a minute."

"I think we need to talk about what the fuck happened," Sam snapped and scowled at Savage through the rearview mirror, which was miraculously still intact.

"Hell, if I know." He shrugged and continued to glance back to check that they weren't being followed. They weren't, not immediately anyway. The other man took a moment to check their six as well before he settled into his seat and checked his rifle the way any good sniper would do after an engagement.

"This was planned," Terry said as they pulled into a nearby underground garage that didn't have any security in it and parked the bullet-riddled Beemer. "Someone was waiting for us to enter the city. Who?"

Savage shrugged again, hauled his duffle bag out, and slung it over his shoulder once he'd made sure the weapons were hidden. None of them appeared to be injured beyond a couple of scrapes from the glass. That was more luck than any of them had any right to at this point.

He had questions too, but they would have to wait until his team was in a safe location again.

CHAPTER TWENTY

I t was Thanksgiving and people weren't supposed to be working today. Restaurants and most of the service establishments would be open, of course. Hospitals and police stations would be open too, although they would probably run on skeleton crews. Most of the folks in the city—the nine to five workers and everyone in between— would head home or to a parent's place, or a friend's to enjoy the holiday. They would eat too much food, drink copious amounts of beer, wine, or other alcoholic beverages, and watch some bastards who did need to work for the holiday fight over a ball they could all afford to buy for their own if they chose to do so.

Banks didn't like feeling like this. He normally didn't mind sports. His college and high school both had teams and he enjoyed watching them play, even if it was more of a pastime and a way to meet the cheerleaders, and the sports themselves weren't horrible to watch. He happened to prefer soccer and baseball, though.

His mood had much to do with the fact that he had

been up all night in his effort to keep track of the person or people who would inevitably arrive to kill him. He was, quite plainly, exhausted and had a hard time feeling charitable toward anything or anyone. From the looks of it, Savage had been in Seattle and had dealt with the situation there in person. He wasn't sure if the man would remain close to his family to ensure that no other teams made a second attempt. The operative might well know the situation online was a little bogged down, however. He was thought to work with a team when he ran operations like these, but despite his client's best efforts, she hadn't actually been able to find anything useful. They could already be with him for all he knew.

Which was why he was tempted to stay in the office for the entire day. He couldn't stay there forever, of course. There were people who expected him elsewhere once the work week resumed the next day, but there wasn't anything that said that he couldn't simply hide out there for as long as was necessary. To his mind, it would be the last place anyone would expect him to be on a national holiday. While the prospect of being holed up there alone had little attraction in and of itself, it certainly had appeal when it came to preserving his own skin.

There was, of course, the small matter of food. He had to eat, but to do so, he would have to leave the office. Aside from that, he needed something to do. Banks wasn't the kind of person who would be comfortable sitting around all day, and from the way he was already climbing the walls before he'd even made it to midday, he knew he needed to get out of there. He would stay on the move, he decided. That was what he could do. Hadn't he heard somewhere that a moving target was safer than a stationary one? Well, that was what he'd do. He'd buy something at a drive-through, keep moving for the day, and return to the office to spend the night again. There were rooms in the building where witnesses could stay for a couple of days when they had to testify. He knew there were legal ramifications around the matter of people staying in the building long-term—building codes and the like—but it would do for the short-term, right?

Banks sighed and shook his head in frustration as he tried to come to terms with his plan. He was living on the edge and to be stuck with only himself for company seemed like the worst option ever. Being on the move seemed like the right thing to do.

He closed his office and took care to lock it behind him before he hurried to the elevator that would take him down to the garage. He froze and considered the wisdom of that. After a moment's thought, he decided he would have the car delivered to the lobby entrance for him to take from there. He never took advantage of most of the perks that came with being a partner, but if there was ever a time to actually enjoy them, it was now, right?

The elevator doors opened and the lawyer stepped cautiously into the lobby, where he took a moment to inspect his surroundings. He doubted he would be able to see Savage if the man were actually waiting for him, but anxiety made a man justifiably cautious. The unforgivable error would be if he was caught because he had simply not been careful enough.

He stepped farther into the lobby, still cautious although he tried to appear confident. He received a couple of looks from the people who were on the job. Of course, he knew what they were looking at. Quite frankly, he looked like shit. His five o'clock shadow had grown for another five or six hours, his suit was a little wrinkled, and his tie sat loosely and a little skewed. He didn't look great. but he didn't have to, right? He was a partner and could fucking well do as he pleased.

"Mr. Banks, sir." The man running security at the front desk nodded when he realized who approached. "Happy Thanksgiving, sir. Gobble gobble and all that."

"Right." Banks chuckled although he wasn't sure why. He was a little sleep deprived, he supposed. "I'm heading out for some lunch, but I'll be back. I have work I need to get done over the weekend. Would you mind sending someone down to bring my car up?"

He left the keys on the counter, which gave the man no choice other than to either go down and do it himself or make the necessary call to bring the car up pronto.

The guard called one of his underlings and relayed the instructions. The lawyer waited at the front desk and kept his head on a seemingly constant swivel to inspect his surroundings.

"If you don't mind my asking, sir, is everything all right?"

He eyed the man, a little startled, and for a shocking second, he felt the temptation to simply tell him everything. It would be a relief to tell someone everything he'd been forced to face since the beginning of this fucking week and let it all out. It wasn't like anyone would believe him if he were to tell them he was a minion to a global player who had all the fingers in all the pies. Nor would they believe that he had worked to get a CEO out of jail in order to eliminate another CEO, her underling, and their guard dog, which had resulted in him having to threaten the man's family. And, of course, no one would ever believe that the bulldog had his scent and would soon move in for the kill.

Thankfully, the moment passed, and he forced a smile onto his lips and shook his head. "I'm simply under pressure. As one of the newer members of the partner board, it means all the work is dumped on my desk. I'm sure it'll change once there's someone else for the rest of the board to bully, but for now, it'll be many weekends and working on holidays, I'm afraid."

"Well, that's a little above my pay grade, I'm afraid, sir," the man said softly. He gestured to the front where one of the security team turned valet had parked his car and now waited outside with the keys.

Banks dropped a handful of bills on the countertop and chuckled. Most were Benjamins, which would go a long way in making sure none of these men talked about what they saw to the board.

"I appreciate it, sir." The man chuckled. "You have a nice holiday now, you hear?"

"You too," he replied and hurried out toward the car. As he cleared the door, though, a van approached at a frantic speed and screeched to a halt directly behind his car. He took a step back, a hint of panic in his features as two men disembarked from the vehicle and marched over to him. Neither of the men was Savage and both looked like professionals who were paid for their work.

"Mr. Banks?" asked the lead man as he stepped closer.

The lawyer hadn't shown any sign of hostility, which meant that neither man reached for the weapons under their jackets. "Mr. Mason Banks?"

"That's me," he replied, not sure if he should bother.

"I'm afraid I have to insist that you come with us, sir," the man said with a small, professional nod. "Client's orders."

It was a short drive but a long walk to reach the abandoned building Sam and Terry used as a base for their surveillance of Banks. They stayed on the move and took all the roundabout routes they could find while Anja made sure they weren't followed. The ploy was effective, but it was also an exhausting way to spend most of the afternoon. The sun had already begun to set when they finally reached the location. His teammates were clearly more comfortable with the place than Savage was.

"So," Sam said, rolled her shoulders, and drew in a deep breath. "Is now the right time for serious questions about what the fuck just happened?"

Terry nodded and looked at his boss. "You seemed to know about what would happen almost before they did. Is there anything else you'd like to share with us, Savage?"

"It's not that we don't trust you." She folded her arms. "But if you know more about the situation than we were led to believe, it would be a shitty move to leave us out of the loop."

"Shitty move," the sniper agreed.

"I don't actually know anything solid." Savage placed

the weapon-filled duffel bag on a nearby table. "I do know that Banks worked as an intermediary for a client. We assumed this client was Carlson, but he's still in police custody. There is no way he could have arranged for something like this, not this quickly. He has connections, though—people who have watched his back from the beginning. It could be one of them who arranged this."

He breathed deeply and shook his head to try to regain focus. The other two exchanged a look and moved over to where he stood.

"Is everything okay?" Sam asked. She gripped his shoulder and squeezed it. "We've been here working with you. We're on the same damn side. Why won't you simply open up to us? A little? Come on, we already know about Abby, Jules, and the annoying jackass lawyer Andy. We're on the same side."

"Anja really shouldn't have told you about them," he responded belligerently and winced when he rubbed alcohol over the cuts and scrapes he'd accumulated thanks to the glass shattered all around him in the car. They definitely wouldn't get the deposit on the Beemer back, but he supposed Monroe would have to eat that too. Savage had a feeling he would be getting yelled at, though.

"If you're waiting for an apology, I think that'll be a long wait for you," Anja said into the earbuds they now all wore.

"You really shouldn't be so clamped up about shit." Sam moved to help Terry clean his wounds. It looked like he had actually been grazed around the hips, likely from when he had helped to clear their perimeter. There was a little blood but not much, and it had been covered by the leather jacket he wore.

"Really?" Savage said and raised an eyebrow. "You think I'm the one who needs to open up more?"

"Don't be gross," she snapped in response. "We're friends and we're in the same line of work. We're all in this together. I'd do the same thing for you if you were injured."

"Do you really think I would get involved with someone as foul-mouthed as her?" Terry asked and winced when she pressed a dressing to the wound.

"Fair enough, although I could argue something along the lines of how opposites attract," Savage said with a small smile.

"Well, if you would all like to can it," Anja interjected, "I'm afraid we have serious business to discuss. The business that brought us all here? Banks, right?"

"Right," the operative said. "There might have been a setback, but I was told there was a plan in the works to get our hands on him. My hands on him."

"There appears to have been a hiccup on that end." The hacker sounded a little more worried than usual, and a trace of irritation also colored her tone. "It's something of a tactical boo-boo, a semantics mix-up."

Savage sucked in a deep breath. She wasn't usually one to bandy words like this, and the way she tried to justify and soften the blow before delivering it said she thought the blow would be something he didn't want to hear. That aside, she usually liked to annoy him, which meant that whatever this was, it was serious.

"What's up, Anja?" he demanded.

"Well, I've run over the cameras on our friend Banks,

and it looks like he might have been…uh, kind of ever so slightly…nabbed."

"Nabbed?" Terry asked.

"You know, kidnapped, absconded with, turned into a movie with Liam Neeson, the kind that ends with a multitude of bad people all beaten up," she replied, rambling again. "The man's gone. I can't find him anywhere. He's not at his offices, or at his apartment, or any of his regular haunts."

"Is he on the run?" Savage asked. "He might have gotten wind that he's in our sights and tried to make a run for it."

"His car is still at the office, and from what I can see, it was brought up for him to use a couple of hours before you were ambushed. I've been dealing with that, so when I turned to get on track with our plans for Banks… Well, he was no longer there. His car was returned to the garage, from what I can tell from the camera across the street. It's not a great view from up there and doesn't actually show the entrance itself. It focuses primarily on the street frontage for the building it's on, so anything beyond that is limited. Plus, there was a fair amount of traffic with cars and trucks coming and going around that time."

"Shit. Couldn't you get access from another camera with a better view?"

"All the cameras with better views are owned by the building," she pointed. "I've worked with traffic light cameras to get us the information we have now. I'm the best, but I'm not God."

"Tell your ego that," he said with a grin. Anja's only response was a fake laugh.

Not the time. Understood.

"Wait, why can't you simply access the building's cameras?" Sam asked. "A place like that has to be brimming with security."

"And it's all kept off the grid to prevent people like me from getting access."

Savage fought back the rising tide of frustration. This wasn't how he wanted the day to go.

CHAPTER TWENTY-ONE

Savage rubbed his eyes and dropped back into the chair. The building where Terry and Sam had set their base up looked like it had been abandoned for a while. Most of the windows had already been broken either by the elements or vandals looking for something destructively entertaining to do. The top floors had been taken over by billboards that could be seen by the rich and successful of New York, which made him wonder why they hadn't put any effort in to develop the building more. There had to be a whole horde of people who wouldn't mind living and working in an unused building in the middle of Manhattan.

It didn't really matter at this point, though. They had a place to set up shop and one that overlooked the general area that Banks lived in. The downside was that it was about a quarter of the way across the island from the building where the man worked, which meant they had to rely on Anja to keep an eye on the place.

The trio had spent a very long night with little to do

except eat something and try to get some rest with the endless drone of the generator they used for lights and all the other electricity needs fulfilled. Thankfully, considering where they were and the time of year, this included heating. As Savage didn't want to move too far away from the action while they searched for Banks—who really had mysteriously disappeared—he had spent an uncomfortable night together with his teammates and huddled on a small cot in a corner of the building that was still mostly intact.

Having to choose between a loud generator and freezing to death was a shitty scenario but not one that had always been available for any of them during their time out in the field. The loud generator won the vote without protest from anyone. The rumble grated and scratched at his already irritated state of mind, but after a few hours, faded into the background and worked to drown out all the fucking noise in the city that never fucking slept.

All in all, it wasn't the best night of sleep he'd ever had but not the worst either. There had been some restful moments here and there, and he had managed a nap on the plane on the way over so it wasn't as bad as it could have been.

Sam helped to change the bandage on Terry's side as Savage coaxed the ancient-looking coffee machine on the table to life and finally made them all something thick, strong, and warm to drink before they focused on making a good start on the day.

That said, as he tasted the brew he'd made, he thought that perhaps good was a strong word for the start that they would have.

"Don't worry." Sam rubbed her eyes and shook herself a

little as if to dislodge the remnants of sleep. She seemed to recognize the look on his face. "It's not your fault. We skimped on quality when we bought coffee and the coffee machine doesn't help either."

Terry shrugged. "It works. The coffee wakes us up, and the after taste is enough to keep us awake until we can buy a proper breakfast on the way. There's a nice little diner-style place around the corner we've frequented. We've also saved the receipts for Anderson and Monroe to refund us since we are technically on the clock here."

Savage chuckled.

"Morning guys, gal," Anja said and came to life in their earbuds. "I hope you slept well."

"Well enough," he replied. "Did you get any sleep?"

"I'll sleep when I'm dead." The hacker laughed. "Well, not really, but I'll sleep when I crash, anyway. That's how I do it. I've tried to get a trace on Banks. I see him heading into the building the day before yesterday but there's no sign of him anywhere in the area around the building until yesterday. As I mentioned, there was considerable traffic around that time and it blocked most of the already limited view I had. All I was able to see was a quick snippet that showed security returning the vehicle to the garage again."

"Were there any other vehicles going in or out of the area at the same time?" Savage asked.

"Literally hundreds over the same time period," she said. "You'd think a place like that would be almost deserted on Thanksgiving, but nope. They still had a lunch-hour traffic jam for miles. If he left the building using one of the vehicles that entered that area, we'll need to narrow it down. I'm good but I can't track twenty-seven different vehicles across the city at the same time. Believe me, I've tried."

"How do we narrow it down?" Sam asked.

"It seems obvious to me," Savage said and took another sip of the questionable coffee. "If the security tapes for the firm's building are held offline, isn't the only option we have to go into the building and get the tapes for ourselves?"

"Ironically, it probably would have been easier to do that yesterday," Terry pointed out.

"Is that irony?" Sam wondered with a small frown.

"It doesn't really matter," Savage said. "We need to case the place if intend to break in. It will take a couple of days, by which time Banks could already be out of the country."

"Not to worry," Anja said. "I've helped Sam and Terry with surveillance over the past few days, so I think we already have all the details we need. They had actually planned to approach Banks at work. I'll send you all the details you need while you find breakfast."

"Why wouldn't he be out of the country already if he got out of the building yesterday?" Terry asked.

"It's a little complicated," the hacker said. "The basics are that it would be possible to get him out of the country but not without using his own passport, which would ping me. If they intend to use a fake, it would take them a couple of days to set it up. Passports are a little more complicated than IDs."

"Right," Savage said. "Well, you lost me at breakfast. Send us the details and we'll discuss how we get into the building while we drink some decent fucking coffee."

"Language," Terry grumbled under his breath as they prepared to leave their little base.

"Don't get me wrong," Sam said. "I'd rather be out here, in the field, instead of watching from a mile out."

"Yeah, rub it in, why don't you?" Terry grumbled. He sat in a car about three hundred yards out on the top of a parking garage, which gave him a good view of their location. He was their overwatch, which was a vital job, of course, and best done by someone who could make use of the high-powered rifle Savage assumed he carried. But he knew from experience that as jobs went, it was about as boring as things could get, despite the fact that they had managed to acquire another rental car, a Mercedes SUV this time.

"But why can't Anja run overwatch for us and we can have three people in here with us?" she asked to extend the thought as the taxi they'd called pulled up at the entrance. Savage turned to check the positioning of the camera Anja had used. It was low and skewed to the right, which made it easy to block, especially during heavy traffic hours. It seemed like a design flaw, but things weren't always well-thought-out when it came to building in such close proximity. He turned his attention to the cameras belonging to the law firm that covered the entrance. If Banks had left via the front door, they would be the ones that picked him up.

The operative was dressed in a suit and tie, acceptable attire for a visit to legal counsel during business hours. Sam was similarly dressed and had actually gone with makeup suggestions from Anja and worked herself into a professional-looking pantsuit, with her hair drawn up in a rigid bun above her head. She completed the outfit with a pair of non-prescription glasses.

"Don't say it," she snapped warningly.

He recalled Anderson's brief on what happened to the last man to say the evil phrase to Sam, and as much as he enjoyed teasing, they were on the job now. Being emasculated by a high heel was not on his bucket list of things he wanted to do before he died.

"I didn't intend to," he replied and fiddled awkwardly with his tie. It was suffocating to have to wear this bullshit, but it was expected by the people who worked in buildings like these. He had cleaned up rather well too, he supposed. His brown hair now boasted a neat comb-over, and the grey suit and tie combo suited him, even if he didn't particularly like it. If he were to pick a color for his suits, it would be black for the intimidation factor, but they didn't need him to attract attention today. He merely needed to be one of the hundred or so legal aides who came and went from this place every day.

They moved into the pleasantly air-conditioned lobby and the duo surreptitiously examined the building's security. They all looked like pros, but the kind that came from years on a police force, not military and definitely not special forces. They were there to provide a bureaucratic barrier between the people outside and the people inside, with a handful of weapons in reach to allow them to be a little more than simply that if they needed to be.

The doors could be locked from the front desk, and

there were pistols and shotguns in the room behind the reception, just in case.

The guard at the front desk, a tall, lean man with a suggestion of baldness amidst greying hair, greeted them with a small, professional smile.

"Good afternoon," he said.

"Hi," Savage said and returned the gesture with one of his own. "Tom Davison, and this is my associate Mary Jane Baker. We have an appointment with Gideon Andres on the eighteenth floor."

"Can I see your IDs?" he asked, and both Savage and Sam presented the IDs Anja had arranged for them to collect only a few hours earlier. He gave them a quick look and handed them back, then checked to make sure there was, in fact, an appointment for them in the system. Once that was done, he looked at them and handed them a couple of visitors' badges. "The elevators are right there to your left. Have a nice day."

"Right back at you," Savage replied with a nod and they wandered toward the elevators.

"So, Anja," Sam said once the elevator doors closed. "A bit of a Doctor Who fan, are we?"

"Doctor what?" he asked.

"Who," the hacker replied. "And yes. I thought you might like that, being British and all."

"Well, color me appreciative." Sam chuckled and glanced at the visitor's badge hanging from her lapel.

"What are you guys talking about?" Savage asked.

"Remind me to tie you down for a binge-watching session later," she replied with a grin. "So, what happens when we don't show up for the appointment we're supposed to have with this Gideon Andres?"

"Oh, don't worry about that," Anja replied. "I isolated the request to make sure only the security schedule showed it."

"And when the security guard calls them to say that we're coming up?" Sam asked.

"Oh, I fed that call into a recording I have of the secretary taking the call," Anja replied. "Their security feeds are all offline, but everything else is kept on the main servers to maximize efficiency. It does work, I have to say."

"Are we in the clear here?" Sam frowned at her reflection in the mirrored interior. "I can't shake the feeling that all this is a little too easy."

"It's a law firm in the middle of Manhattan, not Fort Knox," Savage pointed out as they reached the eighteenth floor. "That said…yeah, let's keep our eyes open. Something may go sideways in the most colossal ways."

"You two are paranoid."

"Yeah, it's almost like we're breaking into a building to steal security tapes." Sam laughed as they left the elevator and made their way through the building. Anja had explained that the system with the visitor's badges included implanted chips that allowed the security team downstairs to keep track of where they were. While she couldn't help them with that directly due to the system being offline, there was a simple way around it. They slipped both into an envelope marked *invoices* and handed it to the office assistant to deliver to Andres' office. It was already too late in the day to handle invoices and it was

Friday, so anything that was marked as such would be ignored until Monday.

The hacker knew more about office work than either of them combined, so they simply trusted her orders and handed the envelope to the young man who pushed a trolley full of similar envelopes before they continued toward the secure server room. Most of the other servers were in the basement levels, but they were kept separate from the security servers for the very reason why they were there.

"Well, I don't know what you're looking at, but I see a very nice, very big, very locked door," Sam said. "I could probably pick it or maybe blow it up, but I think either of those options would attract too much attention."

"If you two could wait out there for a few minutes?" Anja said. Waiting was as necessary a part of any infiltration as any other skill, so Sam leaned quickly against the wall next to the door and pulled Savage in a little closer.

"What are you doing?" Savage asked.

"Don't get any ideas," she said softly and smoothed the wrinkles she'd caused in his jacket. "People get uncomfortable when they see something they think is intimacy. We don't actually have to be intimate. We only need to be close enough to be perceived as intimate."

"So…we can pretend to be intimate on the job but if I make a joke, I get kicked in the nuts?" He focused on trying to look a little more relaxed. People would know they were faking if he was too stiff.

"Well, not you, per se," she replied. "I don't like people to simply see me as nothing more than…well, you know. I would kick you if you tried it, though. But not in the nuts. Maybe in the shins."

"Fair enough," he said with a nod. "I would never, though."

"I know." Her grin was full of sass. "That's why I'd only kick you in the shin."

"Excuse me?" a voice said behind them. It sounded timid, young, and more than a little uncomfortable. Savage turned to see the office assistant they had run into before.

"Sorry, I'm new here. Miss Baker?" he asked and looked at Sam, who hastily reminded herself of her assumed identity.

"That's me," she said and smiling as an envelope was handed to her and the kid hurried away, a hint of a blush on his cheeks.

"See what I mean?" Sam asked. She opened the envelope and a key fell out. "I swear to God the woman has superpowers."

"Not really," Anja replied. "When office security is run almost entirely online, you'd be surprised by what you can do when you have unlimited access. Getting your hands on the keys for secured areas and have them sent to new employees, for instance."

"That's basically a superpower," Savage said as they slipped into the server room. "So, what are we doing here?"

"You simply have to plug that USB drive into the servers and let me work," the hacker replied.

He shrugged and did as he was told. Some of the nearby screens lit up and a handful of programs appeared on them. The lights on the drives came to life one by one.

"Can I ask…what you're doing?" he asked as he studied

the room. He couldn't see any cameras, which helped him relax a little.

"I'm uploading all the footage to the servers that do have Internet access and transferring it all to me," Anja replied. "Which is already done. Nice work, my little puppets. I think you can manage to get out on your own?"

"Right," he said. "We'll need to get the visitor badges back, though."

"We have a problem," Terry said when they returned to the base. He was the first one back and had already begun to examine the security tapes. Savage doubted that Anja had the time to check all the footage they had gotten to her, superpowers or no. She probably ran most of it through an algorithm that identified Banks and worked from there.

"What kind of problem?" Savage asked and crossed immediately to where the man watched everything on a laptop.

"The serious kind," Anja said. "Show them the footage I sent you, Terry."

Savage narrowed his eyes as he watched Banks come down to the lobby, take a moment to chat with the same security guard who had greeted them, and then headed out to where his car waited. He stopped halfway to the door of his car and looked up when a van came into view. The man looked terrified at first, but no weapons were brandished. The new arrivals talked to him calmly for a few seconds before he followed them quietly to the car.

"Do you notice something strange about that video?" the hacker asked.

"Yeah," Savage replied. "The security guard didn't give Banks the car keys. He was in on the kidnapping."

"Well, yes, that too," she said. "But that doesn't look exactly like a kidnapping, right? There is no sign of a struggle. The men turn their backs on him, and he followed them into the van."

"So it's not a kidnapping," Terry said and looked at his teammates. "A rescue?"

"Shit." Savage smacked the desktop with his palm. "Can we track the van?"

"Already done," Anja said. "But I'm afraid that's the good news."

"This is one of those good news-bad news situations, isn't it?" Sam grumbled.

"Yep." Anja brought more footage up on Terry's laptop of the same van going through an industrial area—the docks, maybe—until it turned into a secure location with high fences and a horde of security staff. Banks was led from the vehicle and followed as willingly as he had before. The group strode across to what looked like the entrance to an underground bunker.

"I'm looking into the specs of that place now," Anja continued. "That place is an old cold war bunker. New York is littered with them, apparently, but that one has been repurposed into a safe house of sorts, with the emphasis on safe. It's a fortress, physically and digitally. All the security functions are kept off the grid, of course, including water and electricity. I could crack them, but…"

"Let me guess," Savage said as her voice trailed off.

"We'll need to get inside. Like that Pegasus lab way back when."

"Exactly."

"How the hell are we supposed to get inside?" Terry asked, genuinely nonplussed. "These specs…that place is locked up tighter than—"

"Please say a nun's pussy," Sam said and stared at the ceiling with a small grin.

The sniper merely shook his head and dragged in a deep breath. "Innuendos aside, how will we get in there?"

"I have a couple of ideas about that," Savage said thoughtfully. "But I think we need to spend a little time evaluating the surface security first."

CHAPTER TWENTY-TWO

The little hide they'd put together definitely wasn't a great place. Savage sighed, shook his head, and sat beside Terry with a grimace. It was drafty and cold, thanks to the time of year and time of day, but complaining about it would simply earn him shit from all three of them. Terry, Anja, and Sam would lay into him for getting soft.

The real problem, of course, was that he actually thought he might be.

He placed the paper cup of coffee carefully near where Terry stared through a pair of binoculars. They had found a small crane that currently wasn't in use, probably due to the fact that it was late on a Friday on Thanksgiving weekend. This afforded them an overwatch position over the bunker where their target had been taken.

"Do we know for certain that Banks hasn't already left the country?" he asked. The sniper sipped his coffee calmly without looking away from the binoculars.

"Well, Anja studied the camera feeds in the area, and it doesn't look like he's left the premises," Terry responded as the hacker appeared to be too busy to do so. "There aren't any secondary access points in the plans, either the original or improvements, although I suppose it's possible they simply added them without applying for any permits. Either way, the heavy security is still in place, which indicates that someone's still down there. Or something that needs lots of protecting."

"Yeah." Savage cracked his back and sipped his warm coffee. For once, he'd asked for a little of half and half and sugar to be added. He needed something to make him feel better about the boredom. "It seems our chances of pinning Banks down inside are looking better and better."

The other man finally turned his attention away from the bunker to look at him. "Are you sure you want to do this, man? We can simply wait for him out here. He needs to leave eventually. He'll be at his most vulnerable in transit anyway, so we can wait until he's being transported again and that'll be that."

"We don't have the advantage of time." The operative shook his head decisively. "We delayed his contract on my family but eventually, someone will be capable or stupid enough to make another attempt. I can't risk that. We need to take care of Banks here and now—or as soon as possible, anyway."

"Why doesn't Anja take the ad down?" Terry resumed his surveillance.

"They'll simply put it up again. If we eliminate Banks, we won't need to constantly take the ads down only for someone to post them again."

"I guess that's true. So you're dead set on doing this, then?"

"I am," Savage answered with a small smile. His mind was made up. While he wasn't suicidal, he needed to take some risks at this point. He was the one with skin in the game, as it were, and he wouldn't simply sit around and wait while his family was in danger.

"And there's the change of the guard." The sniper gestured for him to look at the target location as two SUVs pulled up outside. They greeted the five men who were stationed outside but headed down in the elevator that went into the bunker. About three minutes later, the elevator returned with another group of ten men, who climbed into the SUVs and drove away.

"What time do the men up top change?" Savage asked.

"Every eight hours, so about three hours from now." Terry frowned in thought. "They stagger the changes to make them more effective at the job or something like that."

"That'll probably be the best time," he muttered and made a mental note of the times. "The guys who are newer on the job will be easier to evade, I think."

"Well, if you're dead set on it, there's no way we'll let you do it sober," the other man said. He looked away from his binoculars and started to pack the hide up.

"What do you mean?" he asked. "You want me to go in there drunk?"

"Of course not." Terry chuckled. "We want to get you sloshed today, get you un-hungover tomorrow, and then we'll make the run."

"I don't think that's a good idea." He narrowed his eyes.

"It's adorable that you think you have any say in it, boss man." His companion grinned and patted him on the shoulder. "Come on, Sam's already starting the shots for us. And she said there might be some visitors joining us later in the evening too, although she didn't give me any specifics."

Savage shrugged. He didn't like the idea of getting sloshed right before a difficult mission, but it wasn't like it was his first time doing it.

Under any other circumstances, Banks didn't think he would mind spending excessive amounts of time there. Bunkers were usually portrayed as dull, dark places where people hid in fear, but he was... Well, he was hiding and afraid, but the structure wasn't dull or dark. Very little sunlight made its way inside but there was plenty of light and nicely paneled walls and elegant furniture. It was like someone had designed the place to be their own little hideaway if the time came to retreat from the world as a whole.

His wanderings through the facility had revealed a fully stocked kitchen, a gym, a small swimming pool, and tanning beds, as well as three different bedrooms—all suites with enough space to put most apartments in New York to shame. Hell, his client could make a fortune by renting this place out. He knew people who would quite literally kill to have this much space available right in the middle of Manhattan. Well, maybe not right in the middle, but still.

The bunker also contained fully stocked bars, which he had taken the liberty of using. He'd had a long nap for almost a full day, but after that, lacking anything else to do, he decided to attack the stock of gin they had on hand. The whiskey was good, but gin had always been his poison of choice. He'd become far less picky once he realized Savage was coming after him, though.

There was an Internet connection, run through about fifty VPNs to keep Savage's computer expert off his scent, but the men who ran security for him had told him it was still a risk. He had taken that warning seriously. Even with this many people to keep him safe, there was still a very real trace of fear in the back of his mind. He was in danger as long as he remained in the same place.

Banks closed his eyes, leaned back in his seat, and took a sip of his gin and tonic. It was the soft kind of drink he had grown accustomed to. Others tended to think it was the drink people ordered when they didn't know what they wanted. He would have disagreed.

But now wasn't the time to think about trivialities.

His phone buzzed. He had been told there would be no signal down there, so he was understandably confused when he retrieved the device and confirmed that there was a call coming over the line. Weird. He pressed the accept call button and his eyes widened with surprise when an image accompanied the voice. He'd seen the client before—only once when she'd met him for coffee. She still had that luscious, long black hair, but it was tied up in a braid this time, and she wore glasses too. The area around her was dark, which made him wonder if she was in a time zone where it was night, or if she was merely in a dark room. Either was an option, he assumed. She wasn't the kind of woman to share much, which left his mind occupied with trying to work out any detail he could.

"Mason," she said, greeting him familiarly by his first name. "How's the new place? Up to your standards, I hope?"

"More than up to them, thanks," Banks replied cautiously. He had been told when he'd met in the flesh that it would be the last time he ever saw her, which made him curious as to why she called him on a video call.

"Well, it's one of the best safe houses money can buy," she replied and leaned forward into the screen. "It's only fair that it should provide a few creature comforts."

He smiled. "I still feel like I'm a sitting duck here. As secure as it is, Savage is still out there, gunning for me. It can't be long before he finds me here, right?"

She chuckled. "I'll be honest with you, Mason, that is half the reason why I have you there. Savage has shown himself to be rather resourceful, and I don't doubt that his arrogance will lead him to try to get his hands on you himself. He will most likely fail in the attempt, and that loose end will be effectively tied. I do want my people—and you, if you like—to make it a very slow, painful death and record every moment. I'd like to use it as a lesson for all those who might annoy me the way he has. Of course, if he decides to wait or can't find you, I'll have all the papers necessary to get you out of the country in a couple of days and you'll be in the clear. I still have a need for you to work for me out here, Mason."

The lawyer nodded. "I…appreciate that."

"Try to stay alive, and I'll be in touch." She cut the connection before he could respond.

He didn't appreciate the woman trying to be sweet. She had manipulated him and tried to soften the blow. The reality, though, was that he was being used as bait to bring Savage in. While he could understand that he wasn't as important to her cause as eliminating the operative, it still sent a chill down his spine to know it. He'd had his suspicions before, of course, but to have them confirmed so blatantly was enough to stir all his fears back to life.

It was all good, though, he thought sarcastically as he raised his glass to his lips and took a nice, long sip. He would simply drink himself into a blackout and test his liver's ability to process the poison until it was time to leave. Or be attacked by Savage, whichever came first.

CHAPTER TWENTY-THREE

Savage and Terry arrived at the Irish bar where Sam told them to meet her, and by the looks of it, only the woman herself was there with no unannounced visitors to join them. Terry hadn't been joking when he said she would start on the shots for them. She had also ordered what looked like nachos and cheesy fries for the table too, which she had already dug into by the time they arrived.

"Hey, you're here," she shouted, a little loudly and with a slight slur. "You're all fucking late, so I had to start without you."

"Well, this is a charming little place." Savage looked around. It seemed too small to have a kitchen in the back, but New York had a way of teaching people to be efficient in the use of space. Still, it wasn't anywhere near as big as most other establishments he'd been in. Of the fifteen or so tables, about half were full, although more people trickled in as the hour grew later. Most had the look of regulars who were there almost every night. The room was dark. A couple of TVs above the bar showed sports channels

Savage didn't think he had time to catch up on. He had been out of the loop when it came to sports and simply saved all the games on his TV at home, so when he eventually had the time to get back to it, he could.

Not just yet, though.

"So, is everything in place?" Sam asked. Her gaze encompassed them both as she started to pass the first round of shots.

"We have a plan to work with, yeah," Savage said with a grin as he took the first shot of Irish Whiskey and his companions followed suit.

"It's a crazy fucking masterpiece of a plan," she said and actually shivered as the burning liquid moved down her throat. "And that's the highest compliment I can pay, so you'd better be all impressed and shit."

He looked at Terry, who bristled visibly at the profanities she used. Thankfully, the man had spent a fair amount time around her over the past few months, so he had begun to build up a tolerance to her foul mouth.

Kudos for him, he thought as he downed another shot and scowled. Sam pushed the plates of nachos and fries over to him.

"What?" he asked.

"Oh, you know, a working dad and all that. I assumed your tolerance is all the way down since you don't drink that much," she replied cheekily.

"I'll kick you in the shins," he retorted, but he decided to go with the starchy foods anyway. She was wrong about his tolerance, but he didn't want to actually try to get drunk. He wanted to drink and celebrate. Libations were important before a big fight.

He grabbed a couple of the fries and shoved the nachos over to Terry, who chuckled.

"Unlike the two of you, my tolerance for alcohol is actually rather low," the sniper said. He chewed on a couple of the nachos while Sam called the bartender over. The man took the empty glasses, set up another group, and poured until they were full.

"Leave the bottle," Sam said. "And bring another round of beers. It'll be a long night."

"My kind of night," Savage said with a grin. He pushed a couple of the shot glasses to Sam and Terry and took another for himself. It would definitely be a long night. His gaze drifted to scan the bar as they all did despite the relaxed occasion. It was in their blood to constantly assess their surroundings and learn the exits no matter how drunk they were.

His gaze wandered a little. The shots had begun to affect him but he was able to refocus when the bartender brought their beers to the table and jolted him back to reality. He glanced at the bar again and the stools around it. More precisely, the brunette in a criminally short skirt who had just perched on one of the seats. He craned his neck slightly to try to get a view of the rest of her.

"I think we lost Savage," Sam pointed out as she looked at Terry, who dug into the starches to help his body process the liquor he had consumed.

"Well, we were bound to eventually," he replied, leaned back in his seat, and stretched. "I suppose I was hoping we would get to hang out for a while longer, at least until we were all equally drunk."

Savage turned to his group. "I'm not lost. Promise. Merely…appreciating the view from over here."

"I think we should make a drinking game of it," Sam said with a firm nod and took a sip of her beer. "You know, something like…drink when Savage's eyes start to wander, long sip when he loses track of the conversation, and we all take a shot when he decides he'll get our refills at the bar?"

"That sounds about right." Terry chuckled.

"Yeah, you two are playing it off like an old married couple." He raised his glass in a mock toast and took a big sip to taste the beer they'd ordered for him. It wasn't the best he'd ever drunk, but it was ice-cold, which made up for that.

"Ugh, for the last time, we're not fucking sleeping together," Sam protested.

"Like I said, an old married couple." He grinned and ducked when the woman tossed a handful of chips at him.

The bartender sent them a couple of dirty glances, which was really all he could spare as the place had filled up. Still, they took the hint and the two men quickly cleaned up Sam's mess.

Savage did notice that the brunette he'd noticed before sighed and looked around the room, a classic indicator that she was looking for someone to come along and buy her a drink. The chances were good that she simply wanted a way to kill time until her date, boyfriend, or group of friends showed up, but at this point, he really didn't care. His inhibitions were lowered by the sudden intake of alcohol, and dammit, he would take advantage of that.

"You two," he said as Terry and Sam continued to argue about not being an old married couple. "Drink, and drink."

He pointed at the beer first, then the shots, as he pushed himself clear of the booth they shared and wandered to the bar. His beer didn't need refilling. It would still be there for him when he returned once he'd been shot down. Or maybe not. In which case, Sam would be there to finish his beer for him. She seemed the type to not waste good alcohol.

It took a while to push through the crowd that now filled the small pub but he reached the bar without mishap. He wasn't attended to immediately, so he took his time before he approached the young woman. She noticed him and offered him a tentative, invitational smile as he sat down beside her.

"Not to be cliché or anything, but can I buy you a drink?" he asked.

She was about to answer when a hand touched his shoulder. Well, grab was more appropriate. He was dragged around to face the person in question. As drunk as he was, it took him a second to realize who it was.

"Anderson!" he said, a little too loudly. "What the hell are you doing here?"

"I came in to try to talk you out of doing something stupid," the man said with a grin. "And then maybe get you to avoid going into a heavily fortified bunker on your own."

"What are you talking about?" he asked and glanced at the brunette. "By the way, meet my friend… What was your name again?"

It looked like the woman was about to answer, but Anderson cut in first. "Whatever her name is, she came in with her boyfriend who's sitting in the corner over there."

"Hey, thanks a lot, asshole," the woman snapped and pushed herself up from her seat.

"You're trying to steal drinks from gullible, drunk guys," he retorted, his tone sharp. "Get lost, asshole bitch."

Her eyebrows raised but she knew he was in the right in this particular situation. All she could really do was huff, act offended, and return to her boyfriend, who looked annoyed at her inability to score him free drinks.

"Well, I think I owe you one for that," Savage said with a grin.

"There was the one in that other bar," the former colonel reminded him as they shuffled through the crowds to the table where Terry and Sam waited.

"I paid you back for that one by saving your life a couple of hours later, so that doesn't count," he said and shook his head decisively.

"Well, I'm cashing in on this favor right now to get you to rethink your current strategy," Anderson said. He slid into the booth beside Terry, which forced Savage into the opposite seat with Sam, who draped her arm over his shoulder. "It's suicide and you know it. Suicide's a sin, Savage. It should be me going in there."

"Not if you're not Catholic," he pointed out and reclaimed his beer. "I'm not Catholic. I can do crazy shit all I want. Besides, it has to be me. Otherwise, the plan doesn't work."

"I disagree with that," she said. "I like you, Jer. You shouldn't do any crazy shit. Leave that to me. I'm the crazy one. Everyone knows that."

"The woman has a point," Terry said with a chuckle.

"I'll drink to it." He grinned, picked his beer up, and

added the contents of the last shot glass that was still full before he raised it in another silent toast.

———

Savage staggered out of the bar, but by the time he reached the street, he had managed to straighten his steps and his clothes. He was drunk, more or less. His tolerance for alcohol was still strong, and it took him more than five or six shots and a couple of pints of beer to bring him to the strip down to his underwear and sing kind of drunk. He'd starched up, hydrated, and taken his time, and he was done with the drinking part of the night in less than an hour and a half. That was a personal record.

Of course, he'd had to sell the whole schtick of having a low tolerance Sam had hinted at or outright goaded him into, but he didn't mind. He did his best drinking in smaller, safer locales with fewer people around. He'd never bought into the appeal of a crowded bar—too much noise and too many people he hadn't specifically chosen to be around. Terry, Sam, and Anderson were all well and good, but the same couldn't be said about the literally dozens of people who crowded into the place. It had reached a point where he simply hadn't been able to enjoy himself.

He had booked a room in a hotel for the night as he didn't want to sleep in the cot in the abandoned building where Terry and Sam were still headquartered. He was sure they had rooms elsewhere too and had only set the cots up in case they needed to hunker down there for the night or take a nap in the middle of the day.

It wasn't the best accommodation but was within

walking distance, so he didn't need to take a cab. Besides, a brisk walk in the chilly New York evening had a shocking effect and would dispel the warm, drunken feeling he was filled with at the moment. A ten-minute walk was enough to exorcise most of it and to make his nose and ears numb before he reached the hotel.

Check-in was a quick and easy process. He used the ID Anja had provided him with earlier that day in the name of David Baker. Sam had mentioned something about a doctor, but she hadn't actually given him an explanation so he was none the wiser. He would ask her about it later if he had the time and remembered something so inconsequential. There were other more important things, like requesting a room with a queen-sized bed.

"Of course, sir. The room was already selected in your reservation," the night manager said with a polite smile.

Savage didn't remember doing that, but maybe he had pressed the button and simply not noticed it.

He asked for a full mini-bar and about the kitchen. Food was a definite requirement in order to keep his stomach settled. He was informed that the room service menu was available all night long.

The man remained quietly polite, but the operative wondered if he could tell he was halfway to drunk—or maybe a little more than half. It seemed likely that he could, if only from his breath. He liked to think he would have been able to tell if someone as drunk as he was approached. Besides, these guys dealt with drunk patrons all the time, right?

With check-in complete, he located the room and unlocked it with the key that had been handed to him. Too late, he realized he should have noticed that the light inside was already on. His hand instantly found the pistol under his jacket. It might not have been the best idea to bring a gun to a bar, but he hadn't really thought all that much tonight.

Compared to most of his life, the night had lacked uncomfortable surprises. That alone meant he should have seen this one coming.

"You can put the gun away," Dr. Jessica Coleman said with a smile, still seated on the single chair in the room which had been pushed into the corner beside the night light.

Savage realized he'd drawn the piece halfway out of his holster, his thumb already on the safety, ready for a fight.

"Sorry," he said and shook his head as he shoved the piece away and covered it with his coat. "I'm still a little jumpy. It's been one of those…weeks."

"So I've heard," Jessica said with a chuckle.

"How did you hear that?" he asked and narrowed his eyes. "Actually, how are you here in my roo— Damn it, Anja!"

"What? I said I liked her," the hacker said over the comm link he still had in his ear. "You might want to take the earbud out, though, if you don't want me listening in."

"You'll simply hack into my phone," he reminded her.

"Well, I'm curious, but I'm not that curious," she protested. "You kids deserve some privacy. Have fun!"

He took her advice and removed the device from his ear and placed it on the bedside table before he sat on the bed. "Kids. Yeah, right. I'm reasonably sure I'm older than she is."

"I don't think that's what she meant," Jessica said softly, her gaze assessing but not challenging.

"What are you doing here, anyway?" he asked with a little more heat in his tone than he'd intended.

"Anderson filled me in on what you were doing, and… well, I assumed everyone would tell you to reconsider."

"And you won't?" His question was a little curt as he removed his jacket and placed it on the bed.

"No, I'm here to wish you good luck." She grinned cheerfully. "If there's one thing I've learned about you it's that once you settle on the course of action you think is right, you're the only one who can convince you to change it. That and the fact that fortune tends to bend herself over backward to accommodate your schemes."

"Fortune, huh?" He snorted derisively. "Is that what you call me getting shot and beat up in that hotel in Charlotte?"

"Not that specifically, but me being there to bail you out and help you out with your injuries was fortunate, wouldn't you say?"

Savage nodded. "What happened later that night of course was…" He didn't know how to finish that sentence, mainly because he wasn't at all sure what it was. It continued to elude his attempts to explain it.

"We both needed each other that night," she said. "It was a moment of crisis and danger, and we found comfort in each other. There's nothing wrong with that."

"It did make things complicated, you have to admit that," he pointed out.

"Sure," she responded but her small shrug was almost dismissive. "But complicated doesn't always mean worse. It was an enjoyable evening for us both, but that doesn't mean anything needs to come of it. We're both adults, we should be able to move on and keep things in context."

He needed a moment to compose himself as there was still a little too much alcohol in his system for him to trust whatever came to his mind first. "I'll be honest, I really did want something to come of it. It's been tough, and being with you was one of the best things I've had in this short new life I've lived. The only problem I see is that…well, I don't think it'll be what you're looking for. I won't be able to engage myself fully if that makes sense. There's too much baggage on my end. Too much Savage, and not enough Jeremiah left—I suppose that would be the best way to explain it."

She nodded and pushed up from her seat. He stood as well and assumed that as she hadn't heard the answer she'd wanted, she would therefore take her leave. It was entirely understandable, and he didn't blame her. He wasn't the family man he'd been before—or at least someone who tried to be—and the truth was that he had moved way past normal or even halfway committed relationships.

"I understand," she said softly, but instead of making her way to the door, she moved closer to him. There was a moment where he thought she might want a goodbye hug or something. While he wasn't much of a hugger, he could make an exception for her in this instance. She had made it worth it, he thought.

It seemed he had completely misinterpreted her intentions. She hesitated for only a moment, then draped her arms over his shoulders and pulled him in. He didn't resist when she pressed her lips to his with a warm, tender touch. The kiss was soft at first, but the longer it lasted, the more intense it became. He realized that she used the opportunity to push him slowly into the bed behind him.

Savage landed roughly and it creaked loudly beneath him. Jessica clambered after him and straddled his hips in a smooth motion. She pressed her lips onto his neck and ran her hands under his shirt to find and trace his hard-planed torso.

"I thought you said—" He tried to voice a protest but his words were cut off by a sudden and almost electric shiver up his spine.

"Well," she replied to his unfinished question, her lips still close enough to his bare skin that he could feel her lips move and the vibration of her voice and the heat of her breath on his neck. "I decided that I'd come all this way, so I might as well have something to remember you by, right? And I don't mean something from the JFK Airport souvenir shop."

He couldn't really argue with that as she already busied herself with removing his holster, followed quickly by his shirt. She added her own to create a growing pile of discarded clothes and shifted a little over his hips to compensate for the disparity in their heights. He drifted his hands down her sides and she grinned at him from her perch.

It would be a long night, as Sam had predicted. Still, as long nights went, this was far more enjoyable than he had expected.

CHAPTER TWENTY-FOUR

The day before, his teammates and Anderson had told him constantly how dangerous and ill-conceived his plan was, but it was the only one that had presented itself. He had his own doubts about how well it would work or the unseen variables they might encounter. There were many risks, mostly for him, but Banks had made it quite clear that Savage was the target of his vendetta when he accessed his file and threatened his family specifically.

The logic behind it was indisputable. They wanted to eliminate the man who worked as an enforcer for Anderson and Monroe's team. Given the history, they obviously realized they wouldn't effectively be able to remove either of them while they had him to throw wrench after wrench into their works, and they targeted him directly.

Which meant he was the one who had to pull this off in order for it to work. He needed to get into that bunker himself and make sure people were distracted long enough in their attempt to either entrap or kill him to allow the rest of the plan to unfold effectively.

Most of the day had been spent running surveillance from a distance. Savage, Sam, Terry, and Anderson alternated who was in their hide on the crane that was still unused. Work continued along the docks during the weekend, but it took place on the far side and so left their location all but abandoned, for the most part. The lack of traffic and activity was probably why their adversaries had chosen this bunker to build their secure location in. If he were someone rich who wanted a safe hideaway that would enable them to keep potential attackers at bay, he would have wanted somewhere that wasn't used until the peak seasons.

The light had begun to fade and his phone vibrated in his pocket to notify him that it was almost time. He moved his car closer to the target in a slow crawl and inched toward the fences before he finally stopped about half a klick from the bunker.

It was all too easy to slip into an overthinking mindset—the kind that made him wonder about the hundreds of different ways in which all this could go wrong. He was acutely aware of the possibilities if not the probabilities. His death was one of the worst ways in which it could go wrong. He would essentially go in there blind, with maps created from the bunker plans that were at least a decade old as his only reference for orientation once he entered.

A half-hour remained before he could move toward the bunker itself on foot. The operative took the time to enter the dark, cold place within, the place where the plan was irrevocably settled and cast in stone. Questions would only come along when he was in a position where he had to deal with them in the moment and only had a split second to make choices. It didn't guarantee that he would make the best decision, of course, but it certainly meant he wouldn't have too much time to overthink the problem and probably revert to his original decision anyway.

"Savage, are you good to go?" Anderson asked from his position on the crane where he functioned as a spotter for Terry. "Fifteen minutes and counting. Run a quick weapons check."

It had been a while since the former colonel had conducted a field operation, but he still knew how to do it. He assumed Savage would be in his car, stewing over his own possible demise. At this point, it was too late to call the operation off, which meant they were all in this together. Part of his role was to be there to help and give the man on the ground something to do with his hands to keep his mind off of the bad shit that very likely lay ahead.

Savage actually did run a quick check on the weapons he'd brought with him. His Glock was fitted with a suppressor Terry had somehow acquired, although he hadn't explained the details. The shotgun was essential too—close quarters, up close and personal, was what he aimed for and anticipated. From the plans he'd seen of the bunker, there was little in the way of open spaces. In other words, the fortress was the kind of place where he wanted to have as much lead spewing downrange as possible.

"Locked and loaded, boss," he said. He wore a vest of body armor but would have felt more comfortable with one of the full helmets they issued as standard gear to the Marines these days. They'd provided him with a ski-mask laced with some light shit they'd pulled out of the Zoo that apparently worked almost like body armor. Still, the fact remained that if he took a headshot, the bullet might not punch through but it would be a kill shot, nine times out of ten. Of course, it was better than going in there with nothing.

He was dressed in dark camo to help him remain unseen as much as possible. Anja and Anderson had explained that the light tech in it allowed him to be more difficult to see in weak light or dim situations. There had been far too much science involved for him to really assimilate, and all he had really come away with had been the fact that Pegasus actually developed these kinds of things. What government would want some kind of active camo?

Savage didn't really want to know the answer to that.

"You're good to go in three…two…one," Anderson said, already patched into the earbud comm system Anja had set up for them.

A second after one, the operative stepped out of his vehicle and didn't bother to shut it behind him before he moved on. The faint sound of cars approaching on the road created a steady background hum. He stayed low and remained close to the mostly abandoned warehouses around his target. Headlights lit the area well enough, but any noises he might have made were covered by the two engines of the security vehicles and wheels on tarmac. He had sufficient time to continue his advance as the group of men seemed in no particular hurry once they'd arrived. They stood around and exchanged pleasantries that he could hear from the position he'd managed to reach at the fence.

As a group, they stepped into the elevator and the door closed. He hefted his pistol in readiness and hugged the ground.

The elevator doors opened a few minutes later to reveal the men who protected whoever was in there and who had been relieved by the newcomers to head back to their homes. Hopefully, the whoever was Banks.

The five men who stood guard outside waved the group goodbye and watched as the SUVs left the area at a slow, steady speed.

"Are you good to go, Savage?" Anderson asked, momentarily forgetting that he couldn't actually say anything without giving his position away. "Oh...right. Ready to go, Terry?"

"Call them," Terry said in the soft voice snipers used when they were in their quiet, dark place. It wasn't the same kind of dark place Savage went to—or, at least, he didn't think so—but it was similar enough that he could understand it. You needed somewhere like that when you knew you were about to kill people.

"Five targets," the former colonel said. "About seven hundred yards out. Fire when ready."

An almost frozen silence hung over the area a few seconds before it was shattered by a distinct crack. By the time the operative heard it, the man closest to him was already dead, his brains splattered across the gravel around him. A headshot from seven hundred yards out was an excellent shot. A second crack followed and another body thudded to the ground. Savage withdrew a pair of bolt cutters from his pocket and went to work on the fence to create an opening large enough to allow him in.

Two more cracks preceded loud footsteps that alerted him as he stepped through the hole he'd made. He immediately drew his Glock and held it at the ready. The man who had been on the other side of the elevator tried to circle while he called for backup. There was no answer on his comm device—at least that Savage could hear—but it was still best to not permit him to enlist further help on the surface. He raised his weapon and squeezed the trigger a couple of times. Both shots struck their target, but the man appeared to be wearing some kind of body armor. He grunted in pain and stumbled out of the limited cover provided by the entrance to the bunker. There would be no prizes for guessing what would come next.

Another sharp report followed a dull thump as the bullet pounded through the man's skull. The operative had already moved on toward the elevator.

"Do I have any company coming up?" he asked while he made a hasty assessment of the area.

"There's no sign of any movement on the elevators," Anja replied. "Wouldn't they want to confront you up here to ensure as much distance as possible between any attackers and the person they're protecting?"

"I doubt it," he responded caustically and peered more closely at the elevator doors. "If the communication reached the people down there they know someone will eliminate them from long range. They'll probably stay down there and try to bring in reinforcements to deal with the sniper. It's the standard protocol for anything like that. Although in the field, they would simply call in a mortar strike on the general location and hope to flush him out that way."

"I don't think that'll work in the middle of New York fucking City," the hacker replied. Terry would no doubt be relieved to hear that. "But either way, I've blocked comms in and out of the place. It won't matter if they have a landline, but either way, I think I bought you five minutes. Do you feel like using it?"

Savage positioned a device that had taken most of the day to acquire but which was fairly important to the success of the operation. The doors were supposed to be magnetically sealed in case of an attack, but they functioned on electromagnets. He had listened as closely as he could when she explained it to him, but all he really understood was that it was some kind of focused EMP that worked to disengage doors exactly like these. It locked magnetically to the elevator door, and he pressed a button on the center of the disk and took a step back.

A soft snap and crack indicated success and the device fell with a dull thunk. He narrowed his eyes.

"Is that it?" he asked and retrieved a small, compact crowbar from his pack.

"What did you expect?" she asked, but he was already focused on the next step. Sure enough, the doors pulled apart easily and the magnets kept them disengaged. The shaft opened and he pulled climbing gear from his pack. He leaned inside to find the steel wires and attached the rope grabs to them, clipped them to the harness he put on over his suit, and dragged the ski-mask down over his face. Cameras on the outside would have already identified him as the invader. There was no need to keep them in the loop any longer.

"Good luck, Savage," Anja said as he began his descent

of the shaft. The grabbers worked automatically and lowered him faster than he was comfortable with, but when he turned his flashlight on, he realized it was actually a fairly decent speed. In less than a minute, he reached where the elevator had stopped.

He'd examined the plans over and over again and now confidently applied the bolt cutters to the lock that kept the hatch at the top of the elevator closed.

His heart hammered loudly in his chest as he retrieved a flashbang from his pack and cradled it in his palm for a moment. He kept both weapons within easy reach as he pulled the hatch open briefly to confirm that the elevator's door was open. After a long, deep breath and a slow exhale, he primed the flashbang, pulled the pin, and opened the flap to lob it through and toward the open door. Quickly, he shut the hatch again.

A loud bang shuddered through the sturdy insulation of the elevator as Savage yanked the hatch open one last time and pushed through. He landed on his feet, dropped smoothly into a roll that carried him clear of the box, and found his feet, his shotgun in hand.

"I'm in, Savage," Anja said softly, but his focus was elsewhere, and he didn't respond. The roll had felt smooth, but it still shocked his whole body into a sluggish response he had to work through in these critical moments. He swung the shotgun barrel toward two guards who stood nearby and stared at the doors. Fortunately, the flashbang appeared to have incapacitated them somewhat, which bought him precious seconds. The weapon kicked back into his hands and buckshot powered through the body parts that weren't protected by armor. The first man fell with most of his throat missing.

The operative pivoted in place and identified a second target before he jerked the pump action in the weapon and squeezed the trigger again. This man was close enough that he was able to aim all the pellets toward his mostly exposed head, which rapidly became a smoking red mess.

The effects of the flashbang wouldn't last much longer, he reminded himself and darted behind what looked like a refrigerator when a concerted volley drove him into cover. The slugs battered his temporary shield, but it seemed to hold up. There should be about eight of them now, plus Banks if he was there.

"Savage, get out of there now," the hacker shouted into his comms, but he couldn't comply. Well, he could have, but almost any movement would bring him under fire from the eight defenders who positioned themselves for maximum engagement.

One of the men circled and tried to get a shot in but Savage fired his shotgun at him. It wasn't a clean hit, but he pumped the action quickly and fired again. A third shot shredded the tables nearby and the man finally fell. Blood seeped onto the floor beneath him. The operative let the weapon fall and drew his Glock clear of its holster to open fire as the remaining guards launched into a concentrated attack.

A defender collapsed when a bullet hammered into his body armor and Savage fell back with a curse. A round had winged him in the arm but the wound, thankfully, wasn't serious although it left him disoriented.

Now out of his cover, he tried to find something to

stabilize his balance, but one of the men barreled forward and tackled him before he could initiate a defense.

Why did they not shoot to kill?

He landed hard and the breath expelled painfully from his lungs. His adversary pushed to his feet and seemed to forget for a moment that he still had a gun in his hands. He pointed it vaguely in the man's direction and pulled the trigger—once, twice, and three times until his target sagged over him and a red splash erupted out the back of his head.

Before he had managed to shove his victim off him completely, a hard kick to his wrist careened the weapon out of his hands.

"Savage!" Anja yelled, but when he tried to answer, another boot pounded into his gut and he curled into a fetal position.

Ah, that was why they didn't try to kill him. They wanted to beat the shit out of him first. The thought provided little comfort as punches and kicks battered him relentlessly from all sides. He tried to fight back and managed a couple of blows of his own, but they made little impact. All he really could do was smile as he watched the elevator doors close as if of their own accord.

CHAPTER TWENTY-FIVE

The phone rang insistently.

Banks scowled at it and tried to think of a good excuse to avoid answering it. This hadn't been his best day. Most of it was spent staring at that same damn phone while he waited for the client to call. First prize would be to tell him his papers were ready and it was time to head to the nearest airport with first class tickets and a plane that would take him anywhere that wasn't fucking New York.

Well, not literally anywhere. Somewhere with no extradition treaty, as well as most of the best comforts that modern society could buy. Switzerland was apparently very pleasant in this season. Their ski resorts would be open although it was still early in the year and wouldn't be as packed as they would become during the winter months. The client would be able to put him up somewhere comfortable and allow him to continue his work for her and for the firm from afar.

But he'd waited all day and the phone hadn't rung. Not once. He ran out of gin and started on the bourbon, and still, the stupid device remained obdurately silent. The guard changed two and even three times without the communication he hoped for. He was stuck underground with a strong likelihood that someone would try to kill him, and all he was expected to do was wait. By now, though, he was halfway sure the guards assigned to protect him would forcibly keep him a prisoner or shoot him in the back if he tried to escape, which meant he was not going anywhere. He wasn't a naturally courageous individual.

That was when it had all started. He was into his third rum and coke of the evening, about five minutes after the guard shift changed again, and the newcomers listened to the comms in their ears. Something had gone desperately wrong up top, and they tried to identify the details. They had hustled him quickly to the securest room in the bunker —which resembled a safe with an oxygen pump to draw air in from the top.

Thankfully, a fully stocked bar—as ridiculous as the idea was—mitigated any other discomfort. They sealed him inside and told him they would alert him when it was safe to come out again. All his questions had been rebuffed with repetitions of their previous statement and he had been shoved into the damn room like unwanted merchandise.

And now, finally, the phone rang. They would either tell him it was safe to come out of hiding, or it was Savage to assure him he would find a way into the safe too and he should simply wait for his inevitable arrival. The lawyer wasn't sure which was the more likely of the two scenarios, although he did know which he preferred.

He sighed as the phone continued its incessant demand. It had become annoying, and because not knowing was worse than anything else, he leaned over in his seat and snatched the receiver up from the cradle.

"Yeah?" he said, a slight slur in his voice.

"We caught him, sir." The voice he already recognized as belonging to one of the men who had pushed him into the safe room sounded smug.

Banks needed a second to process that. "What do you mean, you caught him?"

"We have him here, disarmed and secured," the man said and sounded like he almost didn't believe it himself. "The area is clear if you would like to come and see him for yourself."

There were no camera feeds to confirm that what he heard was the truth. For all he knew, it was an elaborate trap to entice him out of the safe room, but at this point, he didn't really care. It was probably the alcohol in him, but he wanted this whole ordeal to be done and finished with, one way or another. Anything was better than simply sitting around and stewing in his own fear for hours.

"Fine," he said and shook his head in a futile attempt to clear the fuzziness. "I'll come out."

He punched in the code that would unlock the door and pushed it open, not sure what he would find waiting for him.

Somehow, it looked exactly how he imagined it would. The safe room had been soundproofed to keep the occupants completely isolated so he hadn't heard the battle that had caused the very obvious damage. Bullet pockmarks marred the walls and pieces of furniture were wrecked beyond repair. A handful of bodies still seeped red. He grimaced instinctively at the gory scene, one all too clearly visible as most of the lights in the ceiling were still intact.

And there he was—the cause of the fears that had hounded Banks all week. Savage looked like he'd had the almost literal shit beaten out of him. His face was bruised, swollen, and bloodied and his right eye all but completely closed by ugly, purple swelling. Blood trickled from his lips, which were split in several places. He was secured on his knees, held up by a pair of burly bodyguards who watched him closely to make sure he didn't try anything.

He studied the prisoner for a moment, a little nonplussed, and reminded himself that this man had disabled four trained guards on his own. His record was impressive, but the man himself didn't align with the larger than life persona he had created in his wild imaginings. He'd expected something like a force of nature or straight out of a Schwarzenegger or Stallone flick. This man, with his brown hair and average height and nondescript build and was even a little disappointing.

His file contained innumerable details that defined him as a lethal and efficient killer, but for some reason, the lawyer had expected something…more.

Banks sighed and accepted the weapon that was placed in his hands almost without question. It was a Glock, and it had been fitted with a silencer—no, suppressor was the right word for it. His time as a criminal defense attorney had taught him that much. It was a little too big for his hand, but in a pinch, it would do fine.

"You should know something, Savage," Banks said and didn't care that his voice still slurred from the sheer amount of alcohol he'd imbibed over the past few days. "I hope you know that it wasn't anything personal against you. Your family wasn't ever in any real danger. It was all to remove you from the equation so we could eliminate Monroe and Anderson, you pain in the ass."

Savage looked at him, and despite the pain it had to cause him, he smirked and took a moment to spit blood onto the floor before he spoke.

"Somehow, none of what you said makes me feel any better about this." He chuckled, which triggered a hint of annoyance to creep in beneath the lawyer's smugness. The man who had turned his whole world upside down was on the wrong end of a gun and unbelievably, didn't seem to give a shit.

Give a shit, damn it!

Suddenly, he simply felt very, very tired. He didn't want to have to care about any of this. He wanted to go back to work and continue with his life.

"You know," he said and inspected the weapon in his hand, "my client wants me to make an example of you and to record it, too, and capture you suffering all kinds of unimaginable shit. Waterboarding, acid, electricity, the works. She wants it to be distributed far and wide to drive the point home that she's the one everyone has to fear, not you."

Savage's eyes narrowed, but Banks ignored him. He raised the weapon and pressed the elongated barrel to his bruised and battered forehead.

"But I don't think that'll happen," he said. He tilted his head to study his captive and enjoyed the feeling of power that holding a gun to someone else's head filled him with.

"I think I'll say you resisted and I had to shoot you a couple of dozen times to make sure that you were annihilated, once and for all."

"I can respect that," the operative said easily and actually leaned into the barrel of the gun.

"Don't think I don't want to, though," the lawyer continued with a smile. "I'd like nothing more than to fill you in on the kind of hell I've been put through over the past week or so, but I don't want to give you the opportunity to find a way to escape. That would be too—"

He lost his train of thought when the elevator doors dinged behind him to signal that someone was coming down. It was safe to assume it was a team sent by the client when she found out that Savage had raided the bunker himself. They were here to ensure the job was done. He could appreciate that and wasn't at all sure he wanted to go against the woman's wishes. If these men wanted to take the man away and deal with him themselves, there wasn't much he could do. All he knew was that if it were up to him, he wanted to Savage dead and be done with it.

Banks blinked when the door opened to reveal only two people in the elevator, a man and a woman. The man was on his one knee and looked down a scope attached to what appeared to be a very powerful rifle aimed directly at him.

"Shit!" he yelled before he could control himself and turned instinctively to face the elevator. He swung the gun away from Savage in the precise moment that the hand holding the weapon exploded in a spray of blood.

CHAPTER TWENTY-SIX

People had constantly told him this whole plan was suicidal from the beginning. While aspects of it remained the same as when he'd snuck into Carlson's base on a previous occasion, the target was much smaller and far better defended this time. Anja had said that the bunker had a similar wireless connection as the other facility and that it would require her to have a transmitter in range of the connection to allow her into the system. Since the plans indicated that most of the security system was automated, she would be able to work her way through it and take control. All it took was for them to have someone inside.

Given that Savage had been their target all along, the only person they were likely to allow inside without much resistance would be him.

Knowing he was the one they wanted dead all this time meant he also knew he'd effectively head in there on a suicide mission. The hope was that he would be able to get back into the elevator in time for Anja to close it, bring him to the surface, and allow the team to properly assault the bunker.

That was the plan, anyway, but as anyone could have told them, things very rarely went off without a hitch. Counting on the plan going wrong probably wasn't the best way to go about it, but he was well aware of the fact that his chances of walking out of that bunker at all, much less unscathed, were basically nil. Sending two people in would have been worse than only one. They would have been outnumbered anyway.

Maybe he should have simply tossed his earbud inside from the elevator hatch. In retrospect, it could have avoided a significant amount of unnecessary pain for him. Either way, it would be a learning experience.

When Terry and Sam arrived in the elevator to rescue him, hope stirred that his chances at actually living to learn the lessons from the mistakes he'd made were a little higher.

Most of the guards turned to deal with the new threat and forgot for the moment that their prisoner was close to them and still unbound. He glanced quickly at them as one dropped almost immediately after the spray from what had been Banks' hand spattered Savage's face. He was battered, bruised, and maybe even broken in some places, but a fire roared up inside him. The need to survive and thrive pushed through the pain and discomfort.

His right elbow connected with the jaw of one of the guardsmen beside him. Maybe standing wasn't the best choice in the middle of a crossfire, but he trusted his teammates to try to shoot around him.

The man he struck fell and another collapsed a few feet

away when a couple of bullet holes appeared in his forehead. Sam's work, the operative thought. Terry's big fucking rifle had a habit of severing heads or leaving much larger holes.

Savage quickly remembered where he was and why and used all the power he had in him to move behind cover. A pillar now shielded him from the remaining—Four? Three?—however many guardsmen. He hadn't had time to count. Sam and Terry followed his lead and ducked behind a bar and another pillar, respectively. She drew the operative's needle gun from under her arm and tossed it to him.

If he had been in better condition, he would have been able to catch it smoothly, maybe even with one hand, although he wouldn't have risked that when the situation was this dire.

As it stood, though, he didn't manage to catch it the first time and cursed when the weapon slid between his fingers. He flailed and snatched it by the barrel before it reached the floor.

"Are you a little off your game, Savage?" she asked as he swung it toward their adversaries.

"Yeah," he conceded and pressed his back against the pillar. His right ring finger was dislocated, and he wouldn't be able to shoot anything like that. It was weird how things like that slipped your mind when you were on your knees, ready to die with a smile on your face.

He gritted his teeth and tugged the finger roughly back into place. A strangled roar of pain followed by a deep, ragged breath accompanied the painful process. He'd done it before. You were expected to simply deal with small injuries like that during boot camp. Of course, it still didn't change the fact that it hurt like a whore's ass on a busy night.

"Feeling better?" Terry asked as he set his rifle down gently and drew his sidearm. Savage assumed it was because he was out of ammunition, although it also could have been that they were now in close quarters, which made the range factor on the weapon less useful.

He needed to stop overthinking this. They had a job to finish.

Sam spun around her corner first and opened fire on the dumbasses who still were ranged against them. Terry followed a second later to deliver a swift volley while Savage circled his pillar as quickly as he could. He groaned in pain as he pushed his battered body to continue and peered out to find his targets out of position. His weapon already raised, he fired three shots before he ducked behind the pillar again seconds before a barrage of bullets pounded into the narrow barrier.

His aim wasn't up to his usual standards, but he'd managed to wound a couple of them when the needles drilled easily through their body armor. Neither were kill shots, but from the way his two teammates both pounced, it was enough to draw them out of their cover and into the kine of fire. Two bodies thudded to the floor almost simultaneously, and as he darted around the corner, Sam and Terry circled the remaining guard. It wasn't fair, really, but they still played it safe, remained in cover, and waited for the man to make a mistake.

He did, sooner rather than later, when he tried to shift his position behind the bar he crouched behind and exposed his foot. The sniper responded quickly and decisively and his target screamed in pain. Sam vaulted over to finish the job with a double tap.

She took a second to make sure the man was dead, then looked at the two men. "All clear over here."

"Should we clear the place?" Terry asked. "We surmised there were only ten inside, but we could have been wrong."

"It wouldn't be the worst idea," Savage said softly and his gaze shifted toward the only movement in the room that wasn't from the three of them. "Why don't you guys handle that? I have a bone to pick with a motherfucker who just lost his best gal."

Terry narrowed his eyes and he wondered if he would tell him to watch his language too. The sniper never tired of that, but Sam grinned. It appeared the other man was only a little confused by Savage's terminology.

"You took his best gal away," Sam explained and gestured with her hand near her hips and closed it in a fist. She jerked up and down a few times and finished with what probably was intended to represent a splatter.

"Oh," Terry said as understanding dawned. "Oh…" He finished with a grunt and a disgusted face. "That's disgusting."

"And appropriate." She grinned. "He must love it. Look at how he's still going after it like it owes him money."

She wasn't wrong, actually. Banks, still bleeding from his ruined hand, crawled pitifully to where a few of his fingers lay on the ground. Savage had reached a point of exhaustion and he simply wanted this to be over, but there were things he needed to take care of before went in search of treatment for his bruised…everything.

"Where do you think you're going, Banks?" he asked

and limped over to the man. He checked his weapon as he reached him. The lawyer wasn't a complete idiot, apparently, and had managed to staunch the blood from his hand with his tie and part of his shirt. The wound still bled noticeably but it had slowed, which explained why he wasn't dead yet. What Savage didn't understand was why he wasn't in shock yet. Most civilians went into shock when they were shot for the first time.

Banks, however, hadn't succumbed to a wound that might have been life-threatening to others. He wasn't really in his right mind either, though, judging by the way he reached for the pieces of himself that weren't attached. Still, he didn't need much of the man to be around anymore, only the parts that needed to be taught a lesson— the kind he wouldn't forget in a hurry. Of course, it was likely that he wouldn't be in a position to use his newly acquired wisdom much or even pass it on to others. Still, that notwithstanding, the lesson was due.

"Where do you think you're going?" he asked again and stepped in front of the man who looked at him now through eyes wide with the terror he clearly felt.

"Away…from you," the lawyer said in a trembling voice. "It…wasn't…personal. Merely…business. You have to understand that."

"You attacked my family, dickhead," he accused balefully. His quarry pushed onto his knees to see him better. "How businesslike did you think this conversation would be?"

"Not personal," Banks repeated and shook his head.

"It looks like Terry broke this one." Sam chuckled as she approached.

"We'll fix him up well enough." He pressed the needle gun to the man's head and grinned at her. "We need him healthy and hearty if we want him to live through the nightmares I have in store for him."

Terry didn't look amused by what he implied, but his opinion was irrelevant. People needed to stop targeting families, and there was only one way they would get that through their thick skulls. Sam looked like she agreed with him, but her expression changed in an instant and she aimed her weapon at the captive. Savage took a step back out of instinct, followed her lead, and aimed his needle gun at Banks.

He realized why a second later. His Glock, suppressor and all, was in the man's hands. Terry had shot it out of his grasp, so it made sense that it was where the fingers were. How had he missed that? He was a little under the weather, but that was no excuse. It was unforgivable that he'd allowed his target to get his hands on a weapon while he had been gloated and planned for the future.

"What the fuck do you think you're doing?" he asked.

The lawyer smiled distantly at him, his eyes a little glazed. "I'm only…taking a .45 nightcap."

He thrust the elongated barrel into his mouth and pulled the trigger. The back of his head exploded outward and he slumped, his eyes open to stare lifelessly at the ceiling.

"What the fuck?" Terry asked.

Savage shook his head. He hadn't planned to do anything extreme and honestly didn't have the stomach for actual torture. Kneecapping or maybe a gut shot—or a groin shot—before a quick end. Well…yeah, maybe suicide felt like the best option for the man who was out of any others.

"Shit," he cursed. How had he missed that? He was off his game. Somehow, he'd allowed his emotions to get the better of him and so made stupid mistakes.

"Right?" Sam asked. "That's clearly a Glock 17 that fires 9 mm rounds. I don't know what he was talking about with all that .45 bullshit."

"Don't 17s have a mod that lets them shoot .45s?" Terry asked.

They were bantering, but Savage wasn't in the mood. He leaned against one of the nearby pillars. A phone rang somewhere. He could hear it over their bickering, and he moved to the bar where a phone was situated. It was an old-fashioned bright red hardline, the kind used in spy movies in the 80s that the US used to contact the Soviets to persuade them not to blow everything up.

He scowled and glanced at his companions, who both shrugged. With another muttered expletive, he shook his head and snatched the receiver from its cradle.

"Banks." A woman's voice spoke over the other line without preamble. He had no opportunity to speak to let her know that Banks was indisposed. "The paperwork came through. I have a team on the way to get you to the airport and maybe we can start to unravel this mess you've made of things ."

Her accent wasn't American, but he really couldn't place it. There was a hint of the Mediterranean with some German and maybe Russian too—and possibly other Asian accents. He'd never been good at placing people by accent. Maybe Anderson would be better at it.

"Banks?" the woman asked, her tone suddenly suspicious.

"Sorry," he grumbled into the silence. "Banks can't make it to the phone right now. He's…permanently indisposed. Rest assured, though, that you and he will have a nice, long chat before too long."

"Savage, I presume?" she asked.

"Banks' mysterious client, I presume?" he replied. "You know, here I was thinking Carlson was his client but—hello?" The line went dead, and he rolled his eyes. It hadn't been much of a conversation anyway.

"Who was that?" Sam asked, her eyes narrowed.

"Banks mentioned that his client was a she when he explained why he had to kill me quickly," Savage said and touched his eye cautiously. "I assume I just had my first conversation with her. The first of many, I hope."

She smirked, and Terry shook his head.

"She did say there was a team on the way," he added. "I'd advise that we get out of here before they arrive. Anja, is our exit clear?"

"Anja told me to tell you that she's not talking to you on account of you being a suicidal maniac," the sniper mentioned as the three of them returned to the elevator. The doors closed behind them. "She'll come around, though."

"No, I won't," Anja retorted. "I hope you learned your lesson, Savage."

"What, that you'll come around faster than expected?" he asked.

"Don't test me," the hacker hissed.

"Sorry." He leaned gingerly against the wall of the elevator. The adrenaline had begun to fade from his system, and the pain of his injuries rushed in like a freight train. "Yeah. Next time, we'll find a way to connect you without my having to get inside."

"Good boy." She chuckled. "Anderson's waiting outside for you. I hear you're in a hurry."

"You could say that." He grimaced as a wave of pain surged through him. Terry offered his shoulder to lean on as they hurried toward the car Anderson had started as soon as they emerged.

"You look like shit," the ex-colonel commented as they all scrambled in.

"I feel it too," he muttered. "I think a hospital might be in order right about now."

"Good call." Anderson put the car in gear and pressed the accelerator.

"*Merda*," she shouted and slammed her phone down on the table. It wasn't a landline like the one Savage had answered, and the device wasn't built for this degree of abuse. It shattered on the second strike and fell into pieces after the third. She had a couple of other phones in the mansion, though, and there was something incredibly satisfying about destroying a phone when the news wasn't what you wanted to hear.

She brushed the broken pieces off her fingers and shook her head.

"*Cazzo*." She continued to curse and headed to the pool area where a group of models she was helping to prepare for the catwalk tomorrow were currently sunbathing and enjoying the warmed pool. "*Figlio di puttana*."

Her outburst was noticed by the crowd nearby and they tried to make out what had upset her. They'd been around her long enough to know that she was kind and generous when she was in a good mood, more than willing to spread the wealth and make sure everyone around her shared in her good fortune. They also knew people tended to go missing when she was in a bad mood. Thankfully, that didn't happen often enough to drive them away, but there was a collective look of fear and apprehension in their eyes as they exchanged a few glances. They tried to agree between themselves whether or not it was time to call an end to the sunbathing and find something to do on the other side of the estate.

But it looked like she had calmed a little and so they relaxed and returned to their business and fun, enjoying the food, drink, and entertainment that was provided in lavish amounts. No expense had been spared, not for the party last night and not for the after-party in the morning. She wasn't the kind to skimp.

She regained her customary benevolent smile and a handful of guests turned their attention toward the pool. A few moved to where a couple of masseuses waited for them to make use of their services.

Elena shook her head. This was a setback, but not a large one. She was sure Banks thought he was one of a kind when it came to his usefulness. And yes, he was rather useful and the fact that he didn't need to be bailed out of some controversy or another every two weeks had been a plus. But it wasn't like he was the only person in the world who could do the job of keeping track of all of her investments in the US.

No, she thought as she gazed at the Ibiza beach her estate overlooked. There were hundreds in the city of New York alone who would literally kill for the position. And now, they wouldn't have to. The position was vacant.

She let the silk robe that she wore drop from her shoulders and reveled in the sensation as it slid all the way down with almost no resistance. Someone stepped forward a second later to retrieve the expensive piece of fabric.

Her looks were a source of smug pride. Everything about her shouted exotic, the rich femme fatale and full of mystery. Her raven-black hair, long, natural eyelashes, almond-shaped eyes, and well-tanned skin, all combined to place her easily in nearly a hundred different locations. It was a rare advantage to be able to blend into any culture. There had been a time a decade and a half ago when she'd dreamed of being a model, singer, or famous actress with hundreds of people to adore her for everything she was and strove to be.

Her ambitions had shifted after her father died and left her everything, which included the responsibility to fight off the attempts of the twelve or so siblings who had been denied their claim to the man's financial fortune. She'd succeeded, however, and became the sole heiress of the wealth and the vision that had come with her father's money.

And now, there she was, adored by the people whom millions adored in turn. She never would have thought it, but it was by far the superior option.

Yes, there were bumps along the road, but that was par for the course, to use the golfing term. It was to be expected at this point in the game. Anderson, Dr. Monroe, and their attack dog, Savage, had proven to be an interesting obstacle to her visions. They had allowed her to take her mind off of the grand scheme of things and focus on the minutia of the operations she worked with. She had even let her people convince her to send an attack team to intercept the operative when he was caught on facial recognition landing in New York, for all the good that had done them.

They wouldn't last long of course. They knew about her, which was unfortunate, but they had nothing but a voice and an untraceable call from halfway across the world to a landline in a bunker. There was no real information to follow. They knew what they were looking for but didn't know where to start. She could live with that. Let them keep chasing their tails for years to come. She would be waiting for them to finally give up.

Her mood was restored, and she could see her guests now felt a little more comfortable as she moved over to one of the poolside recliners and sprawled elegantly across it to enjoy the sunlight. Everything seemed swathed in a warm, golden glow, visible through her custom-made Dolce and Gabbana sunglasses. Considerable effort went into maintaining her appearance, but it was immensely satisfying to simply sit back and let the sun do some of the work.

One of the hard-working house servants moved closer, a single champagne flute on the gleaming tray in his hand. There wasn't any champagne in the glass, of course, although it was chilled to the point where she could already see condensation on the outside. The liquid inside was bright blue and appeared to swirl and move of its own accord. She scowled at the glass but took it in her perfectly manicured fingers. It was a necessary evil these days, and she had to admit that it had made her life of looking good a whole lot easier.

It didn't change the fact that it tasted like death, though.

She took a sip. "*Cazzo di inferno.*" She scowled and shook her head. "This Zoo shit is disgusting."

"So why do you drink it?" one of the tall, lean, and handsome male models whose name escaped her at the moment asked. He settled easily into the recliner beside her.

"You don't look this good without a few sacrifices," Elena replied and allowed herself a moment to appreciate the perfect form of the man beside her. "But I have to say that it's been worth it."

"I really didn't want to go back to the hospital," Savage said and glowered at his surroundings. The room was private with an appealing view of a small creek and the trees that had started to turn all kinds of colors between red, yellow, and orange. It was a pleasant place to spend time in, even if it was a hospital. "I'm serious. A couple of bruises. A concussion, maybe. A few cracked ribs, and…" He raised his right hand still bound in a couple of black wraps. "I relocated my finger badly, so they had to pull it out and put it back in again correctly. It was as painful as hell, but I should get out of here within a couple of days."

He was lying of course and had been in a great deal of pain when they checked him into the hospital. There had also been a few complications. He had still been dealing with the problems that had put him in hospital the last time, and the beating he'd taken had made those injuries worse. All had been exacerbated by the fact that he hadn't taken his medication for the past week.

As hard as it was to accept, he needed to stay in the hospital and get better. He wouldn't survive if he didn't allow himself to recover between beatings.

"So, you're saying this is all a formality?" Jessica asked skeptically as she studied him on the hospital bed.

"Sure," he replied with a shrug. "I would have been told to walk this off if I was still in boot camp."

"Well, do it for me, okay?" she asked, a bite of sarcasm in her voice when she squeezed his shoulder "It'll make me feel so much better knowing the doctors and not some drill sergeant have given you a clean bill of health. Please, do it for me, okay?"

"Will do." He smiled a little sheepishly and she turned, made her way to the door, and gave Anderson a quick hug before she stepped out of the room.

"And now that the ladies aren't present?" the former colonel asked and moved closer.

"Hey, what am I?" Anja asked through their earbuds.

"I would have thought you didn't like being called a lady," Anderson replied with a chuckle.

"True, but you should always check first."

"How are you feeling, Savage?" The man returned to his original query. "Really feel, not that crap you fed Coleman."

"I feel like shit," Savage responded morosely. "The meds the doctors are using have been reduced because they don't want me to develop a dependency on the stuff. Which means most of my recovery will be spent on the very, very edge of what can be considered tolerable pain."

"I'm sorry."

"Don't be. I acted on emotion and did the very thing I tend to criticize others for doing. I made mistakes a lot of people don't usually survive and with some help from you, Anja, Terry, and Sam, I managed to live long enough to be able to learn from those."

"You would have done the same for any of us," Anderson reminded him.

"That's not the point," he stated bluntly. "I'm supposed to be the one to keep you all safe, alive, and well enough to do your jobs. I'm the one who needs to keep his head on his shoulders so everyone else can afford to get emotional."

"Like I said, you would have done the same for any one of us," his companion repeated with a small grin.

The operative shook his head. "I swear to God I've started to wish this job didn't get me beaten up so much."

"You volunteered for it, dumbass," the ex-colonel reminded him and punched him gently on his shoulder. Despite the lack of force in it, he still grunted in pain and scowled at the man.

"Yeah, I guess that's true," he admitted after a moment.

"Do you want to hear some good news?" He didn't wait for the patient to answer before he pulled his phone from his pocket and brought up a news article. "The police in Seattle are still baffled by the attack on the Devers household and more baffled by their apparent protector. Sources of an undisclosed nature shed some light on the man—one man, according to those claims—who is known as The Savage, a killer and protector for hire. The only questions that remain are who this Savage is and whether what happened at the Devers house was protection or assassination."

Savage chuckled. "You have to love tabloid journalism. That sounds like Anja's work to me."

"Yes and no," the hacker replied. "Yes, because I did plant the news about a mysterious international hitman of James Bondian proportions as a protector to the family to make sure nobody touched Banks' contract. I wasn't the one who leaked the name to the press, though. That has to be someone who looked into the contract and probably spread the name around to try to get more info on you."

"On that note," Anderson said, "I had a quick chat with friends of mine at the Pentagon. I shared some—not all—of the details of what happened regarding your leaked information, and they made sure your file was reclassified under the National Security Act of 1947. That protects the identity of soldiers acting as liaisons to American intelligence agencies, living or dead. Admittedly, the file was already leaked, so whoever already has it still does, but it will prevent anyone else from acquiring it."

"Speaking of that," Savage said. "Anja, were you able to trace the call we had after Banks died?"

"That was on a landline," Anja reminded him. "I didn't even have access to it, and I only managed to listen in because of your earbud. I've tried to get voice matches, but the copy I have is a little garbled. I can't make any promises."

"There's someone else who knows about who this client of Banks' could be," Savage said and glanced at Anderson. "That is who we're guessing she is, even if it's a little premature?"

"It's the only lead that we have," the former colonel said and shook his head dubiously.

"Who's this lead?" the hacker asked.

"Someone who's still in federal custody," Savage said. "This isn't over. You know you need me on this, right?"

"I do," Anderson replied.

"Well, I'll get right on that then." He started to push himself up from his bed, only to stop when the other man placed a firm hand on his shoulder.

"You need your rest, Savage."

"You know I can break that hand right off, right?" he asked, his eyebrow raised.

"In the condition you're in, I'd give even odds to you not being able to break a toothpick in half," his boss replied with a chuckle.

"I can get to Carlson in my sleep," he protested. "With Anja's help, of course. Minimum security prisons are a cakewalk to break out of and even easier to break into."

"All the more reason for you to give yourself time to recover," Anderson insisted. "Carlson isn't going anywhere, and Anja's already on the case. When she has something for us, I'll be the first to break you out of this hospital, got it?"

He leaned back on his bed. After all that talk about being stupid and putting his emotions ahead of his intellect, he was ready to jump into the deep end again. There had to be a special place in hell for people as stupid as he was right now.

Still, he had a lead on the person who had put his family in danger. It was almost torture to simply sit around and wait for his body to finally piece itself back together again.

"Yeah, I got it." He relaxed and took a few deep breaths, resigned to the truth.

"I need to go put fires out back in Philly," Anderson said. "Stay alive, Savage. And don't do anything stupid."

He nodded as the man headed out of the room.

It wasn't all bad, he mused. He would be released in a couple of days, and from that point forward, he could probably start working again. Like he had said, breaking into a minimum-security prison would be a cakewalk and even easier if he had Anja's technical skills on his side. There was no need to rush this. Not yet. And he had Wi-Fi in the hospital. Why would he want to leave?

CHAPTER TWENTY-EIGHT

Carlson couldn't see himself living out the rest of his life in this place.

Admittedly, he couldn't describe it as absolutely terrible. There were many resorts he'd seen advertised that had fewer amenities, for one thing. It had been a golf resort, he had heard. Considerable money had gone into developing the area around it to make it a pleasant place to play during about three-quarters of the year, with enough alternatives offered in the premises to make it appealing even during the months where golfing wasn't an option. Indoor swimming pools, tennis courts, billiard rooms, and lounges didn't even begin to sum up the whole experience.

No drinking was allowed, of course, but there was a good supply of contraband that the guards liked to turn a blind eye to in order to enjoy it themselves. He even had his own cell, his own space that he didn't have to share with anyone. While the room had two bunks in it, the prison wasn't heavily populated, and a substantial amount of money had gone into a variety of accounts in exchange for making sure he had his own space in the prison.

But it still wasn't good enough. He believed in what he had done on the outside. The world needed to be saved from itself, and thanks to the efforts of a handful of individuals, the Zoo was a treasure chest of things they could use to do exactly that.

Despite his frustrations, he still had justifiable fears about a life out in the world. Banks had assured him that the Savage problem was all but resolved but he hadn't heard from the man in almost three weeks. He hadn't heard from any other lawyers, either, which meant the client was starting to get antsy about their whole operation. Or at least, he hoped that was what it meant. She wasn't the kind of person to worry unnecessarily, which meant Savage had proved more troublesome than anticipated.

People had a bad habit of underestimating the man, and Carlson hated the fact that he was the first of what appeared to be a very long line of fools.

Banks was probably dead or in hiding right now. The client would pull back and disengage. She liked to operate from the shadows and having someone like Savage on her trail would ruin that.

Ultimately, the ex-CEO was more than happy to remain precisely where he was. The bunks were a little small and a little uncomfortable. The lack of female company was also a drawback, although he was sure he could arrange conjugal visits if things became really dire. He could still engage in most of his vices, even if he did have to buy enough for himself as well as the guards who would show up unannounced at his cell, their hands extended, waiting for a payoff. He was more than willing to oblige, but it was still a gritty, dirty business.

He didn't want to stay there for too long, but it wasn't like it was a hellish place to be.

Right now, for instance, was evidence of the brighter side. Carlson looked around the abandoned golf course. He didn't have a caddie with him, which meant he had to carry his own equipment, but that was good exercise—something he hadn't had enough of since his incarceration. It was winter, which meant it was too cold for most of the regulars to play, but Carlson didn't mind playing on his own and regarded it as a good opportunity to work on his handicap. Besides, the quiet solitude allowed him to play pretend, as if he were actually on his favorite golfing course in Florida, chatting with like-minded folks and talking big money while enjoying nature and sunshine galore.

And it was a gorgeous day. The fall made it even better, he thought. The sun shone brightly but the air was still crisp and pleasantly cool. The trees were bare of their leaves, of course, which spoiled the view a little. There had been a problem with the leaves on the course, but after enough complaints, they had brought in teams to clear the area regularly. Even then, while the autumn carpet had been a minor hassle, it wasn't enough to remove his enjoyment of the game.

He tilted his head and eyed the ball in the grass. It still lay where he'd hit it last, about fifty yards from the hole he aimed for and he acknowledged regretfully that the quality of his game was declining. The former CEO could complain that it was due to the poor quality of balls and clubs they were provided with. There was a security risk involved in giving prisoners fully weighted golf clubs, even in minimum security facilities, since they could be used as weapons against the guards. It was one of the few perks that even all his money couldn't buy, so instead of the fully weighted and perfectly balanced clubs he was used to, he had to make do with light aluminum replicas that were considerably less durable than what they would have been on the outside. The weight was off and he was left trying to compensate for that.

But it was a poor craftsman who blamed his tool. Carlson was the kind of man to adapt, no matter how bad the situation became, and that included his golf game. He primed himself, balanced, checked, and swung.

He scowled again as he watched the ball fly. It wasn't a terrible shot and actually came within striking range of the hole, but it would probably take him a couple more hits to get the ball in.

This wasn't a great game for him. He would have to talk to the warden about at least getting some secure clubs that were better quality.

Never one to give in when things didn't go his way, he set off to where his ball had landed, his bag slung over his shoulder, and whistled cheerfully. He had another conversation planned with the FBI next week, and at that point, they might even agree to move him to a secure safehouse of his own choosing. Already, he knew of a couple of places scattered across the US that were perfect for what he had in mind. They had fewer amenities but far more luxuries to be enjoyed. There was one place in Hawaii he really looked forward to trying.

He reached his ball and tried to calculate what he needed to at least get it closer to the hole when he heard footsteps crunch the dried leaves underfoot as they approached.

"I'm almost finished with my game," he said and turned, expecting to see a guard who would inevitably ask him why he played the holes farthest from the prison. He'd had to explain it a couple of times. It helped him live in his fantasy of actually being a free man again.

But it wasn't a guard. The man who approached wore what looked like camouflage. He wasn't overly tall or powerfully built, but the keen green eyes that stared at him were enough to make sure he would recognize him anywhere in the world.

"Savage," he gasped.

"What's up, doc?" the operative replied with a small smile and stepped close as he tried to raise his club to defend himself. The man mostly ignored his attempts and simply pounded his fist into the prisoner's jaw hard enough that he literally saw stars by the time he realized he was already on the ground.

"Nice to see you again, Carlson," Savage said and rubbed his knuckles. It appeared he'd hit Carlson a little too hard and wasn't wearing any punching gloves. "It's been a while. What have you been up to?"

"You can't be here," he protested, shaking his head vehemently as if that would dispel the illusion.

"Sure I can," he responded with a small grin. He

retrieved the club his quarry had dropped with a lazy movement.

"There are cameras out here," he explained and pushed himself onto his hands and knees. He shook his still woozy head in an attempt to clear it. "They'll see you and they'll come running."

"Damn, I hadn't thought of that." The twinkle in his eye belied his apparent regret and concern. "If only I had a technically gifted computer wizard working on keeping the cameras in a loop feed so the guards at the prison only see footage of the last time you came out here to golf on your own. Oh, and I wouldn't bother to scream for help, either. While sound carries out here, you know that everyone inside is busy with movie day, right? Seriously, what the fuck kind of prison has a movie theater? With actual popcorn handed out to the inmates?"

Savage had a point. The movie theater had been one of the reasons why Carlson had selected this particular facility.

The man's expression turned a little less delighted when he hefted the club again and brought it down hard on Carlson's back. The ex-CEO uttered a scream of pain. The poor quality of the clubs meant it didn't hurt as much as it could have, but damn it, the pain was still real.

His attacker scowled, tossed the ruined club away, and chose another from the golf bag. "I warned you."

"I had…nothing to do with them targeting your family." He tried hastily to justify himself. "I swear, I even tried to talk them out of it, but Banks and—"

"Banks and…who?" he asked, picking up on Carlson's

error immediately. The inmate's eyes widened when he realized what he'd done.

"See, I'm not here to kill you, Carlson." Savage dropped to his haunches and pressed the club's head to Carlson's cheek. "I know about the client. I know it's a woman, and I know she's the one behind all this crazy shit I've dealt with since I took a day job. The only thing I don't know is anything about her, and that's where you'll fill me in."

"And why would I do that?" he challenged and made a reasonable attempt to appear brave, although his racing heart contradicted it.

"Because you know who I am and what I'm capable of. I don't give a shit about you, but you know that if you don't change your situation quickly, you'll be caught in the crossfire when I finally eliminate your precious client. I'll give you the option to change your situation. You're clear to leave here and the FBI will set you up in a nice little safe house far away. Better yet, your client will be so busy with me she won't have the time to worry about you."

Carlson eyed the club in the operative's hands. He knew the man was right, but a sinking feeling still lurked in his gut when he looked into the man's icy, expressionless green eyes.

"That's not good enough," he said finally. "If I'm ruin everything I built my life around for this, you need to offer me something better."

"Well, I'm not in the most generous of moods," Savage responded coldly. "Besides, I am offering to spare your life in this deal. But name it and I'll see if I can do it."

"That's what I mean," the man stated with almost unnatural calm. "You, Anderson, and Monroe ruined everything. I've been left with nothing but bullseyes on my back, and I want an end to it. I'll tell you everything I know about the client, but I need you to kill me when I'm finished."

"Hell," the man said with a small grin. "I would do that for free. But start talking."

The ex-CEO pulled himself up to sit on the grass. "Her name is Elena Molina. She's a billionaire heiress to a huge casino fortune out of Monaco. In addition, she's worked toward saving the world using the tools pulled out of the Zoo. She's a little crazy like that. Honestly, she's a fucking psychopath who doesn't care who she hurts in the process. And that is all I know, I swear to God."

Savage stared at him for a few seconds and looked like he tried to decide if he believed him or not. A second later, though, he tilted his head and his gaze shifted skyward. Carlson realized he was talking to someone else.

"It looks like what you've said adds up, Carlson," the operative said and stood.

"Your side of the bargain," he demanded when it seemed his nemesis was about to walk away.

"Oh…right, I almost forgot." He casually drew what looked like an elongated, technologically advanced revolver from a holster under his arm. With little ceremony, he leveled the weapon at Carlson, who only had time to close his eyes before Savage pulled the trigger.

CHAPTER TWENTY-NINE

There was something about driving that met a need within him.

Of course, there were those who talked about how people should use public transport and thus save fuel resources and reduce emissions that inevitably caused all kinds of problems around the world.

Then again, the talk about how the Zoo would ultimately solve all the problems in the world could make that particular argument irrelevant. Savage didn't know who was right in the grand scheme of things.

On the bright side, with most people becoming more conscientious about saving the planet, the roads were comfortably less populated, which left more room to drive without the stress of dealing with too many other people.

And besides all that, the open road had all kinds of benefits, for him anyway. It let his mind settle while it still had something to focus on to keep it from stewing. He'd decided it was kind of like meditating while seated behind an about four-hundred-horsepower engine.

"Savage?" Anja's said through the comms. "Savage, are you there?"

No, it wasn't through the comms, he realized after a moment. It was through the speakers of the car. He had taken his earpiece out once he left the upstate facility where Carlson had been incarcerated. The man had died—which had been the original plan—but he had walked away with additional knowledge about who had really been the power behind him.

Elena Molina. It wasn't a name he'd heard before, but he didn't expect to have known it. People who operated in the kind of business she was in were the kind who liked to work in the shadows. They lurked away from the spotlight, where they could manage everything without ever being held accountable.

His next task would be to trace her and bring her into the spotlight—to find out more about her so they could move against her. Until then, of course, he needed to keep digging and find a way to let Anderson and Monroe in as well, all without telling them he had killed Carlson to get the information.

Savage had a feeling that taking on solo assassination missions would be frowned upon by both his superiors, even if it was more or less what they had hired him for. He was the Savage, after all. They wanted people to be dealt with and didn't ask too many questions about how.

Then again, they tended to be the ones who decided who would actually be dealt with, not him. He was merely the blunt instrument in their hands. People didn't like it when their weapons worked autonomously without their masters' minds to guide them.

But it was something that needed to be done. Carlson hadn't been the kind of man who would simply sit around and watch everything he had forged in his life to be whittled away by the likes of Monroe and Anderson. He would sit and bide his time, wait for his opportunity, and retaliate. The Pegasus leaders would have assumed that the man was no longer a threat due to being in prison and moved on to bigger and better things. They would ignore the problem he presented until it became a real issue again.

His purpose, on the other hand, was to push ahead to that time and solve the problem in advance while he also obtained intelligence on the people who had put his family in danger. Whether his bosses disapproved or not was their problem in his opinion.

Still, it was best if they didn't know about it.

Well, maybe the word would spread that Carlson was dead. Or maybe not—the FBI didn't exactly like to advertise that their star witnesses were killed in custody.

"Goddamnit, I know you can hear me, Savage," Anja all but yelled through the speakers. "The traffic cameras picked you up miles back and I have a connection to your car's Wi-Fi. Don't think you can stay away from me."

He shook his head. This was time for himself, and while he was more than willing to exchange barbs with the hacker most other days, he needed space right now. Honestly, she needed to respect that.

"Savage, you know that you're driving one of those new-fangled smart cars, right?" she asked, still through the speakers. "The kind that has most of its engineering connected to its electronics, which means I can pull you over and make sure that Triple-A comes to take the car away. I don't want to have to do that, but I will. This is important and I need to talk to you. So stop sulking and put your earbud in."

Savage rolled his eyes and finally retrieved the earpiece from where he'd tossed it onto the passenger seat and shoved it in his ear.

"I wasn't sulking," he protested, his tone a little curt. "I was only…uh, meditating."

"While you were driving?" she asked and her tone suggested disbelief.

"Yes, while driving," he grumbled. "Well, less meditating and more pondering the crazy shit my life has been lately. And yeah, I was also trying to think about how we can fill Anderson and Monroe in on what we learned from Carlson without spilling the beans about us…well, killing him dead."

"I can understand that," Anja said. "That is something of a pickle, as you Americans say."

"You say that like you don't speak perfect English without so much as a hint of an accent." He chuckled.

"Be that as it may, you are right that we might want to fill them in on this Molina person," the Russian said. "I've looked around, and if I'm honest, there's really not much to find out in the open. We'll need to dig to find her, and we won't be able to do that in secret. You'll need them to sanction you."

"Besides, it seems like she's the source of all the problems we've faced over the past couple of months," he added. "It only makes sense to make sure this Molina character isn't still out there to cause more trouble over the next few months. If Carlson and Banks were the types of people she had working for her before, who knows who she'll send to target us next?"

"Yes," she agreed. "However, I'm afraid that'll have to be a problem for another time."

"What do you mean?"

"Well, not to be the proverbial wet blanket, but there is a reason I called while you're driving from upstate New York," she continued. "It seems like Anderson and Monroe have already found something for you to do, and while I managed to cover for you to head to Carlson's prison, I told them I didn't know where you were and would try to contact you."

"I appreciate that." Savage leaned back in the seat. "I doubt you'll let me live that down, though. You don't seem the type to not dangle something that someone owes you over their head for as long as you can."

"You know me so well, Savage." She laughed smugly. "And yes, I will remind you about this time that I covered for you when no one else would. And believe me, it will be for a while. But for the moment, they have something for you to do. While I did tell them you are out of reach and I'll keep trying to pick you up, the longer it takes, the more time there is for them to doubt my abilities."

"We can't have that," he responded quickly without even a trace of sarcasm. Anja was, by a massive margin, the most valuable member of their little team and it would be an absolute disaster for everyone if people began to doubt her.

Not that he would ever admit it openly, of course. She was the best, and she knew it. There really was no need to inflate her ego any more than it was already.

"What do they want me to do?" he asked after a moment

of silence, eased back in his seat, and pressed the accelerator.

"Well, see...I don't know that yet," she responded and he had the distinct impression that she hated to admit it.

"What? You don't know? And here I was thinking you had all the angles in the world."

"Well, maybe I've been so busy covering for you that I haven't had the time to dig into what they wanted you to do," she snarked acerbically.

It was good-natured ribbing between friends, of course, and he didn't mind letting her hold onto that. "Well, that is a good point. What did they want you to tell me if they didn't want me to know what it was I actually have to do for them?"

"They sent me the address to an airstrip where there will be a plane waiting to ship you to your mission," Anja explained. "Which tells me that whatever it is they want you to do, it's something far, far away—far enough that you won't need to drive back."

"Where is the airstrip?" Savage asked.

"I'm already putting it into your GPS. But it is outside Philly, so I think you'll have to step on it if you don't want to be late."

"When are they expecting me?"

"Well, I did say I didn't know where you were," the hacker reminded him. "So Monroe said that the plane will be on standby to pick you up. However, the longer you take, the longer it'll cost her, which means she'll definitely be pissed right the fuck off if you take your time."

"So, the message is...step on it and get to Philly as quickly as possible. Got it." He was already over the speed limit, but the lack of speed traps and police patrols in the area meant he could probably go a little faster.

"Well, yes, obviously," Anja confirmed. "But remember, not Philly itself. The airstrip is just outside."

"Right, it's already in my GPS," he pointed out. "I'll simply follow that."

"Try not to kill anyone, Jer. And especially not yourself. I would hate to have to explain that to our bosses."

Savage nodded, not entirely convinced that she couldn't see him. It was difficult to imagine that after all the crazy, life-threatening shit he'd been through, he might realistically go out in a car crash. How fucking mundane would that be?

He grasped the wheel a little tighter and eased his foot slowly down on the accelerator. It was a powerful car he'd selected from the rental agency, even if it didn't look it. Many of the rental places liked to put powerful engines in simple-looking sedans to be used for official business—the kind that might require people to move someplace in a hurry.

Three hours was a record time to reach his destination and apparently, Anja had already advised Monroe of his travel time, if not where he was coming from. As he pulled up to the airstrip, the plane was already prepared for departure, which meant he would only have to wait a couple of minutes before he could board and they would take off.

The crew was as polite as he had come to expect from these people, although they did seem a little annoyed at having to file another flight plan to correspond with their new departure time.

They were in a hurry as Monroe had probably stated that they wouldn't be paid to dawdle, and in under half an hour, they were in the air at cruising altitude.

Once they were airborne, the TV in the cabin came on and pulled his attention to the screen, from which Monroe looked at him.

"So nice of you to join us, Savage," she said but didn't sound particularly pleased. "I hope I haven't taken you away from anything too important?"

He narrowed his eyes and wondered if she somehow knew what he'd been up to. Logic told him the chances of that were minimal, but she probably had her suspicions that he'd headed off to kill someone on his own. She merely didn't know who.

That, or he was being paranoid.

"I had things that I needed to take care of," he said finally. "Personal business and nothing really important, merely far away. How about you?"

"I'd say I'm further away than you are," she replied with a soft chuckle. "But that's not the point right now."

"I assume the point is that you have something you want done." He changed the subject as smoothly as he could. "Which is why we're currently in the air, flying somewhere I know nothing about, although the crew does."

"You're heading out to Portland, Oregon, for starters," she said, picked her phone up, and studied what looked like notes. "The cliff note version is that we have specialists traveling around the country, working with local authorities and companies to look into most of the labs recently opened around the country. Since we still have so much equipment missing after Carlson's antics, many of the places are opening using stolen merchandise. Some might have bought them cheaply off the market, but others might have obtained it directly from Carlson's people."

"This is the cliff note version?" he asked and toyed with his seat.

"Yes," Monroe replied, her expression deadpan. "Now, the situation in most cases is that people head in—usually code officials and the like—and get pictures and details on the items inside. This makes them a matter of public record, which allows us to have a look. Unfortunately, in this lab in Portland, we picked up the specs of not one but three of our stolen devices. Any attempts to get them to turn the devices over to us legally have been rebutted, and they've quietly put their money into improving internal security to prevent anyone from gathering further evidence. They're dead set on keeping what they stole."

"Let me guess," Savage stated calmly. "You want me to get in and get your shit out."

"Are you crazy?" she asked and laughed. "The collective weight of all three devices is over fifteen tons. No, we fully intend to recover the devices in the legal way. Of course, the evidence need not be collected legally."

"There isn't a problem with the fruit of the poisonous tree and all that?" He was genuinely curious.

"That's where you come in, technically," she clarified. "If you're in there legally—even if infiltrating—any data you collect can't be proven to be acquired illegally. They did allow inspectors in there recently, and therefore, with a little help from Anja, it can be used."

It was all too complicated for him to care about. Then

again, a company-run lab would want to avoid having their company dragged into a long, expensive, and potentially damaging litigation. They were clearly up to playing dirty when they acquired the devices in question, and the last thing they would want was to have people digging into their businesses.

From that perspective, it made sense.

"You said you have specialists in the area, working the case," Savage said. "Would I be able to meet with them and look at their notes?"

"Of course," Monroe said. "And I have good news on that front, actually. It's someone you have worked with before."

He narrowed his eyes and had a bad feeling about where this was going.

"Jessica?" he asked.

"Yes," she replied. "How did you know?"

"I don't know that many of your specialists," he said and folded his arms.

"Will that be a problem?" she asked. "I thought you two were on good terms."

"We...well, it's complicated," he mumbled. "We're exes, more or less, but it shouldn't be a problem. We're both professionals and won't let personal feelings get in the way of the job."

"I'm very glad to hear it," Monroe said. "I need to head off. Have a nice flight, Savage."

CHAPTER THIRTY

Well, Jessica was a professional anyway. Even in his first mission when he'd dragged her into his shadowy world of corporate backstabbing, she had quickly adjusted to the situation. After a short time spent freaking out about professional assassins trying to kill her—as anyone would—she had adapted quickly and even helped him when he needed extra bodies on the job.

Savage for his part, had bad memories about how professional he really was when she was involved. Their last encounter had been at a meeting he felt he had stuttered his way through and looked like a complete dumbass. He was sure it wasn't as bad as he felt it was, but it felt seriously damn bad. There were a few social situations he was good at and others where he wasn't quite so good.

In a less preoccupied moment, he might have stopped to consider the thought that there was probably something telling about the fact that the social situations he was comfortable with involved mostly people whom he didn't know very well, if at all.

But now was not the time for introspection. He needed to get his game face on and see if it held through this meeting with Jessica, who was already waiting for him in town when his plane touched down in a small private Portland airport. Anja had told him that they would meet for coffee at a shop inside the city. The situation being what it was—around Jessica this time, not him—there apparently did need to be some anonymity regarding where they met.

A car was waiting for him at the airstrip too. Monroe really wanted this mission done, no matter the cost. He could understand why she needed it. People constantly looked to her for guidance. Stock sales were coming up, and they needed to present a show of strength to power through the repairs to all the damage Carlson's arrest and imprisonment—and inevitably, his death throes—had caused to Pegasus. Strong leadership would increase both the prices and the trust her shareholders had in her.

Which meant she would give him any resources she could get her hands on as long as he accomplished the mission as quickly as possible.

He slid into the electric BMW that waited for him and drove the annoyingly quiet vehicle into the city past what he supposed counted as a beautiful forest on the way in. Oregon was usually annoyingly cloudy at this time of year, but they apparently had a few rather sunny days ahead of them.

He wasn't a stranger to the city, yet he still needed the help from the GPS Anja had already programmed to find his way to the coffee shop where Jessica was supposed to wait. Savage wasn't sure if she had chosen it for any particular reason, but he still paused and waited in his car for a few minutes to make sure there weren't any signs that she was being surveilled. Gone were the times when someone in a van with binoculars and a parabolic mic would hang around, but he had to make sure.

Not only that, but he also needed to trust that Anja would make sure no one was watching them in the ways more traditional to the age of information.

"Do you have anything on your radar, Anja?" he asked. "And before you say it, yes, I know that you're not actually using a radar. It's merely an expression."

"I wasn't going to bitch about that," she lied and chuckled sheepishly. "But I don't see any taps on any of the nearby cameras that you should worry about. Well, none more than the usual. NSA, FBI, and their other alphabet friends have a couple of taps in the area, but I don't see anything directed at you or Jessica."

"Fantastic." He stepped out of the vehicle and locked it before he strode into the coffee shop.

There were enough people inside that made two people meeting for something to drink in the early afternoon inconspicuous. He scanned the room quickly while he ordered something to drink—something that would last them a while since he wanted to be around for as long as was necessary without attracting attention.

Jessica sat in the rear of the shop as if she tried to not be seen by anyone who walked in. He scowled and collected his drink. She looked around when she heard his name called. There obviously weren't too many people called Jeremiah walking around Portland these days, he assumed.

He smiled and placed a hand on her shoulder for a

moment before he took his place across from her in the booth she'd chosen.

"For future reference, you might find it's better to position yourself in a position that has a better view of the whole shop and easy access to a couple of available exits," Savage said and kept his voice low and pleasant.

"I'm sorry," she replied and toyed nervously with her long brown locks. "I'm not used to being in this kind of situation. Anja told me there are bugs in my hotel room, so I'm trying to be as paranoid as possible."

"I get that," he replied and sipped his overly sweet coffee. "And your instincts are right. But the chances are that if they come into the coffee shop, they already know you're here anyway so the priority becomes identifying threats and escaping them as quickly as possible. It's merely some constructive criticism is all."

She nodded and now tapped nervous fingers on her mug of tea. "I appreciate it. And it's nice to see you again, Jer."

"You too, Jes," he replied with a small smile. "It's not actually been that long since we last saw each other, though."

"So," she said after a slow sip of her beverage. "In the effort to avoid any awkwardness, shall we get into the meat of what you're here for?"

"I don't know what awkwardness you're talking about, but I'm ready to move on if you are," he said with a grin.

Jessica chuckled and rolled her eyes playfully. "Well, I'm glad there's no awkwardness. Anyway, shall we talk about the lab?"

He nodded, and she withdrew a laptop from her bag

and showed him what she had worked on since she had left Philadelphia. He assumed, anyway, as he honestly had no idea how much work she had done in the weeks it had taken him to recover from his little song and dance with Banks.

Savage studied the pictures first. The facility was smaller than the labs he was usually involved in raiding, and he noted that there were actually buildings surrounding the lab.

"It doesn't look like they put any effort into isolating it," he said and narrowed his eyes. "Is that safe? Legal, even? Aren't there codes in place to keep precisely that from happening?"

"Well, they're pushing new codes through the regional lawmakers' offices that will make sure any labs handling stuff from the Zoo need to maintain certain standards," she replied. "Believe me, I asked the same question. Either way, until they come through sometime in the next decade, it's perfectly legal as long as they stick to the codes already in place. It's not in the city proper, where the codes are stricter, so they're barely straddling the line of legality to keep themselves in business, which is why there are inspectors going in and out of there every other week. And they were happy to show that they complied with the local regulations until the pictures of the stolen items came out. Since the inspections are actually voluntary on the part of the lab, they closed the place off."

"Who thought of that?" It seemed to defeat the purpose of having inspectors in the first place.

"Probably lawmakers talking to lobbyists who work for the companies that don't want to be inspected regularly," she said. "But that's neither here nor there. The point is that as soon as they heard that we had identified them and the items, they sealed their facility to unannounced visitors and began to quietly upgrade their security to keep anyone from trying to do precisely what you want to do."

"Fun times," Savage said and glowered suspiciously at his coffee. He'd ordered something off the overhead menu and now regretted it. It honestly was way too sweet for his tastes. He would need to talk to the barista.

Either that or simply sit and sip it gingerly like most people did and never come back here again.

"Anyway, Courtney thinks that since they've gone through that much effort to keep their stolen items, they are probably leftovers from what Carlson tried to do when he was still in charge of the resistance against the new leadership. Either way, she wants you to get in, get a few pictures—the kind you would only get if you were working there—and get out before anyone notices you're in there."

"I understand what I need to do," he responded and recalled his chat with Monroe on the plane. "I have a hard time deciding how I'll get in, though, if they're upgrading their security."

"Oh, that's actually easier than anticipated." She pulled up schematics that could not have been acquired legally. "It seems like all the money they invested recently has gone into electronic security measures, working from the inside out. They're still hiring from an outside security company to get the people who are actually there in person."

"And that's where I come in," Anja interjected over their earpieces. "I've worked on getting you hired by the company in question to let you step into the lab as a security guard. It's a little more complicated than I thought it would be. I'll keep you guys updated on my progress."

"I appreciate it, Anja," Jessica said, her head tilted although she did manage to resist the urge to press her finger to her ear to hear the Russian a little better. "Anyway the outside security company does seem to be a weak point in their defenses. It's only a matter of time until they have money to upgrade that too, so we need to act on it now."

"Well, that explains the time constraint," he noted.

"Yes." She chuckled. "But anyway, that is our way in."

"It looks like they've used smaller and smaller facilities to keep us off their scent," the hacker added and sounded unhappy about the development. "These people are really determined to maintain their research. We no sooner close one place and another one appears in a couple of days. It's like they want something in particular and won't let anyone else stop them before they have whatever it is."

"How do you know about that?" he asked.

"It's mostly only assumptions based on available evidence," she said. "There's plenty of evidence, though."

"Don't worry, Anja," he said softly, finished his coffee, and winced. "Your assumptions have brought us through enough hard times to earn our trust."

"I appreciate that, Jer," she said but sounded a little uncomfortable with the positive reinforcement. "Anyway, again, I'll let you know when I make any progress on the job front."

"You know how badly I need this job," he said with a chuckle. "I'm done with my coffee, and your tea is cold. Do you want to take a walk outside?"

"We're a couple of weeks away from winter starting in

earnest," Jessica pointed out. "It's forty degrees out."

"A nice, brisk walk will be good for us," he said with a nod. "Besides, it's always good to stay on the move when people are trying to keep tabs on you. If you simply stay in one location, they can easily zero in on you. Change what you do and keep them guessing."

"You merely want to get out of here, don't you?" she asked.

Savage shrugged. "Honestly? I can't say I'm a fan of the environment. But I do like staying on the move. And taking brisk walks."

"Fine," she agreed reluctantly. "But I'll warn you right now that I'm as cold-blooded as fuck and we'll duck into another coffee shop before too long."

"I'm okay with that," he said. "But no more...caramel lattes. I'll go with black and maybe a little Irish. That stuff is still coating the inside of mouth."

"You obviously don't have a sweet tooth," Anja said as they shrugged into their coats. "Unlike me, of course. I kind of need the sugar to keep me going, as well as the caffeine. Nothing is better than combining the two."

"I'll bet your heart disagrees," he grumbled and stepped out into the chilly afternoon.

"My heart is what wants all the sugar," she retorted.

"No, I mean your literal heart. Research indicates that sugar-filled beverages cause high blood pressure, among other things."

"Psh, don't sully my love with facts." She laughed.

Jessica shook her head. "I've missed listening in on you two bantering."

He smiled. "I guess we have missed having you around

too. I still remember when it was only the three of us, running around the city and trying to make it work."

"It feels like a long time ago," she said. "But yes, I do miss it, I guess. Maybe not the shooting and the ducking and trying not to die but being in the middle of it with the two of you? Definitely."

"Well, yeah, I guess no one misses being target practice," he concurred. "Even if you do shoot back. But then you look back at the whole thing a couple of days later and all you remember is the adrenaline and you kind of want it again."

"Well, I guess that is why you wanted to keep doing this job of yours," she pointed out with a slight edge to her voice. "At the expense of being with your family. At the expense of being with someone who you care about."

Savage looked at her out of the corner of his eye. "It sounds like you have something you want to say."

She shrugged. "Nothing that hasn't already been said. We wanted to be together and then we didn't. Something drew us apart long before I decided to start working for Courtney full time. You would never stop being this...savage you so desperately need to be."

"It's not that I want to be this," he protested. "It's more along the lines of...not really knowing what else I can be. It's been a part of my identity for so long that I don't know what else I can be. I can't even remember what I might have wanted before I was Savage or before I was even in the army and the government decided to invest a couple of million dollars to turn me into the kind of killer they needed me to be."

Jessica turned to face him and place her hand on his

shoulder. "I'm sorry, I never realized."

He shook his head. "There's no need to apologize. It's only...like, even when they decided I needed to die to, I spent weeks in physical therapy thinking about what I could do with my life. I had a fresh start and a healthy bank balance. What would I choose to be? An investment banker? Would I buy my own bar? Paint?"

"In fairness, I'm reasonably sure you would have been an awful painter, anyway," Anja pointed out.

"I'm a killer," he said and decided to simply state his point. "There is no way to change that and no way to avoid it. Doing something else would simply deny my true nature. I could join a security company, but that would only be a tamer version of what I did before. This way, I at least know I'm working with someone who cares about the folks in the field. I trust Anderson. I trust Monroe—to an extent, anyway. They seem like they have good intentions. If it means I have to be a killer to save lives...well, it's a sacrifice I told myself that I would make anyway. I might as well stick to it."

Jessica nodded and squeezed his shoulder. "Well, as explanations go, I guess that's a damn good one. I'm sorry I pushed you into it, though."

He smiled and rested his hand over hers. "It's okay. I guess I needed to say it loud and get it out there."

"Well, now that all the mushy stuff is over with," Anja interjected as the silence threatened to draw on, "I guess we can get started on breaking into the lab, right?"

"I guess," the other woman agreed. "Do you have any updates?"

"As a matter of fact, I do." The hacker sounded smug.

CHAPTER THIRTY-ONE

"Are you sure that this is a good idea?" Savage asked.

"Well, after you spilled your purse for Jessica's benefit, I guessed that you needed a way out, so... I suppose that depends on your definition of a good idea," Anja replied.

He leaned back in his seat and stared through the windshield of his car. "Well, while I appreciate you getting me out of that conversation without me having to get more involved with my feelings and spilling them, I'd still like to think that I'm not heading into a trap."

"I know I like to rib you about it and we all have fun with it," she said, her voice a little softer than usual. "But do you really think that getting in touch with how you feel about shit is that terrible?"

"If I wanted to be psychoanalyzed, I'd find a professional who would hopefully be able to point me on a decent course," he said. "Getting it out there is beneficial, I suppose, but I'm not here to impress people with my emotional depth. I'm here because we need to retrieve shit that was stolen from Pegasus."

"Right. Well, all the emotional discussion aside, I still think it's a very good plan. Jessica did a ton of research into the facility, but since you'll be the one who heads into the damn place, it's probably a good idea for you to get a feel for it yourself before you do so."

"And how is it going on that front?" he asked.

"I'm still working on it," she answered quickly. "But get ready, would you?"

He sighed and donned the pair of non-prescription glasses he'd purchased from the dollar store. For this visit, he was dressed in a cheap suit, the kind people wore for work when their job wasn't managing a multi-billion dollar company—the kind that lasted for a long time and could be quickly and cheaply replaced. His hair matched the suit—split down the middle and swished back the way someone would if they were in a hurry to leave the house.

After yet another hasty look in the mirror, he scowled. He looked like the kind of guy who had a nine-to-five job he hated to support a wife he'd never intended to marry, except that they'd been teenagers and not informed on proper sex ed. She'd gotten pregnant, and they were both incredibly bitter about being forced together.

"I don't like this guy," Savage said and stared at his reflection. Getting into character would certainly be interesting.

"Which guy?"

"Me," Savage replied. "It turns out I'm a bitter nine-to-fiver who hates his life. I'm seriously not sure what he does to cope. Either he drinks or has a mistress his wife knows about but pretends not to. What do you think?"

"I think you're taking this a little too seriously," Anja said, her tone tinged with humor.

"When creating a legend, the small details are important," he explained as he stepped out of the car and adjusted his tie. "Getting into character requires you to adjust to being the person you look at in the mirror."

"Hey, you don't need to convince me. I'm not the one walking up to the guards at the end of the workday," she reminded him. "I merely wonder why you need to think about what your character's vices are."

"Again, the small things," he said. "I think about what kinds of questions I might be asked in there, consider them, and build back from there. These guys might ask me about a wife and kids. I say yes and roll my eyes and let my shoulders sag wearily and I'll bet you a solid seventy-five percent of those guys will be able to relate on at least some level. And believe me, they'll be able to tell when someone's faking it."

"Huh." She grunted. "I hadn't thought of that."

Savage shrugged and adjusted the glasses again. "It's only something to think about when you're out here, talking to the people. You can see it when they don't fully buy what you're selling, and you learn to change your pitch."

He cleared his throat, brought his voice up an octave, and let a nasal quality slip in. As he approached the booth where a couple of security men waited for him, he tapped his ear lightly.

"No... What's wrong with the wallpaper we have in

there now?" he said and sounded like he was about to lose it. "Yes, I did like the damn coloring, I simply don't understand why... Look, can we talk about this when I get home? I need to get to work... No, don't tell the contractor anything until I get there."

He tapped the earpiece he wore again lightly to end the "call" before he turned his attention to the men who watched him closely.

"Hey," he said and withdrew the badge Anja had delivered to him not twenty minutes before. "Chris Podolski, Health and Safety. I'm here to have a chat with your boss—a Dr. Gains?" He paused before he said the name to check a notebook like he'd added a list of names he needed to check off his list for the day. The tired, bored tone of voice completed the sense of an onerous workload.

"I'll check with him. Wait a moment," one of the guards said, took the badge, and headed to a nearby phone, likely to call and see why a Health and Safety inspector tried to gain entry.

The other, presumably rather bored, rolled his chair to the window of the booth.

"Is there a problem at home?" the man asked.

"You don't know the half of it," he replied and shook his head. "I've got to finish with this interview here and head home to have my ear yelled off because my wife doesn't like the wallpaper in the study. My study."

The guard laughed. "It sounds like you have a firecracker on your hands."

"I used to," he said with a sigh. "But I don't want to bother you guys while you're on the job, especially not with my family problems."

"Hey, man, don't worry about it," he said cheerfully. "I've been divorced for three years now, and I can tell you that I've never been happier. Seriously. Having someone tell you constantly how to live your life is a quick way to serious problems with the bottle if you know what I'm saying."

"I hear you. I don't know what to do. It's not like we were ever 'in love'"—he added the air quotes for effect—"but there was a time when she let me do my thing and I let her do hers. Long, long ago."

"Here's my advice," the guard said as his comrade hung up. "Get out of it as quickly as you can. The longer you stick around, the more likely it'll be that she finds someone and walks away with all your money. If you move first, she'll be surprised and less able to find a good lawyer to fuck you over."

Savage nodded. "I guess that makes sense. I don't think we're quite there yet, though."

"Believe me, you'll get there soon," he said as his partner returned.

"I'm sorry, but it looks like Dr. Gains is gone for the day," the other guard said. "You can always schedule an appointment with his secretary, though."

"I've tried for the past three weeks with no luck," Savage replied and shook his head regretfully. "I honestly hoped to catch him here since I think he's avoiding me. You know the deal—everyone thinks the government's out to get them, and they start playing hard to get. In reality, there are only a couple of forms I need his signature on, and all the troubles that have circled this facility can finally go the way of the dodo bird. My boss has been riding my ass to get this case closed so everyone can go home."

"I bet that's all the riding you'll get, though, so maybe you should stop complaining," the first guard said and laughed. "Hey, Jeff, are you married?"

The second guard looked up from where he flipped through some paperwork. "Nah, I'm not married yet. I have a girlfriend, though, who I love very much, so watch what you have to say, Harry."

Jeff and Harry. Savage made a note to remember their names and faces.

"Well, I didn't plan to say anything bad about the love of your life, Jeff." Harry chuckled and rolled his chair to see what his friend was looking at. Savage took the moment where he was unattended to scan the booth they were in. It contained two desks and was fairly small and cramped, definitely on a budget. Most of their cameras were on what looked like a closed-circuit network and fed into the two screens on the desk closest to him.

The two turned back to face him and he settled into his previous position.

"Look, I'm sorry we can't help you, man." Jeff handed his badge back. "The people who run this place aren't exactly open about their schedules with the security staff, so we either know they're here, or we don't. If you like, I can keep your name and number and when the good doctor decides to come to do his job, we'll let you know."

"Are you sure you can do that?" he asked. "I don't want to get you guys in trouble. And again, this really isn't that important. It's only some paperwork for him to sign, is all."

"Hey, man, we're all doing our jobs here," Harry said

with a chuckle. "It's not like you're any kind of a security threat, so if there's anything we can do to make sure our little lab here keeps running, I don't see why not. He'll probably be in tomorrow."

"I'll have to work a couple of other cases tomorrow," he said thoughtfully so they wouldn't think him too eager to jump at their offer. "I don't know... I can leave you my name and number and you can pass it along to his secretary. Maybe then he'll understand that there's nothing to be worried about from us."

"That sounds good to me," Jeff agreed. "I'll do that."

"Thanks for your time, gentlemen," Savage said with the tip of an imaginary cap. "You wouldn't believe how many people in your position would make my life difficult simply because they can. I really appreciate it."

"Hey, us guys have to stick together, am I right?" Harry said and turned to look at his comrade for support.

Jeff nodded but only offered a noncommittal grunt.

Savage laughed and patted the man's shoulder through the window of the booth. "Don't worry, kid. You'll know what I'm talking about before too long."

"What we're talking about," Harry added and patted his comrade on the other shoulder. "Sticking it out against the crazy bitches is what we do around here."

"If you say so," Jeff said. He clearly didn't want to be involved in the conversation but didn't want to be ostracized from it either.

"Anyway, I'll leave you guys to finish your shift." He looked from one man to the other before he raised his hand in farewell and walked casually back to where he'd parked his car.

"How the fuck did you do that?" Anja asked when he stepped into the vehicle. "I don't think I could even get those guys to talk about their sports teams, much less get them to talk about their personal lives."

"I don't know," he said as he closed the door and assumed his natural voice tone. "You could probably distract enough to get the job done if you were willing to dress the part. I'm not saying that you need to dress like a hooker, mind, but even having something a little too low on the neckline would be enough for them to want to keep talking to you. It's not great on dignity, I know."

"Well, I don't think I have the body to pull that off anyway," she grumbled.

"In this case, it was mostly to keep them talking," he explained. "I saw a little interest from one of the guards, if not the other, and I pushed myself into that little crack. They're friends—or are at least on good terms with each other—so they drag each other into the conversation and I have an opening with both of them."

"You didn't do much with that opening though," she commented as he started the car and pulled away.

"I did enough," he countered. "First of all, I couldn't press them for more information or they would sour on me. They knew what I was there for and they tried to help because they felt generous. It turned into a conversation, which gave me time to look at their security system. They have a small example of it in the booth to keep the team outside updated in case they need to lock the building down."

"So, what do you think about these guys?" she asked.

"The security guards themselves? They aren't exactly

the best that money can buy. Professionalism is down the toilet since they did actually try to talk to me instead of keeping a reserved silence. I'd say rent-a-cops who aren't being rented for much."

"Do you think they'll recognize you when you show up later?" Anja wondered.

"It's unlikely," Savage said. "Guys in their position tend to remember distinctions rather than facial features. They'll remember the cheap suit, the glasses, the hair, and the high voice. When someone shows up with none of the above, they will think it's a completely different person."

"You say that with the kind of confidence I don't think you should have."

"Okay, yes, there is a possibility that they might be able to recognize me," he conceded. "But it's not like we have any other options here. We go in tonight, which means I need to play this as safe as I can but still accomplish it in under twenty-four hours."

"Fair enough," Anja said as he pulled the car into a garage nearby.

He paid the hourly rate, found a space near the back, and took a moment once he was parked to remove the glasses and ruffle his hair to its natural state before he removed the suit.

In minutes, most of what anyone would recognize him by had been shoved in a black garbage bag which he carried away from the stolen car he'd used. Following the hacker's instructions, he went down the steps that weren't covered by cameras into a back exit, where Jessica waited for him.

The car was already reported as stolen, probably, and

garages like these tended to give the records on their cars to the cops when asked. It wouldn't be long until they found the vehicle again, with nothing much changed in the car itself other than a full tank of gas.

"What about the rest of their security?" Anja asked as he stepped into the other car.

"There are improvements," he said. "But from the cameras, I can tell they're still working on it. I noticed a fair number of blind spots and overlaps here and there. More importantly, I couldn't see any coverage on the big boss man's office. I'd say that's where we'll be able to get the data we need without being seen."

"That sounds like a plan," Jessica agreed.

CHAPTER THIRTY-TWO

"So, this can't be easy, huh?" Anja asked.

Savage looked up at the rearview mirror of his car. He'd chosen to obtain this one legally since having a vehicle he drove reported stolen would end the mission before it started. For now, things were simple and under control. They wouldn't have to look at the more difficult aspects of the mission until he was inside and actually had a better view of what was happening and what could be done.

All that they needed to focus on was getting him in without incident.

"What can't be easy?" he asked and scrutinized the mostly deserted streets.

It was past ten in the evening, and while there was still activity this late in the world, people mostly headed home for the night since it was a regular workday the next day.

"You know...spending time with and talking to your ex," she said. He guessed that she'd clearly noted that he wasn't doing much other than driving and wanted to strike up a conversation.

He had missed her. "Well, considering that we're not technically exes, it's not too bad."

"Don't bullshit me, Jer," she grumbled.

"No bullshit," he assured her. "Everything we could have said or done was said or done. It's time for both of us to move on."

"Would you feel that way if she was already seeing someone else?"

"That sounds like you trying to trap me," he retorted. "Like you're trying to get me to jump on that with a 'what, who is she seeing' and show that I care."

"Psh, people do that?" the hacker said weakly.

"Sadly, they do," he confirmed. "For the record, if she was seeing someone, I would think that was great. She deserves all kinds of happiness, even if I couldn't deliver on it."

"You know that she's not plugged into this conversation, right?" Anja asked.

"Oh." He grunted, unaffected even though he hadn't realized—although it made sense. "Well, the sentiment still stands. I don't have any right to be jealous in any way."

"Sure, it does," she said, her chuckle low in the background. "Well, anyway, everything's set up. You have the badge for the security company and the uniform. You'll drive in the same way you approached when you had that chat with the guard booth. If the gents in there recognize you, get ready to run. Just in case you want me to change the subject away from your ex."

"They won't recognize me," he insisted with more confidence than he actually felt.

The real truth was that he really didn't like heading into a mission like this with so little prep time.

Savage scowled suddenly. "Wait...come on, she's not my ex."

"You keep saying that," the hacker replied. "But I simply don't believe you. You need to put more feeling into it."

He narrowed his eyes. "She joined the chat, didn't she?"

"How did you know?" Jessica asked.

"Anja seemed a little too insistent." He growled his annoyance, then thrust it aside. "Are we all clear on your side of things?"

"I have everything set up for them to think I'm still in my room," she assured him. "In the meantime, the computers are ready for the transfer of data. All we need now is data to transfer."

"And that's where I come in," Savage stated as he approached the lab in question.

"Most definitely," she agreed.

The facility didn't look much different at night than it did during the day. It wasn't like he expected it to since most of the afternoon and evening had been spent studying as much of the schematics as possible and committing them to memory. Some dissonance was expected since putting what was on paper to reality always came with that.

Maybe he was merely becoming better and better at this job.

"Okay, the moment of truth," Anja said through his earpiece.

He knew what she was talking about and leaned back a little in his seat when he pulled up at the booth.

Fortunately, it appeared that all their fears were for naught. The two men who manned the booth were not the guards he had encountered previously. These were a couple of overweight old-timers, from the looks of it and had the look of former law enforcement, either state or local police. He assumed that they probably needed the work to supplement their retirement income.

Savage retrieved the new ID card Anja had obtained directly from the office of the security company for him and handed it over to the man.

"You work for ICU Sec?" the older man asked and narrowed his eyes.

"Yes, sir. I'm a recent addition to the team," he explained calmly. "They said that Perkins was taking time off so I needed to cover for his shift."

"Military man, are you?" the guard asked and leaned over the edge of the booth to try to match the picture to the face.

"Yes, sir. Three tours with the Corps."

"Yeah, well, your service is appreciated," he grumbled but sounded less than enthusiastic about it. "Head down into the garage. There's a locker room to the right. It's clearly marked. That's where we all get changed for the shift."

"I appreciate it," he said politely and took his badge.

He parked in the first underground parking garage where, as the old man had said, the locker room was clearly marked. Quickly, he changed into the black-and-blue uniform he'd been given before he moved to the first floor where his shift team already waited for him.

"Well, it may not be the usual kind of nine-to-five job, but hey, in this economy, you have to take what you can get, right?" Anja asked through his earpiece. "Even if it is the graveyard shift."

Savage didn't answer. He couldn't since most of his shift-mates would think he was weird for talking to himself. Of course, Anja knew that. It simply made it fun for her.

"Well, boys." The shift leader of the group of five called them into the common work area. "It looks like we have a new face joining us since Perkins has apparently taken time off, the lucky bastard. Anyway, introduce yourself, fresh meat."

Fresh meat? Could the guys not have come up with something a little more creative than that? Then again, he reminded himself, they were on the graveyard shift for a reason.

"Lawrence Palmer," he said and introduced himself by the name on his ID card. "It's my first day with ICU Sec and they said they needed extra bodies here."

"Palmer, nice to have you with us," the man replied. "I'm Matt Guy, these are Hisako, Brown, and Cutter. I'll be honest, we usually only have four guys here, even though the recommendation is six, so it's nice to have someone extra to work with us. Brown will show you the ropes. There really isn't that much to do. Two guys will hold the fort down in the booth, but that's for me and the vets. The rest of you need to scan the grounds and check all the doors and the building, so it means you three have to stay on your feet for most of the night. This place ain't that big, but for three guys patrolling the whole area, it damn well feels big."

Savage nodded. He was the new guy, so most of the work would be dropped on his shoulders. He didn't much mind that, however. If this were his real job, he would want to work his way to sitting down for a living. But he needed to be unsupervised in order to get to the back office of the man in charge of running the facility to access the information he was there for.

"See?" Anja asked. "Nothing to worry about. Okay, sure, there would have been if the two you met before were still on duty, but since they weren't, you had nothing to worry about. I love living in a time when everything's computerized. It's like people are begging someone like me to step in and appropriate all the knowledge they have."

She almost sounded like she didn't know that Jeff and Harry wouldn't be on duty but he wasn't able to process that thought. Brown was talking him through the hallways he'd committed to memory barely a couple of hours before.

He would have time to himself while he patrolled the hallways and made sure nothing unexpected or untoward happened between the third and fourth floor as well as the rooftop. That was the job the newbie got, he was told since they were closing in on winter and it would be cold out.

"It's not too bad if you're a smoker, though," his partner explained as they began the walk through the third floor for the first time.

Most of the work appeared to be delegated to the newcomers since it lay on him to check the alarms deeper inside the facility. They weren't allowed in there and most of the security for those areas was delegated to the closed-circuit systems, which made their job easier.

Brown appeared to know that they were being phased out of the security division, which was why they had to deal with a lack of personnel. ICU Sec didn't want to over-commit to a contract they would probably lose in the next few weeks.

The people working at the lab appeared to have already left for the day. When he began to patrol the hallways, he was able to see that most of the offices and testing rooms were locked and closed for the evening. He would need to plan his way around any of the people who had stuck around for longer hours than they needed to.

"Are you clear on what you need to do?" Brown asked. "It's simple. But make sure you're at each of the checkpoints at least once every hour. We have a little time off at around three in the morning, but it will be staggered and you'll be the last one, since—"

"Since I'm the new guy, I get it," Savage said with a chuckle. "Believe it or not, I have done this kind of shit before."

"In the Marines, right. Greg told us about it," the other man said.

"Yeah, patrolling the bases had a similar set of duties, and I was paid about a quarter of the hourly I get with ICU Sec. I guess I might get tired of being the new guy eventually, but for now, I'm only happy to have a job."

"Well, I do know our bosses like that kind of thinking, so keep at it, I guess." The guard laughed wryly. "For now, though, I need to get to my sections of the building, so...have fun, I guess."

Savage nodded. He doubted there was much he could do if someone planned to break in. While he was equipped with a radio and an alarm button should something go wrong, the people running the facility had apparently not gone for the full security package. ICU Sec supposedly had packages where their security people were armed, but not in this case.

Brown was right. They were being phased out.

"So, what's your next step in there, Savage?" Jessica asked. She'd obviously noticed the silence that now surrounded him and assumed he was on his own.

"I've made my peace with the fact that Anja will be a voice in my head for the foreseeable future," he quipped and kept his voice low as he began his rounds. "I guess I never thought I would have a second voice as well. People will begin to think I'm crazy."

"They're only starting to think you're crazy now?" Anja snarked. "Come on, you've charged head-first into life-threatening situations for a while now, so you have to assume that people have known you're nuts for much longer than you pretend."

"True," he admitted. "But the voice—singular—in my head kind of crazy. Not the voices plural kind."

"Well, we all know you are all kinds of nuts, Jer," she retorted and he thought he heard her quiet chuckle in the background.

"Can we get back to the mission, please?" Jessica sounded a little annoyed.

"Sure thing," Savage replied.

"Now, what kind of plan do you have?" she said and repeated her previous question.

"Nothing much in the way of plans," he said with a casual shrug. "I'm here to find evidence and to do so, I need access to one of the computers. It's a game of patience. My cover is still good and no one suspects a thing. The more suspiciously I act, the more they'll suspect me and the more my cover will be in jeopardy."

He had no idea why the woman was being this overbearing about the mission, but he could guess. It seemed logical that word of Carlson's death had reached Monroe and she was able to put two and two together and realized that he had killed the man.

She wouldn't say he shouldn't have done it since she had to know that the ex CEO was still a threat, even while in custody.

Monroe merely wouldn't like that he had gone off-schedule and had probably called and told Jessica to be as on top of the mission as she could be. And Jessica, not used to being that kind of person, would overcompensate and carry it over onto him.

The only question was whether or not Monroe had told Jessica about what he'd done. Still, that was a thought for another day. For now, there were other more important things to focus on.

He headed into the lab and moved quickly through his checkpoints to give himself time to move around the lab areas in his search to find any of the areas where they might use the materials he was supposed to obtain pictures of.

And, surprisingly, he found evidence in a handful of

them. They were out in the open, and while he couldn't get into the labs themselves without triggering any alarms, Jessica's directions were enough for him to make out which devices he was there to locate.

A couple of these even still displayed the Pegasus logo on their sides.

"Well, it's safe to say they have the devices here," Savage said and made a note of where the third one was on the fourth floor. "I don't think there will be any on the roof, so how do I get to the other devices?"

"From the paperwork we have from the inspectors, the other two devices we are looking for are in a storage area in the back," Jessica said. "Unfortunately, it is in the first basement, so you'll likely have a little difficulty getting there without alerting the other people working security."

"It's not really necessary either," Anja interjected. "There should be many cameras in the storage areas since this place does seem like the kind of place that would make sure their employees can't steal the smaller, more expensive items. If you can get me into the camera streams, I should be able to find them myself."

"How can he access one of the security streams?" the other woman asked.

"I actually have a couple of ideas on that," he said.

CHAPTER THIRTY-THREE

It would definitely be a long night. Savage hadn't had much sleep on the plane, and he had spent most of the day either preparing or studying the information for the mission. He'd had coffee and a fifteen-minute nap to take the edge off before the mission started, and it had been go, go, go from that point forward.

Somewhat morosely, he reminded himself that he really needed to stop doing this to himself. It would go badly for him eventually and considering the life he currently lived, he would be lucky to be able to learn from that mistake. The chances were, though, that Pegasus would ultimately find some way to cut all ties from him and they would find some other poor schmuck to do their dirty work for them.

Maybe Jessica, Anja, and Anderson would lament his loss. Monroe would probably miss him too, although he doubted that the rest of the Heavy Metal team really knew enough about him to care that he was gone.

His own family thought he was long gone. When he thought about it, the state of mind was a somewhat depressing one to be in. He needed to simply stick to the mission and focus on keeping himself alive and undetected. That should be all that he did in the lab.

There would be enough time to think about how fucked up his life was when he was out of this with the mission accomplished and his bosses happy.

Unfortunately, he caught a little flack when he checked in with Guy at the end of his first two hours. The man didn't like how quickly Lawrence Palmer, as he was known by these people. had gone through his first few checkpoints. He was supposed to make them last the hour and so ensure that the people who ran the lab knew there were people all around the building at all times of the night.

It was a lie, of course, but an effective one that was easily sold to the folks who didn't know much about how security was run. The team didn't want a newbie to make it look like they hadn't been pulling their weight or lacked enthusiasm for their work.

"You need to take your time," Guy said. "Which is why, if you go through the paces a little quicker than usual, take a break on the roof. It's why the guy who has that part of the patrol usually takes a smoking break."

"I don't smoke," Savage said. "Who the hell smokes these days anyway?"

"Or...vape. I don't know, play games on your phone," the man snapped, clearly not in the mood to be talked back to by the new hire. "My point is that you need to take your time is. We're selling a product here as much as running security."

"Well, with security in the name..." he started to say.

"Look, we're obviously not the best that ICU Sec has to

offer. We're the guys they send to punch numbers and make them look good at the end of a quarter in front of shareholders with a smile on their faces. The guys who are the real professionals will make far more than we do, have guns, and actually do something important. You can bet your ass they won't work the graveyard shift like we do. Do what I tell you and stop asking stupid questions."

Fortunately, he remembered that he wasn't there to attract attention—and what he did right now was attracting attention. While he could think of all kinds of snarky responses, he needed to move on. He had a job to do, and it sure as fuck wasn't being a security guard.

He bit his tongue and headed to the third floor, following the map he had committed to memory and made sure to stick to the plan they had insisted he follow. That schedule gave him minutes between checkpoints, give or take, which meant he would have a small window between the fifth and sixth point that would place him directly in front of Dr. Gains' office.

If he hadn't already had the key, it would have been a complex lock to pick and there would also be no help from Anja. There didn't appear to be any electronic connections to the door she could manipulate from her side. It was a double-edged sword—which worked in his favor—since it meant there would be no alarms connected to the door, which would enable him to enter without being seen due to a security blind spot in the area.

That definitely wasn't a coincidence. Someone with Gains' history of harassment lawsuits—which had been a subject of curious study for part of the afternoon—would want to show people into his office at odd hours, given that he had a wife at home who had no idea of his legal problems.

They assumed, anyway. There wasn't much Anja could find about the woman herself aside from a couple of social media accounts that were filled with pictures of her cats. But still, it was a good assumption. No self-respecting woman would stay indefinitely with a husband who had a history of getting handsy with receptionists.

Savage hoped, anyway, but reminded him that human beings were strange creatures.

Thankfully, none of that mattered much at the moment. He wouldn't need to force his way into the office since he was given the keys to all the doors on his floor, and after a couple of attempts with incorrect keys, he finally managed to enter. He was careful and quiet and shut the door behind him before he slipped behind the desk. A personal laptop had been left on the surface and a couple of work computers and a tablet also provided possibilities.

Savage didn't have time for all of them. Thankfully, he didn't really need to do that much. He turned them all on but only plugged the dongle Anja had delivered to him into one of the work computers and turned all the screens on when the dongle glowed red.

"I'm connected," Anja said.

"See what you can get," he said. "I need to keep moving through the building."

"Will do," she replied quickly. "Good luck on keeping your new job, Savage."

"Once they realize I'm here as a spy, I'll get the boot anyway." He left the room hurriedly and left the hacker to do what she did best while he continued with his rounds.

"Okay, I'm in the system now," she said. "There are numerous firewalls here. It looks like their first line of spending when it came to security was to pour everything into their electronic security."

"Will it be a problem?" he asked and maintained his measured pace along the hallway.

"It would have been about three or four years ago," she said. "Given that I wrote and sold most of this code myself, I know my way around it. It merely takes a little while. I guess that means I should have some pride in my work."

"Don't you always?"

"Well, yeah, but it's nice to know that my work remains effective even after three or four layers of inferior work has been added into it," she said. "Okay, I'm into the system, so if you want to do one more round of the checks, I can remote activate them from that point forward and let you get back to your day—or night—job."

"That sounds like a plan," Savage said as he reached his next checkpoint.

Over the next few minutes, he made sure not to rush his way through before he returned to the office. As much as he wanted to continue his career as a security officer in order to maintain his cover and avoid detection, there was a job he needed to do in there, and it wouldn't be done by punching checkpoints every five minutes. He turned toward the office as Anja took over control of the devices that would monitor his progress.

"What's the situation on the data?" he asked as he closed the office door behind him. "Did you get everything you need?"

"I think so," the hacker confirmed. "I have images of all

of the devices we need to retrieve, but there are other things I think you should take a look at really quickly."

He circled the desk, sat, and woke one of the screens up as she called up some of the images she wanted to share with him. Most of these were of the devices they were looking for and had been made to seem like they were collected by people who were actually meant to be there to cover them against any fruit of the poisonous tree legal defense. Her task was to manage that side of things.

Savage was thankful that he wasn't actually a part of the legal team who had to actually put all this work together. His role was really as close to legal work as he would ever get while working for Pegasus and there was a reason for that. He was there for the dirty work. That was what he was good at. If they wanted him to go legal, they needed to pay him far more than he received right now.

Going legal would definitely be much more expensive to his mind.

"Wait, wait—come back to that one there," Savage said and leaned forward to focus on one of the images on his screen.

"That's an...electronic microscope?" Anja said tentatively but didn't sound too confident about it. In fairness, it didn't sound right.

"An electron microscope," Jessica corrected her. "It's not one of ours, though. Anja thought that it had a Pegasus logo and sent it to me, but it's definitely not one of ours. It looks like it's top-of-the-line, though."

"No, that's not what I mean." He narrowed his eyes for better focus. "What's with that glass wall in there?"

"Uh…it looks like it's something they use to contain live

test subjects," Jessica said. "But that's much bigger than what they usually have for those things. It actually looks like it's a cage for a chimp or something similar, which is interesting since this lab isn't authorized for any live testing."

"Is this vital to the mission?" Anja interjected. "Because if we're wasting time out there to satisfy personal curiosity, I think that shit can wait, don't you?"

"Call up the footage on that room," he insisted in a tone that demanded compliance.

He had only seen a tiny little portion of the room from the picture, but it was enough to tell him there was no chimp inside there. Since when did chimps need a toilet and sink?

The hacker did as she was told with a huff of annoyance and called up the camera feeds that monitored the room. Sure enough, it was definitely a cage, six feet by eight feet and maybe seven feet tall, all made of clear glass.

A small bathroom occupied one corner of the room, and the other held a narrow little cot where he could see what looked like a young woman wrapped in a white blanket.

"What the fuck?" Jessica asked when she saw the same thing he did.

"Is this what I think it is?" he asked.

"If you think that this is human testing then...yes. Yes, it is," Anja said after she pulled up a couple of files connected to the room.

It took her a few seconds, which Savage supposed spoke to the sheer amount of encryption that went into what they attempted to hide here as well as to the skill of the woman who worked on a keyboard from the other side of the damn planet.

"Her name is Jenna Castle," she said finally and displayed the files up for both Savage and Jessica to see. "It looks like she suffered from childhood leukemia—of the terminal kind—and her parents signed her up for some revolutionary and experimental new treatment coming from the Zoo, both the stuff coming out of it and some attempts to replicate it too."

He nodded. "Well, that doesn't sound too bad. I have the feeling that it's about to get worse, though."

"You should trust that instinct." The hacker did not sound happy about what she was reading. "Well, as it turns out, the treatment cured her leukemia...more or less."

"What do you mean?" he demanded. The medical work was called up on the screen next, and he wasn't too proud to say he was one hundred percent out of his depth.

"Well, it would probably take us all night to explain," Jessica said. "Basically, the cancerous cells were altered while inside the body, pushed out and expunged, and returned different but still functional. The people running the treatment shrugged, said that altered is merely cured with another name, and called it a win."

"Were there any side effects?" Savage asked.

"You'd better believe there were," Anja said. "Which is how they justified keeping our gal in the treatment for longer than she was allowed to be by the contract her parents signed for her. They tried to get her back from the company involved, but both parents died in an iffy car crash before they could file the case with the local authorities. They then changed the company name and moved

Jenna to another state once they realized she had no other legal guardians."

"Fuck me," Savage said. "It looks like they really want Jenna on the roster."

"It sounds like they had someone they could keep running tests on indefinitely and decided they had no intention to give her up," Jessica said angrily. "Despicable assholes."

"They've changed their company name about three times a year since they brought Jenna in, and they've moved her regularly," the hacker continued. "She's always kept in that cage, though, which sounds like a very specific kind of hell to me. Currently, she's recovering between experimental treatments."

"Huh." Jessica grunted. "What are these files signed off on? It looks like they're delivered to someone off-site. As in made into physical copies and sent via parcel service to someone outside the country."

"To one Edwina Smith," Anja said.

Savage raised an eyebrow. The name was too similar to Edward Smith—the moniker had been used by numerous men who had been employed by Carlson as a means to obscure his involvement in various unethical and down-right criminal activities. Aside from that, a few had been part of a team that tried to eliminate him and Anderson. According to the one he'd questioned, they'd all gone by the name Edward Smith.

"Do you know who that is?" Jessica asked.

From Anja's silence, he gathered that she had reached the same conclusion he had but didn't want to discuss what could also as easily be a simple coincidence.

"Nope," he said quickly to ensure that they weren't diverted down a rabbit hole that might require far more time and attention than they had right now. "Fuck this shit. We can't leave this kid here at the mercy of these assholes. We need to get her out. Well, I need to get her out of here."

"Agreed," Anja said. "Although I guess I should warn you that it won't be as easy as getting into this office."

"I guess I should cover my ass and tell you that while she might agree with the sentiment on a personal level, Courtney would absolutely not approve of this change to the mission from a business perspective," Jessica pointed out. "With that said...good luck, Savage."

"Thanks," he replied and pushed resolutely from his seat.

CHAPTER THIRTY-FOUR

"Do you have any idea as to how you'll do this?" Anja asked as he continued his rounds.

Savage did not, in fact, have any idea at all, only a certainty that he would do it. He knew more about the building than most of the men tasked with keeping it safe, but that didn't mean there was a way in and out of every area that would enable him to accomplish his purpose undetected.

The first problem he faced, of course, was the fact that the room where Jenna was held was on the second floor, which meant he would need to time his actions around the guard who patrolled that floor. Cutter, if memory served, looked like a man who had seen better days and probably only did this job part-time. Maybe to help a kid get enough money for college? He didn't look old enough to have grandchildren in need of support.

Unfortunately, that was the easy part. Anja would be able to track him through the system by timing his checkpoints to allow him to reach the room after the guard had passed it, which would give him an hour to get in and out of the place.

And that was where the good news ended. She would be able to open some doors for him but without the use of actual physical keys, he would trigger all kinds of alarms throughout the building since those rooms were specifically designed to not be opened unless there was some kind of emergency inside.

The kind of situation that would activate warning sirens throughout the facility, he assumed.

Which meant that if he intended to enter, he needed to ensure that he had a nice and well-established way out if he wanted to clear the building before all hell broke loose. The easiest way out would obviously be the garage, where he could get back to a car and drive away, but he would need people to be out of their position to enable him to break out past the security booth. There were other options too. The roof had easy access to the fire escape, but that would leave them exposed and easy to locate by people on the ground.

It was a solid option but definitely a plan B.

First things first, he needed to get the girl out of the cage she was in.

"I have something like a plan in my head," he said. "But it has to be fluid and open to on-the-spot changes if I need them. I don't usually do this kind of mission without enough time to plan it thoroughly. This way...there's too much shit that can go wrong."

"Well, I'm only reminding you that this was your idea in the first place," Anja said. "I originally intended to suggest that you head off and call the cops on these motherfuckers.

Legal does seem to be the way these people want you to operate, which means you need to kind of follow their plan—one that was in place before you even rolled around."

"A plan begun by people who don't know shit about being the boots on the ground," he retorted. "In other words, flawed from the start."

"I know you don't know much about Courtney and the team here, Savage," she said, and suddenly turned serious. "So, I'll let that pass without giving you the kind of lecture your mom would give you. Suffice it to say, though, that Courtney knows what it's like to be boots on the ground. Maybe cool it on trashing her."

Savage nodded. "Fair enough. No more trashing Courtney and the team over there in the Sahara. With that said, she brought me on here to save lives and I can understand that sometimes, sacrifices need to be made for the greater good, especially when it comes to this Zoo shit. But not kids, though. Never kids."

"I can agree with that," the hacker said. "Which is why I'll help you with this and not simply find a way to emotionally blackmail you into getting your ass out of there. I agree with what you're doing, although you have to admit that it comes right out of the bag of your worst ideas ever."

"I won't argue that. It's right up there with my barreling into a heavily defended bunker on my own to get attention."

"Yeah, that was stupid," she agreed. "Anyway, are we doing this?"

"Let's fucking go."

He moved into the stairwell and headed down to the

second floor where Anja had already unlocked the door for him. Cutter had passed through the area some fifteen minutes before and was not expected to return for another forty-five minutes, which gave him about as much time as he could ask for. From there, she was able to open a couple more doors for him to move deeper into the facility.

"Okay," she said when he stopped outside one of the more secure-looking steel doors. "I can open it and there should be a straight route for you to the cage. But once I do, alarms blare, I will be locked out of the system, and it's more than likely that guards who aren't rent-a-cops with radios will stream in to make your life miserable."

"Sounds about right," Savage said and shook his head at the thought.

There was time to rethink this. He could simply leave her there and tell Courtney she needed to work to get the girl out the legal way. That was an option but not a realistic one. In all probability, the moment these people realized they had infiltrated, Jenna would be moved and they would have no hope of finding her again. Aside from a second, massive stroke of luck, she would be lost to them.

Which meant he needed to do this now or risk losing her for the foreseeable future. He reminded himself that he had obtained the name of the woman responsible for the attacks they had experienced on Anderson and Savage's own family. That added the kind of leverage he would need to negotiate his way through clearing this with his bosses— and also for killing Carlson.

He would already face their disapproval over the ex-CEO's death so might as well add this little adventure to the list of sins. Facing them would be its own challenge, but it was one for another time. For now, he needed to get himself into the sectioned-off portion of the building and get Jenna out. Once that was done, they could start thinking about how he would explain it.

Fortunately, he had always been a fan of the asking for forgiveness instead of permission approach to these kinds of situations, and there was no need to make it uncomfortable for anyone. Rescuing Jenna might actually prove to be less of an issue than killing Carlson, given the moral ground. If so, he would tell them what he had done, tell them that it had been a tactical decision based on the man's own request, and add that they wouldn't talk about it further since they did need to deal with another threat now.

"Savage, you ready?" Anja asked and interrupted his temporary distraction.

He realized that he had mentally wandered off in the middle of their conversation. It probably wasn't the politest thing to do, but he still needed to find a way out of the whole situation.

"Right," Savage said and took a deep breath. "Yeah, I'm good to go. You can open the door on my mark. Three...two...one...mark!"

He pressed against the door. It didn't budge.

"Mark?" he said again and peered up at one of the cameras she could probably see him through.

"It's a process," the hacker said. "The code is working. You merely have to wait until it's ready to be used."

A scowl settled on his face and he shook his head and rubbed his shoulder until the steel door clicked loudly enough for him to hear.

"There you go," she informed him unnecessarily. "The alarms will go off the moment you open it. So...be ready for that."

"Would it be too cheesy to say that I was born ready?" he quipped as he placed his hand on the knob.

"It would be cheesy and utterly inaccurate unless you were born ready to specifically infiltrate a lab to rescue a girl they've been performing tests on. That said, though, if you want to tell me about how you were able to get into the mess of things while you were still a kid that got you into the situation you are in now, I guess we have time for it. It's not like there's a ticking clock on this or anything."

Savage rolled his eyes, drew the magnetic pistol he had hidden under his uniform, and made sure it was ready for a fight before he turned to the door and pushed it open. He didn't need to do it slowly and honestly, that would only steal precious seconds away from his escape.

Sure enough, the moment that he was through, klaxons blared across the rest of the facility. He couldn't hear much of anything beyond the noise. Red lights flashed around the room and made it very clear that the whole building would definitely be on alert. The clock was ticking.

He moved toward the cage at a near sprint, hefted his weapon, and held it ready.

"Oh...shit, how do I open the cage?" he asked, his tone rough.

"I'm locked out of the system, remember?" Anja said. "I can look up the cage locks, but aside from that—"

"Never mind," he said with a chuckle. "It's only a bolt."

"Are you kidding me?"

"I guess they didn't think they needed a lock to keep her

in." He yanked the bolt and stepped into the cage where Jenna was already awake and stared curiously at him.

"Hey...Jenna, right?" Savage said, careful to approach her slowly. There was no need to scare her more than she probably already was. "I'm Sa—Jeremiah, and I'm here to get you out of this place. If...if you want, that is."

He didn't know why he asked her if she wanted to come. When he'd entered, he was ready to take her and didn't really care about what the girl wanted to do. Now, though, when he was suddenly faced with the actual person, he suddenly realized there was no way he could get her out of there if she didn't want to leave. Dragging her out against her will would ultimately mean fighting both her and the forces that probably already on their way to stop him.

"I...well, did you have to come this late?" Jenna asked and rubbed her eyes. "I'm tired."

"You and me both, kid," he replied. "Are you in, or out?"

She shrugged. "I'd like to get out of here. Let's go."

"Fair warning, though, we might need to fight our way out of here," he said.

"That's what that gun is for, right?" she said and indicated the weapon that he had in his hand.

"Well...yes. Yes, it is." For a teenager who had barely woken up from sound sleep and suddenly confronted by a stranger saying they needed to get out of there, she seemed surprisingly calm. Not that he really knew much about her to judge one way or the other.

"Then let's go," she asserted, pushed up from the cot and straightened her white clothes down. She was much shorter than he had first thought, which made him wonder exactly how old she was. Not only that, she had been pumped full of the blue stuff from the Zoo, which meant that all kinds of changes could be happening to her body that he couldn't understand.

With that said, it wasn't his job to work out what the hell was wrong with her. He needed to focus on getting her out so that Jessica could take care of that side of things.

He nodded, led her out of the cage, and kept an eye out for any of the other guards who might have moved in. None were approaching, but there was considerable talk on the radio. Guy wanted to know exactly what the fuck was going on the second floor, and Cutter responded that he had no fucking clue. He sounded winded like he tried to rush to the area in question, but the fact that he was out of shape made him slower on the response time than he would have preferred.

"Let's go," Savage said, tugged Jenna by the arm, and headed toward the stairwell door that he had propped open to give them a way out.

"I can see them!" Cutter shouted from the end of the hall.

"Repeat. Them?" Guy asked over the radio.

"Yep!" the man said. "A man and a wo—oh, shit!"

Savage jerked back to open fire at a point above the man's head. It didn't have the same effect as a normal gun would have, but the shower of sparks that erupted when the piping in the roof was struck was enough for the guard to get the picture. "They are armed. Repeat, armed and dangerous and heading up to the third floor."

He had already closed the door of the stairwell and

sealed it behind him. What he could hear now was through the radio.

"Roger that," Guy called. "We have people on the way who can handle these sons of bitches. Palmer, do you have eyes on them?"

Oh, right, that was him. He yanked the radio from his belt. "Yep, I can see them. They're going up the stairs. I think they're heading for the roof. Is there any way out that way?"

"The bastards are trying to use the fire escape. Let's go," their team leader replied.

Well, that was one way to clear the security booth, he supposed. In the meantime, they would race down into the garage to find a car to escape in. He could use the car that he'd come in, but he had to hope that Anja would be able to wipe any footage of it from the databases. If she didn't, there would be a way to track it to the agency he had rented it from, and there was a long line from there that would lead to people finding a picture on the fake driver's license they had copied.

It was best to keep things on the down-low, though. They reached the garage and jogged toward the car.

"Do you still have eyes on them, Palmer?" Guy asked and he sounded out of breath as well. "I don't see anyone coming down the fire escape."

"They're still on the stairs," Savage replied and tried to emulate the man's breathy tone of voice. "For now, they're trying to keep me away and shooting down the stairs. I think I'm slowing them down, though."

"Don't you dare get shot on the job, you hear me rook-ie?" the man ordered.

He turned to Jenna, who watched his interaction with the security guards who thought he was there to pursue himself. "It's nice to know they care, anyway."

"Sure," Jenna said with a nod, although her attention was drawn away when a loud diesel engine roared and a vehicle careened into the garage. The ICU Sec logo on the side of the armored car confirmed the arrival of reinforcements.

"Trouble?" the young woman asked and tensed beside him.

"You bet," he replied with a grin.

CHAPTER THIRTY-FIVE

"Savage." Anja said in his earpiece. "I think you're about to have company."

"Think so, do you?" he asked in a hushed whisper.

"Oh...they're already there?" she asked. "They have impressive response time, I have to say."

"I'm glad you're impressed," Savage retorted.

"Who are you talking to?" Jenna asked.

He didn't respond aloud. Instead, he simply turned his head to the side and tapped his right ear, where she would be able to see the tip of a skin-colored earpiece hidden inside. It was meant to be mostly invisible to the naked eye but still simple to pull out when he wanted to. All in all, it was one of Anja's best inventions, considering that it was connected to her without the need of any cell phones or outside connecting devices.

"Oh," she said. "Who are you talking to, though?"

"My man—or woman, in this case—in the van," he replied. "Tech support. Eyes and ears in the sky. Is now really the time?"

She shrugged and leaned against the car that they hunkered behind. Again, she seemed too calm for a girl in this kind of situation, although he wasn't sure if she was maybe in some kind of shock or if it was merely an effect of the stuff they had pumped into her. Either way, her calm helped him remain calm, and that was always a good thing.

"Can you access any of these cars?" he asked and directed his question to Anja this time.

"I told you, I'm out of the system," she said.

"Yeah, but can you access any of these cars?" he insisted. "So you can perhaps unlock any of the cars that would allow us to get out of the garage without having to fight our way through the damn place?"

"Oh...right, but why don't you use the car you came in?"

"Because they're parked between me and it." Savage growled his frustration.

"Fuck...what are the odds?" the hacker muttered.

"Murphy's fucking law. Now, can you access the cars or not?" He struggled to keep his voice down.

"What do you think I'm doing while I'm talking to you?" she asked and still managed to keep her cool as she worked and bantered with him.

He would have appreciated it more if he weren't looking at dealing with the six men who disembarked from the armored car. They still didn't know where the intruders were, but it was only a matter of time until they realized that Palmer was full of shit. They needed another plan. Another way out, preferably, and he wracked his brain for a possible solution while he waited with growing impatience.

"There's an Audi three cars down from you," Anja said.

"I've already turned it on and unlocked the doors. It's waiting for you, so get over there now."

Savage nodded and gestured for Jenna to move with him as he moved in a rapid crouch toward the Audi in question. Moving between the cars would let them get to their escape vehicle but moving it out would certainly not go unnoticed.

"Hey!"

Shit.

"What are you doing down here?" the guard who had seen him asked. He'd clearly only seen the uniform and not the gun. "You're supposed to be inside, keeping an eye out for the people breaking in!"

He looked around hastily and wondered if he could somehow twist this in his favor. Unfortunately, the group of men was far more professional than the men upstairs looking for him.

And definitely more observant as well. All the man needed was a moment to see the gun in his hand and the white-clad young woman with him.

Thankfully, he was fairly experienced at being observant as well and he had already raised his weapon in response to the man's sudden realization of the truth.

"They're here!" the guard shouted as a loud whine filled the garage and two of the needles fired from the weapon.

The target fell immediately when the needles punched easily through his body armor and into the soft flesh beneath it. He really didn't want to hurt them, but if they stood between him and Jenna getting clear of this lab, he had to act.

Well, he could only hope he didn't kill any of them, but he definitely wouldn't pull his punches.

"Get to the Audi," he commanded Jenna. "I'll cover you!"

She moved quickly and decisively, stayed low, and scrambled into the Audi that had been unlocked for them. He maintained a steady stream of needles, thankfully without needing to reload. The other guards had seen what happened to their comrade and decided they wouldn't put themselves or their body armor to the test against this weapon.

"We need to go!" the girl called.

"Do you think I don't know that?" he retorted and took a last couple of shots before he slid into the driver's seat.

Anja noted that they were in, took control remotely, and pulled it out of the parking spot. She had also already lowered the window on his side to enable him to continue to fire at the guards and pin them behind cover. A couple of them stepped out to stop the car but quickly fell back and clutched their legs when several needles drilled into them.

"I'd love to see how they'll manage to pin this shit on gang violence," Anja quipped.

"Who the fuck is driving this thing?" Jenna yelled and looked terrified for the first time that night as the car was guided toward the exit. The barrier was still down.

"Well, our tech support is," Savage said.

He wasn't exactly relaxed but he trusted the hacker to know her way around this situation. On more than one occasion, he had trusted her with his life and he was still around. There would be time to panic later if she didn't prove herself worthy of his trust, although even the possibility seemed comfortingly remote.

He still grasped the steering wheel as she accelerated into the barrier, though. His eyes closed as the vehicle pounded into. The wooden bar splintered and they emerged cleanly.

"Huh." Jenna grunted and suddenly relaxed against her seat once more. "Seriously, you have good tech support."

"Right?" he agreed as Anja released control of the car into his hands.

"You have to love living in an age where everything's electronic, right?" the hacker commented and laughed.

"You're goddamn right," he said with a chuckle. "I never doubted you for a second, Anja."

"Anja?" the girl beside him asked. "That's the name of the technical support?"

"What's wrong with Anja?" the Russian asked.

"She's asking if you have a problem with it," he told Jenna.

"Nothing," she replied. "It's a nice name, is all."

"Damn right it is," Anja said smugly.

"She's happy you think so," Savage said and wished he could carry a spare earbud wherever he went.

Jessica had really forgotten exactly how stressful this whole business could be. Of course, she had been involved in a peripheral way, and she had heard from Courtney and the people still at the Pegasus HQ that Savage still worked and thrived in the world he had been thrust into. There were more than enough people who seemed determined to make it a difficult life to live.

And from what she had learned, he was the only one who had walked away from a number of violent interactions he'd been involved in.

Not that she was really surprised.

She had seen him in action. While she wanted to think there was something inhuman about the way he was able to successfully kill people and get shit done, that wasn't quite accurate. The better description was that what he did was utterly human. Saying otherwise almost detracted from how truly amazing it was.

There was something utterly unbeatable about him. Like he knew how to flip the little switch that made him go berserk, attack his enemies with everything he had, and reach fearlessly into the dark side within him. She was honest enough to acknowledge that all humans carried their own version of darkness in one way or another, and yet they liked to think that they were somehow different and had nothing like it.

He skipped that part. It was exhausting for him and he simply accepted the dark side and let it emerge when it was needed.

That gave him an advantage over the people who thought they could outmaneuver or outmatch or outgun him. They forgot that if they let him come within striking distance, he would strike. She couldn't really understand why they would think he might act like a regular human being when he wasn't. He was beyond that and he would continue to teach them that lesson until they learned it for good.

Either that or until Pegasus ran out of people for him to shoot, beat up, or intimidate. For the moment, that looked like it was a long way away. And she never really doubted that Savage would be able to get Jenna out of the lab. He had said he would do it in that way that sent chills down her spine and in her mind, that essentially sealed it. There was nothing more to be done other than watch, help as much as she could, and stay out of his way.

Honestly, there wasn't much Jessica could do from this side of things. It was still a real privilege to watch Savage and Anja work together on this in the way that only they could. The two were the best in their businesses and it brought them together with the kind of chemistry that had made some of the greatest teams in sports history.

They would inevitably have a difficult time dealing with it all, of course, but they were able to work through the problems while still keeping the banter up. It often seemed like they both tried to keep the other focused and calm at the same time. They knew how to work together. Jessica hadn't been there from the beginning so she couldn't tell if there had been a learning period between them when they first started, but they were a well-oiled machine now.

And it was a real pleasure to watch them work, especially from the side of the operation that wasn't under fire. That was the best part of this mission. While it would be sheer stupidity to assume there weren't still people who would target her—when did they not?—she was comparatively safe in this hotel room. Besides, the people running that lab would have bigger problems than her from this point forward.

"It looks like they're in the clear for now," Anja said. "I'm working on scrubbing all evidence that Savage was in the building. There's not much as he was good at keeping his face off the cameras, but there's the car I need to deal with."

Jessica relaxed into her chair and only then realized that she had been on the edge of it and had grasped the armrests tightly enough that she could see the white in her knuckles showing. It was a tense escape, especially since she couldn't see all the things Anja and Savage did. But they were out now—he and Jenna, the new addition to their little team.

That was assuming she would stick with them. They still didn't know who the hell she was and what she wanted out of life.

It was interesting, though. Jessica had wanted to learn about the Zoo stuff for as long as she had been around but absolutely couldn't stomach the thought that human testing was going on—especially when it came to teenagers who couldn't consent to anything done to them. The benefits did not overcome the blatant violations of human rights.

With that said, there would be side effects to that treatment, and she was already reading up on the details Anja had stolen from their files. It wouldn't be as good as having Jenna in the room with her, but that probably wouldn't happen in the foreseeable future. They would need to make those kinds of decisions later.

Something buzzed…vibrated…no, rang, which meant a phone. Her phone, to be precise, and since Anja and Savage could contact her through the earpiece she still had from their first adventure together, it could only mean it was someone who wanted an update.

"Oh, I'm not looking forward to this," she said softly and rubbed her eyes for a moment before she answered and let the screen pop up to display both Anderson and Monroe.

"Hey, Jessica," Courtney said, and her tone of voice clearly indicated that this wouldn't be a pleasant, catching-up type of conversation. "I received a news alert on my phone that tells me that the lab Savage was supposed to break into was broken into."

"I really hope that's not news to you at this point," Jessica said in an effort to lighten the tone.

It didn't work.

"Well, the idea was for him to be in and out like a ghost, unseen and unheard," the woman continued. "So imagine my surprise when I see alarms have gone off all over the place and police are scrambled to the location to deal with it."

"Well, the situation unexpectedly became a little more complicated on the ground," she explained. "Savage discovered they were holding a young girl there—Jenna Castle—and running human experiments on her with stuff from the Zoo as well as attempts to replicate it. The whole situation was extremely shady, and Savage decided to break her out."

"What?" Courtney asked and a vein pulsed on her forehead. "I thought we hired him to be the guy who makes the correct tactical decisions while in the field, not to charge in, act like a white knight, and save people."

"In fairness, that sounds very much on par with what we know about Savage," Anderson interjected. He leaned back in his seat and looking a good deal calmer about the situation than his companion. "He charged in head-first to save members of my family and his own. I think that's something we should have expected from him in that situation. Honestly, I think I would have probably made the same call. Which is not to say it's necessarily the right call from a tactical perspective, but it is the right call from a moral point of view."

The woman took a moment to calm before she finally sighed and rubbed her temples. "Fine, he made the right call. From...some points of view, anyway. And given that there's no news about them catching the intruder yet, I suppose I can save him a tongue-lashing until he gets himself caught. In the meantime, what's the damage? What kind of blowback are we looking at?"

"For the moment, not much," Anja said and joined the call. "I've managed to erase most traces of his existence from where it could be easily accessed, and I've worked on getting him clear of the location. There are already police on-site who responded to the shots fired calls from the area. While they don't have any images on the security footage of him—you're welcome for that, by the way—the cops were able to talk to the security guards that he met and they gave a description and even have a sketch circulating."

The image came up on Jessica's phone, and from the looks on the others' faces, she had to assume it was on everyone else's as well.

"That...doesn't quite look like him," Courtney said and narrowed her eyes as she studied it.

"They have the jawline all wrong," Anderson agreed.

"His hair isn't like that," Jessica added.

"Actually, it was while he was working there," the hacker explained. "He gave some spy-craft mumbo-jumbo about it but apparently, that's really all the sketch focused on."

"Well, that's good news for us," the former colonel said. "How can we help him?"

"We can't," Jessica replied. "Not in any official capacity anyway. There's considerable paperwork and fancy legal tricks involved, but what they were doing to the girl was perfectly legal since her parents signed off on it." Both Monroe and Anderson listened intently while she gave them a brief explanation of the situation, and they looked as disgusted as she felt when she described the human testing. "So no, officially, we can't help him, despite that I feel he made the right moral choice."

"Agreed," Courtney said. "While having human testing on their resume would be a PR nightmare for the company running the lab, Pegasus would still be on the hook for breaking and entering if it ever came back to us."

"So, what do we do?" she asked, knowing that she wouldn't like the answer.

"Under no circumstances are you to extend any official help Savage's way, at least not until he's clear of the situation," her boss instructed. "We can help him in subtle ways —like Anja's doing—but for the most part, they're on their own out there."

"Understood," Savage said with a nod and placed his hand over his right ear so he could hear better. "Thanks for the update, Anja. We'll be in touch."

He gripped the steering wheel of the car a little tighter and tried not to let his frustration show.

It did, however, despite his good intentions. Jenna appeared more than attuned to his emotional state and narrowed her eyes. "What's the matter?"

"Nothing much," he replied and made an effort to keep his tone light and jovial. "I got word that the people who sponsored this mission would rather not be involved in any of the illegalities of it, so they would rather keep themselves clear of the situation—which leaves us, for the most part, high and dry."

"That doesn't sound good," the girl replied. "It does sound like they're looking out for their own skins, which wouldn't be something people who sent you to save me would do."

"They didn't send me in to save you, technically," he

clarified. "I was sent in to find stolen merchandise to help them shut the place down. We saw you on one of the video feeds, and I decided to act on my own initiative and get you out since... Well, I don't really care for people who like testing their new stuff on other human beings. There are some other reasons on top of that, but…well, you probably don't want to talk about that."

Jenna shrugged. "I do know they were doing it for someone in particular—the person who sponsored the lab, at least. And I know it's a woman they were working for. Over the past couple of months, I've heard people talk about how the testing on me wasn't progressing fast enough and that they needed to up the schedule, all while talking about how 'she' wouldn't be happy about it."

"She is a woman called Edwina Smith, apparently," he explained. "Unfortunately, I don't know much more about her or why she's so interested in testing the shit that came from the Zoo, aside from the obvious monetary aspect to it. It seems like there's something bigger involved, but I'd need to know more about it before I come up with any new assumptions."

"Why are you interested in her?"

"Well, aside from my overall dislike of the people who profit from the oddity that is the Zoo and the fact that people are dying to get to that stuff out for them?" he asked, not sure how in tune with what was happening the girl was. "She may be connected to people who made very pointed threats against myself, my family, and people I care about as well as their families."

"How pointed were those threats?" She was a sharp one, he realized.

"Killers targeted me and my friends," he replied and forced his gaze to remain on the road and his hands to ease their vice-like grasp on the wheel. "When they failed, teams of killers attacked my family and another family, all while trying to convince us to get off their backs and talking about how they were really the good guys in this whole debate."

The girl nodded. "Did you do anything to deserve that kind of treatment from them?"

Savage shrugged. "Probably enough to have them send someone to kill me. But there are lines. The kind that if people cross them, they get crossed right the hell back."

She nodded but didn't say anything further for a moment. He realized that he probably hadn't come off as a fantastic person to the young woman, but he didn't really need to. If she didn't want to be around him, that would be her decision to make.

"Are you a good person?" she asked suddenly.

"What?" he snapped in response and narrowed his eyes, although he still focused on the road. "You ask a lot of questions, you know that?"

"Sure," she replied. "But if you like, we can make it an exchange. You answer a question, and I answer a question. And I know you have some."

He nodded. "That's fair enough."

"So, do you think of yourself as a good person?" She repeated her question calmly.

"I don't know." He shrugged. "I'm sure there are people in the world who would have good reason to say I'm not. They might even have a solid case to state that I'm an outright terrible person."

"That's not what I asked, though," she said. "Do you think of yourself as a good person?"

"It depends on the day and time if you ask me," he said, which was dumb because she had asked him. "I'd say the most flattering way to say it is that I try to be as good a person as I can. I fail often in that regard, and honestly, it's almost unavoidable in my line of work, but I do try."

She smiled. "I guess that's as honest an answer as someone can give. What line of work is that, exactly?"

"I think it's my turn to ask you a question now," he pointed out. "Isn't that how this game is supposed to work?"

"Sure."

"Did you really want to be rescued from the lab?"

She paused and scrunched her eyes for a moment like she hadn't actually thought about it. He wondered if she had obeyed instructions from other people for so long that simply following him when he said that he was there to get her out seemed natural.

It was, he thought suddenly, like resisting or questioning him hadn't even occurred to her. It made him wonder if they had used conditioning and brainwashing techniques to make her a more pliable test subject. They would have had to be careful about it since mental tricks like that could get in the way of medical testing.

"Okay..." she started to say, then paused, leaned back, and toyed with her seat. "Well, yes, I wanted to get out of there. But contrary to what some people might think, they didn't actually treat me badly in there. They're not monsters."

"Aside from the whole keeping you in a lab against your

will and using you basically as a human guinea pig?" Savage pointed out.

"Something like that, yeah." Jenna laughed. It was a clear and happy sound, free of the kinds of weight that he normally would have expected to be present in a girl like her. "But yeah. I had my own room. I had three meals a day and all kinds of things to do between the testing. They brought in a couple of tutors here and there and kept me up to date on my studies and larger global events. I even have a TV in my room most nights. I know, I must sound like some lost Stockholm syndrome case to you."

"Do you want me to lie about that?" he asked bluntly and watched her from the corner of his eye. "Because...well, honestly, yes, there are some serious red flags about that."

"I know," she replied. "I remember that they didn't even tell me that my parents were dead until a couple of months later. And they gave me this whole speech about how I would be remembered for decades to come as the girl who helped to cure cancer, and that if we stopped now, my parents would have died for nothing."

"Yeesh." He growled, the sound heavy with disgust. "So many red flags."

"I know." Jenna shook her head. "I don't consider myself the sharpest of kids, but that speech immediately made me think about how they might have killed my parents."

"Yeah, I glanced at the details, and they were as shady as fuck," he agreed.

"Okay, my turn." She sounded genuinely excited. "What do you do for a living that gets you into random labs where you rescue girls from glass cages?"

"Now that you mention it, you kind of remind me of Hannibal Lecter," he pointed out.

"Who's that?" she asked.

"A— Never mind." He decided to avoid that particular pitfall for now. There would be time to educate the girl on horror classics later. "I used to work in special forces for the military. These days, it's more along the lines of hunting the assholes who make a profit any way they can, including killing or harming innocents. Technically, I work for folks who make the profit as well but also fight unofficially to make sure that those who profit off suffering are out of the business altogether."

"Okay," Jenna said and tilted her head in query when he eased over to the side of the road. "Why are we stopping?"

"We need to find another car," he explained. "This one is burned and will be out on a hundred APBs by now."

CHAPTER THIRTY-SEVEN

Anja had been the one to alert him that the car was now reported as stolen from the scene of a crime. They were inside the city of Portland now, and the police would obviously patrol the areas with far more intensity. If they found a stolen car associated with a robbery, their capture would be inevitable.

They would be penned and caught. Savage wasn't sure what would happen to Jenna in this case since she was very literally innocent of all charges. He would be locked up for breaking and entering, but she would probably be signed into the hands of a social worker or something.

It depended on how old she was, really. He remembered details in the paperwork he had briefly looked at, and they probably included her birthday, although he hadn't thought to check.

He merely hadn't seen it for some reason. It hadn't been his best moment of being sharp and clear-headed. Grateful for the hacker's warning, he eased over to the side of the road, stopped the car, and stepped out quickly.

"So, you're like this super-cool super-spy?" Jenna asked as they began to walk down the street. "Like Jason Bourne, or James Bond?"

"I like to think I'm a little better at my job than James Bond and certainly better than an amnesiac killer from the cold war," he retorted, his eyes narrowed.

"Since when is he from the cold war?" she asked. "The movies have him all CIA and very, very modern in a 1984 kind of society. You know, with Matt Damon?"

"Oh...no, I was talking about the books," he said. "OG Jason Bourne was a CIA-sponsored assassin to hunt an actual dude called Carlos the Jackal. It was a good book but ended up being bullshit and Carlos merely a fat dude with considerable luck and as many connections."

"OG?" Jenna asked. "What are you, a fan of nineties rap or hip hop?"

"As a matter of fact, I do like me some Notorious BIG and a little Tupac too," he said with a nod. "But that's not the point right now. It is my turn to ask a question, right?"

"Right," she said and took a couple of rapid steps forward to stand in front of him, then walked backward to face him as they moved. "What do you have for me?"

"You seem really upbeat about this whole thing," he pointed out casually.

"I haven't had the opportunity to talk to people aside from the scientists who ran tests on me," she replied. She seemed to manage her backward walk without colliding with anything, although it unsettled him. "You're damn right I'm upbeat about this."

"All right," he said. "What kind of shit did they give you

in there to do? Someone your...approximate age would be bored to tears in a place like that."

"Most of my time was spent being tested on," she said. "They did give me time off between tests, though. A couple of days. That's when they wheeled the TV in on the other side of the glass to let me watch movies or the news. I had no Internet access, which I guess should have been another major red flag in my mind. They worked overtime to keep me isolated from the rest of the world."

"Which kind of segues me right into my next question, but it's your turn," he said and reached out without thinking as she approached a nasty crack in the sidewalk.

She was about to trip over it when he caught her arm and turned her to face the right way. Her little stunt had been enough to set off all kinds of anxiety flags in his head.

"Oh, okay," Jenna said and sounded like she wouldn't have minded another question from him. "Okay, so why did you leave the military if you still wanted to work at saving people? I don't know much about it, but they probably don't make you retire if you don't want to—it doesn't seem very logical. They spend money training you and they like to have people with your kinds of skills working for them. It tells me you chose to leave of your own volition, which begs the question of why?"

Savage paused to consider this for a moment before he increased his pace to make sure that he didn't lag behind her. There were enough problems with their situation now, and losing her was not one that he wanted to deal with. If she wanted to leave, she could. He wouldn't drag her around against her will.

But if she did want to stick around, he needed to make sure she didn't get herself into more trouble. She was his responsibility at this point, and he intended to take that very, very seriously.

"Jeremiah?" she asked when the silence threatened to drag on interminably.

"Oh," he said and shook his head to bring himself back into the moment. "Sorry, I was distracted. You can call me Savage, by the way."

"Your name is Jeremiah Savage?" Jenna asked and raised her eyebrows. "Your parents must have hated you. That's not even fair."

"Maybe, but that's a question for another time," he responded with a small smile. "Regarding your question... Well, I did retire from the military, but suffice it to say that it wasn't entirely my choice. I worked in black ops all around the world and they needed me to step away when keeping me around would cost more than they thought I was worth. So, I stepped away."

"You simply did it without any questions?" She sounded incredulous.

"I can't go into the details but there were certain carrots offered as well as certain sticks," he said. "The US government doesn't really take kindly to people who threaten their bottom line."

"I can see that. Although, again, most of my experience revolves around movies, so that seems like what they would do."

"It was a little more complex than that, but okay," he said with a shrug. "My turn for a question, though. Why did you follow me when I said that I was there to get you out, and why were you so calm and…well, composed when the breaking out became dangerous?"

Jenna shrugged her shoulders. "I heard you talking from the outside. Also, when you broke in, you told me what you were going to do, and asked me to follow you. You didn't insist that it was what was needed and you didn't keep anything from me. In my eyes, that made you far more trustworthy than the people who had been around me for the past couple of years. I had begun to think that I needed to get out anyway, and I had half made my mind up that if you tried anything, I could break away when you were distracted and do my own thing."

"That seems fair." Savage grinned. "Although, in the interests of full disclosure, I wouldn't have been totally against dragging you out. Having said that, given that it was only me with no support and the necessity to get out as quickly as possible before the proverbial cavalry arrived, I kind of needed you to be on board with the whole rescue. It wouldn't have worked otherwise."

"I appreciate your honesty." Her chuckle contained real humor. "I guess we're both lucky we were on board with what the other wanted when the time came. Okay, my turn?"

"Sure."

"How the hell does someone get a name like Jeremiah Savage?"

"You remember how I told you about the armed forces basically telling me to drop off their radar or else?" he asked and she nodded. "Well, in that package, they offered a decent amount of money in exchange for my disappearance and they needed me to change my name."

"So, you changed it to Jeremiah Savage?" The girl stared at him as if waiting for him to tell her it was a joke.

Savage could hear Anja laughing though his earpiece and he narrowed his eyes. "Well, yeah. Jeremiah was my first name anyway. I thought the name Savage seemed appropriate at the time. It still is, honestly. There was context."

"I'm sure there was," Jenna commented. "Still, though. I don't think I'll call you either of those. Do you have any nicknames? Like...Jer?"

"Damn, not you too," he said with a sigh.

"What?" Anja protested. "No, Jer is my name for you."

"I'm sure you didn't trademark that shit," he said and tapped his ear to indicate who he was talking to.

"Nope, but it's still my name for you," she insisted.

"Anja says you can't call me Jer," he explained to the now somewhat bewildered girl. "That's her nickname for me."

"Well, you can tell Anja she can come over and tell me that herself," she replied with a grin.

He paused and waited for the hacker to respond. After a few long seconds, he realized that none would be coming.

"Did you hear that, Anja?" he finally asked.

"Yes," the Russian grumbled and sounded less than happy.

"You're not buying tickets for yourself to fly out to Portland, are you?" he asked warily.

He doubted that she would, but you could never tell with Anja. She was capable of doing something crazy about the whole situation merely to prove that she was right. Although he was still about ninety percent sure she was simply playing around.

Mostly sure, anyway.

"No, that would be stupid," Anja said. "But know that the moment that Jenna gets a phone or some other method of communication, I'll fill her in on what she can and can't call you."

That would definitely not end well.

"Anja says that this isn't over," he said for Jenna's benefit.

"Sounds good, Jer," she said with a cheeky grin.

"Either way, do you guys plan on merely walking around the city all night, waiting for cops to notice you, or do you have a plan about what to do next?" Anja asked.

"I've mostly been improvising ever since we went off schedule at the lab," he said. "Why do you ask?"

"Well, in case you want to look into finding a place to stay for the night, I'd suggest you guys find a car and get off the streets. The guards talked to the cops, and they have a full description of you. and should already be on the prowl."

"Huh," He cast a hasty glance around the area.

The city was usually busy during the day but it was rather dead at night. If there were any cops in the area, the two of them would stick out like a sore thumb. The hacker was right. They needed to get off the road.

"I have to ask, though," he said. "If Pegasus isn't supposed to help us to escape, why are you still around on the line helping us?"

"Come on, you know I don't work for Pegasus," she said with a laugh. "There are enough problems for you guys to deal with without questioning why I'm helping you. Besides, it's not like they can actually prove that I'm involved anyway. I'm better than that."

"I guess you are," he said and shrugged. "At the same time, how would Monroe feel about you helping us? I don't think she really approved of what I did back in the lab."

"Well, no, she didn't approve," Anja replied honestly. "But she understood. And actually, she felt that it was the right thing to do, so you don't have to worry about too much backlash from her on that. There might be backlash from other sources, though—merely a heads up."

"Right, I think I know what those sources might be. But back to the matter at hand. Since you can help us, is there any way to get us a car out here?"

"I'm already working on it," she assured him. "Not many of the cars parked out in the open are accessible for me, so I'll let you know when I have something for you."

"That sounds like a plan," Savage said. "In the meantime, we should probably stay off the street, right?"

"I'll let you know if there are any cops on the way," she said.

"Don't you think it's a little weird how quickly the word has spread?" he asked. "I realize that someone breaking into a lab can't be a great thing, but they should have better things to do than hunt us, especially since we haven't actually taken something they would openly admit to having."

"You know, just because I'm standing here doesn't mean that I know the context of the conversation," Jenna pointed out. "With that said, saying I'm something that was taken really doesn't endear you to me."

"She's as sassy as fuck," Anja said.

"No shit." He grimaced and rubbed his eyes. "Still, you don't think it's a little suspicious how quickly they were onto us?"

"And the fact that they had armed guards on standby waiting for someone to break in?" the hacker asked. "But yeah, I'm looking into that shit already, so you don't have to worry about it. You only need to worry about getting the fuck out of sight. Speaking of which, I've managed to get your picture that's been circulating."

"I thought you erased all the images that they might have of me," he said.

"I did. Seriously, the lack of faith around here is disheartening. No, I meant the sketch they made of you for the cops."

Savage's phone buzzed and he pulled it out of his pocket and studied the picture that had been sent to him. "Well, that's a sketch, but I don't think it's one of me. Do I really look like that?"

"Let me see," Jenna said and peeked at the screen before she narrowed her eyes and peered at his face. "I don't know. There are some things they got right, but the hair and the jawline are all wrong."

"How will they find us using this?" he asked.

"Well, it doesn't really matter, does it?" Anja pointed out. "Cops are still on the lookout for you, and that means you need to keep moving. I'll let you know when I have a car for you."

"Thanks, Anja."

He stepped forward quickly and Jenna caught his hand to help her keep up with his pace. It was an odd thing, one that made something warm settle into the pit of his stomach but not a bad sensation, he decided. Rather, it was something he had been missing and he never actually realized it.

CHAPTER THIRTY-EIGHT

There were some things in the world that really made life worth living. A nice sunny day when it wasn't too hot or too cold was one. Also good was a song with the kind of beat that managed to get you moving whether you liked it or not, depending on where you were. A good fuck that left you sore and satisfied in all the right places maybe topped the list. Another favorite was a cool drink on a warm day, especially when you were out in the open, enjoying the best of both worlds as the sun blazed over your skin.

Today was a mixture of all those things. For her, anyway. There were people who liked staying where it was snowy and cold during the winter, but as the icier months rolled in, Elena always gravitated toward the sandy beaches where she would find endless sun and surf to enjoy.

Most people in Ibiza lived in a world where seven in the morning was something only seen when one stayed up that late. It made the whole place far quieter, which gave her the time to enjoy the beginning of the day. There was generally a significant amount of business to attend to for the rest of the day, which left her with only a couple of moments to herself.

She enjoyed her work, but to merely sit and relax while she watched the sun rise over the ocean was one of those things that couldn't be replicated.

"*Buenos días, señorita Molina,*" the young man said as he carried in a tray with the breakfast she had ordered.

He placed it on one of the nearby tables and set it out for her to enjoy at her leisure, although the coffee would only remain warm for a limited time. Her meal consisted of an egg-white omelet, a couple of cinnamon rolls covered in a chocolate glaze—something she simply couldn't start the day without—a couple of freshly baked rolls and sliced cheeses, and a selection of fruits to go with the coffee, which was served in white porcelain with milk and sugar waiting beside it.

"Thank you, Diego," she said softly, not quite ready to move from her seat.

"*Tienes una llamada esperandote,*" he said and inclined his head slightly. "*Cuando puedas.*"

"I'll take the call out here, please." She shrugged her sunglasses off and stretched gracefully.

It seemed that work wouldn't actually wait for business hours. Since her phone was something of a tether that constantly brought her back to the international business that had been left to her by her father, she found it preferable to leave it behind when she tried to relax.

With that in mind, however, she was never far enough

away from the phone that she couldn't be reached in case of an emergency. And there was always an emergency.

Diego went inside as Elena moved to the table and took a sip of her coffee. There were people who needed the caffeine every morning and simply guzzled any swill they could get their hands on. For her part, she always tried to treat herself when she drank it. There really was no point in drinking hot bean water when you could have something that was delicious and good for you.

The man returned quickly with her phone on the tray, which he left on the table before he walked inside. She would spend time with him later or maybe later in the evening when he was off work. For now, though, duty called.

She pressed the button on the phone to set it to speaker.

"Yes," she said and took another sip of coffee.

"Miss Smith, I'm sorry to bother you at this time of the night," said a vaguely familiar voice.

"It's morning here, so there is no need to apologize," she said brusquely. "Who is this?"

"This is Dr. Gains," he replied and after a pause that made him realize she needed more than a name, he added, "You put me in charge of your laboratory in Portland. The specialized lab you requested to be informed about regarding any changes?"

"Oh, yes, of course, Dr. Gains," she said and shook her head. "It must be late in Portland. Why do you feel the need to contact me when you could call me in the morning?"

"Well, it's about the lab itself," Gains said. "And...well, the special subject you wanted me to keep a close eye on."

Molina narrowed her eyes, crossed her legs, and tapped

her fingers on the table. "I have the distinct feeling that you'll give me bad news. Is this bad news that you want to give me, Dr. Gains?"

"Yes, I'm afraid so," he said and apparently didn't quite realize the dangerous position that he had put himself in. "Unfortunately, it would appear that someone broke into the facility, and... Well, there are many problems, actually, as you would expect from this kind of...uh, infiltration. However, when we investigated the break-in, it would appear that they made off with your special subject."

Made off with? It was like the guy tried to be in some kind of TV show and he was supposed to be the cop while she was some kind of victim.

She was afraid that he had wildly misread the situation.

"Explain made off with," she snapped although she did make an effort to keep her voice calm.

"Well, the details are still coming in, but from the reports we've been able to get from our security people, he managed to infiltrate the company we hired for security," Gains explained. "Using that as a cover, he connected himself to the wireless network of the building and from there, was able to access the rest of the security without too much trouble."

Molina closed her eyes when her heart began to thud in her chest and beat after beat thumped a little faster than the last. Her mouth had gone suddenly dry, a situation not helped by the coffee she sipped. Every word he said merely made all the sensations worse.

Of course, she was infuriated by the news, but there were certain things she couldn't share with the people who worked for her. There was still a certain stigma associated with a woman in business, and any sign of weakness would be pounced on by everyone, from tabloids to economic news to the members of her own collective boards. She needed to constantly maintain a strong and sometimes terrifying front.

"Is there anything you'd like to add to the report?" she asked and drew a deep breath.

"We'll send the details in full to your email," Gains said. "The guards who were on duty actually remember the break-in as well as what the perpetrator looked like."

"From those rent-a-cops?" she snapped. "Spare me. Please do what you need to do to keep the local law enforcement away from the damn facility and stay out of their way. I'll put someone on this immediately. They might arrive and ask for the details you mentioned and if so, you'll cooperate and give them everything they need to know, understood?"

"Yes, ma'am, but—"

"But nothing." Molina growled a warning. "That's all that you have to do if you want to keep your job. And believe me when I say that I know you well enough to know that you need this job more than you'd like to have to confess to that wife of yours. Understood?"

"Ye...yes, ma'am," Gains said as she killed the line and shook her head furiously.

Well, now that she was up and awake, it was about time she got to work. She searched for a number on her contacts lists, called it, and finished her coffee as it dialed.

Diego emerged and topped her coffee up while she waited for the call to be answered.

"Hello?" The man's voice sounded crisp and almost cheerful.

"Mr Stevens," she said. "This is Molina."

"Miss Molina, so pleasant to hear from you again," he replied. "Are you still in Switzerland?"

"Ibiza, actually," she responded.

"I don't think I'll be able to make it to Europe this season, unfortunately," he said.

"That's fine. I actually have a job for you right there in Portland. The pay is your usual plus expenses. Are you in?"

"Of course." He almost sounded surprised that she'd asked.

"Someone broke into my facility in the city, and I need you to track them and retrieve what they stole," Molina said. "They have someone covering for them and doing an extremely good job at it. I'll need you to find out if you can recover anything that was erased. I want your best team on this, understood?"

"Completely," he said. "I'll contact you when we have more information for you."

"I look forward to it." She smiled and hung up.

Her mood was ruined and she would need to find a way to improve her spirits before the day began in earnest.

A glance at her arms didn't help. It merely provided a nagging reminder that the growing blue veins were now more and more visible through her well-tanned skin.

Maybe she needed to spend time with Diego to help distract her from the problems. Assuming he had recovered from the night before, of course.

"Savage, are you there?" Anja asked.

"Where else would I be?" he retorted.

Things had gone from bad to worse and more than once, they'd had to duck into a couple of alleys to avoid the patrol cars that had begun to cruise up and down the streets with far more regularity. It made their progress much slower than they needed it to be, and they really had to get off the streets and into a car.

"I think I've found a car for you guys," the hacker said. "How the fuck do people live without all the electronics in their cars? Also, I sense considerable sass in your tone, and I don't think you've earned that."

"I think I've earned more than enough tonight," Savage countered smartly. "Where is the car?"

"Continue down the street and take the next left," she said. "You'll reach a parking lot, where you'll find a Mercedes I've unlocked for you."

"Great, that sounds good." He glanced at Jenna. "We have a car. Then, we'll find someplace to spend the night."

"Awesome," she replied. "You know, you two should really think about getting me one of those earpieces of yours. Hearing only the one side of a conversation that relates to me and my safety does feel a little irresponsible."

"Yes, we'll work on that right away, okay?" he said wearily. She had a point, and he was heartily over being the man in the middle.

"Well, it takes me a while to make these devices up, but I'll see what I can do," Anja said through the earpiece. "For now, though, get to the fucking car."

Savage couldn't agree more. It had been long enough since his last good night's sleep that even walking began to feel like a chore. While he had been trained to operate on minimal sleep, food, and water, that still meant he now operated at reduced capacity.

They finally reached the parking lot and Anja, who appeared to be in a hurry, flashed the lights of the car they would take.

He and Jenna jogged over and she scrambled into the passenger side of the car.

He was about to join her when the sight of flashing red, white, and blue lights caught his eye and a patrol car pulled into the parking lot.

"Oh...fuck me sideways," he said softly as the siren wailed for a couple of seconds. The cops appeared to want him to pay attention to them.

"What do we do?" she asked from inside the car.

"Don't worry about it," he said. "I'll handle this. Stay inside the car, okay?"

She nodded and looked at him with the terrified yet trusting light in her eyes that made him feel all warm and fuzzy again. He really needed to stop with that. The chances were that he wouldn't actually see much of her once he turned her over to the people who would actually be able to take care of her. Getting attached would only cause problems for him down the road.

The police car came to a stop in front of the Mercedes and both officers stepped out. They were beat cops, young and obviously hadn't been on the force long enough to know that they needed to keep one man in the car in case someone did precisely what Savage planned to do if they decided to be a problem.

Well, technically, he was the one who was the problem, but he couldn't think about that right now.

"Sir?" the first officer asked and his hand hovered at his hip, already reaching for his weapon. "Sir, please step away from the car now."

His gaze followed the officer's movement. The buckle was still on, and while his hand rested on the grip of the weapon, it would take him a few seconds to draw it.

The other hung back, closer to the car.

"I won't ask you again, sir," the first officer now yelled and tried to sound intimidating as he approached.

"Roger that. Yes, I have someone who looks like the sketch standing outside a car," the second officer said into the radio on his shoulder. "I don't know…the jawline is a little off but it's close enough. There's a young woman inside the car. She looks scared so it's possibly a hostage situation."

"The sketch looks nothing like me," Savage grumbled under his breath and raised his hands as he complied and stepped away from the car.

"What was that?" the officer asked and approached cautiously.

"What is the problem here, officer?" Savage said a little louder so the man could hear him although he kept his tone of voice calm and showed no aggression as he kept his gaze lowered.

"We need to ask you a few questions," the officer said and stepped in closer still. "What are you doing here at this time of night?"

He shook his head. "I'm not discussing my day."

"Why not?" the officer asked and moved forward. "Do you have something to hide, sir?"

"Am I being detained or am I free to go?" he asked and deliberately ignored the man's questions.

"We're only talking here."

"Am I free to go?" he repeated.

"We merely need to ask you a few questions and then you'll be free to go," he said and took another step.

"I'm not discussing my day," he repeated and inched closer as well, although he kept his gaze lowered. "Have you ever heard of the fifth amendment?"

"Do you have something to hide, sir?" the officer asked, grasped Savage's arm, and tried to push him over to the car.

It was all he had waited for. The hand that was supposed to have been on his weapon now fumbled for a pair of cuffs on his belt. The other man peeked into the patrol car, probably to make sure their doughnuts were still edible.

Or something. He had no idea what would make the officer look inside the car rather than keep an eye on his partner while he attempted to make an arrest.

Either way, it made for the kind of perfect storm he could work with. He turned with the insistence of the officer's hand but he overworked it and spun a full one-eighty to drive his elbow into the man's jaw.

The cop looked stunned by the strike, not quite limp but he also didn't react when he moved behind him, unbuckled the firearm, and drew it out of the holster before his partner realized that something was wrong.

"Oh, shit!" the man shouted.

Savage had no intention to use the firearm. Firing it now would unleash all kinds of hell on them when people called the cops for shots fired. That wouldn't be an ideal outcome.

He also wasn't interested in a prolonged standoff with these two.

Instead, he drew his pistol from under his jacket and aimed it at the second officer, who still stood behind the car door, obviously thinking it would provide him with some kind of cover.

"Think about what you're doing!" the man shouted as if trying to sound like the decisive officer of the law he told himself he was while he stared at himself in the locker room mirror. "Do you really want to piss the whole Portland PD off?"

"Nope, but that doesn't mean I won't if I have to," he replied, aimed his weapon below the car door, and pulled the trigger twice. A couple of needles were launched magnetically into the officer's legs.

A scream from the other side of the door told him the man was still alive, at least.

"What the fuck?" the first officer asked, still a little dazed.

He didn't respond and instead, thunked the grip of his pistol into the back of the man's head. As he fell, he aimed at his knees and pulled the trigger of his weapon twice. Another scream followed.

There really was no time to feel sorry for these guys. They were working-class men, maybe a little unprofessional and in need of more training.

On the bright side, they would receive all kinds of

compensation for this and would probably be heroes in their local precinct for being injured in the line of duty.

Savage disabled the radio on the first man and walked over to the other one to do the same. Neither put up much of a fight to stop him. They weren't trained for this kind of shit. He wondered if they were maybe in their first five years with law enforcement. This had to be the worst kind of rude awakening.

Still, he was in this business to get shit done, not feel bad for the people who got in his way, intentionally or otherwise.

Calmly, he leaned over the cop and disabled the radio in the car too. The officers would know they could simply use their phones to call for backup, but from the state they were in now, they would have a hard time remembering it. He finished off by putting a series of needles into the hood of the car, hopefully disabling that too before he walked over to where Jenna still watched him from inside the car.

"We need another car, Anja," he said, opened the door, and gestured for Jenna to get out. "This one is burned."

"There's one on the other side of the parking lot. I've already brought it online for you," she responded quickly.

"I appreciate it." He looked quickly at Jenna. "Are you okay?"

"I only...I need a second," she replied and stared at the two officers on the ground.

"Take a second while we're getting away," he replied, took her arm, and walked her toward their new car.

"There's a problem, Savage," she said as he stepped into the car, a Nissan electric.

"What kind of problem?" he asked as he checked to make sure Jenna had her seat belt on.

"The someone intercepted the footage from the patrol car camera kind of problem," she said. "I erased it like I always do, but there were signs of tampering. Someone got their hands on it before I did. And it definitely wasn't law enforcement."

"Shit." He scowled as he started the car. "Is there anything we can do about it now?"

"Get the fuck out of dodge," she replied.

"Roger that."

CHAPTER THIRTY-NINE

It already promised to be an extremely long day.

By the time she looked through her phone after the call to Portland was completed, there were dozens of messages waiting for her. People needed her input for spending reports, they needed to know what she wanted to do with a certain item, and certain cash payments that had come in.

It wasn't that she didn't like the fact that she was needed in the day-to-day operations of the businesses. Molina was the kind of person who would feel at a loss if she didn't have something to work on. She would find something to do if she lacked a constant demand for her efforts.

The problem was that there weren't enough people she trusted in her line of work to take the work over. She really needed someone to take responsibility for the comparatively smaller details and manage them effectively in order to free her up to work on the bigger picture problems her company faced. It was a trust issue. Given the fact that much of the work that was done by her companies and investments tended to have shady elements, it was difficult to find people who could handle it who weren't shady themselves.

She wasn't really complaining—not much, anyway—but there were times when she really wished she could delegate the work to someone else and dive into the aspects of her work she genuinely enjoyed. The concept that when one worked at doing something one loved, one never worked a day in their life was one close to her heart.

But until that moment arrived, she would have to take the good with the bad and force herself to oversee most of the smaller details of the companies she had control of.

When she had finished with Diego, a limo had already waited to take her to the local headquarters of her company, with a handful of aides who needed her approval and signature on a veritable library of documents.

What was the company called these days? She had flown under the Pegasus banner for a while until Carlson lost control of the company, and she needed to make changes to keep them invisible to the public eye. Was it...Minotaur? She liked working with mythical beasts, specifically from Greek mythology. It was displayed at the front of the building so that would remind her, but she kicked herself for forgetting.

For now, though, there were things that required her attention more than merely knowing about the name of the company she was the de-facto leader of at this particular time of the month. It was always fluid since people tended to pick up on what she was doing and they would have to slip under the public radar again. It really was an unfortunate necessity.

"Ma'am?" one of the aides said and leaning across the small partition between her and the other three men she shared the car with.

"What is it..." she asked and paused as she tried to remember the young man's name.

"Santiago, ma'am," he replied with an understanding smile. "Your phone is ringing insistently, and it appears to be important. Or insistent, at the very least."

Molina yanked her purse open and tugged her phone free. The phone was buzzing, as he had said, and she didn't recognize the number that was being used. She had more than a few people on her payroll who didn't like to be tracked. They changed their numbers from time to time and kept her on her toes—and irritated the living crap out of her.

Well, it was best to find out what they wanted.

She sighed and shook her head before she pressed the device to her ear. "Hello?"

"This is Mr Stevens," said the thick male voice on the other line. "I thought you might want to keep yourself free from connections with me for the duration of this operation."

"You thought right," she said, leaned back in her seat, and crossed her legs. "How can I help you, Mr Stevens?"

"Well, it's more about how I can help you, Miss Molina," he replied. "We've conducted a preliminary tracking investigation into the team that attacked your facility."

"Broke into," she corrected him. She didn't need word that one of her facilities had been attacked spreading. It was all about the doublespeak when those kinds of things were concerned. It was why she had publicists working around the clock to keep them in business.

"Broke into, of course," he said, understanding completely. "Anyway, we have used our connections in the local police force to keep track of the investigation and pursuit of the burglars, and something we thought was interesting came up. An encounter between the burglar, your prize specimen, and a couple of local law enforcement officers came to light and was captured on video. Someone was there to quickly scrub the incriminating evidence in his favor, but our specialist was able to intercept the recording beforehand. I thought you might want to see what we are up against yourself."

"I would," Molina said with a nod.

"The footage is already on its way to your inbox. We are currently using it to try to track your burglar. I will let you know if there are any new developments."

"I appreciate your efforts, Stevens," she said. There was a reason why she had trusted the man with this mission, after all. On top of being discreet, he also knew that she liked to be on top of proceedings, not because she wanted to micromanage them but because she needed to know what was happening in case there was anything that she needed to do herself.

She hung up and sure enough, a new message waited for her in the encrypted inbox she maintained for her more delicate transactions. These were of a kind she didn't want found should investigators in any of the investigations currently in progress against her in various countries decide to get smart and not be open to bribery.

With an inward sigh, she opened the video of the

footage and studied it closely. The quality wasn't quite up to her admittedly high standards, but it was good enough that she could at least see what was happening. A man stood outside a car and looked both surprised and annoyed by the two officers talking to him. He wasn't quite what she had pictured, if she was honest, but things rarely lived up to what she thought they should. He wasn't overly tall or muscular but there was something about him—what sports coaches called the intangibles. She decided it might be the way he positioned himself and how he kept his center of gravity low and ready for a fight while looking like he had no intention to cause any trouble.

His body language fooled the officer who moved closer to him as well as the second cop, who disappeared from the footage, possibly looking for something inside the car. When the man attacked, it wasn't anything flashy and it didn't need to be. After he delivered an elbow into the jaw of the man closest to him, he calmly disarmed him and used him as a body shield to protect himself from the other officer.

Leg shots? Why would he choose leg shots instead of killing them? They were witnesses who would be able to identify him as the man who had shot them. But no, he left them disabled but alive and worked quickly and calmly to make sure they couldn't call for backup.

His method was fast, efficient, and got the job done— not unlike how she wanted her people to operate. This guy was good.

"That's hot," she said, surprised that she had voiced it aloud as she set the video to play again. It was that kind of must-see material.

"Ma'am?" Santiago said, leaning forward. "I'm afraid that we still need your input on the Chernobyl issue. The local authorities are being particularly difficult regarding the salvage attempts."

Molina waved him away. "They're being difficult because they forgot that I own them. Those who matter, anyway. Remind them of the kind of leverage we have over them and I can assure you, they will crumble."

It was a bold claim but one that she had sufficient confidence to make. Those who had tried to come between her and Chernobyl had learned that hardball was the only ball that she played.

"Of course, ma'am," the young man said and typed furiously on his phone.

She restarted the video, feeling that she hadn't given the few seconds she missed the proper attention while dealing with her assistant. It was necessary to learn more about this man and why he had positioned himself against her like that. More importantly, she needed to find out if he could be brought over to her side.

As they escaped the parking lot through another exit and found the open roads, there was silence in the stolen car. Savage was mostly focused on making sure they weren't being followed by any of the local cops. Anja, for her part, said she would try to track whoever had taken their footage before she had managed to erase it.

He didn't mind the silence, but a few glances at Jenna told him that something was on the young woman's mind.

Something was bothering her, and it would only get worse if she held it in. Maybe it was a coping mechanism. She had been submitted to the kind of shit no teenager should endure, and there was bound to be residual damage there.

He merely didn't think it was his place to play therapist so he said nothing.

A few more minutes passed before he finally sighed and shook his head. "What's the problem?"

She perked up and turned to look at him. "Are you talking to me? Or to Anja?"

"You," he said. "You have that look on your face that says something is wrong but you don't want to talk about it or don't know how to address it, so you're keeping it in. Trust me, kid, when it comes to issues, it's always better to get it out in the open."

"Oh," she said and tilted her head like she hadn't realized that her emotions were written all over her face. "Okay, well, I guess I was a little surprised by how you handled those police officers back there. You kind of think they would be able to help us and instead, you were on them almost immediately."

"I told you what I was about, kid," he said. "I didn't mince any words or spare you any details. I'm not the greatest guy in the world, and in the eyes of those two we left back there, I'm in the running for the worst. I did leave them alive, though."

"I know, I know," she said and rubbed her temples furiously as if that could somehow alter her thoughts. "And yeah, you were honest about who you were and yes, you left them alive. It's only...you hear something and you accept it, but seeing it in person is a whole different thing."

Savage nodded and kept his gaze focused on the road. "Does that change what you think about me? Would you rather step out and continue on your own? Honestly, the cops in the city are after me because…well, yes, I did break the law here and there. They'll also be after me with more intensity now that I left a couple of their finest needing crutches for the next six months or so. They won't really care much about what you do."

"I'm fine sticking it out with you," Jenna asserted. "Besides, I have the feeling that if I leave, the people running the lab will simply be able to pick me up again. I only need a little time to process it, is all."

"I understand that," he replied and drew a deep breath. She was right. Hearing about it was always considerably less intense than seeing it. Nothing could really prepare her for seeing what he was capable of, no matter how well he put it verbally.

"Am I interrupting something?" Anja asked through the speakers of the car as well as through his earpiece.

Jenna looked surprised by the development.

"What?" the hacker asked. Clearly, she'd seen the young woman's reaction. He chuckled when he considered the wonders of modern electronics. "You said you wanted to be part of both sides of the conversation. Until I can get you an earpiece, this will be as good as it gets."

"Okay," the girl said softly and looked at him for guidance.

He simply smirked and shook his head. "Roll with it. Like me, Anja is a lot to take in at first. Unlike me, though, she's far more lovable with each successive serving."

"Damn right." The Russian laughed, which prompted a

smile from his passenger at long last. "Anyway, as much as I want to tune in and chat with you beautiful folks, I actually do have updates on the situation. Courtney approved the use of a private plane to get you out of town, but it won't be available until tomorrow. You'll need to stay alive until then, and I'd suggest maybe finding someplace to hunker down for the night."

"What's left of it," he grumbled under his breath.

"Right," she said. "There's a motel not far from your location. They're the kind you pay for by the hour, and they don't need credit cards or ask for names or IDs. It seems like the kind of place the two of you need."

Jenna narrowed her eyes as if she sensed there was some kind of reference she was missing. She had to have been locked up in that lab for a while for her to not understand what Anja was insinuating.

"We're on our way," Savage said. "I guess I can't use my corporate card to cover the expenses?"

"You're hilarious, Savage." The hacker chuckled. "But no, you can't. You have cash on hand, though, right?"

"Correct," he said. "Thanks for the update, Anja. Talk to you soon."

"No problem." The speakers immediately went dead.

"What will you do when we've gotten you safely out of here?" Savage asked Jenna when the silence threatened to take over again.

"I don't know," she replied. "There's not much out there for me in the world. My folks are gone and I didn't have much in the way of extended family or friends I can fall back on. I guess I could always find something to do with my life—maybe go to college, but considering that I never technically finished high school, there are challenges there too."

He glanced quickly at her, not liking the suddenly negative world view she espoused. "How old are you?"

"Nineteen," she said. "Why?"

"Kid, you have your whole life ahead of you," he said with a small smile. "Choose something that you want to do —anything really—and go after it like life owes you some good karma."

"Is that what you did?" she asked.

"That's not the point." He shook his head. It wasn't what he did. Sure, he'd wanted to be something of a hero when he was a kid, but he'd grown up and realized that bankers made more money. "The point is, you need to find out what it is you want to make of your life and go after it."

"It sounds like you read that on a poster that had a little cat on it," she pointed out.

"That's also not the point," he grumbled.

CHAPTER FORTY

He had to admit that he liked working with Molina.

Stevens wasn't the kind of man who was all that selective about the work that came his way. His firm was relatively new, anyway, and he wasn't in a position to be persnickety about who wanted his services. He had left the military and had more than a few years in the private sector to his name. People had told him he would make more money if he branched out and worked for himself.

They had all been the kind of people who were interested in having him on the payroll themselves. Considering the obscene amount of cash he had made working for private security companies, that was saying something.

And damned if they hadn't been right. Three years after he cut away from the business and started out on his own, he cleared more than he had as an employee to the tune of six figures. He could look into selling his firm and retiring in another couple of years.

It helped that he had connections from his time

working as an employee. It was important to cultivate relationships with the people you worked with as well as those you worked for, even while an employee. When he had parted ways with the company that had employed him, it had been with the assurances that they would send any freelancer work they had his way, which was really all he needed to hear from them.

They were good people—solid people—and kept their commitment to send all the freelancing recommendations his way. That had certainly helped with his retirement ambitions.

Molina had been one of those who hadn't even needed to be recommended to him. The ultra-billionaire liked to do her own research and find the people who worked out best for her. He wasn't surprised or even arrogant in saying that if she wanted work done in the Midwest and western areas of the US, he was the man for the job.

He had the best people working for his firm, and when they weren't enough, he had enough connections with the freelancers in the area to be able to supplement his resources.

There had been a mission from her not that long before that he had thankfully turned down. For one thing, it hadn't been from her directly—which meant she might not even be involved—merely someone who worked for her. Secondly, they had to capture a small civilian family.

While Stevens would never claim to have much in the way of morals, there were certain things he didn't do. Involving families in a capture-not-kill situation would always be a problem since it involved people he didn't know much about. Those who weren't civilians tended to have enough of a history that he could get a good picture of what they were capable of.

Prolonged involvement with civilians meant that there was more time for something to go wrong. You always knew what professionals would do but not what amateurs would do. For one thing, they tended to call the police, while pros disliked having law enforcement involved.

He felt safe in saying that he had made the correct decision in leaving that bounty for someone else. They had ended up annihilated by a pro who protected the family and who went on to destroy the other team that had tried it. Word on the street was that the man who had laid the bounty out for Molina had been dealt with as well to take the money off the table. Further intelligence had told him that it was a team that had gone after Banks, although not much was known about that yet.

His connections were mostly situated on the west coast, while the attack had happened on the east. Still, the fact that the money had been withdrawn without any paydays processed said all it needed to.

Thankfully, she was involved this time. She had already paid his upfront fee, ready to shell out more if it was needed. He would definitely not overcharge her, though. She was a good client, sent a fair amount of good, rich work his way, and it was a cash cow he fully intended to milk for as long as possible.

Of course, he had needed to bring some of his free-lancers into the mission. He had enough muscle on his team already and didn't need to bring outsiders in for that, but the technical support that had been required for the operation could only be called in from the outside.

Chaos was the guy's online handle, and Stevens wasn't sure if he liked the man. They had worked together before but it had always been from a distance, far enough away to keep the human aspect out of their relationship. Admittedly, he was a one-of-a-kind talent, but he appeared to know it. To his mind, he was an arrogant little shit who couldn't be older than twenty-five but acted like the whole world owed him everything.

He would make sure they wouldn't need to work with him in person again. Without a doubt, he wanted to have those skills on his side instead of with the competition and would be willing to pay for it too. The kid looked like he was more comfortable on his own ground anyway and was simply made up for it by being an asshole.

"Christ, lurk much?" Chaos asked and glared at Stevens. In fairness, he had peered over the kid's shoulder, but he was entitled to at least have a basic idea of what he was doing.

Or at least make him think he had a basic idea. The asshat worked on three screens and a laptop and Stevens honestly couldn't tell what was happening on any of them.

In fairness, he wasn't great with all the IT crap. It was why he had hired the kid in the first place. Next time, he would be hired to stay in his room and work from there.

"Sorry, I'm simply wondering what the fuck you're doing here," he said. "And wondering if you've moved past the twenties, using lines like that."

"Hey, man, no need to hate," Chaos responded. "You

need my skills so let me talk however the fuck I want. Do you have any complaints about the use of said skills?"

"Well, no, but—"

"Then don't hate," the younger man cut in and shrugged. He hadn't bothered to turn his attention away from the screens in front of him for the full exchange. "Let the C-man do his work."

"You have to know how that sounds, right?" he asked and shook his head.

"Of course, I do," Chaos said, laughing. "Why the hell do you think I use it?"

Stevens opened his mouth to say something, but he blinked and shook his head. He had no idea why he spent so much time with this, and frankly, it didn't matter.

There was no point in antagonizing the glorified technical support—which they needed to track the burglar, of course, but still merely support. He wouldn't go out there and put his life on the line for the team. Once they had the man located, he wouldn't be used for more than simply making sure that whoever ran interference for the burglar wasn't on their back as well.

It had all the makings for one frustratingly long night. The man had disappeared after the footage had come up, but Chaos had decided he would try to track them using the footage from the traffic cams in the area. Someone in the position of the man they were hunting wouldn't run any red lights as he needed to remain as unseen as possible, but he would still be in the area.

And with the city as abandoned as it was at this time of night, there was a reduced number of cars they actually needed to track.

Four dozen, from the looks of the screens, Stevens noted. Given that they were talking about a city with over a million occupants, it wasn't that much, but it was still enough to cause a headache. Chaos didn't look like the stress was telling on him, though. He had programs running the tracking of the cars, and all he needed to do was select which of the people needed to be ruled out from their little search.

"Something tells me our guy doesn't work at a Seven-Eleven, so I guess that rules him out," the tech said, having narrated everything in order to impress his employer. "He probably doesn't live in the suburbs either, so we can rule him out too. We're down to about three dozen cars. Easy, right?"

"What the hell do you want us to do about it?" one of Stevens' muscle men asked. They had begun to get annoyed, not only at the youngster's attitude but the fact that they waited for him to give them a target.

Stevens could see why that was infuriating since he felt it himself, but there was no need for animosity to build in his team.

"I don't know…maybe stand there, slack-jawed, and watch me do the impossible?" Chaos asked and glanced at the rest of the muscle. "Or stand there and not understand. See, that's why IT guys think anyone who doesn't at least have a decent grip on Java is merely a Neanderthal."

He knew he'd have to step in. The idiot had to know that as skilled as he was with his computers, being an asshole would get him torn to pieces by the people he antagonized.

If word got out that the IT folks who worked for him

were killed, no one would work with him again. That was the most annoying part of freelancing, of course. Reputation was everything, not only for his clients but for the people who would work with him.

Having to kowtow to people like Chaos was one of the downsides. There were a few, but the upsides more than made up for it—mostly with zeroes added to his bank account, but that was neither here nor there. Right now, he needed to step in as his people had begun to surround the kid, who merely stared infuriatingly at his screens with a small smile on his face.

"Okay guys, back the fuck off. Go check your weapons again," Stevens ordered and the men nodded, eased away, and headed toward where they had their weapons stashed. He remained with the younger man. "You need to start rethinking your business strategy, kid."

"Why is that?" Chaos asked and looked at him. "I'm the best in the business and you know that. You need me on this operation."

"You're obviously not the best in the business," he retorted. "The best in the business is the person who's covering for our burglar since they're running you in a merry circle. There are other people in the business too—those who might not be as skilled as you but charge far better rates and are less antagonistic to the people they're working with."

The IT man clearly didn't like having his flaws pointed out to him. He also didn't like that the person on the other side of the computer had blocked all the ways to find the burglars, and he knew that he'd been lucky to intercept the footage from the patrol car attack before his nemesis had.

But, as Stevens well knew, he had a point. Chaos had more than only a paycheck on the line here. He was up against one of the best, and that meant he needed to bring his A-game. It explained why he was being such an ass, but the man could work without being an asshole.

He didn't want to say his survival depended on him acting a little more like a civilized human being, but given the dirty looks his boys still directed at the hacker, there was really no telling what might happen.

"Now sit there and give us someone to follow. And for your own safety, shut the fuck up," Stevens said.

Chaos didn't reply. Maybe he knew he was right, or maybe he had a lead he needed to work on. The hacker did shut up, however, which meant that he no longer needed to play nice. He moved away to the corner where his laptop was open, still playing the only footage they had of the burglar.

"Hey, Jackson, get over here," he called to his second in command, a tall, bald bastard who was nearly a foot taller than he was. "Help me out and look at this guy. What are you seeing here?"

Jackson narrowed his eyes and studied the footage intently while the lean man dealt with the cops. "He's fast. He was ready for a fight almost before the cops pulled up. He had every step of the fight played out in his head before the cop even approached him. He could have killed those guys if he wanted to, but he didn't. Instead, he left them alive for some reason. That's a nice little custom piece he has there too. I'll bet that's not even on the market yet."

"Conclusion?" Stevens asked.

The man shrugged. "The guy's a pro. Maybe he's

working with an agenda, which is why he didn't kill the cops. He's slick, though, and he has the right skillset. I'd say special forces, probably American from that particular style, although definitely not Marines."

"How do you think we'll be able to defeat him?" he asked and rubbed his chin in thought.

"Change the rules of the game—put him on his back foot and force him to ad-lib," Jackson said and folded his arms in front of his chest. "Once he doesn't know what he'll do next, we'll have a split second to pin him down somewhere and make him suffer. It'll only be a second, though."

"A second's all we need, honestly," he said as a car pulled into the warehouse they used as a base.

They would definitely never run an operation like this from his firm's headquarters, not when they would do shit that was this illegal. Especially when they brought people in from the outside.

The man who stepped out of the car was the sixth member of their team—not counting Chaos aside—and he had worked from the police front and tried to get everything that had been passed along to them back to the team.

"Jesse," he said in greeting to the smaller, stouter man. "What do you have for us?"

"Honestly, the cops are fairly lost about it," the man replied and shook his head. "I needed to feed info to my contacts to get them to connect the two wounded cops to the break-in. After that, all they really had was a sketch and witness reports from the folks who were there when he broke in."

"Let's see the sketch." He took the tablet from his man's hand and compared the two.

"It looks nothing like him," Jackson muttered and narrowed his eyes.

"No wonder these cops are completely fucking clueless." Stevens shook his head in disgust. "Oh, well, their incompetence is our gain. At least we won't need to work our way around the boys in blue this time."

CHAPTER FORTY-ONE

They pulled up to the motel, situated beyond the edges of the city proper. It looked a little run-down but honestly, Savage had seen far worse over the years. Even during his time with the folks at Pegasus, he had been forced to stay at a couple of verified dumps.

"This'll do," he said with a scowl and shoved the car into park. "Barely."

"Hey, don't hate. This was the best that could be done on short notice," Anja said.

"I'm not hating, only pointing out that it's not exactly the Ritz," he said and made a careful scrutiny of their surroundings.

"Well, you can't stay at the Ritz, since they would ask for an ID," she pointed out unnecessarily. "Oh, and need I remind you that, without access to company funds, you can't afford to stay there either?"

"Yeah, I get the picture." He muttered an imprecation under his breath. His surliness came down to a lack of sleep and as long as there was a bed for him to use—and maybe something to eat before they collapsed for what was left for the night, he would be happy. Well, less annoyed, anyway.

They made their way to the front desk, which was covered by a heavy frame of bulletproof glass. There were obvious reasons for that, the most logical being that it prevented people from reaching in to snatch the cash while the person working the register wasn't present.

Person being the keyword, he supposed. No one was actually present at the front of the desk when they arrived, which forced him to tap the bell that rang a soft alarm in the back room.

A young man rushed out and looked very much like he had been woken up from a nice long nap.

"Hey, man, sorry for the delay," he said, his words slurred enough to raise the question of whether sleep had been the only thing he'd indulged in. "Queen bed, right?"

"My daughter and I need a place to stay for the night," he said and narrowed his eyes. "Two beds, if you please."

"Oh...right," the clerk said but tilted his head curiously. He appeared to doubt that his newest guests were related and could be excused for thinking that. Savage didn't care, though. If the guy thought they were here on some kind of tryst, it would perhaps make them even more forgettable.

It didn't really matter.

"Two beds and two people will be seventy bucks for the night," the young man said. He punched the details into a computer that looked to have been bolted to the desk two decades before. "A clean hundred if you want a late checkout."

"We're fine for the early checkout option." Savage

peeled a few bills from his wallet and slid them through the partition.

The clerk counted the money and studied them closely for any signs that they might be fake currency before he put them in the drawer to his right and took a key from the wall above it. "Room 108. Climb the outside stairs and follow the numbering on the doors and you'll find it."

"Thank you kindly." He retrieved the key from under the partition and gestured for Jenna to follow him. "Do you want something to eat before we sleep?"

"Sure, I could eat something," the young woman said with a firm nod. "Could we order something? Can we order pizza?"

She sounded excited enough by the option to make him turn to look at her. "Sure. Is there any particular reason why?"

"I don't know, except that it's been a while since I've had pizza," she said with a shrug. "It was my favorite before the whole leukemia thing, and the doctors kept me on a very strict diet before I even entered the lab. They kept me on the diet there as well to make sure there were no regressions."

"So you miss pizza, then," he said and nodded. "Sure, let's order some. They probably have brochures in the room to order from. Either that or we'll find some online."

"I'm already working on that for you," Anja said. "I ordered a couple online that should be headed your way in fifteen minutes."

"Oh...thanks." He grinned as he unlocked their door. "Anja is already on the pizza delivery."

"Don't judge me. I was bored and needed something to do," the hacker said and chuckled.

"Well, I guess we owe you for all the little things." He stepped cautiously into the room and made sure it was secure before he motioned Jenna in and locked it behind her. "That on top of the whole saving our bacon thing."

"Oh, stop, you'll make me blush," Anja responded, her voice coquettish.

Maybe he was becoming a little too mushy for his own good. Or maybe he was merely a little too tired to be snarky.

The room was relatively clean—much cleaner than he expected it to be, anyway, and while he wouldn't actually get too comfortable on the beds, it was still better than snoozing in the car.

Still, even optimistically, it barely passed acceptable levels. Thankfully, it would only be a short night of sleep, after which they would take the roundabout route to the airstrip where he'd originally arrived. From that point forward, he assumed Jenna would be Monroe and Jessica's problem. He could acknowledge, at least to himself, that he had become a little attached to the girl but, like it had been with Jessica, it would be better for her to find someone more stable to stay with.

Someone like Jessica, he thought as a knock on the door announced that the pizza had arrived five minutes early.

Savage made sure to check that it was the pizza man and no one else before he opened the door. He paid for the meal and left a decent tip—enough to make sure that they were not remembered as cheapskates, but not so much that they would be remembered for being overly generous.

Jenna hadn't lied about having missed pizza. Anja had ordered pepperoni and meat lover's, along with soda for them, and he hadn't even had a chance to sit before she attacked both with the kind of gusto he remembered seeing in himself when he was taken to a fast food joint as a kid.

It was nice to watch, but by the time he got around to it, there were only a couple of slices of the pepperoni left—not nearly enough, but he could make do.

"Sorry," Jenna said and wiped her mouth politely. "I guess I was a little hungrier than I thought I was."

"Don't apologize. I'm actually a little impressed," he said around a bite of the second to last piece. "At this rate, you could probably make a good living from prizes at eating competitions."

"Still, I don't think that only two pieces are enough for you," she pointed out but still stared at the piece he hadn't eaten with a hint of greed.

He laughed and pushed it toward her. "I can get something from the vending machine later. Honestly, I'm more tired than hungry at this point, anyway."

"I get that." She attacked the slice with the same fervor as she had the others. "Can I ask you something?"

He looked at her and tilted his head in query. "I think it was your turn anyway, so sure, go ahead."

"I don't want to pry or anything, but I don't think you covered this in our previous question and answer session," she said, finished her food, and took a sip of her soda. "Why did you decide to help me escape from the lab when it would jeopardize your mission so thoroughly?"

Savage narrowed his eyes. "How did you know about

that? I didn't tell you that rescuing you would compromise what I was really there for. I only said I was there to find merchandise."

"Well, I did hear you talking about it before you broke in and set all the alarms off," she said. "I could hear what was being said in your earpiece."

"I...wait." He scowled and closed his eyes. "You could hear what was said through my earpiece the whole time? Why didn't you tell me?"

"Loud and clear, yes." Jenna grinned and shrugged a little sheepishly. "I guess I didn't want to seem impolite, snooping around in your private conversations like I was."

"That's impossible," Anja said. "I've tuned these earpieces to be heard by the person wearing them and no one else. How the fuck did she hear us?"

"The doctors said there would be side effects to the treatment they gave me," the girl explained. She'd obviously clearly heard what Anja said through Savage's earpiece, which meant she did an excellent job of faking ignorance earlier. "One of the first that I noticed was that my hearing improved dramatically over the first couple of months. While they tried to reverse the effects, that one never went away. I told them it did, though, to keep them from panicking about it. Don't change the subject, though."

Savage rubbed his temples. He really didn't have the time—or the inclination—to get into this. "Well, the operation was for something else, but when we saw they were keeping you in there and against your will, from what we could see, I didn't feel right leaving you there to be used as a human guinea pig any longer."

"Why not?" She placed her elbows on the table were

seated at and yawned. "I thought you said you were a bad man."

"I also told you that I have a family," he reminded her, his voice a little softer than he meant it to be. "A wife and a daughter. My wife divorced me and married someone else —someone better—but they'll always be my family, to my mind, anyway. When I saw you in there, I couldn't help thinking about my little girl."

"Do I look like her?" she asked curiously.

"No, she's still fairly young. It's more like...my mind went to the thought of what would happen if she was subjected to the things you were. It burned me up inside, and I would like to think that if someone saw my daughter in that cage, they would act and get her out of it. Once I had the thought, I could only act on that instinct."

"You sound like you are a really great dad." She finished her soda and stretched on her seat. "What happened to your family, though? Did they die? Is that why you're doing this?"

"No." Savage shook his head. "No, hell no. Why would you think that?"

"I don't know. It's what usually happens in the movies," Jenna said. "You know, hero retires from active duty to be with his family. Someone comes after him but kills his family instead, so he vows vengeance. Alternatively, they go after his dog, with similar results."

"Depressing movies," he retorted. "Although I guess the reality isn't that much more uplifting either. Remember when I told you I needed to disappear for the benefit of the government?"

She nodded.

"Well, yeah, one of the conditions is that I have to stay away from my family and not let anyone from my past life know I'm still kicking," he explained. "After the divorce, though, I wasn't that close to them anyway. I...well, she told me to leave and I did. I signed up for another couple of tours—kind of a way to show her, I guess. It doesn't really matter, though. I wasn't a great dad or husband. She married another guy, and I can't honestly say she made a mistake. Guy's a fucking lawyer."

"That has to hurt, right?" Jenna said.

"Yeah," he agreed roughly and kept his gaze focused forward while he tried to keep his emotions in check. "But the guy's a great dad and a decent enough person."

"You stalked your ex-wife's husband?"

"Of course, I did," he confirmed with a chuckle. "You don't think I'd let some random dude move in with the two people I care about most in the world, do you?"

"Well, I think it's creepy, no matter your good intentions," she countered.

"You're probably right. But I'm a paranoid dude for a reason. Folks have targeted me and have gone after my family to do it so, creepy or not, I stalked and checked up on the guy. I guess I also hoped to dig up a little dirt but it was, for the most part, for safety reasons."

"You're a tough man to get a read on, you know that, Savage?" Jenna stood from her chair and stretched again. "First, you're honest about what you want me to do and you're nice and chat to me, but then you beat up a couple of cops. You say you helped me because you hope someone would do that for your girl if she were in trouble, but you stalk her new stepfather."

"I know," Savage said. "Like I said, many people would have good reason to believe I'm not a great guy and they might be correct. I'm only doing what I think is right."

She smiled and shook her head. "You don't have to defend your actions to me, Jer. Only think about them before you do them."

"I try," he replied. "Thinking isn't usually the kind of thing I have the luxury of doing. Like with the cops. If I hadn't acted instead of thinking, I would probably be sitting in a jail cell right now and they—whoever 'they' are —would haul you off to another facility, far out of the reach of anyone who might be able to help you."

"Okay, you say that, but if it had happened, I would have put some effort into helping Jenna," Anja interjected. "And there's not much in the world that I can't find when I put my mind to it."

"I appreciate that, Anja," the girl said and moved over to her bed, the one farthest from the door.

"I still can't get used to that kind of hearing," the hacker muttered as he collected the trash and left it in a neat pile for housekeeping to collect in the morning, assuming they had housekeeping there.

"You know I can hear that too, right?" Jenna asked.

"Get some sleep," Savage said quickly. "It seems like we both need it."

"I'll keep working on trying to find the folks who inter-cepted the video," Anja said. "Stay safe, Savage."

"Will do," he replied and removed the security guard uniform to reveal the jeans and shirt he'd worn under it. He remained fully dressed and stretched on the bed, tucked his pistol under the pillow, and kept his hand close, even if the safety was on.

He was paranoid, but he had good reason to be. Weariness settled in and he shifted to find a more comfortable position and turned the lights off before the exhaustion from the long day finally took control.

CHAPTER FORTY-TWO

"Sir?"

Stevens grumbled in his sleep. It was too early to head out. They would spend an hour waiting for approval from the brass and merely play with their thumbs while they could have been sleeping. He wouldn't sit around and wait for them, damn it. They would have to wait for him.

"Stevens!"

He snapped awake and bounded to his feet from the seat that he'd chosen. He wasn't sure how long it had been but there was a faint light through the dirty windows of the warehouse, and that was enough to tell him he had been out for a while.

Too long. If there was one way to know he was getting old it was when he told himself he would close his eyes for a few minutes, only to wake up a few hours later. That was a typical old-guy thing—the kind he'd told himself would never happen when he got old, and yet there he was. An old fart who was doing all those annoying old fart things.

What was he doing next? Oh, right.

"Jackson?" Stevens said and shook his head to clear the remains of fog. "Sorry, didn't... What's up? Why did you wake me?"

"Chaos came through," his second in command said and sounded like he resented having to say that. "We have a location on our burglar and, as it turns out, he's still traveling with the girl we saw in the footage."

"Huh." He grunted. "You'd think he would have turned her over to his handlers already. We are working under the assumption that he broke in there to get her out, but things could have gone badly and forced him to go to ground for the night?"

"That seems to be what he's done," Jackson said. "Chaos tracked them to a motel outside Portland, which they haven't moved from for the past few hours. It looks like they have a room and are laying low."

"Smart. It's what I would have done," he said. "Thankfully, it's also precisely what we're waiting for. Do we have any idea where they might be headed afterward?"

"I've had no luck in identifying our burglar," Chaos said and looked rather exhausted himself. He had worked all night, but he wouldn't be part of the actual operation. His part of the job was done for the moment. None of them were really sad about that. Despite Stevens' words, the kid was the best available on such short notice, but he was exceptionally difficult to work with.

"No worries, I didn't think his name would be easy to find," Stevens said. "When you're as good in the business as he appears to be, and when you have support like that on your side, the chances are you will be as hard to find as your average ghost."

"Yeah, well, as nice as that is, I do have a couple of leads," the hacker said. "I've looked into that weapon he used, especially when talking to the cops who were shot by it, and I was able to connect the use of a weapon like that to a few isolated incidents around the country."

His boss narrowed his eyes. "Around the country?"

"Yep. When I overheard Jackson talking about how the weapon was custom and probably not even on the market yet, I wondered if I would be able to pin it down as being used anywhere else, and sure enough... I have them around Vegas, DC, Philly, and in a half-dozen other locations. They are all isolated incidents where a professional was cited as entering and leaving quickly. Here's the interesting part, though. In every single one of those instances—even those with eyewitnesses involved—there was no available footage of the man himself."

"How did something like this pass under the radar?" Jackson asked. "You'd think a guy walking around the country killing people with a space-age weapon would raise a few eyebrows."

"The thing is, many of the cops involved in the cases seemed to think there were gang elements involved," Chaos explained. "Gang violence was cited in an unbelievably high percentage of the cases. I guess the cops involved either didn't want to get in deeper with a guy like our man —which, let's be honest, is a perfectly valid approach—or they were merely lazy. It's also a valid approach if you're prone to being lazy."

"Sure," Stevens said. He didn't really agree with either point, but there was no time to debate that right now. "Do we have a plan of attack in place?"

"There isn't really much to plan, to be honest," Jackson said. "It's a motel. We have six people."

"Not me," the hacker said quickly. "My job's done and I'm heading home."

"I know. There are six of us," his boss said and shook his head impatiently. "Your money is already in your bank account and we will let you know if we want to work with you again. Although I think we can all agree that it'll be over long distance."

"Please, God, I hope so," Chaos said. "Later, breeders, and you all have a very happy new year or whatever."

He moved out of the warehouse and the group studied him for a few moments in something close to disbelief.

"Is he drunk?" Stevens asked finally.

"Nope. His pupils were dilated," Jackson muttered. "My bet would be on Xanax or some other kind of anxiety medication. For a guy who doesn't interact with people much and deliberately makes that an intentional part of his life, he would need to almost overdose on the stuff in order to not have a panic attack around us. Which explains why he was such an asshole."

"I'm reasonably sure he was an asshole already, but the drugs simply brought it out with a little more intensity," Jesse grumbled. "Anyway, will we take some dude out in a motel?"

"That's right," their leader said. "We'll teach this guy a lesson while hopefully not wake the dirty bastards who are too cheap to find a real hotel to have their affairs in. We're in quick and quiet. The guy will be the more dangerous of the two but thankfully, we are under no orders to take him alive. That does not extend to the woman he has with him. If she dies, we don't get paid, got it?"

The crew understood the stakes. They were there to watch each other's backs like they were all still in the military, but they were there to get paid too. While the consequences for failing a mission like this in the armed forces was maybe a suspension and time away from the field to clean the barracks for a few months, failure now would be the lack of money. Worse, though, would be the infamy of failing the mission that would keep them off the lists of potential employers for years to come.

They absolutely would not fuck this up.

"Let's load up and get the fuck out there," Stevens said, and the whole crew stepped into the van they'd collected for the occasion. It was a rental and had been rented under the name of a shell corporation in case they needed distance from what was about to happen.

He doubted that they would have any problems, though. They would attack the man while he was in his safe place, and while he was unlikely to go down without a fight, he would focus on defending the girl and therefore would be easier to eliminate.

To capture the girl alive without her screaming up a fuss would be a little more complicated, but as long as they kept her under control, they would be able to dose her with chloroform. It would knock her out and not only make it easier to get her out of there, but it would end any screams she might make fairly quickly.

Stevens couldn't help but feel a twinge of anticipation, however, as they began the drive toward the motel. It hadn't been easy by any means, but he still couldn't help the feeling that things were about to become considerably more challenging.

After what had been a long night filled with all kinds of mission-related stress, Savage had looked forward to getting at least four or five hours of solid sleep. The reality, however, didn't meet the expectation. While he had fallen asleep quicker than he thought was possible on a foreign bed, it was a light sleep and not overly restful.

Every little sound Jenna made kept him hovering between deep sleep and dozing and as annoying as it was, she seemed to sleep soundly and he didn't want to disturb her.

She was most likely used to being on her own. Any sound he made would probably disturb her or even make it difficult for her to sleep at all.

He grimaced in the darkness at the odd thought that plagued his brain while the night dragged on.

A few hours in, he finally accepted the realization that he would not get a good night's sleep. All he could do was try to get as much rest as was possible, after which he could maybe snatch a nap on the plane Anja had told him Monroe would have ready for them.

The thought sustained him through the long dark hours.

It was all he could do not to bound from his bed when he heard a van pull up outside. He wasn't sure why it had alarmed him so much, but something that had him almost fully awake a few seconds after the loud diesel engine cut off.

His instinct told him something was wrong. He turned to look at Jenna, surprised that she was awake as well. Maybe she'd had the same difficulties as he had with sleeping.

No. There was something else in her eyes—fear and terror. She didn't look like she had been kept up all night and hated him for it in the way the sleep-deprived tended to.

Something was wrong, and she obviously hoped that he knew it too.

She could see how alert he was already, and he could tell that his instincts had been right to bring him awake.

"They have guns," she whispered under her breath.

Maybe twenty-four hours earlier, he would have had a hard time believing her. It was complete and utter insanity to even think she could hear weapons from out in the parking lot, right?

Normally, the answer would be a resounding affirmative, but they had already established that she could hear what was said in an earpiece buried in his ear. Anja had confirmed it too, which negated the difficulty he had to accept it based on his own logic.

He had no problems believing that she knew exactly what was happening outside. A van had pulled up in the early hours of the morning before the sun had even peeked over the horizon, although faint light filtered through the thin curtains closed over the motel's windows.

Savage moved out of his bed as quietly as he could, his

weapon already in his hand. Jenna seemed surprised to see him already in action, armed, and ready for a fight. He assumed that she hadn't seen someone act on any of her warnings before or maybe she realized that the most terrifying times of the night before had returned with the morning.

With quiet, cautious movements, he eased toward the room's door. A small peephole enabled him to see if anyone was on the other side but for the moment, it appeared that the door was not yet covered.

That would definitely change if the two fugitives decided to make their way out of the room. Anja had said someone had intercepted the recording from the patrol car's camera, which meant they probably had his face and Jenna's too, depending on the quality of the image. There was no way they would be able to sneak out of the motel.

Not out of the front, anyway, but there had to be some other way to exit the room. Places like these needed to have a fire escape, right?

He flicked the safety off his weapon as the back door of the only van in the motel's parking lot opened. A couple of men spilled out and they immediately moved toward the front desk.

"Are they here for us?" Jenna whispered, already up from the bed. She pushed her blonde hair down over her shoulders as if to straighten it.

"I'm not sure," he replied, his voice low as well. "But my money's on yes."

The two men looked like pros. Boots weren't that uncommon considering the time of year, but the ones they wore weren't exactly the kind that would protect one from falls on patches of ice. They were undoubtedly those used in combat that allowed for quick movement as well as hard kicks should they be needed.

Not only that, he would put his money on them having steel tips too for added effect.

With that said, he didn't really plan to get into a fist-fight with them. There were more waiting in the van, of course, and from Jenna's warning, he could expect them to be armed to the teeth as well.

Savage wouldn't take any chances, not with her on the line. He doubted that the men were there to kill her, but things tended to quickly get out of hand when bullets were exchanged.

No, he wouldn't risk it.

The two men reached the front desk. His gaze followed their movements through a crack in the blinds and he watched while they stopped in front of the bulletproof glass and appeared to have a pleasant conversation with the man on the other side.

There would be a policy of sorts to prohibit talking about the guests in the motel since the people who frequented it tended to like their privacy, but the two men appeared rather insistent. The transaction ended when they slid a couple of bills through the partition and the clerk pointed them toward the room he surveilled them from.

"Shit," he muttered as the two men began to approach and gestured for their team in the van to join them. The door opened again, and the group spilled out. Two more of them headed toward the motel room, while the others remained with the van as backup should they be needed.

"Get into the bathroom," Savage told her sharply. He'd

seen enough and decided they wouldn't wait in the bedroom for the goons to attack. He would prefer to engage them away from where Jenna was and hopefully, keep her away from the fighting altogether.

She followed his instruction without protest and ducked hastily into the bathroom, where he looked around and identified their exit. Rooms like these were required by law to have a secondary exit in case the primary one was blocked by a fire, which meant the front door wasn't their only way out.

He pulled the window open and she didn't need any further encouragement from him before she scrambled over the sill.

It took only a moment to lock the bathroom door behind him before he attempted to escape through the window. While it was the right size for his companion, it was a little small for him. He needed desperation to surge power into his arms to squeeze through when he heard the front door kicked open.

It wasn't a long fall to the ground, and she was already there waiting for him.

"Where to now?" she asked.

"Good question."

CHAPTER FORTY-THREE

Savage tapped his earpiece lightly to activate it. "Anja, how the fuck can we get out of here?"

"What—" she mumbled on the other side of the line. "Who's getting what out of where now?"

"Anja, truly, I'm so happy you're awake," Savage snarked. "If you're not too busy, I don't suppose you could help us get the fuck out of here? And please tell me you guys have a plane waiting for us somewhere?"

"What?" she grumbled and sounded like she had just woken up herself. "Who? Goddammit, Savage, are you in trouble again?"

"You bet your ass I am," he replied and beckoned for Jenna to follow him when he heard them attempt to break into the bathroom, obviously still trying to find them. "Someone found us at the motel and they are not the friendly types who want us to talk to them about their lord and savior. Well, maybe they do, but it seems more likely that they want to introduce us to him. So, if you don't mind, could you find us a way out of here?"

"Ugh, fine," she snapped. "You two will make my hair go grey."

He didn't bother to reply to that and guided the girl toward the edge of the building, away from where their attackers would be able to see them from the window. From there, they would have a decent view of the parking lot without being overly visible themselves.

"I've turned the car on for you guys," the hacker said. "It seems like you should be able to make a clean getaway. I've intercepted communications in the area, but they're hard to break through. Someone encrypted it for them, how adorable..." The silence was broken by what sounded like an attack on her keyboard for a few seconds. "Okay, they know you're not in the room, and they're trying to establish where the hell you are. You have a few seconds before they swarm the motel grounds."

"Thanks for the warning," he said and gestured for Jenna to follow him and not make a sound.

"What?" she whispered.

"For fuck's sake." He immediately regretted it when he remembered that she would have no clue how to read the motions he'd made. "Follow me. Be quiet." He punctuated the words with the hand signals that were meant to represent them, and she nodded.

She didn't look happy about it, but now was not the time for petty annoyances to be aired. They needed to get out of there first. Once they were free and clear, she could tell him he would have saved more time if he had simply told her what he wanted instead of making hand gestures.

They moved toward the car, which was thankfully parked a good way away from the van, although they would have to drive past it to reach the exit of the parking lot. That wouldn't happen without incident, but he didn't mind that as much since it meant they would already be on the move.

Anja hadn't been kidding about them knowing already that they were gone and would want to search the motel. The two men waiting in the van apparently had orders to make sure they had been given the right room, and they exited hurriedly and ran a quick weapon's check.

They were barely ten yards away from where he stood with Jenna directly behind him. He did not intend to wait for them to see him or even hope they wouldn't. These guys were pros, and if they didn't see them immediately...well, they would have a little help to do so.

Savage already had his weapon in hand and he raised it. There was no thought to simply injure them in this situation. They were there to stop and hurt him and Jenna, which meant they wouldn't receive any preferential treatment.

The first one fell and clutched his throat when a pair of needles drilled through it. His comrade gaped, confused and shocked as his partner succumbed to what almost seemed like a non-existent assault.

He was sharp enough to realize that they were under attack, however, and reached quickly for the weapon he had stowed in his jacket. The layers were his undoing, and Savage pivoted in place, grasped his pistol with both hands, and opened fire. The soft whoosh of the magnets in the pistol was all that could be heard before the second man dropped with three holes in his chest.

The other team members responded immediately and

raced from inside the room. They knew their prey had turned hunter, and he pushed the girl down between a couple of cars for cover when they reached the vehicle they had used earlier.

Barely in time too as their assumption that their adversaries had come armed and ready for a fight was confirmed when suppressed weapons opened fire behind them.

The clerk would regret his decision to tell these guys where Savage and Jenna were spending the night. Some nosy guest might have noticed the activity and possibly already reported it to the local police. When it became known that the motel would be shut down due to it being a fucking crime scene, it was unlikely that it would be reopened. People tended to avoid sleazy motels as a rule, and those that didn't mind the sleazy appearance of the place would most definitely object to the police presence.

Then again, he had no time to waste on considering that or the future of the clerk. He wasn't sure how much money had been spent to get the man to talk, but it hadn't been much. Certainly not enough to sell out the lives of two people, including one nineteen-year-old.

Maybe it had been enough for only Savage, but that wasn't the point.

Jenna slid into the back seat of the car and he stepped in behind the wheel. As Anja had said, the car was already on and waiting for them. He reminded himself that they were lucky the owners hadn't reported it stolen yet. Or maybe the hacker had stepped in to help them there too and had blocked any attempts to find the vehicle while they still needed it.

He put the car into gear and stamped on the accelerator. The electric motor was silent except for a low whir, but the tires squealed loudly as they suddenly reacted with the cold pavement.

"Stay down!" Savage roared, turned the vehicle, and located the men who continued to fire at them, still attempting to reach their quarry despite the distance between.

A couple of rounds did strike and impacted with the body of the car, but it appeared that the suppressors on the sub-machine guns they used compromised any degree of accuracy they might have hoped for.

"Why didn't you give me a hand signal to stay down this time?" Jenna asked, even though she did as she was told and kept her head down in the back seat.

"This is not the fucking time," he responded roughly, his gaze focused intently on the way ahead as the car hurtled toward the exit of the parking lot and onto the road.

They would have time to talk about it later, but for the moment, he needed to concentrate on getting them out of danger.

"Fuck," he said when he glanced over his shoulder and realized that the four men who had broken into their room now sprinted toward their van. "I should have disabled that. I don't suppose you have anything that could help with that, Anja?"

"Sorry. That might as well be from the stone ages for all the electronics it has," she said. "It doesn't even have a GPS. Who the hell doesn't have a GPS in a working van?"

"The kinds of guys who don't want people like you to peek in on what they're doing, I guess," he replied, his tone edged with frustration.

They were already in pursuit, and the sound of police sirens in the distance could now be heard. The cops wouldn't follow the cars, not for a while at least, which meant the only problem he would have to deal with was the team behind him.

Logic told him they wouldn't start a firefight, not this close into the city. The traffic was hellish, even this early, with enough people heading in and out of town for work. The mercs who had arrived would try to avoid the sheer number of variables involved in a high-speed shootout on a busy street.

For now, they would simply bide their time and follow as he headed farther and farther from the city.

"Jessica's up, and she has a plane ready for the two of you," Anja said. "It's at the same airstrip you came in on, Savage. Do you know the way back there?"

"Sure, but I won't be able to head that way without bringing unwanted company," Savage said and tried to increase speed. Unfortunately, the electric motor wasn't able to gain any significant lead on the diesel-powered van.

"Can't you lose them?" the hacker asked.

"It doesn't look like it." He dragged in a deep breath and fought to regain his calm. He needed it to ensure he wouldn't yell at anyone again. "I suppose it would be too much to hope that Monroe sent Terry and Sam to help us, right?"

"Sorry, she was serious about not having Pegasus involved in any way," the hacker confirmed.

"Fuck."

They were on their own out there. He had managed to eliminate two men, but they would still have to defend themselves against four more. All would be trained and possibly as well-armed as he was himself.

There was a limited number of needles he could launch manually, and it wasn't anywhere near the nine hundred RPM of the sub machine-guns their attackers carried.

He needed to come up with creative ways to shake them off of his back. When they began to move away from the suburbs and deeper into the mountains around the city toward the airstrip, their pursuers opened fire again. This time, they didn't bother with the suppressors.

There did seem to be one small advantage in the situation, however. Either they were merely terrible, terrible shots, or they tried not to accidentally shoot Jenna.

The latter scenario would probably be the one to go with. It was the most likely of the two, after all. Besides, making assumptions one way or the other wouldn't make that much difference to their predicament.

The important thing was that he had to get clear of them. That was all he needed to focus on.

Savage grasped the wheel a little tighter when he saw them attempt to overtake him. Thankfully, their engine was no more powerful than his own and appeared to pull a heavier load. As they began to climb higher, they apparently had a harder and harder time keeping up.

That, he realized, would increase their desperation. They would overreact and he had to be ready for it. A man edged out of the passenger side window and attempted to hold himself in place while he eased his weapon out and attempted to fire.

The attempt wouldn't be that accurate, to begin with, and if he attempted to avoid shooting anyone inside the car and aiming for the tires instead, he had even less chance to achieve his purpose.

With that said, he raised an eyebrow when one of the sensors told him that their right back tire had begun to lose air fairly rapidly. It would last until they reached the airstrip, hopefully, but it would also make the car a little more difficult to manage.

"Try to strap yourself into something," he called to Jenna.

He couldn't see how bad a time she endured back there but given that she stretched and retrieved one of the seat belts to strap herself in while she also tried to hunker down safely, he could at least confirm that she was still alive.

Sometimes, that was all you could really ask for.

The airstrip came into view and the barrage grew more and more erratic. Two tires leaked air now and the vehicle had become even more difficult to control. It seemed that their pursuers still hadn't come to terms with the fact that they might have to shoot to kill, though. Hopefully, that little fact would enable the fugitives to make it out alive.

They careened onto the tarmac, where the plane already waited for them—although there was no sign of any of the crew who normally waited outside for the arrival of the guests. The steps were down, however, and ready for them to board, but there was no sign of anyone around them.

Those questions were answered quickly when Jessica stepped onto the first step from the top and brandished what looked like an assault rifle in both hands.

It was an impressive sight, he had to admit, but a terrifying realization touched him. He had no idea how well she could shoot, and she intended to fire at a van that was almost two hundred yards from where she stood.

Not only that, the two of them were directly in the firing line.

"Fuck." He jerked the car to the side as she opened fire.

The crack of the assault rifle was easy to hear and it launched bullets in an interestingly collected pattern toward the van. Maybe she had practiced since he had seen her last, but there was still no way he would allow Jenna to stay in the line of fire.

The same could not be said for the men in the van, who appeared to not realize that they now faced a retaliatory barrage. Tires screeched behind him, a clear confirmation of the exact moment when they did.

Jessica had been training, and the rear-view mirror showed him the holes punched in the windshield of the van, although he couldn't see if any of the occupants were down. Either way, this was the opening they needed.

Savage yanked the handbrake to bring the electric car to a sudden halt. That had actually been the intention, but while the stop was sudden, it wasn't nearly as sudden as he'd hoped it would be. They finally came to a standstill a couple of paces away from the stairway leading into the plane.

"Get out and get up there," he instructed as he stepped out and opened her door.

Their rescuer needed to reload, which would give their attackers the opening they needed. It was now up to him to close that opening as the van had already resumed its approach. He drew his pistol, pulled the trigger as quickly as he could, and rocketed needles at the enemy vehicle as rapidly as he could while Jenna sprinted up the steps.

She had reached the top when the van halted and three men stepped out to both try to reach her and shoot her protector.

He caught one of them three times in the chest and another in the neck and head before he was forced back behind the car. The world around him exploded in pieces of glass and he hastily covered his head to avoid injury.

"Tell them to take off," he said into his earpiece and tried not to yell over the ringing in his ears.

"Yeah, that won't happen," Anja said. "You don't think I'll leave you behind, do you?"

"I can take care of myself. There's only one of them left," he shouted.

"One of who left?"

Savage looked up from where he hunkered and immediately focused on the man who had led the team of mercs during the attack. He was the only one left but he was armed and he looked pissed.

"Oh, fuck." He reacted as quickly as he could and attempted a shot, but his adversary closed the gap between them too quickly, locked his arm against the car, and pounded his elbow into his head. The assault hurled him back and thrust the weapon from his hands.

He fell and tried to push to his feet but was stopped by a boot that thumped into his chest.

"I think it's time we learn a little about you," the man stated coldly and aimed the barrel of his weapon at his head.

Well, the plane would take off now, right?

Rather than look at the gun, he closed his eyes and flinched instinctively at the loud clatter of the sub-machine gun. His ears rang as he looked up to see that he hadn't had his head blasted open. The man had missed.

How had he missed?

Jenna stood over the merc, her fists clenched and a furious look in her eyes.

"Look, kid," the man said and chuckled as he straightened from the car he had been shoved into. "I have orders to leave you alive, but that doesn't mean I'm above shooting you in the leg to get you to come quietly."

"Walk away," she all but growled with a threat Savage wasn't sure she meant. "Walk away, and you'll live."

"Not to be insulting or anything, kid, but you're really not at all intimidating." He punctuated that with a laugh and began to raise his weapon.

She stepped in, moved faster than Savage had ever seen someone move before, and caught the barrel before it had lifted more than an inch.

"I warned you." She hammered her fist into his gut and the breath exploded out of his lungs.

When he bent forward to recover, she tapped him with a perfectly executed uppercut to the head and hurled him with impossible power into the car behind him.

The merc fell without even a gasp.

Jenna turned to offer her hand to help Savage up.

"Thanks," he grumbled and took her hand. "I totally had that covered, by the way."

"Sure, you did." Her grin was both amused and smug.

CHAPTER FORTY-FOUR

Once they were in the air, Jenna moved over to where Savage sat and pressed an ice pack to his head.

"Thanks." He took it from her so she could sit across from him. "Where did you learn to do shit like that, anyway?"

"Oh, I did some Panantukan when I was in my formative years," she replied and rolled her shoulders. "Yeah, I know a thing or two about how to bring the pain."

"That's really not what I meant," he said. He wasn't really a fan of Panantukan himself, but who was he to say anything at the moment?

"Oh...yeah, the docs said there might be physical changes, and they tested for them too," she said with a nod. "Along with altering my bone marrow to get rid of the leukemia, there was higher bone and muscular density with no apparent changes to agility and no loss in speed or stamina. They looked as confused as you do now."

He nodded but winced when the movement made his head hurt. "Well, fuck, kid, is there anything you can't do?"

"She shouldn't go for too long without food, that's for certain," Jessica interjected and patted the girl on the shoulder. "There's breakfast in the back if you want."

"I do, thanks." She bounded up and moved away quickly.

The woman took the empty seat. "How are you feeling?"

"I've been better, but I'll live," he said. "Thanks for the assist there. I didn't know you were that good with an assault rifle."

"I take time at the range when I have some to spare," she responded, her expression thoughtful. "I like her, by the way. She's a spunky kid. She raced down to help you almost before I realized what was going on."

"She's something else," he agreed. "I like her too."

"Well, I know you're not up for it, but Courtney would like a fucking word," she said. "So...steel yourself, or something—whatever you stoic types do when you have to face shit."

"Let's get this over with." He knew it was coming. Monroe would want to make sure her investment would pay out, and there was nothing he could do to prevent that. He would have to simply grit his teeth and wait for whatever it was she needed to get off her chest.

The TV on the side of the cabin came to life, thanks to Anja, and Monroe's face appeared.

"Savage, Jessica," she greeted and nodded at them. "How are you two?"

"Not too bad," he said and continued to press the ice pack to the side of his head. "How about you?"

"It's been a long day, but I'm happy to say it's coming to an end." She sounded tired but upbeat, which he assumed boded well for their discussion. "Thanks to Anderson's contacts, I've been informed that there are currently a handful of warrants executed on the lab you broke into last night. They should be able to shut the facility down as well as recover our stolen devices without too much difficulty."

"Well, that's always good news," Savage said.

"How's the girl?" she asked. "Jenna, right?"

"She's...well, she's something else," Jessica said. "She's having breakfast as we speak."

"I was," Jenna said. She'd clearly heard her name and returned to Savage's side with a plate full of food. "Who are you?"

"Hi, Jenna, I'm Dr Courtney Monroe," she replied and a warm smile crossed her face. "It's good to know you all managed to get out of that whole situation uninjured."

"Thanks...I guess?" the girl said around her mouth full of food.

"Now that you're all in the clear, do you have any idea what we'll do with Jenna?" Monroe asked and directed the question to the other two.

"I'll be honest, I didn't think that far ahead," Savage admitted.

"I'm not surprised," his boss replied with a small smirk, and he chuckled.

"I actually had a couple of ideas on that," Jessica interjected quickly. "I do need to ask Jenna about it first, of course, but I thought that considering the situation she is in, she will still need medical supervision over the next couple of months to ensure that none of the side effects she might run into become life-threatening. It would also be interesting to conduct studies on what was done to her and see the effects of the goop in human bodies."

"How do you propose to do that?" Monroe asked.

"Well—and again, I would need to talk to Jenna about this—I thought she might move in with me and perhaps even be enrolled to complete her education."

Savage glanced at the young woman beside him. "How do you feel about that, kid?"

She shrugged. "Jessica seems cool enough. I don't mind it, so long as I'm not locked in a cage anymore."

"It would take a fair amount of adjustment—for the both of us, I should add—but I think we would have fun getting to know each other better, Jenna," Jessica said.

The girl smiled. "I'd like that. And does that mean Jer will come over to visit from time to time?"

His eyebrows raised hastily. "That...will be a topic for another time."

"Cool." She grinned and headed back to the breakfast table.

"You'll have your hands full with that one," he warned.

THE END

<u>Frankfurt, Germany (Sunday night before Book Fair)</u>

Thank you for reading this series and all the way to the back of this book!

I'm presently in Frankfurt eating at an Italian Restaurant (Fontana di Trevi). Well, I'm actually waiting for my dessert at the moment typing up these author notes.

I like eating in Europe as there is never any stress on rushing to finish. On the contrary, I'm often asking my wife 'where's the bill?' and she replies they won't bring a bill unless we ask. You would think as many times as I've asked the question I would have learned the answer. Apparently not, I asked again at the Steak and Seafood restaurant just last night.

<Sigh.>

We arrived in Frankfurt at about 4:30PM yesterday (9 hours ahead of Las Vegas time.) We left the condo in Las Vegas Friday at 11:30 AM, arrived Frankfurt at approximately 7:30 AM Saturday.

I thought I had been on the road for 24 hours, it was merely 19. It's a good thing I lie for a living, I have some sort of excuse for bad math (other than the obvious - foreign time zones completely mess me up.)

The jet-lag (so far) has been pretty annoying, but not overwhelming. Mind you, this is after a four-and-a-half-hour nap in the middle of the day.

I am not a world-weary world traveler by a long shot. I'm that 'neuvo-world traveler' who hates time changes and has to deal with it everywhere I go. Heck, just going from Pacific to Central time change sucks for me (2 hours difference!). I'm about as turtle when it comes to travel as I can get (you know, the kind that sticks their head in and wants to ignore the world?).

I am the ultimate example of an introvert.

However, once I'm wherever I'm supposed to be, I'm just as happy to call that home as anything. *Until I'm not.*

Then I want my real home with my real restaurants that I am used to eating that are on their way to making me a nice figure… A round figure.

Kinda like a ball with two arms and two legs rolling around. The hands and feet push me off of obstacles.

I'm so damned full from dinner, I am introducing how I feel post food intake into this set of author notes. UHHH-HGGGG…. I need another nap! (It's 9:40 PM, so I suppose that constitutes sleep here, but for my body it believes I am in mid-afternoon.)

Either way, I want to be horizontal and snoozing.

This series is / was the start of projects that are a bit more male oriented. Starting with The Birth of Heavy Metal, then Team Savage and finally Cryptid Assassin (coming in the future, first book finished. I have to decide whether to bring them out some time apart, or close together (and wait on the release.)

If you get a chance, put Cryptid Assassin on your to-be-read pile. It's making me laugh (or at least smile) thinking about the story right now ;-)

Michael Anderle

Ghost Walking (5)

Ghost Talking (6)

Ghost Brawling (7)

Ghost Stalking (8)

Ghost Resurrection (9)

Ghost Adaptation (10)

Ghost Redemption (11)

Ghost Revolution (12)

TEAM SAVAGE

Kill or Be Killed (1)

Dead or Alive (2)

Vengeance or Death (3)

THE BOHICA CHRONICLES

Reprobates (1)

Degenerates (2)

Redeemables (3)

Thor (4)

9 781642 025057